CB128640

EX LIBRIS

VINTAGE CLASSICS

## RICHARD FLANAGAN

Richard Flanagan has been described by the *Washington Post* as 'one of our greatest living novelists', and as 'among the most versatile writers in the English language' by the *New York Review of Books*. He won the Booker Prize for *The Narrow Road to the Deep North* and the Commonwealth Prize for *Gould's Book of Fish*. *The Narrow Road to the Deep North* has been adapted into a 2024 series for television starring Jacob Elordi and Odessa Young. Flanagan's father, who died the day Flanagan finished *The Narrow Road to the Deep North*, was a survivor of the Burma Death Railway.

ALSO BY RICHARD FLANAGAN

*Death of a River guide*

*The Sound of One Hand Clapping*

*Gould's Book of Fish*

*The Unknown Terrorist*

*Wanting*

*Question 7*

RICHARD FLANAGAN

# THE NARROW ROAD TO THE DEEP NORTH

VINTAGE CLASSICS

1 3 5 7 9 10 8 6 4 2

Vintage Classics is part of the Penguin Random House
group of companies whose addresses can be found
at global.penguinrandomhouse.com

Penguin
Random House
UK

This edition published in Vintage Classics in 2024
First published in Great Britain by Chatto & Windus in 2014
First published by Knopf Australia in 2013

Copyright © Richard Flanagan 2013

Richard Flanagan has asserted his right to be identified as the author
of this Work in accordance with the Copyright, Designs and Patents Act 1988

The author gratefully acknowledges the use of the following texts and translations: 'Poem 5, Catullus', from *Bed to Bed*, translated by James Michie, Orion, 1967; *Selected Poems and Prose of Paul Celan*, translated by John Felstiner, W. W. Norton, New York, 2001; *The Essential Haiku*, edited and translated by Robert Hass, Ecco Press, 1994; 'Issa and Kikusha-ni haiku' from *The Sound of Water: Haiku by Basho, Buson, Issa and Other Poets*, translated by Sam Hamill, © 1995 by Sam Hamill, reproduced by arrangement with The Permissions Company Inc., on behalf of Shambhala Publications Inc., Boston, MA, www.shambhala.com; *The British Museum Haiku*, translated by David Cobb, The British Museum Press, 2002; *The Narrow Road to the Deep North* by Matsuo Basho, translated by Nobuyuki Yuasa, Penguin, 1966; *Japanese Death Poems*, translated by Yoel Hoffmann, Tuttle Publishing, Boston, 1986; 'These Foolish Things (Remind Me Of You)', lyrics by Eric Maschwitz and Jack Strachey,© 1976 by Lafleur Music Ltd, reproduced by permission of Boosey & Hawkes Music Publishers Ltd

Every effort has been made to trace and contact all holders of
copyright in quotations. If there are any inadvertent omissions or errors,
the publishers will be pleased to correct these at the earliest opportunity

penguin.co.uk/vintage-classics

Typeset by Palimpsest Book Production Limited, Falkirk, Stirlingshire
Printed and bound in Great Britain by Clays Ltd, Elcograf S.p.A.

The authorised representative in the EEA is Penguin Random House Ireland,
Morrison Chambers, 32 Nassau Street, Dublin D02 YH68

A CIP catalogue record for this book is available from the British Library

ISBN 9781784879860

Penguin Random House is committed to a sustainable future for
our business, our readers and our planet. This book is made from
Forest Stewardship Council® certified paper.

MIX
Paper | Supporting
responsible forestry
FSC® C018179

*For prisoner san byaku san jū go (335)*

Mother, they write poems.

*Paul Celan*

A bee
staggers out
of the peony.

*Basho*

# 1

Why at the beginning of things is there always light? Dorrigo Evans' earliest memories were of sun flooding a church hall in which he sat with his mother and grandmother. A wooden church hall. Blinding light and him toddling back and forth, in and out of its transcendent welcome, into the arms of women. Women who loved him. Like entering the sea and returning to the beach. Over and over.

Bless you, his mother says as she holds him and lets him go. Bless you, boy.

That must have been 1915 or 1916. He would have been one or two. Shadows came later in the form of a forearm rising up, its black outline leaping in the greasy light of a kerosene lantern. Jackie Maguire was sitting in the Evanses' small dark kitchen, crying. No one cried then, except babies. Jackie Maguire was an old man, maybe forty, perhaps older, and he was trying to brush the tears away from his pockmarked face with the back of his hand. Or was it with his fingers?

Only his crying was in Dorrigo Evans' memory fixed. It was a sound like something breaking. Its slowing rhythm reminded him of a rabbit's hind legs thumping the ground as it is strangled by a snare, the only sound he had ever heard that was similar. He was nine, had come inside to have his mother look at a blood blister on his thumb, and had little else to compare it to. He had seen a grown man cry only once before, a scene of astonishment when his brother Tom returned from the Great War in France and got off the train. He had swung his kitbag onto the hot dust of the siding and abruptly burst into tears.

Watching his brother, Dorrigo Evans had wondered what it was that would make a grown man cry. Later, crying became simply affirmation of feeling, and feeling the only compass in life. Feeling became fashionable and emotion became a theatre in which people were players who no longer knew who they were off the stage. Dorrigo Evans would live long enough to see all these changes. And he would remember a time when people were ashamed of crying. When they feared the weakness it bespoke. The trouble to which it led. He would live to see people praised for things that were not worthy of praise, simply because truth was seen to be bad for their feelings.

That night Tom came home they burnt the Kaiser on a bonfire. Tom said nothing of the war, of the Germans, of the gas and the tanks and the trenches they had heard about. He said nothing at all. One man's feeling is not always equal to all life is. Sometimes it's not equal to anything much at all. He just stared into the flames.

# 2

A happy man has no past, while an unhappy man has nothing else. In his old age Dorrigo Evans never knew if he had read this or had himself made it up. Made up, mixed up, and broken down. Relentlessly broken down. Rock to gravel to dust to mud to rock and so the world goes, as his mother used to say when he demanded reasons or explanation as to how the world got to be this way or that. The world is, she would say. It just *is*, boy. He had been trying to wrest the rock free from an outcrop to build a fort for a game he was playing when another, larger rock dropped onto his thumb, causing a large and throbbing blood blister beneath the nail.

His mother swung Dorrigo up onto the kitchen table where the lamp light fell strongest and, avoiding Jackie Maguire's strange gaze, lifted her son's thumb into the light. Between his sobs Jackie Maguire said a few things. His wife had the week previously taken the train with their youngest child to Launceston, and not returned.

Dorrigo's mother picked up her carving knife. Along the blade's edge ran a cream smear of congealed mutton fat. She placed its tip into the coals of the kitchen range. A small wreath of smoke leapt up and infused the kitchen with the odour of charred mutton. She pulled the knife out, its glowing red tip glittering with sparkles of brilliant white-hot dust, a sight Dorrigo found at once magical and terrifying.

Hold still, she said, taking hold of his hand with such a strong grip it shocked him.

Jackie Maguire was telling how he had taken the mail train to Launceston and gone looking for her, but he could find her nowhere. As Dorrigo Evans watched, the red-hot tip touched his nail and it began to smoke as his mother burnt a hole through the cuticle. He heard Jackie Maguire say—

She's vanished off the face of the earth, Mrs Evans.

And the smoke gave way to a small gush of dark blood from his thumb, and the pain of his blood blister and the terror of the red-hot carving knife were gone.

Scram, Dorrigo's mother said, nudging him off the table. Scram now, boy.

Vanished! Jackie Maguire said.

All this was in the days when the world was wide and the island of Tasmania was still the world. And of its many remote and forgotten outposts, few were more forgotten and remote than Cleveland, the hamlet of forty or so souls where Dorrigo Evans lived. An old convict coaching village fallen on hard times and out of memory, it now survived as a railway siding, a handful of crumbling Georgian buildings and scattered verandah-browed wooden cottages, shelter for those who had endured a century of exile and loss.

Backdropped by woodlands of writhing peppermint gums and silver wattle that waved and danced in the heat, it was hot and hard in summer, and hard, simply hard, in winter. Electricity and radio were yet to arrive, and were it not that it was the 1920s, it could have been the 1880s or the 1850s. Many years later Tom, a man not given to allegory but perhaps prompted, or so Dorrigo had thought at the time, by his own impending death and the accompanying terror of the old—that all life is only allegory and the real story is not here—said it was like the long autumn of a dying world.

Their father was a railway fettler, and his family lived

in a Tasmanian Government Railways weatherboard cottage by the side of the line. Of a summer, when the water ran out, they would bucket water from the tank set up for the steam locomotives. They slept under skins of possums they snared, and they lived mostly on the rabbits they trapped and the wallabies they shot and the potatoes they grew and the bread they baked. Their father, who had survived the depression of the 1890s and watched men die of starvation on the streets of Hobart, couldn't believe his luck at having ended up living in such a workers' paradise. In his less sanguine moments he would also say, 'You live like a dog and you die like a dog.'

Dorrigo Evans knew Jackie Maguire from the holidays he sometimes took with Tom. To get to Tom's he would catch a ride on the back of Joe Pike's dray from Cleveland to the Fingal Valley turnoff. As the old draught horse Joe Pike called Gracie amiably trotted along, Dorrigo would sway back and forth and imagine himself shaping into one of the boughs of the wildly snaking peppermint gums that fingered and flew through the great blue sky overhead. He would smell damp bark and drying leaves and watch the clans of green and red musk lorikeets chortling far above. He would drink in the birdsong of the wrens and the honeyeaters, the whipcrack call of the jo-wittys, punctuated by Gracie's steady clop and the creak and clink of the cart's leather traces and wood shafts and iron chains, a universe of sensation that returned in dreams.

They would make their way along the old coach road, past the coaching hotel the railway had put out of business, now a dilapidated near ruin in which lived several impoverished families, including the Jackie Maguires. Once every few days a cloud of dust would announce the coming of a motorcar, and the kids would appear out of the bush and the coach-house and chase the noisy cloud till their lungs were afire and their legs lead.

At the Fingal Valley turnoff Dorrigo Evans would slide off, wave Joe and Gracie goodbye, and begin the walk to Llewellyn, a town distinguished chiefly by being even smaller than Cleveland. Once at Llewellyn, he would strike north-east through the paddocks and, taking his bearings from the great snow-covered massif of Ben Lomond, head through the bush towards the snow country back of the Ben, where Tom worked two weeks on, one week off as a possum snarer. Mid-afternoon he would arrive at Tom's home, a cave that nestled in a sheltered dogleg below a ridgeline. The cave was slightly smaller than the size of their skillion kitchen, and at its highest Tom could stand with his head bowed. It narrowed like an egg at each end, and its opening was sheltered by an overhang which meant that a fire could burn there all night, warming the cave.

Sometimes Tom, now in his early twenties, would have Jackie Maguire working with him. Tom, who had a good voice, would often sing a song or two of a night. And after, by firelight, Dorrigo would read aloud from some old *Bulletins* and *Smith's Weeklys* that formed the library of the two possum snarers, to Jackie Maguire, who could not read, and to Tom, who said he could. They liked it when Dorrigo read from Aunty Rose's advice column, or the bush ballads that they regarded as *clever* or sometimes even *very clever*. After a time, Dorrigo began to memorise other poems for them from a book at his school called *The English Parnassus*. Their favourite was Tennyson's 'Ulysses'.

Pockmarked face smiling in the firelight, gleaming bright

as a freshly turned out plum pudding, Jackie Maguire would say, Oh, them old timers! They can string them words together tighter than a brass snare strangling a rabbit!

And Dorrigo didn't say to Tom what he had seen a week before Mrs Jackie Maguire vanished: his brother with his hand reaching up inside her skirt, as she—a small, intense woman of exotic darkness—leaned up against the chicken shed behind the coaching house. Tom's face was turned in on her neck. He knew his brother was kissing her.

For many years, Dorrigo often thought about Mrs Jackie Maguire, whose real name he never knew, whose real name was like the food he dreamt of every day in the POW camps—there and not there, pressing up into his skull, a thing that always vanished at the point he reached out towards it. And after a time he thought about her less often; and after a further time, he no longer thought about her at all.

## 3

Dorrigo was the only one of his family to pass the Ability Test at the end of his schooling at the age of twelve and so receive a scholarship to attend Launceston High School. He was old for his year. On his first day, at lunchtime, he ended up at what was called the top yard, a flat area of dead grass and dust, bark and leaves, with several large gum trees at one end. He watched the big boys of third and fourth form, some with sideburns, boys already with men's muscles, line up in two rough rows, jostling, shoving, moving like some tribal dance. Then began the magic of kick to kick. One boy would boot the football from his row across the yard to the other row. And all the boys in that row would run together at the ball and—if it were coming in high—leap into the air, seeking to catch it. And as violent as the fight for the mark was, whoever succeeded was suddenly sacrosanct. And to him, the spoil—the reward of kicking the ball back to the other row, where the process was repeated.

So it went, all lunch hour. Inevitably, the senior boys dominated, taking the most marks, getting the most kicks. Some younger boys got a few marks and kicks, many one or none.

Dorrigo watched all that first lunchtime. Another first-form boy told him that you had to be at least in second form before you had a chance in kick to kick—the big boys were too strong and too fast; they would think nothing of putting an elbow into a head, a fist into a face, a knee in the back to rid themselves of an opponent. Dorrigo noticed some smaller boys hanging around behind the pack, a few paces back, ready to scavenge the occasional kick that went too high, lofting over the scrum.

On the second day, he joined their number. And on the third day, he found himself up close to the back of the pack when, over their shoulders, he saw a wobbly drop punt lofting high towards them. For a moment it sat in the sun, and he understood that the ball was his to pluck. He could smell the piss ants in the eucalypts, feel the ropy shadows of their branches fall away as he began running forward into the pack. Time slowed, he found all the space he needed in the crowding spot into which the biggest, strongest boys were now rushing. He understood the ball dangling from the sun was his and all he had to do was rise. His eyes were only for the ball, but he sensed he would not make it running at the speed he was, and so he leapt, his feet finding the back of one boy, his knees the shoulders of another and so he climbed into the full dazzle of the sun, above all the other boys. At the apex of their struggle, his arms stretched out high above him, he felt the ball arrive in his hands, and he knew he could now begin to fall out of the sun.

Cradling the football with tight hands, he landed on his back so hard it shot most of the breath out of him. Grabbing barking breaths, he got to his feet and stood there in the light, holding the oval ball, readying himself to now join a larger world.

As he staggered back, the melee cleared a respectful space around him.

Who the fuck are you? asked one big boy.

Dorrigo Evans.

That was a blinder, Dorrigo. Your kick.

The smell of eucalypt bark, the bold, blue light of the Tasmanian midday, so sharp he had to squint hard to stop it slicing his eyes, the heat of the sun on his taut skin, the hard, short shadows of the others, the sense of standing on a threshold, of joyfully entering a new universe while your old still remained knowable and holdable and not yet lost—all these things he was aware of, as he was of the hot dust, the sweat of the other boys, the laughter, the strange pure joy of being with others.

Kick it! he heard someone yell. Kick the fucker before the bell rings and it's all over.

And in the deepest recesses of his being, Dorrigo Evans understood that all his life had been a journeying to this point when he had for a moment flown into the sun and would now be journeying away from it forever after. Nothing would ever be as real to him. Life never had such meaning again.

## 4

Clever bugger, aren't we? said Amy. She lay on the hotel room's bed with him eighteen years after he had seen Jackie Maguire weeping in front of his mother, twirling her finger in his cropped curls as he recited 'Ulysses' for her. The room was on a run-down hotel's third storey and opened out onto a deep verandah which—by cutting off all sight of the road beneath and beach opposite—gave them the illusion of sitting on the Southern Ocean, the waters of which they could hear crashing and dragging without cease below.

It's a trick, Dorrigo said. Like pulling a coin out of someone's ear.

No, it's not.

No, Dorrigo said. It's not.

What is it, then?

Dorrigo wasn't sure.

And the Greeks, the Trojans, what's that all about? What's the difference?

The Trojans were a family. They lose.

And the Greeks?

The Greeks?

No. The Port Adelaide Magpies. Of course, the Greeks. What are they?

Violence. But the Greeks are our heroes. They win.

Why?

He didn't know exactly why.

There was their trick, of course, he said. The Trojan horse, an offering to the gods in which hid the death of men, one thing containing another.

Why don't we hate them, then? The Greeks?

He didn't know exactly why. The more he thought on it, the more he couldn't say why this should be, nor why the Trojan family had been doomed. He had the sense that *the gods* was just another name for time, but he felt that it would be as stupid to say such a thing as it would be to suggest that against the gods we can never prevail. But at twenty-seven, soon to be twenty-eight, he was already something of a fatalist about his own destiny, if not that of others. It was as if life could be shown but never explained, and words—all the words that did not say things directly—were for him the most truthful.

He was looking past Amy's naked body, over the crescent line between her chest and hip, haloed with tiny hairs, to where, beyond the weathered French doors with their flaking white paint, the moonlight formed a narrow road on the sea that ran away from his gaze into spreadeagled clouds. It was as if it were waiting for him.

*My purpose holds,*
*To sail beyond the sunset, and the baths*
*Of all the western stars until I die.*

Why do you love words so? he heard Amy ask.

His mother died of tuberculosis when he was nineteen. He was not there. He was not even in Tasmania, but on the mainland, on a scholarship to study medicine at the University of Melbourne. In truth, more than one sea separated them. At Ormond College he had met people from great families, proud of achievements and genealogies that went back beyond the founding of Australia to distinguished families in England. They could list generations of their families, their political offices and companies and dynastic marriages, their mansions and sheep stations. Only as an old man did he come to realise much of it was a fiction greater than anything Trollope ever attempted.

In one way it was phenomenally dull, in another fascinating. He had never met people with such certainty before. Jews and Catholics were less, Irish ugly, Chinese and Aborigines not even human. They did not think such things. They knew them. Odd things amazed him. Their houses made of stone. The weight of their cutlery. Their ignorance of the lives of others. Their blindness to the beauty of the natural world. He loved his family. But he was not proud of them. Their principal achievement was survival. It would take him a lifetime to appreciate what an achievement that was. At the time though—and when set against the honours, wealth, property and fame that he was now meeting with for the first time—it seemed failure. And rather than showing shame, he simply stayed away from them until his mother's death. At her funeral he had not cried.

Cmon, Dorry, Amy said. Why? She dragged a finger up his thigh.

After, he became afraid of enclosed spaces, crowds, trams, trains and dances, all things that pressed him inwards and cut out the light. He had trouble breathing. He heard her calling him in his dreams.

Boy, she would say, come here, boy.

But he would not go. He almost failed his exams. He read and reread 'Ulysses'. He played football once more, searching for light, the world he had glimpsed in the church hall, rising and rising again into the sun until he was captain, until he was a doctor, until he was a surgeon, until he was lying in bed there in that hotel with Amy, watching the moon rise over the valley of her belly. He read and reread 'Ulysses'.

> *The long day wanes: the slow moon climbs: the deep*
> *Moans round with many voices. Come, my friends,*
> *'Tis not too late to seek a newer world.*

He clutched at the light at the beginning of things.

He read and reread 'Ulysses'.

He looked back at Amy.

They were the first beautiful thing I ever knew, Dorrigo Evans said.

## 5

When he awoke an hour later, she had painted her lips cherry-red, mascaraed her gas-flame eyes and got her hair up, leaving her face a heart.

Amy?

I've got to go.

Amy—

Besides—

Stay.

For what?

I—

For what? I've heard it—

I want you. Every moment I can have you, I want you.

—too many times. Will you leave Ella?

Will you leave Keith?

Got to go, Amy said. Said I'd be there in an hour. Card evening. Can you believe it?

I'll be back.

Will you?

I will.

And then?

It's meant to be secret.

Us?

No. Yes. No, the war. A military secret.

What?

We ship out. Wednesday.

What?

Three days from—

I know when Wednesday is. Where?

The war.

Where?

How would we know?

Where are you going?

To the war. It's everywhere, the war, isn't it?

Will I see you again?

I—

Us? And us?—

Amy—

Dorry, will I see you again?

# 6

Dorrigo Evans felt fifty years pass in the wheezy shudder somewhere of a refrigeration plant. The angina tablet was already doing its work, the tightness in his chest was retreating, the tingling in his arm had gone, and though some wild internal disorder beyond medicine remained in his quaking soul he felt well enough to return from the hotel bathroom to the bedroom.

As he walked back to their bed, he looked at her naked shoulder with its soft flesh and curve that never ceased to thrill him. She partly raised a face damasked with sleep, and asked—

What were you talking about?

As he lay back down and spooned into her, he realised she meant a conversation earlier, before she had fallen asleep. Far away—as if in defiance of all the melancholy sounds of early morning that drifted in and out of their city hotel room—a car revved wildly.

Darky, he whispered into her back, as though it were obvious, then, realising it wasn't, added, Gardiner. His lower lip caught on her skin as he spoke. I can't remember his face, he said.

Not like your face, she said.

There was no point to it, thought Dorrigo Evans, Darky Gardiner died and there was no point to it at all. And he wondered why he could not write something so obvious and simple, and he wondered why he could not see Darky Gardiner's face.

That's flipping inescapable, she said.

He smiled. He could never quite get over her use of words like flipping. Though he knew her to be vulgar at heart, her upbringing demanded such quaint oddities of language. He held his aged dry lips to the flesh of her shoulder. What was it about a woman that made him even now quiver like a fish?

Can't switch on the telly or open a magazine, she continued, warming to her own joke, without seeing that nose sticking out.

And his own face did seem to Dorrigo Evans, who had never thought much of it, to be everywhere. Since being brought to public attention two decades before in a television show about his past, it had begun staring back at him from everything from charity letterheads to memorial coins. Big-beaked, bemused, slightly shambolic, his once curly dark hair now a thin white wave. In the years that for most his age were termed *declining* he was once more ascending into the light.

Inexplicably to him, he had in recent years become a war hero, a famous and celebrated surgeon, the public image of a time and a tragedy, the subject of biographies, plays and documentaries. The object of veneration, hagiographies, adulation. He understood that he shared certain features, habits and history with the war hero. But he was not him. He'd just had more success at living than at dying, and there were no longer so many left to carry the mantle for the POWs. To deny the reverence seemed to insult the memory of those who had died. He couldn't do that. And besides, he no longer had the energy.

Whatever they called him—hero, coward, fraud—all of it now seemed to have less and less to do with him. It belonged to a world that was ever more distant and vaporous to him. He understood he was admired by the nation, if despaired of by those who had to work with him as an ageing surgeon, and mildly disdained and possibly envied by the many other doctors who had done similar things in other POW camps but who sensed, unhappily, that there was something in his character that was not in theirs which had elevated him far above them in the nation's affections.

Damn that documentary, he said.

But at the time he had not minded the attention. Perhaps he had secretly even enjoyed it a little. But no longer. He was not unaware of his critics. Mostly he found himself in agreement with them. His fame seemed to him a failure of perception on the part of others. He had avoided what he regarded as some obvious errors of life, such as politics and golf. But his attempt to develop a new surgical technique for dealing with the removal of colonic cancers had been unsuccessful, and, worse, may have indirectly led to the deaths of several patients. He had overheard Maison calling him a butcher. Perhaps, looking back, he had been reckless. But had he succeeded he knew he would have been praised for his daring and vision. His relentless womanising and the deceit that necessarily went with it were private scandals and publicly ignored. He still could shock even himself—the ease, the alacrity with which he could lie and manipulate and deceive—and his own estimate of himself was, he felt, realistically low. It was not his only vanity, but it was among his more foolish.

Even at his age—he had turned seventy-seven the previous week—he was confused by what his nature had wrought in his life. After all, he understood that the same fearlessness, the same refusal to accept convention, the same delight in games and his same hopeless hunger to see how far he might push a situation that had driven him in the camps to help others had also driven him into the arms of Lynette Maison, the wife of a close colleague, Rick Maison, a fellow council member of the College of Surgeons, a brilliant, eminent and entirely dull man. And more than one or two others. He hoped in the foreword he had that day been writing—without bothering it with unnecessary revelation—to somehow finally put these things somewhat to rights with the honesty of humility, to restore his role to what it was, that of a doctor, no more and no less, and to restore to rightful memory the many who were forgotten by focusing on them rather than himself. Somewhere he felt it a necessary act of correction and contrition. Somewhere even deeper he feared that such self-abasement, such humility, would only rebound further in his favour. He was trapped. His face was everywhere but he could now no longer see their faces.

I am become a name, he said.

Who?

Tennyson.

I've never heard it.

'Ulysses'.

No one reads him anymore.

No one reads anything anymore. They think Browning is a gun.

I thought it was only Lawson for you.

It is. When it's not Kipling or Browning.

Or Tennyson.

I am a part of all that I have met.

You made that up, she said.

No. It's very—what's the word?

Apposite?

Yes.

You can recite all that, said Lynette Maison, running a hand down his withered thigh. And so much else besides. But you can't remember a man's face.

No.

Shelley came to him on death, and Shakespeare. They came to him unbidden and were as much a part of his life now *as* his life. As though a life could be contained within a book, a sentence, a few words. Such simple words. Thou art come unto a feast of death. The pale, the cold, and the moony smile. Oh, them old-timers.

Death is our physician, he said. He found her nipples wondrous. There had been a journalist at the dinner that evening who had questioned him about the bombing of Hiroshima and Nagasaki.

Once, perhaps, the journalist said. But twice? Why twice?

They were monsters, Dorrigo Evans said. You have no comprehension.

The journalist asked if the women and children were monsters too? And their unborn children?

Radiation, Dorrigo Evans said, doesn't affect subsequent generations.

But that wasn't the question and he knew it, and besides, he did not know whether radiation's effects were transmitted. Someone a long time ago had told him that they weren't. Or that they were. It was hard to remember. These days he relied on the increasingly fragile assumption that what he said was right, and what was right was what he said.

The journalist said he had done a story on the survivors, had met and filmed them. Their suffering, he had said, was terrible and lifelong.

It is not that you know *nothing* about war, young man, Dorrigo Evans had said. It is that you have learnt one thing. And war is many things.

He had turned away. And after, turned back.

By the way, do you sing?

Now Dorrigo tried to lose his memory of that sorry, awkward and frankly embarrassing exchange as he always did, in flesh, and he cupped one of Lynette's breasts, nipple between two fingers. But his thoughts remained elsewhere. No doubt the journalist would dine out on the story forever after, about the war hero who was really a warmongering, nuke-loving, senile old fool who finished up asking him if he sang!

But something about the journalist had reminded him of Darky Gardiner, though he couldn't say what it was. Not his face, nor his manner. His smile? His cheek? His daring? Dorrigo had been annoyed by him, but he admired his refusal to bend to the authority of Dorrigo's celebrity. Some inner cohesion—integrity, if you like. An insistence on truth? He couldn't say. He couldn't point to a tic that was similar, a gesture, a habit. A strange shame arose within him. Perhaps he had been foolish. And wrong. He was no longer sure of anything. Perhaps, since that day of Darky's beating, he had been sure of nothing.

I shall be a carrion monster, he whispered into the coral shell of her ear, an organ of women he found unspeakably moving in its soft, whorling vortex, and which always seemed to him an invitation to adventure. He very softly kissed her lobe.

You should say what you think in your own words, Lynette Maison said. Dorrigo Evans' words.

She was fifty-two, beyond children but not folly, and despised herself for the hold the old man had over her. She knew he had not just a wife, but another woman. And, she suspected, one or two others. She lacked even the sultry glory of being his only mistress. She did not understand herself. He had the sourdough smell of age. His chest sagged into shrivelled teats; his lovemaking was unreliable, yet she found it strangely wholesome in a way that defied sense. With him she felt the unassailable security of being loved. And yet she knew that one part of him—the part she wanted most, the part that was the light in him—remained elusive and unknown. In her dreams Dorrigo was always levitating a few inches above her. Often of a day she was moved to rage, accusations, threats and coldness in her dealings with him. But late of a night, lying next to him, she wished for no one else.

There was a filthy sky, he was saying, and she could feel him readying to rise once more. It was always moving away, he went on, as if it couldn't stand it either.

## 7

When they arrived in Siam in early 1943 it had been different. For one thing, the sky was clear and vast. A familiar sky, or so he thought. It was the dry season, the trees were leafless, the jungle open, the earth dusty. For another, there was some food. Not much, not enough, but starvation hadn't yet taken hold and hunger didn't yet live in the men's bellies and brains like some crazed thing. Nor had their work for the Japanese become the madness that would kill them like so many flies. It was hard, but at the beginning it was not insane.

When Dorrigo Evans lowered his gaze, it was to see a straight line of surveyors' pegs hammered into the ground by Imperial Japanese Army engineers to mark the route of a railway that led away from where he stood at the head of a party of silent prisoners of war. They learnt from the Japanese engineers that the pegs ran in a four hundred and fifteen-kilometre line from north of Bangkok all the way through to Burma.

They outlined a route for a great railway that was still only a series of limited plans, seemingly impossible orders and grand exhortations on the part of the Japanese High Command. It was a fabled railway that was the issue of desperation and fanaticism, made as much of myth and unreality as it was to be of wood and iron and the thousands upon thousands of lives that were to be laid down over the next year to build it. But what reality was ever made by realists?

They were handed blunt axes and rotten hemp rope and with them their first job—to fell, grub and clear a kilometre of giant teak trees that grew along the planned path of the railway.

My dad used to say you young never carry your weight, Jimmy Bigelow said as he tapped a forefinger on the axe's dull and dented edge. I wish the bastard was here now.

# 8

And after, no one will really ever remember it. Like the greatest crimes, it will be as if it never happened. The suffering, the deaths, the sorrow, the abject, pathetic pointlessness of such immense suffering by so many; maybe it all exists only within these pages and the pages of a few other books. Horror can be contained within a book, given form and meaning. But in life horror has no more form than it does meaning. Horror just is. And while it reigns, it is as if there is nothing in the universe that it is not.

The story behind this book begins on 15 February 1942, when one empire ends with the fall of Singapore and another arises. Yet by 1943, Japan, overstretched, under-resourced, is losing, and its need for this railway becomes pronounced. The Allies are supplying Chiang Kai-shek's Nationalist army in China with armaments through Burma, and the Americans control the seas. To cut off this critical supply line to their Chinese enemy, and to take India through Burma—as their leaders now madly dream—Japan must feed their Burmese forces with men and matériel by land. But it has neither the money nor machinery to build the necessary railway. Nor the time.

War, though, is its own logic. The Japanese Empire has belief that it will win—the indomitable Japanese spirit, that spirit that the West does not have, that spirit it calls and understands as the Emperor's will; it is *this* spirit that it believes will prevail until its final victory. And, aiding such indomitable spirit, abetting such belief, the Empire has the good fortune of slaves. Hundreds of thousands of slaves, Asian and European. And among their number are twenty-two thousand Australian POWs, most surrendered at the fall of Singapore as a strategic necessity before the fighting has even properly begun. Nine thousand of them will be sent to work on the railway. When, on 25 October 1943, steam locomotive C 5631 travels the length of the completed Death Railway—the first train to do so—towing its three carriages of Japanese and Thai dignitaries, it will be past endless beds of human bones that will include the remains of one in three of those Australians.

Today, steam locomotive C 5631 is proudly displayed in the museum that forms part of Japan's unofficial national war memorial, the Yasukuni Shrine in Tokyo. As well as steam locomotive C 5631, the shrine contains the *Book of Souls*. This lists over two million names of those who died in service to the Emperor of Japan in wars between 1867 and 1951. With enshrinement in the *Book of Souls* at this sacred site comes absolution from all acts of evil. Among those many names are those of 1,068 men convicted of war crimes after World War II and executed. And among those 1,068 names of executed war criminals are some who worked on the Death Railway and were found guilty of the mistreatment of POWs.

On the plaque in front of locomotive C 5631 there is no mention of this. Nor is there mention of the horror of the building of the railway. There are no names of the hundreds of thousands who died building that railway. But then there is not even an agreed numbering of all those who died on the Death Railway. The Allied POWs were but a fraction—some 60,000 men—of those who slaved on that Pharaonic project. Alongside them were a quarter of a million Tamils, Chinese, Javanese, Malayans, Thais and Burmese. Or more. Some historians say 50,000 of these slave labourers died, some say 100,000, some say 200,000. No one knows.

And no one will ever know. Their names are already forgotten. There is no book for their lost souls. Let them have this fragment.

So Dorrigo Evans had earlier that day ended his foreword for the book of Guy Hendricks' illustrations of the POW camps, having asked his secretary to block out three hours without interruption so he might finish a task he had been unable to complete for several months and which was now considerably overdue. Even finished, he felt it was one more failed attempt by himself to understand what it all meant, dressed up as an introduction to others that might simply explain the Death Railway.

His tone, he felt, was at once too obvious and too personal; somehow it brought to his mind the questions he had failed to resolve all his life. His head was full of so many things, and somehow he had failed to realise any of them on the page. So many things, so many names, so many dead, and yet one name he could not write. He had sketched at the beginning of his foreword a description of Guy Hendricks and something of an outline of the events of the day he died, including the story of Darky Gardiner.

But of that day's most important detail he had written nothing. He looked at his foreword, written, as ever, in his customary green ink, with the simple, if guilty, hope that in the abyss that lay between his dream and his failure there might be something worth reading in which the truth could be felt.

## 9

For good reason, the POWs refer to the slow descent into madness that followed simply with two words: *the Line*. Forever after, there were for them only two sorts of men: the men who were *on the Line*, and the rest of humanity, who were not. Or perhaps only one sort: the men who *survived the Line*. Or perhaps, in the end, even this is inadequate: Dorrigo Evans was increasingly haunted by the thought that it was only the men who *died on the Line*. He feared that only in them was the terrible perfection of suffering and knowledge that made one fully human.

Looking back down at the railway pegs, Dorrigo Evans saw that there was around them so much that was incomprehensible, incommunicable, unintelligible, undivinable, indescribable. Simple facts explained the pegs. But they conveyed nothing. What is a line, he wondered, the Line? A line was something that proceeded from one point to another—from reality to unreality, from life to hell—'breadthless length', as he recalled Euclid describing it in schoolboy geometry. A length without breadth, a life without meaning, the procession from life to death. A journey to hell.

In his Parramatta hotel room half a century later, Dorrigo Evans dozed, he tossed, he dreamt of Charon, the filthy ferryman who takes the dead across the Styx to hell for the price of an obol left in their mouth. In his dream he mouthed Virgil's words describing the dread Charon: frightful and foul, his face covered with unkempt hoary hair, his fierce eyes lit with fire, and a filthy cloak hanging from a knot on his shoulder.

On the night he lay there with Lynette Maison, he had beside their bed, as he always did, no matter where he was, a book, having returned to the habit of reading in his middle age. A good book, he had concluded, leaves you wanting to reread the book. A great book compels you to reread your own soul. Such books were for him rare and, as he aged, rarer. Still he searched, one more Ithaca for which he was forever bound. He read late of an afternoon. He almost never looked at whatever the book was of a night, for it existed as a talisman or a lucky object—as some familiar god that watched over him and saw him safely through the world of dreams.

His book that night was presented to him by a delegation of Japanese women, come to apologise for Japanese war crimes. They came with ceremony and video cameras, they brought presents, and one gift was curious: a book of translations of Japanese death poems, the result of a tradition that sees Japanese poets compose a final poem. He had placed it on the darkwood bedside table next to his pillow, aligning it carefully with his head. He believed books had an aura that protected him, that without one beside him he would die. He happily slept without women. He never slept without a book.

## 10

Browsing the book earlier in the day, Dorrigo Evans had been taken by one poem. On his death bed, the eighteenth-century haiku poet Shisui had finally responded to requests for a death poem by grabbing his brush, painting his poem, and dying. On the paper Shisui's shocked followers saw he had painted a circle.

Shisui's poem rolled through Dorrigo Evans' subconscious, a contained void, an endless mystery, lengthless breadth, the great wheel, eternal return: the circle—antithesis of the line.

The obol left in the mouth of the dead to pay the ferryman.

# 11

Dorrigo Evans' journey to the Line passed through a POW camp in the Javanese highlands, where, as a colonel he had ended up second-in-command of one thousand imprisoned soldiers, mostly Australians. They passed the interminable time that felt like life dribbling away with sport, education programs and concerts, singing their memories of home and beginning their life's work of burnishing tales of the Middle East—of camel trains at dusk loaded with sandstone; Roman ruins and crusaders' castles; Circassian mercenaries in long, silver-trimmed black overcoats and high black astrakhan hats; and Senegalese soldiers, great big men, walking past them with their boots around their necks. They wistfully recalled the French girls of Damascus; yelling out *Jewish bastards!* from the back of trucks to Arabs as they drove past them in Palestine till they met the Arab working girls of Jerusalem; yelling out *Arab bastards!* from the back of trucks to Jews as they drove past them till they saw the Jewish girls of the kibbutz, blue-shorted and white-bloused, pressing bags of oranges on them. They laughed again at the story of Yabby Burrows, with hair that looked as if he had borrowed it from an echidna, going four and twenty at the Cairo brothel, coming back scratching his crotch violently and earning his name by asking, when he looked down, What are these wog yabbies? Have to be something off the bloody gyppo toilet seat, wouldn't they?

Poor old Yabby, they would say. Poor bloody bastard.

For a long time nothing much had happened. Dorrigo had written love letters for friends from Cairo café tables sticky with spilt arak, mortal lusts secreted in immortal boasts that invariably began, *I write this to you by the light of gun fire . . .*

Then had come the rocks and dried pellets of goat shit and dried olive leaves of the Syrian campaign, slipping and sliding with their heavy gear past the occasional bloated Senegalese corpse, their thoughts their own as, far away, they heard the stutter and crack and crump of battles and skirmishes elsewhere. The dead and their arms and gear were scattered like the stones—everywhere, inevitable—and other than avoiding treading on their bloated forms beyond comment or thought. One of his three Cypriot muleteers had asked Dorrigo Evans which direction exactly they were headed. He had not the slightest idea, but he had understood even then that he was obliged to say something to hold them all together.

A nearby mule had brayed, he scratched a mortar ball of grit out of the corner of his eye and looked around the durra field they stood in and back at the two maps, his and the muleteers', neither of which agreed on any substantial detail. Finally, he gave a compass reading that accorded with neither map but, as with so many of his decisions, trusted an instinct that proved mostly right, and, when it didn't, at least afforded movement, which he had come to understand was frequently more important. He had been second-in-charge of the Australian Imperial Force's 2/7th Casualty Clearing Station, near the front line, when they had received orders to pack up their field hospital in the chaos of a tactical retreat that, the following day, would become the confusion of a strategic advance.

The rest of the casualty clearing station had evacuated in trucks far behind lines, while he had remained with the outstanding supplies, waiting for the final truck. He was met instead with a twenty-strong mule train with three Cypriot handlers and fresh orders for him to advance with his supplies to a village at the new front, twenty miles south on their map and twenty-six miles west on his. Small, talkative men, the Cypriots formed yet one more part of the carnival of Allied forces fighting there in Syria against the carnival of Vichy French forces, a small war in the midst of a far bigger one that no one after ever remembered.

## 12

What should have taken two days instead had taken the best part of a week. On the second day, on a steep track leading into the mountains, Dorrigo and the three muleteers had come upon a platoon of seven Tasmanian machine-gunners whose truck had broken down. Led by a young sergeant called Darky Gardiner, they were making for the same destination. They had transferred their Vickers guns and tripods and metal boxes of ammo belts to the spare mules, and together they went on, Darky Gardiner sometimes softly singing as they made their way up and over the rocky slopes and screes, through the mountain passes, the broken villages, past the rotting flesh, the stone walls groggily half-standing, half-fallen, again and again that spilt olive oil smell, the dead horse smell, the scattered chairs and broken tables and beds smell, the collapsed roofs of broken houses smell, as the enemy seventy-fives kept pounding ahead and behind them.

When they had made it back down into the lowlands, they passed dry stone walls that had offered no protection from the incoming twenty-five-pounders to the men who now lay peacefully among their scattered and broken gear and arms and French tin hats. They walked on through the dead, the dead in the half-moon sangars of rocks pointlessly piled up as a defence against death, the dead bloating in a durra field turned to a hideous bog by water spilt from an ancient stone water channel broken by a shell, the fifteen dead in the village of seven houses in which they had tried to escape death, the dead woman in front of the broken minaret, her small rag bundle of possessions scattered in the dust of the street, her teeth on top of a pumpkin, the blasted bits of the dead stinking in a burnt-out truck.

After, Dorrigo Evans remembered how pretty the rag bundle's faded pattern of red and white flowers was, and he felt oddly ashamed that he remembered nothing much else. He had forgotten the sharp taste of stone dust that hung around the broken village houses, the dead skinny donkeys' smell and the dead wretched goats' smell, the broken terraces' smell and smashed olive groves' smell, the sour stench of high explosive, the heavy odour of spilled olive oil, all melding into a single smell he came to associate with human beings in trouble. They had smoked to keep the dead out of their nostrils, they had joked to keep the dead from preying on their minds, they had eaten to remind themselves they were alive, and Darky Gardiner had run a book on whether he himself might get killed, believing his chances were improving all the time.

Passing through maize fields at midnight, they had

come on a broken village lit by green flare light that the French had inexplicably abandoned after seizing it from the Australians in a fierce fight. The mortars the French had used in their attack had transformed the Australian defenders into things not human, drying dark-red meat and fly-blown viscera, streaked, smashed bone and the faces clenched back on exposed teeth, those exposed, terrible teeth of death Dorrigo Evans began to see in every smile.

Finally, they had made it to the village of their orders to find it still occupied by the French and under heavy bombardment by the Royal Navy. Far out at sea warships huffed and puffed, their big guns working methodically to destroy the village one house at a time, moving from a barn to the stone house next to it and then to the outbuilding behind it. Dorrigo Evans, the muleteers and the machine gunners had watched from a safe distance while in front of them the town was transformed into rubble and dust.

Though it was hard to conceive of anything left there that was not dead, still the shells had rained down. At noon the French unexpectedly withdrew. The Australians advanced over the yellow ground scorched by shell-burst, making their way through collapsed terrace walls, over shattered tiles and around broken trees' still intact root balls, twisted guns and artillery pieces; past gun crews already bloating and slashed, some looking as if sleeping in the midday sun, were it not that out of their popped eyes there ran a jelly that formed with the filth on their stubbled cheeks a dirty paste. No one felt anything other than hunger and weariness. A goat had staggered silently before them, intestines hanging out of its side, ribs exposed, head held high, making no noise, as if it might live through fortitude alone. Perhaps it had.

It's Mr Beau bloody Geste himself, said a lanky machine gunner with red hair. They shot it anyway. His full name was Gallipoli von Kessler, a Huon Valley apple orchardist given to greeting others with a lazy Nazi salute. His name arose out of his German father's pretence that he had been something in the old world, adding the aristocratic *von* to the peasant Kessler name, and his later terror of losing everything in the new world when his barn was burnt down in the anti-German hysteria of the Great War. The mountain settlement behind Hobart in which they lived with other German migrants had promptly changed its name from Bismarck to Collinsvale, and Karl von Kessler had changed his son's first name from one honouring his father to one honouring Australia's involvement in the disastrous invasion of Turkey the year before his birth. It was a name too grand for a face that looked like an old apple core. He was known simply as Kes.

In the town, they had walked past a French tank red-hot from burning, overturned lorries, smashed armoured cars, ordinary cars riddled with bullets, piles of ammunition, papers, clothes, shells, guns and rifles scattered through the streets. Amidst the chaos and rubble, the shops were open, trade went on, people cleaned up as if after a natural catastrophe, and off-duty Australians were wandering around buying and scrounging souvenirs.

They fell asleep to the sound of jackals yapping as they came in to feed on the dead.

# 13

At first light Dorrigo had arisen to find Darky Gardiner had lit a fire in the middle of the village's main street. He was sitting in front of it in an opulent armchair that was upholstered in blue silk brocaded with silver fish, one leg tossed over its arm, playing with a crushed box of French cigarettes. In the sea of that chair—his dark, skinny body clad in dirty khaki—he reminded Dorrigo of a branch of bull kelp washed up on a strange shore.

Darky Gardiner's kitbag seemed only half the size of anyone else's, but from it appeared a seemingly inexhaustible supply of foodstuffs and cigarettes—traded on the black market, foraged or stolen—small miracles that had led to his earning his other name of the Black Prince. Just as he threw Dorrigo Evans a tin of Portuguese sardines, the Vichy French began pounding the village with seventy-fives, heavy machine guns and a single aircraft that came in on strafing runs. But everything seemed to be happening elsewhere, and so they drank some French coffee Jimmy Bigelow had found and chatted, awaiting orders or the war to find them.

Rabbit Hendricks—a compact man with an ill-fitting set of dentures—was finishing a sketch on the back of a postcard of Damascus that was to serve as a replacement for a disintegrating photograph of Lizard Brancussi's wife, Maisie. A spiderweb of fine cracks had spread across her face, and what was left of the emulsion had curled into so many tiny autumnal leaves that she was now a woman to be guessed at. Rabbit Hendricks' pencil drawing captured the same pose and neck, but it was a little more Mae Westish around the eyes and a lot more Mae Westish around the chest, suggesting a cleavage Maisie had never boasted, and a look that was somehow more direct and alluring, and that spoke of things about which Maisie rarely did.

Explain to me, Jimmy Bigelow was saying, why we machine-gun waves of black Africans fighting for the French who are equally intent on killing us, Australians fighting for the English in the Middle East?

The drawing—which seemed possibly false, and therefore a strange betrayal—troubled Lizard Brancussi. But because everyone else thought his wife looked wonderful he offered Rabbit Hendricks his watch in exchange, declaring that was his girl. Rabbit refused the offer, took out a sketchbook and began drawing a group portrait of them having their morning coffee.

It's not even fucking east of fucking Australia, said Jack Rainbow. He had the face of an anchorite and the tongue of the wharfie that he, a hop farmer, was not. It's north, he said. No wonder we can't work out where the next village is. We don't even know where we are. It's the far fucking north.

You always was a commie, Jack, Darky Gardiner said. I'll give you twelve to one I'll be dead by breakfast. Can't ask for fairer than that.

Jack Rainbow said he'd rather shoot him there and then.

Dorrigo Evans put down ten shillings at twenty to three that the sergeant would make it through the war.

Rightio, said Jimmy Bigelow. I'm with him. You're a survivor, Darky.

You throw two coins up in the air, said Darky Gardiner, producing a bottle of cognac from a bag at his feet and topping up everyone's coffee, you bet on the outcome, but the fact is, if it's landed two heads three times in a row, it's still statistically just as likely to be two heads again. So you bet two heads again. Every throw is always the first throw. Isn't that a lovely idea?

A moment later the war finally found them. Dorrigo Evans was standing next to the armchair, pouring a coffee, and Yabby Burrows had just arrived from the field kitchen with a hot box containing their breakfast, when they heard a seventy-five shell coming in. Darky Gardiner leapt out of his chair, grabbing Dorrigo Evans by the arm and pulling him to the ground. The explosion passed through them like a cosmic wave.

When Dorrigo opened his eyes and looked around, the blue armchair with its little silver fish had vanished. Amidst the dust fog an Arab boy stood up. They yelled at him to get down, and when he took no notice Yabby Burrows rose on his haunches to wave him down, and when that had no effect he ran to the boy. At that moment another shell hit. The force of the blast blew the Arab boy onto them, his throat slashed by shrapnel. He was dead before anyone got to him.

Dorrigo Evans turned to Darky Gardiner, who was still holding him. Next to them, Rabbit Hendricks was shoving a dusty pair of teeth back in his mouth. Of Yabby Burrows nothing remained.

I like to keep my bets close, the Black Prince said.

Dorrigo was about to reply when an enemy plane came in on another strafing run down their far flank. As it rose above them, the plane abruptly transformed into a puff of black smoke. A speck falling from it blossomed into a parachute, and it became clear the pilot had escaped.

As the winds swept the airman towards them, Rooster MacNeice grabbed one of the Cypriots' .303s and took aim. Dorrigo Evans shoved the barrel away, telling him to not to be so fucking stupid.

And Yabby? Rooster MacNeice yelled, his lips gravel-covered, his eyes wild white balls. Was that fucking stupid? And that kid? Was it?

He had a face that seemed handsome but which, as Jack Rainbow pointed out, looked up close as if it had been built out of spare parts. His accompanying reputation as an inept soldier was such that when he lifted the .303 back to his shoulder, took aim again and fired, everyone was amazed that he found his target. The parachutist twitched as if blown by some sudden, violent wind, then abruptly slumped.

Later that day when they finally ate the now cold porridge that was in the hot box Yabby Burrows had been carrying, no one sat with Rooster MacNeice.

## 14

And on they went—the jokes, the stories, the poor buggers who never made it back, the Tripoli palace requisitioned for an AIF recreational centre, two-up and crown and anchor, beer and mates, working girls in the room off the corridor coming down to the ring to play two-up and see if they felt lucky, the footy in mountain villages against the Syrian kids. And then in Java, after their surrender, the women in wet sarongs picking tea they sometimes saw when they went out on firewood foraging parties, how beautiful they were changing into dry sarongs and picking nits out of each other's hair—Christ, Gallipoli von Kessler said as they walked past, walking past that, that's what I call punishment.

But their punishment was only just beginning. After six months they were trucked down to the coast on their way to a new project in Siam; a thousand of them, three days sardined in the greasy hull of a rustbucket boat to Singapore then marched out to Changi Gaol. It was a pleasant place—white, two-storey barracks, lovely and airy, neat lawns, well-dressed Aussie soldiers, fit and hearty, officers with swagger canes and red tabs on their socks, a good view over the Johor Strait, and vegetable gardens. Emaciated, clad in a motley of Australian and Dutch uniforms, and many without shoes, Dorrigo's men stood out. Java Scum, Brigadier Crowbar Callaghan, commander of Changi's Australian POWs, had christened them, yet, despite Dorrigo Evans' entreaties, Callaghan refused to provide them with clothes, boots and provisions. Instead he tried and failed to remove Dorrigo Evans as their commander because of his insubordinate attitude in demanding Callaghan open up his stores.

Little Wat Cooney came up to Chum Fahey with a plan of escape. It was to get on to a working party down on the Singapore wharves and there get themselves nailed into crates or something and be loaded into a ship and in this way get back to Sydney.

It's a good plan, Wat, said Chum Fahey. Only it isn't.

They played a game of footy against the Changi camp's top side and lost by eight goals, but not before hearing Sheephead Morton's three-quarter-time address that began with words that would become for them immortal—

I've only got one thing to tell you blokes, and the first of them is . . .

Two weeks later the Java Scum left in the same rags in which they had arrived, the uncrated Wat Cooney among their number. Now officially designated as Evans' J Force, they were taken to the railway station and crammed into the small, closed steel-box wagons used for carrying rice; twenty-seven men in each, not enough space to even sit. They travelled in tropical heat through tunnels of rubber trees and jungle, glimpsed through a profusion of sweating diggers and a partly open sliding door, that tangled green endless over them, and falling away from them the Malays in sarongs, Indians, the Chinese coolie women, all in their gay cloth headgear out there working the rice paddies, and them in the close dark of those cruel ovens. They were men like other young men, unknown to themselves. So much that lay within them they were now travelling to meet.

Beneath them, the railway line beat on and on, as in the sweat-wet slither they swayed in each other's arms and legs. Near the end of the third day they began to see paddy fields and clumps of sugar palm flashing by, and the Thai women, dark and buxom, raven-black hair and lovely smiles. They had to take turns sitting and they slept each with his legs draped over the next man, enveloped in a fuming stench of stale vomit, of rancid bodies, shit and puke, and on they went, soot-slicked and heartsick, a thousand miles, five days and no food, six stops and three dead men.

On the fifth afternoon they were taken off the train at Ban Pong, forty miles from Bangkok. They were put in high-framed trucks, thirty men jammed in each like cattle and hanging on to each other like monkeys, travelling through jungle on a road six inches deep in fine dust. A vivid blue butterfly fluttered above them. A Western Australian POW crushed it when it landed on his shoulder.

Nightfall came, and still the road went on, and late that evening they reached Tarsau, covered in filth and encrusted in road dust. They slept in the dirt and were back in the trucks at dawn for an hour heading up little more than a bullock track into the mountains. At the track's end, they got off the trucks and marched until late afternoon, when they finally stopped at a small clearing by a river.

Into the blessed river they jumped to swim. Five days in steel boxes, two days in trucks—how beautiful is water? Beatitudes of the flesh, blessings of the world beyond the veil—clean skin, weightlessness, the rushing universe of fluid calm. They slept like logs in their swags, until the whoop of monkeys awoke them at dawn.

The guards marched them through the jungle three and a half miles. A Japanese officer climbed a tree stump to address them.

Thank you, he said, for long way here to help Emperor with railway. Being prisoner great shame. Great! Redeem honour building railway for Emperor. Great honour. Great!

He pointed to the line of surveyors' pegs that marked the course the railway was to take. The pegs quickly vanished in jungle.

They worked on clearing the teak forest for their first section of the line, and only after that task was complete three days later were they told that they now had to make their own camp at a location some miles distant. Huge clumps of bamboo, eighty feet high, large trees, kapok with its horizontal branches, hibiscus and lower shrub—all this they cut and grubbed and burnt and levelled, groups of near-naked men appearing and disappearing into smoke and flame, twenty men hauling as one on a rope like a bullock team to drag out clumps of the vicious spiked bamboo.

Next they went foraging for timber and passed an English camp a mile away; it stank and was full of the sick, and officers doing little for their men and much for themselves. Their warrant officers patrolled the river to stop their men from fishing; some of the English officers still had their angling rods and didn't want common soldiers poaching what they knew to be their fish.

When the Australians got back to their camp clearing, an old Japanese guard introduced himself as Kenji Mogami. He thumped his chest.

It meana mountain lion, he told them, and smiled.

He showed them what was required: using a long parang to cut and notch the roof framing; tearing the inner layer of hibiscus bark into long strips to lash the joints together; covering the roof with palm leaf thatch and the floor with split and flattened bamboo, with not a nail in any of it. After a few hours' work building the first of the camp's shelters the old Japanese guard said, Alright men, yasumi.

They sat down.

He's not such a bad bloke, said Darky Gardiner.

He's the pick of them, said Jack Rainbow. And you know what? If I had half a chance I'd split him from eye to arsehole with a blunt razor blade.

Kenji Mogami thumped his chest again and declared, Mountain lion a Binga Crosby. And the mountain lion began to croon—

You go-AAA-assenuate-a-positive
Eliminanay a negative
Lash on a affirmawive
Don't mess with a Misser In-Beween
Nahhhh donna mess with Missa Inbeweeeen!

## 15

At that early time on the Line when they were still capable of doing such things, the men staged an evening concert on a small bamboo stage, lit by a fire either side. Watching the performance with Dorrigo Evans stood their commanding officer, Colonel Rexroth, a study in irreconcilable contrasts: a highwayman's head on a butcher's body, a pukka accent and all that went with it in the son of a failed Ballarat draper, an Australian who strove to be mistaken as English, a man who had turned to the army in 1927 for the opportunities that had eluded him elsewhere in life. Though he and Dorrigo Evans were the same rank, by dint of experience and by virtue of being a military man as opposed to a medical man, Rexroth was Dorrigo's senior.

Colonel Rexroth turned to Dorrigo Evans and said that he believed that all their national British strengths would be enough, that their British esprit de corps would hold and their British spirit would not break and their British blood would bring them through it together.

Some quinine wouldn't be bad either, Dorrigo Evans said.

A few Englishmen had come over from their camp and were presenting a short play about a German POW in the Great War. The night air was so thick with swarming insects that the performers looked slightly blurred.

Colonel Rexroth said he didn't like his attitude. Only seeing the negative. This demands positive thoughts. Celebration of the national character. And so on.

I've never treated the national character, Dorrigo Evans said.

The Australians had started cheering for the German prisoner.

But I am seeing, he went on, an awful lot of diseases of malnutrition.

We have what we have, Colonel Rexroth said.

To say nothing, Dorrigo Evans said, of malaria, dysentery and tropical ulcers.

The play ended with jeers and catcalls. Dorrigo finally recalled what Colonel Rexroth always reminded him of: the beurre bosc pears Ella's father used to eat. And he realised how hungry he was, how he had never liked those pears with their rusty skin, and how now he would have given almost anything to eat one.

Diseases of starvation, repeated Dorrigo Evans. Drugs would be good. But food and rest even better.

If their work building the railway line for the Japanese hadn't yet become a madness that would kill them, it was already beginning to take a profound physical toll. Les Whittle, who had lost his fingers to pellagra, was now playing a rotting accordion—held together with stitching and buffalo hide patches—with bamboo sticks tied to his wrist. His singer, Jack Rainbow, had lost his vision. Watching him, Dorrigo Evans wondered if it was avitaminosis or the combined damage of several maladies that had done this—whatever the cause, he was painfully aware that food would cure this and almost all of the afflictions he saw. Jack Rainbow's anchorite's face was now puffy as a pumpkin, and his wasted body below also oddly bloated with beri-beri, lending an ulcer—which had eaten through a swollen shin to the bone—the appearance of a blinded pink iris that gazed out from the wound at the crowd of POWS, many as grotesquely affected, as if hoping finally to see the audience of its dreams.

The performers were now playing out a scene from the movie *Waterloo Bridge*, with Les Whittle as Robert Taylor and Jack Rainbow taking the role of Vivien Leigh. They were walking towards each other on a bamboo bridge.

I thought I'd never see you again, said Robert Taylor, disguised as the fingerless Les Whittle, in a highly affected English accent. It's been a lifetime.

Nor me you, said Vivien Leigh, disguised as the blind, bloated, ulcerated Jack Rainbow.

Darling, said Les Whittle. You haven't changed at all.

There was much laughter, after which they played the movie's signature song, 'Auld Lang Syne'.

You see, Colonel Rexroth continued, it's what we carry within.

What?

British stoicism.

It was an American movie.

Pluck, Colonel Rexroth said.

Our officers are paid by the Japanese army. Twenty-five

cents a day. They spend it on themselves. The Japanese do not expect them to work. They should.

Should what, Evans?

Should work here in the camp. Digging latrines. Nursing in the hospital. Orderlies. Building equipment for the sick. Crutches. New shelters. Operating theatres.

He took a deep breath.

And they should pool their wages so we draw on it to buy food and drugs for the sick.

That again, Evans, Colonel Rexroth said. It is example that will get us through. Not Bolshevism.

I agree. When it is the right example.

But Colonel Rexroth was already ascending the stage. He thanked the entertainers, then spoke of how the division of the British Empire into arbitrary nationalities was a fiction. From Oxford to Oodnadatta they were one people.

His accent was thin and reedy. He had no gift for rousing oratory but a misplaced sense that his rank gifted him with this talent. He sounded, as Gallipoli von Kessler said, as though he were playing a flute out of his arse.

And for that reason, Colonel Rexroth went on, as members of the British Empire, as Englishmen, we must observe the order and discipline that is the very lifeblood of the Empire. We will suffer as Englishmen, we will triumph as Englishmen. Thank you.

After, he asked Dorrigo Evans if he would like to be involved in planning for the building of a proper cemetery overlooking the river, where they would be able to inter their dead.

I'd rather get the Black Prince to steal some more tins

of fish from the Japanese stores to keep the living from dying, Dorrigo Evans said.

The Black Prince is a thief, Colonel Rexroth replied. This, however, will be a beautiful final resting place and worthy of the efforts of all concerned for the welfare of the men and far better than the present practice of just marching off into the forest and burying them wherever.

The Black Prince helps me save lives.

Colonel Rexroth produced a large sketch map outlining the location of the cemetery and the layout of the graves, with different sections for different ranks. Proudly, he told Dorrigo that he had reserved a particularly idyllic spot overlooking the Kwai for officers. He pointed out that the men were beginning to die, and dealing with the corpses was now a matter of the highest priority.

It is an irrefutable argument, he said. It's been a lot of work getting it this far. I'd love you to be part of this.

A monkey screeched in a nearby bamboo grove.

I am only doing it for the men, Colonel Rexroth said.

## 16

The trees began sprouting leaves and the leaves began covering up the sky and the sky turned black and the black swallowed more and more of the world. Food grew less and less. The monsoon came and, at first, before they learnt all that the rain portended, they were grateful.

Then the Speedo began.

The Speedo meant that there were no longer rest days, that work quotas went up, and up again, that shifts grew longer and longer. The Speedo dissolved an already vague distinction between the fit and the sick into a vaguer distinction between the sick and the dying, and because of the Speedo more and more often prisoners were ordered to work not one but two shifts, both day and night.

The rains grew torrential, the teak and the bamboo closed in around them; Colonel Rexroth died of dysentery and was buried along with everyone else in the jungle. Dorrigo Evans assumed command. As a great green weight that reached to the black heavens dragged them back down into the black mud, he imposed a levy on the officers' pay to buy food and drugs for the sick. He persuaded, cajoled and insisted on the officers working, as the ceaseless green horror pressed ever harder on their scabies-ridden bodies and groggy guts, on their fevered heads and foul, ulcerated legs, on their perennially shitting arses.

The men called Dorrigo Evans *Colonel* to his face and *the Big Fella* everywhere else. There were moments when the Big Fella felt far too small for all that they now wanted him to bear. There was Dorrigo Evans and there was this other man with whom he shared looks, habits and ways of speech. But the Big Fella was noble where Dorrigo was not, self-sacrificing where Dorrigo was selfish.

It was a part he felt himself feeling his way into, and the longer it went on, the more the men around him confirmed him in his role. It was as if they were willing him into being, as though there had to be a Big Fella, and, having desperate need of such, their growing respect, their whispered asides, their opinion of him—all this trapped him into behaving as everything he knew he was not. As if rather than him leading them by example they were leading *him* through adulation.

And with him now in tow, they together staggered through those days that built like a scream that never ended, a wet, green shriek Dorrigo Evans found perversely amplified by the quinine deafness, the malarial haze that meant a minute took a lifetime to pass and that sometimes it was not possible to recall a week of misery and horror. All of it seemed to wait for some denouement that never came, some event that made sense of it all to him and to them, some catharsis that would free them all from this hell.

Still, there was the occasional duck egg, a finger or two of palm sugar, a joke, repeated over and over, lovingly burnished and appreciated like the rare and beautiful thing it was, that made survival possible. Still there was hope. And from beneath their ever growing slouch hats the ever diminishing prisoners still made asides and curses as they were swept up into another universe in which they lived like ants and all that mattered was the railway. As naked slaves to their section of the Line, with nothing more than ropes and poles, hammers and bars, straw baskets and hoes, with their backs and legs and arms and hands, they began to clear the jungle for the Line and break the rock for the Line and move the dirt for the Line and carry the sleepers and the iron rails to build the Line. As naked slaves, they were starved and beaten and worked beyond exhaustion on the Line. And as naked slaves they began to die for the Line.

No one could reckon it, neither the weak nor the strong. The dead began to accumulate. Three last week, eight this week, God knows how many today. The hospital hut—not so much a hospital as a place where the very worst were allowed to lie in filth and gangrenous stench on long, slatted platforms—was now filled with the dying. There were no longer fit men. There were only the sick, the very sick and the dying. Long gone were the days when Gallipoli von Kessler thought it punishment to be unable to touch a woman. Long gone was even the thought of a woman. Their only thoughts now were of food and rest.

Starvation stalked the Australians. It hid in each man's every act and every thought. Against it they could proffer only their Australian wisdom which was really no more than opinions emptier than their bellies. They tried to hold together with their Australian dryness and their Australian curses, their Australian memories and their Australian mateship. But suddenly *Australia* meant little against lice and hunger and beri-beri, against thieving and beatings and yet ever more slave labour. *Australia* was shrinking and shrivelling, a grain of rice was so much bigger now than a continent, and the only things that grew daily larger were the men's battered, drooping slouch hats, which now loomed like sombreros over their emaciated faces and their empty dark eyes, eyes that already seemed to be little more than black-shadowed sockets waiting for worms.

And still the dead kept on accumulating.

## 17

Dorrigo Evans' mouth was so full of saliva he had to wipe his lips with the back of his hand several times to stop himself dribbling. Staring down at the badly cut, gristly and overdone steak lying in the rectangular cup of his tin dixie, its sooty grease smearing the rusting tin, he could not for the life of him think of anything he could want more in the world. He looked up at the kitchen hand who had brought it for his dinner. The kitchen hand told him how, the night before, a gang led by the Black Prince had stolen a cow off some Thai traders, had slaughtered it in the bush and, after bribing a guard with the eye fillet, had given the rest in secret to the camp kitchen. A steak—*a steak*!—had been carved off, grilled and presented to Dorrigo for his dinner.

The kitchen hand was, Dorrigo Evans could see, a sick man—why else would he be on kitchen duties?—sick with one or several diseases of starvation, and Dorrigo Evans understood that the steak was to that man too, at that moment, the most desirable, extraordinary thing in the universe. Making a hasty gesture, he told the kitchen hand to take it to the hospital and share it among the sickest there. The kitchen hand was unsure if he was serious. He made no movement.

The men want you to have it, the kitchen hand said. Sir.

Why? Dorrigo Evans thought. Why am I saying I don't want the steak? He so desperately wanted to eat it, and the men wanted him to have it, as a tribute of sorts. And yet, much as he knew no one would have begrudged him the meat, he also understood the steak to be a test that demanded witnesses, a test he had to pass, a test that would become a necessary story for them all.

Take it away, Dorrigo Evans said.

He gulped, trying to swallow the saliva that was flooding

his mouth. He feared he might go mad, or break in some terrible or humiliating way. He felt that his soul was not tempered, that he lacked so many of the things they now needed from him, those things that qualified one for an adult life. And yet he now found himself the leader of a thousand men who were strangely leading him to be all the many things he was not.

He gulped again; still his mouth ran with saliva. He did not think himself a strong man who knew he was strong—a strong man like Rexroth. Rexroth, thought Dorrigo Evans, was a man who would have eaten the steak as his right and, after, happily picked his highwayman's teeth in front of his starving men. To the contrary, Dorrigo Evans understood himself as a weak man who was entitled to nothing, a weak man whom the thousand were forming into the shape of their expectations of him as a strong man. It defied sense. They were captives of the Japanese and he was the prisoner of their hope.

*Now!* he snapped, nearly losing control.

Still the kitchen hand did not move, perhaps thinking he was joking, perhaps fearing an error in his understanding. And all the while Dorrigo Evans feared that if the steak stayed there in front of him a moment longer, he would seize it with both hands and swallow it whole and fail this test and be revealed for who he truly was. In his anger at the men's manipulation of him, in his fury at his own weakness, he suddenly stood up and started yelling in a rage—

Now! It's yours, not mine! Take it! Share it! Share it!

And the kitchen hand, relieved that he might now even get to taste a morsel of that steak himself, and delighted that the colonel was all that everyone said the

Big Fella was, stole forward and took the steak to the hospital, and with it one more story of what an extraordinary man their leader was.

## 18

Dorrigo Evans hated virtue, hated virtue being admired, hated people who pretended he had virtue or pretended to virtue themselves. And the more he was accused of virtue as he grew older, the more he hated it. He did not believe in virtue. Virtue was vanity dressed up and waiting for applause. He had had enough of nobility and worthiness, and it was in Lynette Maison's failings that he found her most admirably human. It was in her unfaithful arms that he found fidelity to some strange truth of the passing nature of everything.

She had known privilege and never spent the night with doubt. As her beauty drifted away from her, a wake receding from a now-stilled boat, she came to need him far more than he did her. Imperceptibly to them both, she had become to him one more duty. But then his life was all duty now. Duty to his wife. Duty to his children. Duty to work, to committees, to charities. Duty to Lynette. Duty to the other women. It was exhausting. It demanded stamina. At times he amazed even himself. He would think there ought to be some sort of recognition for such achievement. It took a strange courage. It was loathsome. It made him hate himself, but he could no more not be himself now than he could have not been himself with Colonel Rexroth. And somehow what gave him sense and direction and the capacity to go on, the duty above all other duty, was what he believed he owed to the men he had been with in that camp.

You're thinking of her, she said.

Once more he said nothing. As he did all his other duties he bore Lynette in a manner he felt manful—which is to say, he covered the growing distance between them with an increased affection. She bored him more and more; were it not that she remained an adventure, he would have stopped seeing her years before. Their love-making had been desultory, and he had to concede both to himself and to her that things weren't as they once had been, but Lynette hadn't seemed to mind. In truth, nor did he. It was enough to be allowed to smell her back, to rest a hand between her soft thighs. She could be jealous and selfish, and he could not help it, but the smallness of her satisfied him.

As she prattled on about the politics and gossip of the magazine where she worked as a deputy editor, the petty humiliations she endured from superiors she regarded as her inferiors, her office triumphs, her fears, her innermost desires, he was again seeing that sky during the Speedo, always dirty, and he was thinking of how he hadn't thought of Darky Gardiner for years, not until the previous day, when he had tried to write an account of his beating.

He had been asked to write the foreword to a book of sketches and illustrations made by Guy Hendricks, a POW who had died on the Line, and whose sketchbook Dorrigo had carried and kept hidden for the rest of the war. The sky was always dirty and it was always moving, scurrying away, or so it seemed to him, to some better place where men didn't die for no reason, where life answered to something beyond chance. Darky Gardiner had been right: it had all been a two-up game. That bruised sky, blue-welted and blood-puddling. Dorrigo wanted to remember Darky Gardiner, his face, him singing, that sly split smile. But all he could ever see, no matter how hard he tried to summon his presence, was that filthy sky racing away from all that horror.

Every throw is always the first, Dorrigo remembered Darky saying. Isn't that a lovely idea?

You are and you won't admit it, Lynette Maison said. Go on. Aren't you? Thinking of her?

I never paid up, you know. Ten shillings.

I know it.

Twenty to three. I remember that.

I know it when you're thinking of her.

You know, he whispered into Lynette Maison's fleshy shoulder, I was working on the foreword today and I got stuck there in the Speedo, when they worked us seventy days and nights without a day off through the monsoon. And I was trying to recall when they bashed Darky Gardiner. It was the same day we cremated poor old Guy Hendricks. I tried to write what I remembered of the day. It sounded terrible and noble all at once. But it wasn't any of those things.

I do, you know.

It was miserable and stupid.

Come here.

I think they were bored with it, with the bashing. The Japs, I mean.

Come. Let's sleep.

There was Nakamura, that lousy little bastard the Goanna with his marionette strut, two other Japanese engineers. Or was it three? I can't even remember that. What sort of witness am I? I mean, maybe they really wanted to hurt him at the beginning but then it was boring for them, as boring as the hammer and tap was for our fellows. Can you imagine that? Just work, and tedious, dull work at that.

Let's sleep.

Hard, sweaty work. Like digging a ditch. One stopped for a moment. And I thought, Well, that's that. Thank God. He brought his hand up to his forehead, flicked the sweat away and sniffed. Just like that. Then he went back to work beating Darky. There was no meaning in it, not then and not now, but you can't write that, can you?

But you wrote it.

I wrote. Something. Yes.

And you were truthful.

No.

You weren't truthful?

I was accurate.

Outside in the night, as though searching for a thing hopelessly lost, a reversing truck sounded a forlorn cheep.

I don't know why it stands out for you, she said.

No.

I really don't. Weren't there so many who suffered?

There were, he agreed.

Why does it stand out then?

He said nothing.

Why?

Lying in that hotel bed in Parramatta, he felt he should be thinking of the world full with good things beyond their room, that blue sky just waiting to come again in a few hours, that great blue sky which in his mind was forever associated with the lost freedom of his childhood. Yet his mind could never stop seeing the black-streaked sky of the camp.

Tell me, she said.

It always reminded him of dirty rags drenched in sump oil.

I want to know, she said.

No. You don't.

She's dead, isn't she? I'm only jealous of the living.

From that woman
on the beach, dusk pours out
across the evening waves.

*Issa*

# 1

Dorrigo Evans was in Adelaide, doing his final training with the 2/7th Casualty Clearing Station at the Warradale army camp in the ferocious heat of late 1940, before embarking to who knew where. And he had a half-day leave pass—good for nothing, really. Tom had telegrammed him from Sydney to say their Uncle Keith, who ran a pub just out of Adelaide on the coast, was keen to see Dorrigo and *will look after you royally.* Dorrigo had never met Keith Mulvaney. All he really knew about him was that he had been married to their father's youngest sister who had died in an automobile accident some years ago. Though Keith had since remarried, he kept in contact with his first wife's family through Christmas cards to Tom, who had alerted him to the news of Dorrigo being stationed in Adelaide. Dorrigo had meant to visit his uncle that day, but the car he had hoped to borrow had broken down. So instead he was meeting some fellow doctors from the 2/7th that night at a Red Cross dance in the city.

It was Melbourne Cup day, and there was a languid excitement in the streets following the race. To kill time before the event, he had walked the city streets and ended up in an old bookshop off Rundle Street. An early evening function was in progress, a magazine launch or some such. A confident young man with wild hair and large tie loosely knotted was reading from a magazine.

*We know no mithridatum of despair*
*as drunks, the angry penguins of the night,*
*straddling the cobbles of the square*
*tying a shoelace by fogged lamplight.*

Dorrigo Evans was unable to make head or tail of it. His tastes were in any case already ossifying into the prejudices of those who voyage far into classics in adolescence and rarely journey elsewhere again. He was mostly lost with the contemporary and preferred the literary fashions of half a century before—in his case, the Victorian poets and the writers of antiquity.

Blocked by the small crowd from browsing, he headed up some bare wooden stairs at the far end of the shop that seemed more promising. The second storey was composed of two smaller rear offices, unoccupied, and a large room, also empty of people, floored with wide, rough-sawn boards that ran through to dormer windows that fronted the street. Everywhere were books he could browse; books in teetering piles, books in boxes, second-hand books jammed and leaning at contrary angles like ill-disciplined militia on floor-to-ceiling shelves that ran the length of the far side wall.

It was hot in the room, but it felt to him far less stifling than the poetry reading below. He pulled out a book here and there, but what kept catching his attention were the diagonal tunnels of sunlight rolling in through the dormer windows. All around him dust motes rose and fell, shimmering, quivering in those shafts of roiling light. He found several shelves full of old editions of classical writers and began vaguely browsing, hoping to find a cheap edition of Virgil's *Aeneid,* which he had only ever read in a borrowed copy. It wasn't really the great poem of antiquity that Dorrigo Evans wanted though, but the aura he felt around such books—an aura that both radiated outwards and took him inwards to another world that said to him that he was not alone.

And this sense, this feeling of communion, would at moments overwhelm him. At such times he had the sensation that there was only one book in the universe, and that all books were simply portals into this greater ongoing work—an inexhaustible, beautiful world that was not imaginary but the world as it truly was, a book without beginning or end.

There were some shouts coming up the staircase, and following it there came a cluster of noisy men and two women, one large, red-haired, wearing a dark beret, the other smaller, blonde, wearing a bright crimson flower behind her ear. Every now and again they would reprise a half-song, half-chant, raucously chorusing *Roll on, Old Rowley, roll on!*

The men were a jumble of service uniforms, RAAF, RAN and AIF—they were, he guessed, a little drunk, and all in one way or another were seeking the attention of the smaller woman. Yet she seemed to have no interest in them. Something set her apart from them, and much as they tried to find ways of getting in close to her, no uniformed arm could be seen resting on her arm, no uniformed leg brushing her leg.

Dorrigo Evans saw all this clearly in a glance, and she and they bored him. They were nothing more than her ornaments, and he despised them for being in thrall to something that so obviously would never be theirs. He disliked her power to turn men into what he regarded as little more than slavering dogs, and he rather disliked her in consequence.

He turned away and looked back at the bookshelves. He was in any case thinking of Ella, whom he had met in Melbourne while completing his surgical training. Ella's father was a prominent Melbourne solicitor, her mother from a well-known grazing family; her grandfather was an author of the federal constitution. She herself was a teacher. If she was sometimes dull, her world and her looks still burnt brightly for Dorrigo. If her talk was full of commonplaces learnt as if by rote and repeated so determinedly that he really wasn't sure what she thought, he nevertheless found her kind and devoted. And with her came a world that seemed to Dorrigo secure, timeless, confident, unchanging; a world of darkwood living rooms and clubs, crystal decanters of sherry and single malt, the cloying, slightly intoxicating, slightly claustrophobic smell of polished must. Ella's family was sufficiently liberal to welcome into that world a young man of great expectations from the lower orders, and sufficiently conventional for it to be understood that the terms of its welcome were to be entirely of that world.

The young Dorrigo Evans did not disappoint. He was now a surgeon, and he assumed he would marry Ella, and though they had never spoken about it, he knew she did too. He thought that marrying Ella was another thing like completing his medical degree, receiving his commission, another step up, along, onwards. Ever since Tom's cave, where he had recognised the power of reading, every step forward for Dorrigo had been like that.

He took a book from a shelf, and as he brought it up to his chest it passed from shadow into one of the sun shafts. He held the book there, looking at that book, that light, that dust. It was as though there were two worlds. This world, and a hidden world that it took the momentary shafts of late-afternoon light to reveal as the real world—of flying particles wildly spinning, shimmering, randomly bouncing into each other and heading off into entirely new directions. Standing there in that late-afternoon light, it was impossible to believe any step would not be for the better. He never thought to where or what, he never thought why, he never wondered what might happen if, instead of progressing, he collided like one of the dust motes in the sunlight.

The small group at the far side of the room began once more to swarm and head towards him. It moved like a school of fish or a flock of birds at dusk. Having no desire to be near it, Dorrigo made down the length of bookshelves closer to the street windows. But like birds or fish, the swarm halted as suddenly as it had begun and formed a cluster a few steps away from the bookshelves. Sensing some were glancing his way, he stared more intently at the books.

And when he looked up again he realised why the swarm had moved. The woman with the red flower had walked over to where he stood and now, striped in shadow and light, was standing in front of him.

## 2

Her eyes burnt like the blue in a gas flame. They were ferocious things. For some moments her eyes were all he was aware of. And they were looking at him. But there was no look *in* them. It was as if she were just drinking him up. Was she assessing him? Judging him? He didn't know. Maybe it was this sureness that made him both resentful and unsure. He feared it was all some elaborate joke, and that in a moment she would burst out laughing and have her ring of men joining in, laughing at him. He took a step backwards, bumped into the bookcase and could retreat no more. He stood there, one hand jammed between him and a bookcase shelf, his body twisted at an awkward angle to her.

I saw you come into the bookshop, she said, smiling.

Afterwards, if asked to say what she looked like, he would have been stumped. It was the flower, he decided finally, something about her audacity in wearing a big red flower in her hair, stem tucked behind her ear, that summed her up. But that, he knew, really told you nothing at all about her.

Your eyes, she said suddenly.

He said nothing. In truth, he had no idea what to say. He had never heard anything so ridiculous. *Eyes?* And without meaning to, he found himself returning her stare, looking at her intently, drinking her up as she was him. She seemed not to care. There was some strange and unsettling intimacy, an inexplicable knowledge in this that shocked him—that he could just gaze all over a woman and she not give a damn as long as it was *him* looking at her.

It was as dizzying as it was bewildering. She seemed a series of slight flaws best expressed in a beauty spot above her right lip. And he understood that the sum of all these blemishes was somehow beauty, and there was about this beauty a power, and that power was at once conscious and unconscious. Perhaps, he resolved, she thinks her beauty allows her the right to have whatever she wants. Well, she would not have him.

So black, she said, now smiling. But I'm sure you get told that a lot.

No, he said.

It wasn't entirely true, but then no one had ever said it exactly how she had just said it. Something stopped him from turning away from her, from her outlandish talk, and walking out. He glanced at the ring of men at the far end of the bookcases. He had the unsettling sensation that she meant what she said, and that what she said was meant only for him.

Your flower, Dorrigo Evans said. It's—

He had no idea what the flower was.

Stolen, she said.

She seemed to have all the time in the world to appraise him, and having done so and found him to her liking, she laughed in a way that made him feel that she had found in him all the things most appealing in the world. It was as if her beauty, her eyes, everything that was charming and wonderful about her, now also existed in him.

Do you like it? she asked.

Very much.

From a camellia bush, she said, and laughed again. And then her laugh—more a little cackle, sudden and slightly throaty and somehow deeply intimate—stopped. She leaned forward. He could smell her perfume. And alcohol. Yet he understood she was oblivious to his unease and that this was no attempt at charm. Or flirting. And though he did not will it or want it, he could feel that something was passing between them, something undeniable.

He dropped the hand behind his back and turned so

that he was facing her square-on. Between them a shaft of light was falling through the window, dust rising within it, and he saw her as if out of a cell window. He smiled, he said something—he didn't know what. He looked beyond the light to the ring of men, her praetorian guard waiting in the shadows, hoping one out of self-interest might come over and take advantage of his awkwardness and sweep her back.

What sort of soldier are you? she asked.

Not much of one.

Using his book, he tapped the triangular brown patch with its inset green circle sewn on his tunic shoulder.

2/7th Casualty Clearing Station. I'm a doctor.

He found himself feeling both slightly resentful and somewhat nervous. What business did beauty have with him? Particularly when her expression, her voice, her clothing, everything about her, he understood as that of a woman of some standing, and though he was a doctor now, and an officer, he was not so far removed from his origins that he did not feel these things acutely.

I worried I had gatecrashed the—

The magazine launch? Oh, no. I think they'd welcome anyone with a pulse. Or even without one. Tippy over there—she waved a hand towards the other woman—Tippy says that poet who was reading his work is going to revolutionise Australian literature.

Brave man. I only signed up to take on Hitler.

Did a word of it make any sense to you? she said, her look at once unwavering and searching.

Penguins?

She smiled broadly, as though some difficult bridge had been crossed.

I rather liked shoelaces, she said.

One of the group of her swarming admirers was singing in the manner of Paul Robeson: *Old horse Rowley, he just keep on rolling.*

Tippy roped us all into coming, she said in a new tone of familiarity, as though they'd been friends for many years. Me, her brother and some of his friends. She's a student with the poet downstairs. We'd been at some services officers' club listening to the Cup and she wanted us to come here to listen to Max.

Who's Max? Dorrigo asked.

The poet. But that's not important.

Who's Rowley?

A horse. That's not important either.

He was mute, he didn't know what to say, her words made no sense, her words were irrelevant to everything that was passing between them. If the horse and the poet were both unimportant, what was important? There was something about her—intensity? directness? wildness?—that he found greatly unsettling. What did she want? What did it mean? He longed for her to leave.

On hearing a man's voice, Dorrigo turned to see that one of the swarm—wearing a RAAF officer's light-blue uniform—was standing next to them, telling her in an affected English accent that they needed her back to *help sort out a discussion we're having on tote odds.* Her gaze followed Dorrigo's, and recognising the blue uniform, her face changed entirely. It was as if she were another woman, and her eyes, which had been so alive looking at Dorrigo, were now, while looking at the other man, suddenly dead.

The blue uniform sought to ignore her stare by turning to Dorrigo.

You know she picked him, he said.

Picked who?

Old Rowley. Hundred to one. Longest odds in the history of the Cup. And *she* knew. She bloody well knew which gee-gee. Harry over there made twenty quid.

Before Dorrigo could reply, the woman spoke to the RAAF officer in a way that Dorrigo understood was charming but without any feeling.

I just have one more question for my friend, she said, pointing to Dorrigo. Then I'll be back over with you to talk turf accountancy.

And, that short conversation done, she turned back to Dorrigo and froze the blue uniform out so completely that, after a moment or two, he returned to the others.

## 3

What question?

I have no idea what question, she said.

He feared she was playing with him. His instinct was to get away but something held him there.

What's the book? she asked, pointing to his hands.

Catullus.

Really? She smiled once more.

Dorrigo Evans wanted to be free of her but he was unable to free himself. Those eyes, that red flower. The way—but he would not believe it—the way she seemed to be smiling at *him*. He pushed one hand behind his back, drummed his fingers on the book spines there, on Lucretius and Herodotus and Ovid. But they made no reply.

A Roman poet, he said.

Read one of his poems to me.

He opened the book, looked down, and looked up.

You sure?

Of course.

It's very dry.

So's Adelaide.

He looked back down to the book and read—

*I felt another hunger poke*
*Up between*
*My tunic and my cloak.*

He closed the book.

It's all Latin to me, she said.

Us both, Dorrigo Evans said. He had hoped to insult her with the poem and realised he had failed. She was smiling again. Somehow she made even an insult of his sound like he was flirting, until he began to wonder if he wasn't.

He looked to the window for help. There was none.

Read more, she said.

He hastily flicked some pages, stopped, flicked through a few more, stopped, and began.

*Let us live and love*
*And not care tuppence for old men*
*Who sermonise and disapprove.*
*Suns when they sink can rise again,*
*But we—*

He felt a strange rising anger. Why was he reading this, of all poems? Why not something else that might give offence? But some other force had hold of him now, was guiding him, keeping his voice low and strong, as he went on.

*But we, when our brief light has shone,*
*Must sleep the long night on and on.*

She pinched the top of her blouse with her thumb and forefinger, tugging it upwards while all the while looking at him with eyes that seemed to say she'd really like it tugged downwards.

He closed the book. He didn't know what to say. Many things rushed through his mind, diverting things, innocuous things, brutal things that got him away from the bookcase, away from her and that terrible gaze, her eyes of ferocious blue flame—but he said none of them. Of all the stupid things he might say, all the things he felt rude and necessary, he instead heard himself saying—

Your eyes are—

We were talking about what a nonsense love is, a stranger's voice interrupted.

Turning, Dorrigo saw that most hapless of pretenders, the close friend, had come over from the ring of admirers to join them and, presumably, take the blue eyes back. Perhaps feeling he had to address Dorrigo as well, the friend smiled at him, trying, Dorrigo felt, to gauge who Dorrigo Evans was, and where he stood with the woman. Undone, he would have liked to have told him.

Most people live without love, the friend said. Wouldn't you agree?

I don't know, Dorrigo replied.

The friend smiled, a twist of the mouth for Dorrigo, a slow opening for her, a complicit invitation for her to return to his company, his world, the swarm of drones. She ignored the pretender, turning her shoulder to him and saying she would be back in a minute; making it clear that he was to leave in order that she might stay with Dorrigo. Because this was strictly, well, *them*, though Dorrigo, watching her silent but clear communication, realised he had not wished for it nor consented to it.

All these conversations about love, continued the pretender, just nonsense. There's no need for love. The best marriages are ones of compatibility. The science shows that we all generate electromagnetic fields. When one meets a person with opposite ions aligned in the right direction, they're attracted. But that's not love.

What is it then? asked Dorrigo.

Magnetism, said the pretender.

## 4

Major Nakamura was bad at cards yet he had just won the final hand, because it was understood both by his junior officers and the Australian POWs playing with him that it was better that he didn't lose. Through his interpreter, Lieutenant Fukuhara, Nakamura thanked the Australian colonel and major for the evening. The Japanese major stood up, stumbled backwards, almost fell, but recovered his balance. Nakamura seemed oddly ebullient in spite of nearly falling flat on his face.

The Mekhong whisky he had provided had also taken its toll on the two Australian officers, and Dorrigo Evans moved carefully in standing up. He knew he now had his part to play as the Big Fella. He had held off all night, but he judged now was the moment to act.

The Speedo has been going thirty-seven days non-stop, Major, Dorrigo Evans began. Nakamura looked at him, smiling. Dorrigo Evans smiled back. To fulfil the Emperor's wishes, we would be wisest to harness our resources. To best build the railway, we need to rest our men rather than destroy them. A day's rest would do an enormous amount to help preserve not just the men's energy, but the men themselves.

He fully expected Nakamura to explode, to hit him or threaten him, or at the very least to yell and scream at him. But the Japanese commander only laughed as Lieutenant Fukuhara translated. He made a quick aside and was already lurching out as Fukuhara translated his reply for Dorrigo.

Major Nakamura say prisoners lucky. They redeem honour by dying for the Emperor.

Nakamura halted, turned back and was speaking to them.

It is true this war is cruel, Lieutenant Fukuhara translated. What war is not? But war is human beings. War what we are. War what we do. Railway might kill human beings, but I do not make human beings. I make railway. Progress does not demand freedom. Progress has no need of freedom. Major Nakamura, he say progress can arise for other reasons. You, doctor, call it non-freedom. We call it spirit, nation, Emperor. You, doctor, call it cruelty. We call it destiny. With us, or without us. It is the future.

Dorrigo Evans bowed. Squizzy Taylor, a major and his second-in-command, did likewise.

But Major Nakamura wasn't done. He spoke again and when he finished Fukuhara said—

Your British Empire, Major Nakamura say. He say: You think it did not need non-freedom, Colonel? It was built sleeper by sleeper of non-freedom, bridge by bridge of non-freedom.

Major Nakamura turned and left. Dorrigo Evans staggered off to the POW officers' hut and his bed there, a cot that was too short for him. The cot was an absurd privilege that he liked because it was in reality no privilege at all. He looked at his watch. It showed the time as 1240 hours. He groaned. To accommodate his long legs he had rigged up a bamboo tripod, on which sat a flattened kerosene tin braced with more bamboo. It frequently tumbled over when he shifted in his sleep.

He lit a candle stub by his cot side and lay down. He picked up a dog-eared book—a precious commodity in the camp—a romance which he was reading before sleep to take his mind elsewhere and had nearly finished. But now drunk, exhausted, sick, Dorrigo Evans had neither the energy to read nor the desire to move, and he could feel sleep already claiming him. He put the book back down and snuffed the candle out.

## 5

The old man was dreaming he was a young man sleeping in a prisoner-of-war camp. Dreaming was the most real thing Dorrigo Evans now knew. He had followed knowledge, like a sinking star, beyond the utmost bound of human thought.

He sat up.

What's the time?

Nearly three.

I have to go.

He didn't dare say Ella's name. Nor the word *wife,* nor the word *home.*

Where's that kilt?

You were thinking of her again, weren't you?

My kilt?

It hurts me, you know.

Bloody damn kilt.

He had arrived in a kilt, following the annual dinner of the Parramatta Burns Society, to which he had belonged since his work had brought him to Sydney in 1974, and of which he was patron for no reason that he could fathom other than, perhaps, his public vice of whisky and his secret vice of women. And now the kilt was lost.

Not Ella, she said. Because that's not love.

He thought of his wife. He found his marriage a profound solitude. He did not understand why he was married, why sleeping with several different women was seen to be wrong, why all of it meant less and less. Nor could he say what was the strange ache at the base of his stomach that grew and grew, why he so desperately needed to smell Lynette Maison's back, or why the only real thing in his life were his dreams.

He opened the bar fridge, took out the last Glenfiddich miniature, and noticed with a shake of his head the new touchpad technology that meant once he had taken the bottle out it was immediately recorded electronically. He sensed the coming of a new neater world, a tamer world, a world of boundaries and surveillance, where everything was known and nothing needed to be experienced. He understood his public self—the side they put on coins and stamps—would meld well with the coming age, and that the other side, his private self, would become increasingly incomprehensible and distasteful; this side others would conspire to hide.

It did not fit with the new age of conformity that was coming in all things, even emotions, and it baffled him how people now touched each other excessively and talked about their problems as though naming life in some way described its mystery or denied its chaos. He felt the withering of something, the way risk was increasingly evaluated and, as much as possible, eliminated, replaced with a bland new world where the viewing of food preparation would be felt to be more moving than the reading of poetry; where excitement would come from paying for a soup made out of foraged grass. He had eaten soup made out of foraged grass in the camps; he preferred food. The Australia that took refuge in his head was mapped with the stories of the dead; the Australia of the living he found an ever stranger country.

Dorrigo Evans had grown up in an age when a life could be conceived and lived in the image of poetry, or, as it was increasingly with him, the shadow of a single poem. If the coming of television and with it the attendant idea of celebrity—who were otherwise people, Dorrigo felt, you would not wish to know—ended that age, it also occasionally fed on it, finding in the clarity of those who ordered their lives in accordance with the elegant mystery of poetry a suitable subject for imagery largely devoid of thought.

A documentary about Dorrigo going back to the Line on Anzac Day in 1972 first established him in the national consciousness, and his position was enhanced by further appearances on talk shows on which he affected the stance of a conservative humanist, another mask.

He understood he was outliving his age and feeling his eternal desire to live more recklessly he unscrewed the whisky miniature lid. As he took a swig, he felt the kilt with his toes near the base of the bar fridge. Pulling it on, he looked over to the bed where, in the strange night-light thrown by the digital clock and green-lit smoke alarms, Lynette looked as if underwater. He noticed that her arm was over her eyes. He lifted it. She was crying. Silently, without movement.

Lynette?

It's fine, she said. You go.

He did not want to say it but he had to say it.

What's the matter?

Nothing.

He leant down and touched his lips to her moss-hued forehead. The taste of powder. The imprisoning scent of jasmine that always awakened in him a desire to flee.

It's hard, she said, when you want something and you can't have it.

He grabbed his car keys. There was a great pleasure to be had driving drunk on back roads, the lights, the game of making sure he wasn't caught, that he might one more time escape. He quickly finished dressing, skulled the last of the last Glenfiddich miniature, spent five frustrating minutes chasing down his misplaced sporran, which he finally found beneath the book of Japanese death poems, and left, forgetting to take his book with him.

## 6

Dorrigo got a forty-eight-hour leave the following week. He hitched a ride on a military flight back to Melbourne, and in the quiet and empty two days and a night with Ella he tried to make as much noise and movement as possible. He was more desperate for her than ever, as a man about to be kicked to death is desperate to cling to the mud beneath him.

Several times he went to tell Ella of the woman who had talked to him in the Adelaide bookshop. But what was there to tell? Nothing had happened. He and Ella danced. They drank. What had happened? Nothing had happened.

He held Ella like a life buoy. He longed to have her in bed to find him and her anew, and was grateful that she would have none of what suddenly seemed to him inexplicably adulterous. Her black hair, her dark eyes, her full figure—she was beautiful, and yet he felt nothing.

What had happened? He was thinking not of hair or eyes but a feeling as baffling as a million dancing and meaningless dust motes. A strange guilt reduced him to bleakness. Yet what had he done? He had done nothing. He had talked, at best, for a few minutes, then had turned and left the bookshop. He didn't even know her name. What had he asked of her? What had she said to him? Nothing! Nothing! He didn't even know her name.

Ella's world—which had until then looked so comforting in its security and certainty that he had wished to belong to it—Dorrigo suddenly found pallid and bloodless. Though he tried to find in it that indefinable sense of ease, that ineradicable odour of power and its privileges, which he had found so attractive before, it meant nothing to him now—worse, it seemed repulsive.

Ella and others explained away Dorrigo's new awkwardness with that great solvent of the time: the war. The war pressed, the war deranged, the war undid, the war excused. For his part, Dorrigo thought that he couldn't wait for the war to arrive, if this was the alternative.

Finally he told Ella, as though it were simply an odd encounter, yet in his telling it somehow sounded to him like an infidelity. He felt an incommunicable shame. Why could he not want Ella? And in portraying this stranger as an overly intense, rather inappropriate woman, he felt that he had betrayed what had happened, as well as her and somehow himself. He finished the story with a shudder.

Was she pretty? Ella asked.

He told her she was unremarkable. Feeling he had to say something more, he said she had nice—and he searched for some feature he had no memory of, that could not be deemed inappropriate—*teeth*. She had nice teeth, he said. And that was about it, really, he said.

Fangs, more like it, said Ella, her voice a little high. And a red camellia in her hair? I mean to say. She sounds a monster.

And yet she hadn't been. She had stood there and something had happened, something had passed between them, and how he wished it hadn't. Because Ella now appeared to him as someone he had never known before. Her chatter that he had once found joyful now struck him as naïve and false, the perfume she wore only for him now stank in his nostrils, and he longed to hurt her so she would leave.

Should I be jealous? asked Ella.

Of what? he said. I can't tell you how bloody happy I was to get out of that bookshop.

A moment later he was kissing Ella. Ella was kind, he told himself. And somewhere within him he pitied Ella, and buried even deeper was an understanding that they would both suffer because of her kindness and his pity. He hated her kindness and he feared his pity, and he wanted only to escape it all forever. And the more he hated and feared and wished to escape, the more he kept kissing, and as their embraces grew more passionate, and as one moment passed into another and that day into the next, as life filled with life, his bleak mood passed, and he almost stopped thinking of the girl with the red camellia altogether.

He grew cheerful, and the furlough seemed at once to go too fast and at the same time be a never-ending swirl of parties, chance meetings and new acquaintances. Everyone seemed to want to meet Ella's man, be they her friends or her parents' friends. And in this way he met much of Melbourne society, and he came to see himself in their image—as a young man who would after the war rise to great things. And everything in this perfect life fitted so sweetly together—he and Ella, and Ella's family, and their place in the world, which would shortly be his place also. And what had been so difficult with Ella now became unexpectedly easy: there were no longer any barriers between them, and it was as it had been before, perhaps even better, and he had completely forgotten both the bookshop and his own doubts.

On returning to Adelaide, he lost himself in the general staff work that he normally so loathed. Outside a Nissen hut in the administration block of the Warradale camp—where he and some of the other medical staff had offices—dust blew in whirls around the parade ground, while inside, in the appalling oven-like heat, he tried to concentrate on the preparations for embarkation—supplies and equipment that were either non-existent or no one had thought necessary, along with a bewildering amount of paperwork of which he rarely saw the purpose or the end. Of a night there was the prospect of slightly cooler weather and parties with cold beer and iced rum punches, and he threw himself into them as well, seeking an oblivion that he sometimes found.

A postcard arrived from Keith Mulvaney, repeating his invitation to come and visit him at his pub, the King of Cornwall. A hand-tinted photo of the hotel featured on the front of the card, showing a grand, four-storey stone building—complete with a three-sided verandah on every level that looked straight out onto a long, empty beach—built, according to the card, in 1886. To judge from the boaters and moustaches worn by the men at the front of the hotel, the card itself was only a little more recent. Dorrigo misplaced it amidst the office files.

There was about everything and everyone a growing sense of frustration as reports came in of the Blitz in London, along with the first reports of the Australians in action in Libya against the Italians, yet they remained in camp in Adelaide. Rumours of impending embarkation and possible destinations—Greece, Britain, North Africa, an invasion of Norway—came and went.

Dorrigo immersed himself in life, the furious work and frenetic partying, and let everything else wash ever further away. Late one afternoon, at the bottom of a pile of stretcher requisition forms, he chanced upon Keith Mulvaney's postcard of his beachside hotel. And the following weekend, when he had a twelve-hour leave pass and nothing better to do, Dorrigo Evans drove down the coast in a coal-fired Studebaker truck he had borrowed from his batman's brother.

Near dusk, he arrived at a small settlement that served as a holiday village for Adelaidians. With the breeze off the ocean, and the sound of waves, the heat became not just tolerable, but something sensual and welcome. If the beach seemed as sweeping as it had been in the postcard, the King of Cornwall was both grander and more rundown than its photograph suggested, and there was about it the alchemical charm of old things fallen on hard times.

Inside was a long, dark bar in the South Australian style: high-ceilinged, and with a pleasant dimness after the brutal light of the South Australian summer. The hues of stained wood and dun colours seemed to soothe and rest the eyes after the blaze of the outdoor world. The overhead fans rhythmically brushed the low drum of drinkers' conversation. Dorrigo went to the bar, where a barmaid was tidying some bottles on the rear shelf. Her back was turned, and he asked her if she could help him find Keith Mulvaney.

I'm Keith's nephew, he added.

You must be Dorrigo, the barmaid said as she turned. Her blonde hair was pulled up in a chignon. I'm—

A cone of dull electric light that shone down onto the bar made her blue eyes glisten. For a moment there was something in them, then they emptied.

I am Keith's wife, she said.

## 7

His eyes darted everywhere, along the top shelf of rums and whiskies, to the other drinkers, to the bar towel that read THE KING OF CORNWALL. Resting on it, a woman's hand, holding a damp tea towel. Elegant fingers with nails painted burgundy. He was seized by a mad desire to feel them in his mouth. He felt himself shimmering, spinning before her.

Tell Keith that—

Yes.

That my leave was shortened. And I can't stay.

And you're—

His nephew—

Dorry?

He couldn't remember his name but it sounded right.

You're Dorry? Dorrigo? Isn't that what they call you?

Well, yes. Yes.

It's . . . *unusual.*

My grandfather was born there. They say he rode with Ben Hall.

Ben Hall?

The bushranger:

*For just as in the days*
*Of Turpin and Duval*
*The people's friends were outlaws*
*And so too was bold Ben Hall.*

Do you ever use your own words? she asked.

Dorrigo's my middle name but it—

Stuck?

I guess so.

Keith's not here. He'll be very disappointed he missed you.

The war.

Yes. That Mr Hitler.

I'll drop by another time.

Do, Dorry. He'll be so sorry you couldn't stay.

He went to leave. Deep inside him was a terrible tumult of both excitement and betrayal, as though he was hers and she had abandoned him, and coupled to this a sense that she was his and he had to take her back. At the door he turned around and took two steps towards the bar.

Haven't we—? he said.

She pinched the top of her blouse between her thumb and forefinger—her two brightly coloured nails like a Christmas beetle splaying its wings—and tugged the blouse upwards.

The bookshop?

Yes, she said.

He walked back to the bar.

I thought, he said, that they were—

Who?

He felt it, something about him and her, but he did

not know what it was. There was nothing he could do about it. He did not understand it but he felt it.

Those men. That they were—

That they were what?

With you. That—

Yes?

That they were—your—your admirers.

Don't be silly. Just some friends of a friend from the officers' club I hadn't seen for a long time. And some of their friends. So you're the clever young doctor?

Well, young, yes. But so are you.

Ageing. I'll tell Keith you called.

She began wiping the bar. A drinker tilted an empty froth-rimed glass in her direction.

Coming, she said.

He left, drove the truck back to the city, found a bar and determinedly drank himself into oblivion and couldn't remember where he had parked the Studebaker. But when he awoke there was no annihilation of the memory of her. His pounding head, the pain in every movement and act and thought, seemed to have as its cause and remedy her, and only her and only her and only her.

For several weeks after, he tried to lose himself by joining with an infantry company's endless route marches as a medical officer, marching up to twenty miles a day—from valley vineyards, where they filled their canteens with muscat and red wine, to coastal beaches where they swam, and then marched back, and then back again—through heat so intense it felt like a foe. He would help carry the packs of men who collapsed with fatigue, he drove himself beyond any sense. Finally, the company commander ordered him to back off a little so that he not seem a fool to the men.

Of a night he wrote letters to Ella, in which he tried to lose himself in the forms and tropes of love that he had learnt from literature. The letters were long, dull and false. His mind was tormented by thoughts and feelings that he had never read. Accordingly, he understood that they could not be love. He felt a swirling of hatred and lust for Keith's wife. He wanted to seize her body. He wanted never to see her again. He felt a contempt and strange distance, he felt a complicity—as though he knew something he should not know—and he felt, strangely, that she knew it too. He reasoned that once his corps embarked for overseas, he would happily never think of her again. And yet he could not stop thinking of her.

He ate little, lost weight and seemed so oddly preoccupied that the company commander, both impressed and slightly concerned by Dorrigo's extraordinary zeal, gave him a special twenty-four-hour furlough. Ella had said that she would come to Adelaide if he received a short-leave pass and lacked the time to travel to Melbourne. And though he fully intended to spend the leave with her, having even picked out a restaurant he would take her to, he somehow never got around to mentioning in any of his many letters and cards to Ella that he was about to go on leave. When the date grew close he reasoned that it would be unfair to tell her, as it would be too late for her to make any arrangements and she would be left only with a crushing disappointment. Having decided on this course of silence, and after solemnly vowing he would never return to the King of Cornwall, he rang his Uncle Keith, who invited him down to stay the night, saying that 'my Amy', as he called his wife, would be as pleased to see him as Keith himself.

My Amy, thought Dorrigo Evans when he hung up the receiver. My Amy.

## 8

After playing cards with the Australian officers, Major Nakamura had fallen into a deep, alcoholic slumber. In his strange dreams he was lost in a dark room and was feeling an elephant's leg, trying to imagine what room such pillars might support. There was an immense maw of shooting tendrils and smothering leaves that formed a blindfold around his eyes, leaving him unseeing. Everywhere around him he felt life, but nowhere did it seem to him was life intelligible. All things in this room were unexpected and uncivilised—be it the endless jungle or the near-naked Australian prisoners, who, he knew, surrounded him like a troop of huge, hairy, threatening apes.

What was this room? How could he get out? The green blindfold was now wrapping around his throat, choking him. His heart was pounding. He could taste a copper spoon in his dry mouth, stale sweat larded his back in a clammy chill, his ribs itched badly and he smelt rancid even to himself. He was trembling, shuddering, when he realised he was being shaken awake.

What? Nakamura yelled.

He slept badly these days, and to be woken abruptly from sleep in the middle of the night left him confused and angry. He smelt the monsoon rain before he heard it slapping the ground outside, and threading through it the irritating voice of Lieutenant Fukuhara, who was calling his name.

What is it? Nakamura yelled again.

He opened his eyes to leaping shadows and shudders of light and began scratching himself. A wet, rubberised cape formed a black, glistening cone that rose from its base to Fukuhara's darkened face, neat as always, even in the most difficult situations, and adorned with his cropped hair, water-beaded horn-rimmed glasses and moustache. Behind him, holding out a kerosene lantern, was Tomokawa, a soggy campaign cap and neck flaps highlighting the corporal's daikon-like head.

Corporal Tomokawa was on sentry duty, sir, Fukuhara said, when a truck driver and a colonel of the Ninth Railway Regiment walked into camp.

Nakamura rubbed his eyes, then scratched his elbow so hard that he knocked off a scab and his elbow began to bleed. Though he could not see them, he knew he was covered in ticks. Biting ticks. The ticks were biting under his arms, his back, his ribs, crotch, everywhere. He kept scratching but the ticks just burrowed deeper. They were very small ticks. The ticks were so small they somehow got under the skin and bit away there.

Tomokawa! he yelled. Can you see them? Can you!

He held up an arm.

Tomokawa stole a glance at Fukuhara, stepped forward, raised his lantern and inspected Nakamura's arm. He stepped back.

No, sir.

*Ticks!*

No, sir.

They were so small that no one else could see them. That was part of their hellish nature. He wasn't sure how they got under his skin but suspected they laid their eggs in his pores and they incubated under the skin, to be born and grow and die there. One had to scratch them out. Siamese ticks, unknown to science.

He had had Corporal Tomokawa inspect his body before with a magnifying glass, and still the fool had said he couldn't see them. Nakamura knew he was lying. Fukuhara said the ticks didn't exist, that the sensation was a side-effect of the Philopon. What the hell would he know? There was so much in this jungle that no one had ever seen or experienced before. One day science would discover and name the tick, but he just had to endure them for now, like he had to endure so much else.

Colonel Kota has brought fresh orders from Railway Command Group to give you before proceeding to Three Pagoda Pass, Fukuhara continued. He is in the mess being fed. His orders are to brief you at the earliest convenience.

Nakamura waved an unsteady index finger at a small field table next to his cot.

Shabu, he muttered.

Tomokawa swung the kerosene lamp away from his commanding officer's face and searched the sooty shadows that swept back and forth over the technical drawings, reports and work sheets that sat on the tabletop, many of them spotted with blooms of dark mould.

Fukuhara, eager, young, gannet-necked Fukuhara, whom Nakamura found increasingly oppressive in his zeal, continued on about how it was the first truck up the near impassable road in ten days, and how, with the rains, it was likely to be the last for—

Yes, yes, Nakamura said. Shabu!

The truck is bogged three kilometres away, and Colonel Kota is worried that natives might loot the truck of the supplies it carries, Lieutenant Fukuhara finished.

Shabu! Nakamura hissed. *Shabu!*

Tomokawa spotted the Philopon bottle on a chair next to the table. He handed it to Nakamura, who these days survived on the army-issue methamphetamine and little else. Nakamura tipped the bottle and shook it. Nothing came out. Nakamura sat on his army cot, staring at the empty bottle in his hand.

To inspire fighting spirits, said Nakamura dully, reading the army's inscription on the Philopon bottle's label. Nakamura knew he needed sleep above all things, and he knew that now it would not be possible, that he must stay up the rest of the night, meeting with Kota and organising the rescue of the truck, and still somehow get his section of the railway finished in the impossible time headquarters now demanded. He needed shabu.

With a sudden, violent action he threw the Philopon bottle out of the hut's open doorway, where, like so much else, it disappeared without a sound into that void of mud and jungle and infinite night.

Corporal Tomokawa!

Sir! said the corporal, and without anything else being said by either, he headed out of the tent into the darkness, his short body limping slightly. Nakamura rubbed his forehead.

He thought of the will that he had to muster every day to continue to make the necessary advances in the railway's construction. At the beginning—when the High Command had decreed that the railway joining Siam and Burma be built—it had been different. Nakamura, as an officer of the IJA's Fifth Railway Regiment, had been excited by the prospect. Before the war, the English and the Americans had both investigated the idea of just such a railway and declared it impossible. The Japanese High Command had decreed that it be built in the shortest time possible. Nakamura's pleasure in his small but significant role in this historic mission, his pride in joining his life with a national and imperial destiny, was immense.

But when, in March 1943, Nakamura had made his way into the heart of this mysterious country, he found himself for the first time beyond the crowds and cities that had shaped him to that point, far from the strange codes of conformity that men in such places live by. They were engineers and soldiers and guards, they were the army code they carried with them, they were the Emperor's wishes incarnate, they were the Japanese spirit made plans and dreams and will. They were Japan. But they were few and the coolies and POWs were many, and the jungle closed in on them a little more every day.

From and of the crowd, Nakamura increasingly found that here his life had taken on a strange and unexpected solitude. And this solitude troubled him more and more. To put an end to these unsettling feelings he threw himself into his work, yet the harder he worked, the more the work became an insane equation. With the monsoon having come, the river was flooded, running high and fast, full of trees and too dangerous to bring heavy loads upriver, while the road—as Colonel Kota had seen for himself—was mostly impassable and supplies had dwindled away to almost nothing. There was no machinery, only hand tools, and these were of the poorest quality. There weren't anywhere near enough prisoners for the job at the beginning, and now the prisoners not dead or dying were in bad shape. To top everything else off, the cholera had arrived a week ago, and even disposing of the dead bodies was becoming a problem, draining fit men away from the railway work. There was ever less food and almost no medicines, yet Railway Command Group expected him to do ever more.

Nakamura worked with Japanese maps, Japanese plans, Japanese charts and Japanese technical drawings to impose Japanese order and Japanese meaning on the meaningless and aimless jungle, on the sick and dying POWs, a vortex seemingly without cause and effect, a growing green maelstrom that spun faster and faster. And in and out of that maelstrom came orders, endless streams of appearing and disappearing romusha and prisoners of war, as undivinable and as unknowable as the river Kwai or the cholera bacillus. The occasional Japanese officer might stay over for an evening of drink, gossip and news, and the men would fortify each other with tales of Japanese honour and the indomitable Japanese spirit and the imminent Japanese victory. Then they too would disappear to their own hell somewhere else on that ever lengthening railway line of madness.

A wet wind swept through the hut, ruffling the damp papers on the field table. Nakamura looked at the luminous hands of his watch. Three hundred hours. Two and a half hours till reveille. He was feeling anxious, the ticks were getting worse, and he began scratching his chest with a growing ferocity while Fukuhara waited for his orders. Nakamura said nothing until Corporal Tomokawa, with the same fawning reverence he showed in all his actions undertaken for his superiors, returned, bowed and held out a full bottle of Philopon.

Grabbing the bottle, Nakamura gulped down four pills. After his second attack of malaria, when he was still exhausted but had to carry on working, he had taken a few shabu pills to keep him going. Now the shabu was more necessary to him than food. To build such a railway—with no machinery and through a wilderness—was a superhuman task. Fired by shabu, he was able to return to it day after debilitating day with a redoubled fervour. He put the bottle down and looked up to see both men looking at him.

Philopon helps me through this fever, Nakamura said, feeling suddenly awkward. It's very good. And it stops the damn ticks biting.

Already feeling his early morning stupour magically dissolving into a renewed alertness and vigour, Nakamura stared intently at the two men until they dropped their eyes.

Philopon is anything but an opiate, Nakamura said. Only inferior races like the Chinese, Europeans and Indians are addicted to opiates.

Fukuhara agreed. Fukuhara was such a bore.

We invented Philopon, said Fukuhara.

Yes, Nakamura said.

Philopon is an expression of the Japanese spirit.

Yes, Nakamura said.

He stood up and realised he hadn't bothered undressing for bed. Even his muddy puttees remained tightly bound around his calves, though the cross tape on one leg had come undone.

The Imperial Japanese Army gives us shabu to help with the work of the Empire, Tomokawa added.

Yes, yes, Nakamura said. He turned to Fukuhara. Take twenty prisoners back down the track and rescue the truck.

Now?

Of course, *now*, Nakamura said. Push it all the way to the camp, if necessary.

And after? Fukuhara asked. Do we give them the day off?

After, they go and do their day's work on the railway, said Nakamura. You're up, I'm up, we continue.

Nakamura's need to scratch was fading. His cock was swelling inside his trousers. It was a pleasant feeling of strength. Fukuhara had turned to leave when Nakamura called his name.

You're an engineer, Nakamura said. You understand that you must treat all men as machines in service of the Emperor.

Nakamura could feel the shabu sharpening his senses, giving him strength where he had felt weak, certainty where he was so often assailed by doubt. Shabu eliminated fear. It gave him a necessary distance from his actions. It kept him bright and hard.

And if the machines are seizing up, Nakamura said, if they only can be made to work with the constant application of force—well then, use that force.

The ticks, he realised, had finally stopped biting.

# 9

The man walking towards him appeared as a vast outline of nothingness, a silhouette, and to that nothingness Dorrigo Evans now held out his hand in greeting.

You must be Uncle Keith.

In the full intensity of the midday sun, his bulky body blocking the light and head hidden in the bitumen shade thrown by his Akubra, he looked little more than forty and not without menace. He had the presence of a precarious telegraph pole. But nothing was what it seemed and everything looked as if glimpsed through an old window pane—bending, bowing, shuddering in the heat waves rippling the bitumen road and cement kerbing, the dust of the Warradale parade ground, the tin-tubed Nissen huts at the front of which Dorrigo Evans had been waiting.

Once in his uncle's car, a late-model Ford Cabriolet, Dorrigo Evans could see just how big a man his Uncle Keith was, and how his face was more that of someone perhaps fifty. With him was a very small dog, a Jack Russell terrier he called Miss Beatrice, which seemed to exist to emphasise the largeness of Keith Mulvaney—his broad back, his wide thighs and great feet behind which the panting dog drooped like a dropped chamois.

It was too hot to smoke but he smoked his pipe anyway. The smoke wreathed a strange smile that Dorrigo later came to realise was fixed, determined to find the world cheery in spite of all the evidence life produced to the contrary. It all might have been intimidating were it not that Keith's voice was slightly high-pitched and reminded Dorrigo of that of a teenage boy. And of that voice there was no more end than there was of the intolerable

Adelaide heat. It became clear to Dorrigo Evans that Keith Mulvaney's world was his own, self-contained, and that it circled three suns—his hotel, his seat as an alderman on the local council, and his wife.

As they made their way to the coast, he bemoaned the hotel trade in the manner, Dorrigo felt, that those who love what they do bemoan their passion the most. *The motorists*, he would say with a sighing sibilant *s*, had been the making and unmaking of him. *The motoristsss*, what with their whingeing about toilets and meals, turning up in a party of eighty one day, all expecting to be fed, while the next Sunday you might be lucky to sell tuppence ha'penny of Afghan biscuits; always whingeing, *the motoristsss*, to their automobile associations and royal bloody automobile clubs about the state of the bathrooms and the dirty soap. Always whining, the motoring crowd. The only thing worse are the travelling salesmen. Why, today a traveller wanted to rent a room as an office to dispense bromides and aspirins, but I suspect the sex thing going on.

The sex thing?

You know, things to do with the women's plumbing and the births and not having babies, French letters and English freethinking pamphlets; you know the drum.

Yes, his nephew said in a sufficiently uncertain way that his uncle felt the need to establish that whatever others thought the King of Cornwall might be, a moral vortex it was not.

Well, I am a broad-minded man, Dorrigo, Keith Mulvaney continued, but I don't want the King of Cornwall to be advertised through the Melbourne *Truth* and the Adelaide law courts as *the* place of assignation in Adelaide. I am not a prude; I am not like those American hotels, insisting on guests leaving their door open if a lady other than the guest's wife is in the room.

You know, he suddenly said, warming to the theme of adultery and hotel accommodation, in America you risk having an advertisement placed in your home town saying *To whom it may concern, Mr X had been requested to leave the Wisteria in Watstoria for entertaining in his room a lady not his wife*. Can you imagine? I mean, they allow people to meet in their rooms, and then blackmail them with the threat of such advertisements. They run hotels there like Stalin runs the damn USSR.

He went on to talk about Dorrigo's family, but his knowledge—gleaned from what little Tom had written in his Christmas cards—was mostly out of date and only Miss Beatrice nearly falling out of the window while biting at the rushing air saved them from his embarrassment on discovering that Dorrigo's mother was dead. He sat leaning forward in the car, strewn over the steering wheel like a gale-fallen tree trunk, his big hands moving incessantly up and down the wheel as if it were a fortune teller's crystal ball and he was forever searching the long, straight, flat roads of Adelaide for something, an illusion that might help him live.

But there was little other traffic, and nothing other than the straightness and flatness and the heat waves rising up in distortions. Keith Mulvaney talked continuously, as if afraid of what silence might hold or what Dorrigo might ask, asking questions of Dorrigo that he immediately answered himself. His conversation returned frequently to a running battle he was having as an alderman on the local council over a proposal by the mayor to introduce a sewerage system. Dorrigo ended up staring out of his window, running his wet hand in the breeze while Keith talked, oblivious to this lack of interest, asking questions he would immediately answer, and every answer concluding with a smile that seemed to brook no disagreement. Like an occasional clarinet solo would come a periodic mention of Amy.

A modern woman. Very modern. Out and about. She does a terrific job. The war, though. Everything's different now. It dissolves everything, this war. You never saw such things before the war. Did you?

Well—

No, I think not. It's not just London being blitzed. No. Things that were a scandal a year ago no one thinks twice of anymore. I am a modern man. But I am so grateful to have some family to keep her in decent company.

Despite his fixed smile, he seemed utterly miserable.

The other night she was with a redheaded woman called Tippy. Can't stand her.

Tippy?

Tippy, yes—you know her?

Well—

I ask you? It's a name for a budgerigar. And I have this damn municipal conference and have to be gone for the night. In Gawler, hours away. Tonight. I am so sorry I can't be with you. Unexpected—the mayor needs me to represent us. Why?

I suppose—

I have no idea why. Anyway, Amy will look after you. And, to be frank, I'm happy you'll be looking after Amy. You don't mind?

Answering was not the point and Dorrigo finally gave up trying.

Well, I am sure you'll get some rest, anyway, said Keith Mulvaney. And a good bed, rather than an army bunk.

At the King of Cornwall Keith took Dorrigo to a room on the fourth floor. As they made their way up the grand staircase with its threadbare runner, they met Amy coming down, carrying a bag of dirty linen. Dorrigo felt a strange elation that was as inappropriate as it was undeniable. She glanced at her husband, a look in which Dorrigo glimpsed a complex mud of intimacies normally invisible to the world—the shared sleep, scents, sounds, the habits endearing and frustrating, the pleasures and sadnesses, small and large—the plain mortar that finally renders two as one.

Her hair was pulled back in a ponytail, ruby-gold in the atrium light. As he was introduced, complicity took hold before anything complicit had happened. In a glance he saw her face unnaturally glowing, a loose lock of hair landing like a trout fly in front of her right ear, and he understood that they had silently agreed to say nothing at that moment of the bookshop.

Well, Amy, said Keith, I hope you have some entertainment arranged for our guest.

She shrugged, and he was conscious of the slight roll of her breasts in her cornflower blue blouse.

Do you like Vivien Leigh? asked Amy. There's a new Vivien Leigh movie in the city called *Waterloo Bridge*. Would you like to—

I've seen it, said Dorrigo, who had done no such thing and suddenly thought what a nasty man he was, his mind abuzz. Was he frightened of being with her? Was he trying to prove his power over her?

That's a shame, said Keith. But I'm sure it's not the only movie.

Dorrigo no longer understood himself, nor why he said such things. But he had said it, and then, equally unexpectedly, he heard himself say:

But I'd love to see it again.

Pushing away, pushing in: the pattern of so much that was to follow.

Amy shrugged once more, and Dorrigo Evans forced his eyes away from her and down the staircase until she re-entered his vision a floor below, the fingers of her extended hand running along the varnished bannister. His gaze followed her ponytail bobbing as she continued stepping down into the void.

## 10

Of the many things Dorrigo Evans expected to happen that evening, he did not expect to be taken to a nightclub off Hindley Street. She said if he had already seen the movie, he would know what was going to happen next, and that would ruin everything. He was in uniform, she in an apricot oriental shirt and baggy black silk trousers. The effect was of something liquid. Her body seemed to him so definite and strong; when she moved, she glided.

The point is in never knowing, Amy said. Don't you think?

He didn't think. He didn't know. The nightclub was a large room, low lit with the blackout curtains all up, full of shadows and uniforms. Dorrigo noticed a yeasty odour, the slightly drunk smell of spring weeds. They drank martinis as a swing orchestra played. There was a strange excitement in the air. After a time, the house lights were turned down, each band member lit candles on their music stands, and waiters lit candles on the tables.

Why the candles? asked Dorrigo.

You'll see, said Amy.

She talked about herself. She was twenty-four, three years younger than him. She had moved a few years before from Sydney, where she had worked in department stores, and had met Keith through her work as a barmaid at the King of Cornwall. He told her about Ella, and every word sounded both a defence against what he truly felt and a betrayal of all that he was. And then he dismissed such feelings.

Dorrigo told himself that the divide between him and Amy was absolute. Theirs was a friendship buttressed on one side by the pillar of her husband, his uncle, and on the other by his prospective engagement with Ella. And there was in this a great security for him that led him to relax with Amy perhaps more than he might have otherwise.

He found himself feeling unaccountably happy with her in a way he could not remember being for a very long time. He watched as the candlelight shadows leapt over a face that made him ever more curious. It was so strange that when he had first met her in the bookshop, it was not her looks that had made such an impression on him. But now he could not conceive of a more beautiful woman. He enjoyed his proximity to Amy, even the way other men looked enviously, covetously, at the woman who so wrongly seemed to be his. Of course, he told himself, she wasn't his, but the sensation wasn't unpleasant. He was flattered.

They ended up talking with some naval officers, who later drifted away to the far end of the table and other conversations, leaving the couple alone. Amy leant across and put her hand over his. He looked down, unsure what it meant. He felt extremely awkward. But he did not take his hand away.

What's this? Dorrigo asked.

He realised that she was looking at their hands too.

Nothing, she said.

Her touch electrified him, paralysed him, and amidst the noise and smoke and bustle that touch was the only thing he knew. The universe and the world, his life and his body, all reduced to that one electric point of contact. He stared with her at their hands. Yet he presumed it all meant nothing. Because it had to mean nothing. Her hand on his. His in hers. Because to believe anything else was a mistake. Come tomorrow, he would once more be her nephew, soon to be engaged, and she his uncle's wife. But it must mean something, he desperately wished to think—

Nothing? he heard himself repeating.

He tried to relax, but he could not stop the excitement he felt at her touch. She ran her index finger over the back of his hand.

I am Keith's, she said.

She continued to gaze absent-mindedly down at his hand.

Yes, he said.

But she was not really listening. She was watching her finger, its long shadow, and he was watching her, knowing she was not really listening.

Yes, he said.

He was feeling her touching him, and the feeling ran

through his entire body and he could think of nothing else.

And you, she said, you're mine.

He looked up, startled. For a second time she had taken him completely unawares. And for a second time, he felt oddly fearful, as he very slowly came to realise that far from mocking him, she was genuine in her strange frankness. And all that this meant terrified him. But she was still looking at her finger, at their hands between their half-empty glasses, at the circles she traced.

What?

And only then did she look up.

I mean, she said, I mean you're Ella's. But tonight. Tonight you're mine.

She laughed lightly, as though it all meant nothing.

As a companion.

Lifting her hand, she waved it behind her ear in a gesture of dismissal.

You *know* what I mean.

But he didn't. He had no idea at all. And he felt both excited and frightened, that what she said meant nothing, that it meant everything. She was elusive. He was lost.

As the table candles were extinguished by the waiters, the band struck up with 'Auld Lang Syne' as a swing waltz. It was a memory being made of coming together and separating, circles forming only to be torn apart. At the end of every few bars another musician would reach forward and snuff out the candle in front of him.

Dorrigo found himself dancing with Amy, and as the dance floor slowly descended into darkness, she somehow came to rest her head on his shoulder. Her body seemed to be inviting his into a supple, shared swaying. As his body cautiously melded into hers, he again told himself it was nothing, that it meant nothing, that it could lead to nothing.

What are you mumbling? she asked.

Nothing, he whispered.

As they circled, their bodies found a strange peace in resting on each other that was also the most terrible anticipation and tension. He could feel her breath, the slightest breeze on his neck.

The last candle was snuffed, there was a bar of darkness, the curtains suddenly dropped from the windows and—to gasps of wonder—a full moon flooded the room. The waltz now circled to its finale, and he understood the whole event as a strange nostalgia for a future that everyone feared would never belong to them, a sense of tomorrow already foretold and only tonight capable of change.

In the quicksilver light and blue ink shadow, couples slowly separated and clapped. For a moment they were looking at each other and he knew he could kiss her, that he only had to lean slightly forward into her shadow and he would fall forever. But then he remembered who they were and instead asked if she wanted another drink.

Take me home, she said.

## 11

At the hotel she took him to the rooms where she lived with Keith. He sat down in a russet armchair. He could smell Keith's brilliantine on the antimacassar, his pipe tobacco in the brocade upholstery. Amy wound the gramophone, put on a record she said she wanted him to hear, placed the needle and sat on the arm of Dorrigo's chair. The piano shuffled, the sax swept in and out with the breeze off the ocean that ruffled the lace curtains, and a voice began to sing.

*A tinkling piano in the next apartment*
*Those stumbling words that told you*
*What my heart meant*
*A fairground's painted swings*
*These foolish things*
*Remind me of you*

It's Leslie Hutchinson, she said. Apparently he is, you know, *familiar* with the ladies of the Royal family.

Familiar?

She smiled.

Yes, she said very softly, looking across at him. *Familiar.*

She laughed again, from her throat, and he thought how much he liked the full-bodied, large-souled feel of it.

The song ended. He stood up and went to go. She put the record on again. He said goodbye. At the door he leant in, kissed her politely on the cheek, and when he went to pull away, she leant her face in against his neck. He waited for her to pull her head away.

You've got to go, he heard her whisper. But she kept her face against his.

The gramophone needle was ch-ch-ing as it circled the record's end.

Yes, he said.

He waited but nothing happened.

The needle remained stuck in its groove, scratching circles of sand into the night.

Yes, he said.

He waited but she did not move. After a time, he put one arm lightly around her. She did not pull away.

Soon, he said.

He held his breath until he felt her ever so slightly press into him. He did not move.

Amy?

Yes?

He did not dare answer. He breathed out. He shuffled his feet to better get his balance. He had no idea what to say, worrying that to say anything more might upset this delicate equation. He let his hand drop and shape her waist, expecting her to push it away. But instead she whispered:

*Amie*. French for friend.

His other hand found the wondrous curve of her buttocks.

My mother, she said, taught me that when I was little.

She did not push that hand away either.

Amy, amie, amour, she used to call me. Amy, friend, love.

A winning trifecta, Dorrigo said.

She turned her lips onto his neck. He could feel her breath on his skin. He could feel her body with his, now hard, and he was embarrassed to realise that she must be able to feel him. He did not dare move in any direction in case it broke this spell. It was not clear to him what this meant or what he should do. He did not dare kiss her.

# 12

Dorrigo felt a warm hand creeping up his legs and jolted awake. It took him some moments to realise it was the early-morning sun stepping across his room. He found a note from Amy under his door saying that she would be busy until mid-afternoon with hotel business—there was to be a lunchtime wedding reception—so she would not be able to say goodbye.

He wrapped a towel around himself, and went out on the deep balcony, lit a cigarette, sat down, and looked out through the Victorian arches to where the Southern Ocean, ceaseless and open, rippled in front of him.

Nothing has happened, she had said when he left her rooms. Those were her exact words. They had held each other, but she had said it was nothing. How could it be anything to him? Beyond a hug, nothing had happened. That much was true. Nothing had happened at the bookshop. A hug? People did more than that at funerals.

Amy, amie, amour, he whispered under his breath.

Nothing had happened, yet everything had changed.

He was falling.

He listened to the waves break and shimmer sand and he was falling. A slight breeze rose from the long shadows of early morning and he still was falling. He was falling and falling, and it felt a wild freedom. Whatever it might be was as unknowable and perplexing as she was. He understood that much. He did not know where it would end.

He stood up, excited, confused, determined. He threw his cigarette away, and went inside to get dressed. Nothing had happened and yet he knew something had begun.

# 13

He returned to the army camp and a life of order and discipline. But that life, for Dorrigo, no longer had substance. It hardly seemed real. People came, people talked, people said many things, and not one was interesting. They talked of Hitler, Stalin, North Africa, the Blitz. Not one talked of Amy. They talked of matériel, strategy, maps, timetables, morale, Mussolini, Churchill, Himmler. He longed to cry out Amy! Amie! Amour! He wished to scruff them and tell them what had happened, how he longed for her, how she made him feel.

But much as he wanted everyone to hear, he could afford to have none know. Their dreary conversation, their ignorance of Amy and the passion she had for him and he had for her, was his insurance against his indiscretion. The day their talk turned to him and Amy was the day their private passion would have transformed into public tragedy.

He read books. He liked none of them. He searched their pages for Amy. She was not there. He went to parties. They bored him. He walked the streets, gazing into strangers' faces. Amy was not there. The world, in all its infinite wonder, bored him. He searched every room of his life for Amy. But Amy was not anywhere to be found. And he realised Amy was married to his uncle, that his passion was a madness, that it had no future, that whatever it was must end, and that he must end it. He reasoned that, as there was nothing he could do about his feelings, he must avoid acting on them. If he did not see her, he could not do anything wrong. And so he resolved never to visit Amy again.

When his next leave—a six-day furlough—arose, he did not return to his uncle's hotel but took the overnight train to Melbourne, where he spent all his money on outings and presents for Ella, trying to lose himself in her, seeking to exorcise all memory of his strange encounter with Amy. Ella, for her part, would look greedily into his face, his eyes, and—with a growing concern in his heart which at moments approached terror—he could see her face straining to discover in his face and his eyes the same hunger. And what had been a beautiful, exotic face to Dorrigo Evans now simply seemed dull beyond imagining. Her dark eyes—which at first he had found bewitching—now appeared to him as credulous, even cow-like in their trust, though he tried very hard not to think it, and loathed himself all the more for thinking it anyway. And so he poured himself with renewed determination into her arms, into her conversations, into her fears and jokes and stories, hoping that this intimacy would finally smother all memory of Amy Mulvaney.

On his last night they went for dinner at her father's club. A RAAF major whom they met there made Ella laugh over and over with his jokes and stories. When the major announced he was leaving to go to a nearby nightclub, Ella begged Dorrigo that they go with him because *he was such a hoot.* Dorrigo felt a strange emotion that was neither jealousy nor gratitude but a strange mingling of both.

I love being with people, Ella said.

The more people I am with, Dorrigo thought, the more alone I feel.

# 14

Now the day began before the prisoners were awake, before the main body of guards and engineers were up, some hours before even the sun had risen; now, as Nakamura strode through the mud, breathing the wet night air, as his nightmares dissolved, as the methamphetamines cranked his heart and mind, he felt a pleasant anticipation. This day, this camp, this world, was his to shape. He found Colonel Kota, as Fukuhara had said, in an empty mess, sitting at a bamboo bench table eating tinned fish.

The colonel was a well-built man almost the height of an Australian, his physique belying a face that seemed to Nakamura to sag and fall away from either side of a shark-fin nose to ripples that trailed down his wrinkled cheeks.

Kota did not bother with small talk but got straight to business, saying he would be leaving in the morning as soon as transport could be arranged. From a soggy leather satchel the colonel produced an oiled japara folder, out of which he took a single sheet of typewritten orders and several pages of technical drawings so damp that they wrapped around Nakamura's fingers as he read them. The orders were no more complex than they were welcome.

The first order was technical: even though the major railway cutting was already half-completed, the Railway Command Group had altered Nakamura's original plans. They now wanted the cutting enlarged by a third to help with gradient issues in the next sector. The new cutting would entail a further three-thousand cubic metres of rock to be cut and carried away.

As Tomokawa poured sour tea for them both, Nakamura

bent down and retied the tapes of his puttee. They didn't have enough saws or axes to clear the jungle. The prisoners cut the rock by hand with a hammer and chisel. He didn't even have proper chisels for the prisoners to use, and when what they did have blunted, there wasn't enough coke for their forge to resharpen them. Nakamura sat back up.

Drilling machines with compressors would help, he said.

Colonel Kota stroked his sagging cheek.

*Machinery?*

He let the word hang in the air, leaving Nakamura to finish it off in his own mind—with the knowledge that there was no machinery, with the shame of having begged, the sense of being mocked. Nakamura lowered his head. Kota once more spoke.

There is nothing to spare. It can't be helped.

Nakamura knew he had been wrong to raise this matter, but was grateful that Colonel Kota seemed understanding. He read the second order. The deadline for the completion of the railway had been brought forward from December to October. Nakamura was overcome with despair. His task was now impossible.

I know you can make it possible, Colonel Kota said.

It's no longer April, Nakamura said in what he hoped would be understood as an oblique reference to when headquarters had approved the final plans. It's August.

Colonel Kota's eyes remained fixed on Nakamura's.

We will redouble our efforts, a chastened Nakamura finally said.

I cannot lie to you, Colonel Kota said. I very much doubt there will be a corresponding increase in either machinery or tools. Maybe more coolies. But even that I can't say. We have over a quarter of a million coolies and sixty thousand prisoners working on this railway. I know the English and Australians are lazy. I know they complain they are too tired or too hungry to work. That they take one small spadeful and stop for a rest. One blow of the hammer, then they halt. That they complain about insubstantial matters such as being slapped. If a Japanese soldier neglects his work he expects to be beaten. What gives cowards the right not to be slapped? The Burmese and Chinese coolies that are sent here keep running away or dying. The Tamils, thankfully, have too far to run back to Malaya, but now they are dying everywhere from cholera, and even with the thousands more now arriving there is still not enough manpower. I don't know. None of it can be helped.

Nakamura returned to reading the typed letter. The third order was that one hundred prisoners were to be seconded from his camp for work at a camp near Three Pagoda Pass, some one hundred and fifty kilometres to the north on the Burmese border.

I don't have one hundred prisoners to spare, thought Nakamura. I need another thousand prisoners to complete this section in the time I have been given, not lose even more. He looked up at Colonel Kota.

The hundred men are to march there?

There is no other way in the monsoon. That can't be helped either.

Nakamura knew many would die trying to get there. Perhaps most. But the railway demanded it, the Emperor had ordered the railway, and this was the way it had been decided that the railway would be made. And he could see that, in reality—this reality of dreams and nightmares that he had to live in every day—there was no other way for the railway to be built. Still he persisted.

Understand me, Nakamura said. My problem is practical. With no tools, and fewer men every day, how do I build the railway?

Even if most die of exhaustion you are to complete the work, Colonel Kota said, shrugging his shoulders. Even if everybody dies.

And Nakamura could see that, in this sacrifice too, there was no other way for the Emperor's wishes to be realised. What was a prisoner of war anyway? Less than a man, just material to be used to make the railway, like the teak sleepers and steel rails and dog spikes. If he, a Japanese officer, allowed himself to be captured, he would be executed on his ultimate return to the home islands anyway.

Until two months ago I was in New Guinea, Colonel Kota said. Bougainville. Heaven is Java, they say, hell is Burma, but no one comes back from New Guinea.

The colonel smiled, and the sags of his face rose and fell, reminding Nakamura of a terraced hillside.

I'm the proof that old soldiers' sayings are not always true. But it is very harsh there. The American air power is incredible. Day after day we were pounded by their Lockheeds. Day and night, bombed and strafed. We would be given a week's rations and expected to fight for a month. If we only had salt and matches in the combat area, we could have coped with anything. But I tell you, what of the Americans and Australians? They can boast only of their matériel power, their machines, their technology. Wait and see! We will wage a war of annihilation. Every officer and man in our army there is churning with the desire to massacre all the Americans and Australians. And we will win, because our spirit will endure when theirs crumbles.

And as the colonel talked, his terraced face seemed to Nakamura to hold within it so much of the ancient wisdom of Japan, of all that Nakamura found good and best in his country, in his own life. Nakamura understood that the colonel, with his gentle voice, was telling him something more than this story: that he was saying that no matter what adversity, no matter what lack of tools and manpower Nakamura might have to put up with, he would endure, the railway would be built, the war would be won, and all this would be because of the Japanese spirit.

But what that *spirit* was, what it precisely meant, Nakamura would have had difficulty saying. It was good and it was pure, and it was for him a more real force than the thorny bamboo and teak, the rain and mud and rocks and sleepers and steel rails they worked with each day. It had somehow become the essence of him, and yet it was a thing beyond words. And to explain what he was feeling, Nakamura found himself telling a story.

Last night I was talking with an Australian doctor, he said. The doctor had wanted to know why Japan had started the war. And I had explained the nobility of universal brotherhood that was our guiding idea. I mentioned our motto, *The Whole World Under One Roof.* But I don't think it came across. And so I said how, in short, it was now Asia for the Asians, with Japan the leader of the Asian bloc. I told him how we were liberating Asia from European colonisation. It was very hard. He kept on about freedom.

In truth Nakamura had had no idea what the Australian had been on about. The words, yes, but the ideas made no sense at all.

Freedom? Colonel Kota said.

They laughed.

Freedom, Nakamura said, and they both chuckled again.

Nakamura's own thoughts were a jungle unknown and perhaps unknowable to him. Besides, he didn't care about his own thoughts. He cared about being certain, sure. Kota's words were like shabu for his sick mind. Nakamura cared about the railway, honour, the Emperor, Japan, and he had a sense of himself as a good and honourable officer. But still he tried to fathom the confusion he felt.

I remember early on, when the prisoners still had concerts, and one night I was watching. The jungle, the fire, the men singing their song, the 'Waltzing Matilda'. It made me feel sentimental. Even sympathetic. It was hard not to feel moved.

But the railway, Colonel Kota said, is no less a battlefield than the front line in Burma.

Exactly, Nakamura said. One cannot distinguish between human and non-human acts. One cannot point, one cannot say this man here is a man and that man there is a devil.

It is true, Colonel Kota said. This is a war, and war is beyond such things. And the Siam–Burma railway is for a military purpose—but that's not the larger point. It is that this railway is the great epoch-making construction of our century. Without European machinery, within a time considered extraordinary, we will build what the Europeans said it was not possible to build over many years. This railway is the moment when we and our outlook become the new drivers of world progress.

They drank some more sour tea, and Colonel Kota grew wistful about not being at the front, able to die for the Emperor. They cursed the jungle, the rain, Siam. Nakamura spoke of how hard it was to keep driving the Australians out to work, and how if they were only a little more accepting of the great role destiny had given them, he wouldn't have to drive them so pitilessly. It wasn't in his nature to be so harsh. But in the face of the Australians' intransigence, he had to be.

They have no spirit, Colonel Kota said. That's what I saw in New Guinea. You charge them, they scatter like cockroaches.

If they had spirit, Nakamura said, they would have chosen death rather than the shame of being a prisoner.

I remember when I first went to Manchukuo, fresh from officer school, Colonel Kota said, clenching his hand as if around a handle or grip. A second lieutenant, very green. Five years ago. How long ago it seems. We had to undertake special field training exercises to prepare us for combat. One day we were taken to a prison for our trial of courage. The Chinese prisoners hadn't been fed for days. They were so scrawny. They were bound and blindfolded and made to kneel in front of a large pit. The lieutenant in charge unsheathed his sword. He scooped some water with his hand from a bucket and poured it over both sides of the blade. I have always remembered the water dripping off his sword.

Watch, he said. This is how you cut off heads.

# 15

On the following Saturday afternoon, the heat had grown to be unbearable. Having finished with the lunch sitting and made sure everything was ready for dinner, Amy Mulvaney decided to get changed and go for a swim. There was a large crowd smeared up and down the beach across the road from the King of Cornwall, and as she walked along the sand, listening to the waves and squeals, straw-hatted and in a pair of blue shorts and a white cambric blouse, she was aware of the gaze of both men and women.

The long, unbelievably hot summer days, the sensual nights, the stuffy bedroom and Keith's sounds and smells filled Amy Mulvaney with the strangest restlessness. She was full of yearning. To leave, to be someone else, somewhere else, to start moving and never stop. And yet the more the innermost part of her screamed to move, the more she recognised that she was frozen to one place, one life. And Amy Mulvaney wanted a thousand lives, and not one of them did she want to be like the one she had.

She had sometimes taken advantage of the war and Keith's lenient nature to escape for a night here and there. There had been some small adventures—a RAAF officer who had pressed her against the wall after a night's dancing, but to her great relief and slight disappointment, had only kissed her wildly and groped her a little. She had gone to bed with a travelling salesman who sometimes appeared at the hotel's back bar and whom she met outside a cinema in town one night. It had been an awful thing that, once begun, she felt could only end by letting it run its course. Compared to Keith, he'd had a strong, young body, and had been vigorous and attentive—too much so. For as soon as she found herself in bed naked with him, she was horrified: she could not bear his touch, his smell, his flesh. She wanted to be gone.

After, she had vomited and felt such a terrible emptiness that she had firmly resolved it could never happen again; a resolution that had helped her deal with the guilt she felt. She reasoned that perhaps, in the strangest way, this infidelity had ensured her fidelity thereafter to Keith. And because she had not loved the travelling salesman, there had been, she came to think, no real infidelity. Her love for Keith—such as it was—was still love: she still cared about him, was amused by him, and appreciated his gentleness and his numerous small kindnesses. The months after that disastrous night had in some ways been the best they had known. And yet even when she slept long and deeply and awoke feeling serene, with Keith bringing her a cup of tea in bed, Amy Mulvaney wanted something else, but what she wanted she was unable to say. As she sipped the tea and watched his large back lumber out the door, she could not help but wonder what that wanting was—the wanting that ate away at her stomach, the wanting that sometimes made her involuntarily shudder, the invisible, nameless, terrible wanting that she feared might be the very essence of life.

And so it had been for the last year, more or less. She flirted, but in a careful way; she made friends with those perhaps she shouldn't have, but again in a way that seemed to her and others, if not entirely appropriate, not inappropriate either. For that reason, because she felt a strange freedom—even a security—in having decided that no acquaintanceship could end in anything untoward, she felt emboldened to sometimes do and say such things to men as she had to the tall doctor in the bookshop. But again she reasoned that perhaps, ultimately, there had been nothing wrong in her behaviour, for in some fundamental way she had loved none of them and she still loved Keith. She felt she had found a balance that would make that love stronger, and she did not know why as she had walked over to that tall doctor in the bookshop, she had slipped off her wedding ring.

And when Amy thought about it, she realised that what she had said to the tall doctor she had never said to anyone else before. She could not understand it, nor could she understand why she had put her hand on his at the club, nor why she held him when he had gone to leave her rooms. She was simply determined never again to do such foolish things. She tried to convince herself that what had taken place with him was already over. But in her heart she feared something else and she tried hard not to allow her fear words or even thoughts.

Throwing her towel down on the blinding sand, straw hat on top, and skipping out of her clothes, she felt her youth and body as power. And despite her insignificance and unimportance, Amy understood that if only for a short time she was somehow special and important. She ran into the water. Unlike many of the other women, who dawdled at knee height, Amy Mulvaney threw herself under a wave just at the point it was about to break on her. And when she burst back up, tasting salt, the sky an unbearable brilliance, all her confusion was gone and in its place she had the strange sensation that she had surfaced into some new centre of her life. For a moment everything was in balance, everything waited.

Amy floated. Far out to sea a small yacht sat listless on the still water. When she turned back around to the beach she saw a middle-aged man in an old-fashioned woollen bathing suit staring at her. He was hairless, his skin like that of a fowl before it went into the oven. He abruptly looked away.

Once more, she knew that strange, haunting emotion that would not let her be: but what Amy Mulvaney wanted she was unable to say. She swam a few strokes further out, and it was as if the sea, the sun, the slight breeze were all willing her to do something, anything, but *something*. As she looked up and down the surf, she saw other people in line with her, so many people, expectant, hopeful, similarly waiting for the next wave to break, hoping to ride its power in to shore. As the ocean began banking up in a rolling wall behind her she noticed that running along its crest was a long line of yellow-eyed, silver fish.

As far as she could see all the fish were pointed in the same direction along the wave face, and all were swimming furiously as they sought to escape the breaking wave's hold. And all the time the wave had them in its power and would take them where it would, and there was nothing that glistening chain of fish could do to change their fate. Amy felt herself beginning to rise back into the wave's swelling, she tensed in anticipation and excitement, not knowing whether she would succeed in catching it, and, if she did, where she and the fish might end up.

# 16

Colonel Kota unclenched his hand and said—

He spread his legs, raised the sword and with a yell swung it down hard. The head seemed to leap away. The blood was still spurting in two fountains when we had to follow. It was hard to breathe. I was frightened of making a fool of myself. Some of the others hid their heads in their hands, one messed his stroke up so badly a lung half popped out. The head was still in place and the lieutenant had to finish off the mess. And all the time I was watching: what was a good stroke, what was a bad stroke, where to stand next to the prisoner, how to keep the prisoner calm and still. Thinking about it now, I can see that all the time I was looking, I was learning. And not only about beheading.

When my turn came I couldn't believe that I was doing everything so calmly because inside I was horrified. Yet I unsheathed the sword my father had given me without shaking, wet it as the instructor had shown without dropping it, and for a moment watched as those water beads rolled together and slowly ran away. You wouldn't believe how much watching that water helped me.

I stood behind the prisoner, got my balance, carefully examined his neck—skinny and old, filth in its folds; I've never forgotten that neck. Before it had begun it was over, and I was wondering why there were little globules of fat on my sword that wouldn't rub off with the paper they handed me. That's all I was thinking—where did that fat come from in such a scrawny man's scrawny neck? His neck was dirty, grey, like dirt you piss on. But once I had cut it open the colours were so vivid, so alive—the red of his blood, the white of his bone, the pink of his flesh, the yellow of that fat. Life! Those colours were life itself.

I was thinking about how easy it had been, how bright and beautiful the colours were, and I was stunned it was already over. Only when the next cadet officer stepped forward did I see that my prisoner's neck was still pumping blood out in two fountains, just like the lieutenant's victim, but only a little, so it must have been some time after I killed him that I noticed.

I no longer felt anything for that man. To be honest, I despised him for accepting his fate so meekly and wondered why he wouldn't fight. But who'd be any different? And yet, I was angry with him for letting me slaughter him.

Nakamura noticed how, as he told his story, Kota's sword hand continued clenching and unclenching, as if rehearsing or practising.

And what I felt, Major Nakamura, the colonel continued, was something so large in my stomach that it was as if I were now another man. I had gained something, that's what I felt. It was a great and terrible feeling. As if I had died too and was now reborn.

Before, I worried about how my men looked at me when I stood in front of them. But after, I just looked at them. That was enough. I no longer cared or was frightened. I just stared and saw into them—their fears, their sins, their lies—I saw everything, knew everything. Your eyes are evil, a woman said to me one night. I would just look at people and that would be enough to frighten them.

But after a while this feeling began to die. I started

feeling confused. Lost. The men would start talking insolently again, quietly, behind my back. But I knew it. No one was frightened of me anymore. It's like Philopon—once you have it, even if it makes you feel lousy, you just want it again.

Can I tell you something? There were always prisoners. If a few weeks had gone by and I hadn't beheaded someone, I would go and find one not long for this world with a neck I fancied. I'd make him dig his grave . . .

And as he listened to the colonel's terrible story, Nakamura could see that even in such terrible acts, too, that there was no other way for the Emperor's wishes to be realised.

Necks, continued Colonel Kota, looking away to where an open door framed the rainswept night. That's all I really see of people now. Their necks. It's not right to think this way, is it? I don't know. It's how I am now. I meet someone new, I look at his neck, I size it up—easy to cut or hard to cut. And that's all I want of people, their necks, that blow, this life, those colours, the red, the white, the yellow.

Your neck, you see, Colonel Kota said, that was what I first saw. And such a good neck—I can see exactly where the sword should fall. A wonderful neck. Your head would fly a metre. As it should. Because sometimes the neck is just too thin or too fat, or they wriggle or squeal in terror—you can just imagine—and you botch it and end up hacking them to death in rage. Your corporal, though, bull-necked, his attitude, you see. I'd have to concentrate on my stroke and placement to kill him quickly.

And all the time he was talking, Colonel Kota went on clenching and unclenching his hand, raising and lowering it when clenched, as though he were readying his sword for another beheading.

It's not just about the railway, Colonel Kota said, though the railway must be built. Or even the war, though the war must be won.

It's about the Europeans learning that they are not the superior race, Nakamura said.

And us learning that we are, Colonel Kota said.

For some moments neither man spoke, then Colonel Kota recited:

*Even in Kyoto*
*when I hear the cuckoo*
*I long for Kyoto.*

Basho, Nakamura said.

Talking more, Nakamura was delighted to discover that Colonel Kota shared with him a passion for traditional Japanese literature. They grew sentimental as they talked of the earthy wisdom of Issa's haiku, the greatness of Buson, the wonder of Basho's great haibun, *The Narrow Road to the Deep North,* which, Colonel Kota said, summed up in one book the genius of the Japanese spirit.

They both fell silent again. For no reason, Nakamura felt his spirits abruptly rising at the thought of their railway delivering victory in the invasion of India, at the idea of the whole world under one roof, with the beauty of Basho's verse. And all these things, which had seemed so confused and lacking in substance when he had tried to explain them to the Australian colonel, now seemed so clear and obvious and connected, so kind and good, when talking with such a kind, good man as Colonel Kota.

To the railway, said Colonel Kota, raising his teacup.

To Japan, said Nakamura, raising his cup in turn.

To the Emperor! said Colonel Kota.

To Basho! said Nakamura.

Issa!

Buson!

They drained what was left of Tomokawa's sour tea, then put down their teacups. And because they were two strangers with no idea what next to say, the silence that returned felt to Nakamura a mutual and profound understanding. The colonel opened a dark-blue cigarette case with the Kuomintang's white sun emblazoned on it, and proffered it to his fellow officer. They lit up and relaxed.

They recited to each other more of their favourite haiku, and they were deeply moved not so much by the poetry as by their sensitivity to poetry; not so much by the genius of the poem as by their wisdom in understanding the poem; not in knowing the poem but in knowing the poem demonstrated the higher side of themselves and of the Japanese spirit—that Japanese spirit that was soon to daily travel along their railway all the way to Burma, the Japanese spirit that from Burma would find its way to India, the Japanese spirit that would from there conquer the world.

In this way, thought Nakamura, the Japanese spirit is now itself the railway, and the railway the Japanese spirit, our narrow road to the deep north, helping to take the beauty and wisdom of Basho to the larger world.

And as they talked of renga and waka and haiku, of Burma and India and the railway, both men felt a great sense of shared meaning, though exactly what they had shared neither would afterwards have been able to say.

Colonel Kota recited another haiku by Kato, and they agreed that it was this supreme Japanese gift—of portraying life so concisely, so exquisitely—that they, with their work on the railway, were helping bring to the world. And this conversation, which was really a series of mutual agreements, made them both feel considerably better about their own privations and the bitter struggle that was their work.

And then Nakamura looked at his watch.

You must excuse me, Colonel. It's already 0350 hours. I must reschedule the work gangs to meet the new targets before reveille.

As he was about to leave, the colonel put his hand on Nakamura's shoulder.

I could have talked poetry with you all night, the large man said.

In the darkness and emptiness of the hut, Nakamura could feel the intense emotion of Colonel Kota as he drew his arm around Nakamura and brought his shark-fin face in close. He smelt of stale anchovies. His lips were open.

In another world, Colonel Kota began. Men . . . men *love*.

He couldn't go on. Nakamura pulled away. Colonel Kota straightened up and hoped he had been misunderstood. In New Guinea they had butchered and eaten both American prisoners and their own men. They had been dying of starvation. He remembered the corpses with their skinned thigh bones sticking out like gnawed drumsticks. The colours. Brown, green, black. He remembered the sweet taste. He had wanted another human being to know. That they had been starving and had no choice. To say it was all right. To hold him. To—

It can't be helped, Nakamura said.

No, Colonel Kota replied, stepping backwards and flipping open his Kuomintang cigarette case to proffer another cigarette to Nakamura. Of course not.

As the major lit up, Colonel Kota said—

*Even in Manchukuo*
*when I see a neck*
*I long for Manchukuo.*

He snapped the cigarette case shut, smiled and, clenching his fist, turned and left, his strange laughter vanishing with him into the noise of the monsoon night.

## 17

Amy Mulvaney was astonished at how easily lying now came to her, and she felt both a shame and a joy in her new ability. Over dinner Keith had begun one of his rants about council politics, when she interrupted to tell him that she was spending the next day with an old girlfriend—they would drive to a distant, isolated beach for a picnic and a swim, and she would borrow the Ford Cabriolet for the purpose.

Of course, Keith said, and then immediately returned to his story about the new council clerk and his antiquated thinking on sewerage.

Say something real! Amy had nearly cried out. But what that real thing was, what it might sound like, she couldn't say anymore, and besides, she didn't really want his attention at all. And the more Keith rambled on about drains and the pressing need for sewers and modern planning regulations and water closets for all and national mechanisms, regulation and scientific administration, the more she longed for the brush of Dorrigo Evans' fingers in the dark.

That night she had difficulty sleeping. Keith woke twice and asked her if she was ill, but before she answered he was asleep again, mouth rumbling, a minuscule salt pan of dry spume in the crease below his lips.

The next day began with her making her face up twice before she was satisfied and changing several times before settling on what she began with: dark shorts and a light cotton blouse cut to resemble a shawl which would show herself to advantage. Then she took the cotton blouse off in favour of a low-cut red blouse she fancied was like the one Olivia de Havilland wore in *Captain Blood*. But she had no skirt that went with it. And when, a little after ten, she picked up Dorrigo Evans from the sentry gate outside the barracks—Dorrigo Evans, who, she thought, with his smile, and his nose and the way he wore his hair a little longer than normal, really wasn't that unlike Errol Flynn—she was wearing a rather impractical but, she felt, fetching light-blue floral skirt and a cream halter top.

With Dorrigo at her side, everything that had seemed to Amy dull and stupid now was delightful and interesting; all that yesterday felt like an ever more claustrophobic prison she had wished to escape today felt like the most wondrous backdrop to her life. But her nervousness was so great that she kept stalling the car and Dorrigo ended up driving.

God, she thought, how she wanted him, and how

unseemly and unspeakable were the ways in which she wanted him. She thought how disgraceful she was, how wicked her heart, and how the world would punish her. And that thought was almost immediately replaced by another. My disgraceful, wicked heart, thought Amy, is braver than the world. For a moment it seemed to Amy that there was nothing in the world she could not meet and vanquish. And though she knew this to be the most foolish idea, it excited and emboldened her further.

The Ford was in a poor state. The engine roared, and the gears made a dreadful crunch whenever Dorrigo used them. In the general racket she felt free to talk, her words nothing, the drift of them everything.

He's a good man, she said. So kind. You have no idea. I mean, I love Keith. So much. Who wouldn't? A good man.

The best of blokes, said Dorrigo Evans, not entirely insincerely.

Yes, said Amy. A good man. And that council clerk! He has no idea at all about sewerage.

She knew she was babbling, that what she really wanted to tell Dorrigo was how Keith never said one word she felt was true to his heart. Every word was a mask. She wanted to tell Dorrigo how she longed for Keith to say real things. Or just one real thing.

But what that real thing might be Amy in her heart didn't know. What Amy Mulvaney wanted to hear just didn't sound like water closets and garden cities and the necessity of sound sewerage planning. She knew she wanted contradictory things. Really, she did not want her husband to talk at all; while she wanted Dorrigo Evans to say so many things to her, and she wanted him to say nothing in case he broke the spell—in case he somehow said it was only an outing, that she was simply a duty he had incurred as part of what passed, at such distance from his home, as his family. And she expressed all this strange contradictory tumult, all this ocean of feeling about the man to whom she was not married, by saying about the man to whom she was—

Keith is Keith.

When they arrived at the start of the track to the beach, Dorrigo lit a cigarette, but had not taken it from his mouth when Amy, stretching awkwardly to protect both her skirt and her dignity as she stepped over a sagging barbed wire fence, scratched her thigh and cried out. She twisted her leg out. A string of minute blood beads was slowly rising on the inside of her thigh, three glistening red ball bearings.

Dorrigo Evans threw his cigarette away and squatted down.

Excuse me, he said in a formal manner, and with a finger slid the hem of the light-blue skirt slightly up Amy's thigh. He dabbed at the wound with a handkerchief, halted and watched. The three blood balls beaded back up.

He leant in. He put a hand around her other calf to steady himself. He could smell the sea. He looked up at her. She was staring at him with a look he couldn't interpret. His face was very close to her thigh now. He heard a seagull squawk. He turned back to her leg.

He put his lips to the lowest blood ball.

Amy's hand reached down and rested on the back of his head.

What are you doing? she asked in a direct, hard voice.

But her fingers were threading his hair in strange,

creeping contradiction. He weighed the tension in her voice, the lightness of her fingers touching, the overwhelming scent of her body. Very slowly, the tips of his lips just touching her skin, he kissed the blood ball away, leaving a crimson smear on her thigh.

Her hand remained resting on his head, her fingers in his hair. He turned into her a little more and, raising his hand, lightly cupped the back of her thigh.

Dorrigo?

The other beads kept growing, and the first began to return. As he waited for her to object, to shake her leg, to push him away, kick him even, he did not dare look up. He watched those perfect spheres of blood, three camellias of desire, continue swelling. Her body was a poem beyond memorising. He kissed the second blood ball.

Her fingers tensed in his hair. The third blood ball he swept up with his tongue, just past the shadow line of her skirt where her thigh grew thicker. Amy's fingertips dug into his head. He kissed her leg again, this time tasting the salt of her, closed his eyes and let his lips rest on her thigh, smelling her, feeling her warmth.

Slowly, reluctantly, he let go of her leg and got back to his feet.

## 18

For the next quarter of an hour, in an awkward squall of silence, they followed an overgrown track to the beach. The day was growing hot, they were sweating, and both were grateful for the relief of that empty beach and ocean, its noise, its purpose, its solitude. After changing at a discreet distance from each other in the dunes, they ran into the sea together.

Amy felt the water reform her into something whole and strong. Things that a day before had seemed at the centre of her being dissolved into trivia and then washed away altogether: next week's dining room menu; the difficulty of procuring new wool blankets for the hotel rooms; the odour of the chief barman; the sickly sucking noise Keith made as he lit his pipe of an evening.

Behind the wave line they turned, wet-faced and diamond-eyed. On the infinite plateau of ocean only their heads broke, they trod water, each gazing at the other. She felt him swim up from underneath and brush her body as he surfaced. Like a seal, like a man.

After, they rested in the cleft of a dune, where the roar of breaking waves was hushed and the wind deflected. As their bodies dried, the heat returned as a stupefying weight. Amy stretched out and Dorrigo followed suit. She let her back soak up the heat and rested her face in the dark shadow thrown by her head. After a time she burrowed around and nestled her head against his stomach. He lit another cigarette.

Dorrigo held his arm up to the white-streaked sky and thought he had never seen anything so perfect. He closed one eye and with his other watched his finger touch the beauty of a cloud.

Why don't we remember clouds? he said.

Because they don't mean anything.

And yet they're everything, thought Dorrigo, but this idea was too vast or absurd to hold or even care about, and he let it drift past him with the cloud.

Time passed slowly or quickly. It was hard to say. They rolled into each other.

Dorry?

Dorrigo murmured.

You know it's when I'm alone with Keith that I can't stand him and I hate myself, she said. Why's that?

Dorrigo Evans had no answer. He flicked his cigarette into a dune.

Because I want to be with you, she said.

Time had gone and everything had halted.

That's why, she said.

Whatever had held them apart, whatever had restrained their bodies before, was now gone. If the earth spun it faltered, if the wind blew it waited. Hands found flesh; flesh, flesh. He felt the improbable weight of her eyelash with his own; he kissed the slight, rose-coloured trench that remained from her knicker elastic, running around her belly like the equator line circling the world. As they lost themselves in the circumnavigation of each other, there came from nearby shrill shrieks that ended in a deeper howl.

Dorrigo looked up. A large dog stood at the top of the dune. Above blood-jagged drool, its slobbery mouth clutched a twitching fairy penguin. He had the strange sensation that suddenly Amy was very far away, that he was hovering above her naked body. His feelings abruptly transformed. Amy, whose body an instant before had made him feel almost drunk with its scent and touch and sweep, its sweet salt rime; Amy, who a moment earlier had seemed to him to have become another aspect of himself, was now remote and removed from him. Their understanding of each other had been greater than that of God's. And a moment later it had vanished.

The dog dropped its head sideways; the penguin's now limp body flopped, and the dog turned and vanished. But the penguin's howl—eerie and long, with its abrupt end—remained in his mind.

Look at me, he heard Amy whisper. *Only me.*

When he looked back down, Amy's eyes had changed. Her pupils seemed saucer-like, lost—and lost, he realised, in him. He felt the terrible gravity of her desire for him pulling him back to her, into a story that was not his, and now that he had all he had dreamt of in recent days, he wanted to escape it as quickly as possible. He feared losing himself, his freedom, his future. What had a moment before aroused him so intensely now seemed charmless and ordinary, and he wished to flee. But instead he closed his eyes, and as he entered her a groan escaped her lips in a voice he did not recognise.

A wild, almost violent intensity took hold of their lovemaking and turned the strangeness of their bodies into a single thing. He forgot those short, sharp shrieks, that horror of ceaseless solitude, his dread of a nameless future. Her body transformed for him again. It was no longer desire or repulsion, but another element of him, without which he was incomplete. In her he felt the most powerful and necessary return. And without her, his life felt to him no longer any life at all.

Even then though, his memory was eating the truth of them. Afterwards, he remembered only their bodies, rising and falling with the crash of waves, brushed by the sea breezes that ruffled the sand dune tops and raked the ash that ate his abandoned cigarette.

# 19

Dying air dozed in the King of Cornwall's corridors. There was a weariness to the dim light. In the hotel kitchen it smelt like gas, though no leak had ever been found. In the rising floors and elaborate staircases, with their dusty carpet runners, there rose and fell odours Amy recognised as disappointment, of dust balls and dryness mixed with the slumping grease of defective meals and the doomed assignations of travelling salesmen and women bored or desperate or both. Am I one of these women? Amy wondered as she made her way to the top floor. Am I one too?

But once inside the corner room that they both now thought of as theirs—where the French doors with their corroding hinges and rusting lock creaked open onto the ocean and the ceaseless light across the road, where the room smelt of the sea and the air seemed to dance, there, where all things seemed possible—she knew she wasn't. She had arranged some ice and two bottles of beer for him, but in spite of the ferocious heat they were unopened when she arrived.

Dorrigo Evans pointed to the green Bakelite clock on the mantelpiece. Though the minute hand had at some unknown point disappeared from its face, the hour hand showed he had been waiting there for three hours past the time she had said she would come.

I had to wait till the day staff were gone, she said. Until it was safe for me to come here unnoticed.

Who's left?

Two barmaids, the head barman, the cook. Milly, the waitress. None of them ever come upstairs.

There doesn't seem to be anyone staying here.

Not tonight. I had all the bookings put in the two floors below so it's only us up here.

They went out onto the deep-set verandah and sat on the rusty iron furniture and shared a bottle of beer.

You're a great punter, Dorrigo said, according to Keith.

Ha, Amy said. Look at those birds. And she pointed to where sea birds would suddenly drop like dead things into the ocean. She went over to the wrought-iron balustrade; all its paint had long flaked away, leaving only an ochre dust. She ran a hand over its gritty oxide, red as old rock.

Keith reckoned you'd have the gun tip, Dorrigo said.

The birds would rise back up, whiting in their beaks. Amy pinched the sandy rust between her fingertips. She turned her gaze to the long beach, which ran for some miles till it reached an ancient eroded headland, bare of all but the hardiest scrub. Her head seemed full of distant things. He went to take her hand but she pulled it away.

Keith said that?

He said you always know the track and the field and the weights and the best bet.

Ha, she said, and went back to her own thoughts. From the street below, the noise of a dog yapping startled her. She looked around uneasily.

It's him, she said, and he could hear panic rising in her voice. He's come back a day early. I have to go, he's—

It's a big dog, said Dorrigo. Listen. A big dog. Not a mutt like Miss Beatrice.

She went quiet. The barking stopped, a man's voice—not Keith's—could be heard speaking to the dog, and then was gone. After a time she spoke up.

I hate that dog. I mean, I like dogs. But he lets it up

on the table after we've eaten. With its obscene tongue leaping out like some awful snake.

Dorrigo laughed.

And slobbering, panting away, said Amy. A dog on a table? Can you imagine it?

Every meal?

Can I tell you something? Just you?

Of course.

It's not about Miss Beatrice—and you can never tell anyone.

Of course.

You promise?

Of course.

Promise!

I promise.

She came back into the shadowed cave of the verandah and sat down. She took a sip of beer, then a long draught, put the glass down, glanced up at him and back at the beaded glass.

I was pregnant.

She was looking at her fingers, rubbing the now damp rust sand between their tips.

To Keith.

You're his wife.

This was before. Before we were married.

She halted and craned her head around, as if searching for someone else along that long, shadowed verandah. Finally satisfied there was no one, she turned back to him.

Which is why we married. He just didn't—this sounds so terrible—he just didn't think it was right to have a baby out of wedlock. You understand?

Not exactly. You could have married. You did marry.

He's a good man. He is. But—when I got pregnant—he didn't want to marry. And I did. To protect the baby. I didn't—

She halted again.

Love him. No. I didn't. Besides.

Besides what?

You won't think me a bad woman?

Why?

Wicked? I am not wicked.

Why? Why would I think such a thing?

Because I said I was going to Melbourne to see the Cup. I said to people I always went. Well, I was new here, what did they know? But—

But you didn't go.

No. Not that. I went. But I also—

Her fingers were moving quickly, trying to rub the rust off. Abruptly, she wiped them on the side of her dress, leaving a red smear.

I also went to see a man—a doctor—in Melbourne that Keith had arranged. Keith said it was the best way to deal with it. It was November. Well. He fixed it.

A silence opened up that not even the crashing waves could fill.

I never had a skerrick of interest in horses, said Amy.

But you picked Old Rowley to win the Cup. One hundred to one. You must know something.

I picked him because he *was* one hundred to one. I picked him to lose. I half expected him to be put down at the starting gate. I picked him because I hate the bloody Cup. I hate everything about it.

She stood back up.

I don't want to talk about it out here.

They went inside and lay on the bed. She rested her head on his chest, but it was too hot and after a time she moved away and they lay side by side with only their fingertips touching.

He sat there—Keith, I mean. Keith sat there with Miss Beatrice in his lap and said he had arranged a man in Melbourne to look after me. A man. What does that mean? A man?

For a moment this question seemed to absorb her, then she spoke again.

And he patted his dog. I never hated anything like I hated that dog. He wouldn't touch me, but there he was, patting and stroking that dog.

So what happened?

Nothing. I went to see a man in Melbourne. He just kept stroking and cooing at his bloody dog.

## 20

The occasional road and beach noises far below were swept up and swirled around by the ceiling fan's blades as it slowly shucked time. He found he was listening to her breathing, to the waves, to the clock on the mantelpiece. At some point he realised Amy's head was back on his chest and she had fallen asleep; at another that he too was asleep with her. The curtain yawned in as the late-afternoon sea breeze picked up, and with it the heat fell away and there came puffs of the smoky light of dusk. When next he stirred, he realised it was night and the lamp was on and Amy was awake, looking at him.

But after that? he whispered.

After what?

After the man in Melbourne?

Oh. Yes, she said, and halted and looked up at the ceiling or perhaps beyond it. It was a look at once of puzzlement and resignation, as though she expected the world to always come back to this mysterious place on the ceiling or in the stars beyond. Yes, she said several more times, still looking up. Finally, she looked back down at him.

I had to pretend I went to Melbourne for the race. I boned up on horses and betting and the like. Maybe I even got a little interested. It was something to think about, I suppose. And after, I didn't care. It was like the horses. I just pretended. I don't know. Anyway, that's why I have a little flutter now and then.

And Keith?

When I came back he was kind. So kind. I suppose he felt guilty. And I was so upset. And he wanted to marry me, even though there was no longer a baby—maybe to make it up. Maybe he was more ashamed than me. I don't know.

And you fell in love?

Just fell. Everything was snow. In my head. Have you ever had that feeling? You have a world and then all your thoughts have turned into snow. Keith was so kind and I was snow. Maybe I was ashamed. Maybe I just thought I was dirt. I did think I was dirt. I know I didn't want to be a spinster. Maybe I thought we could make it right. Get pregnant again. And this time make it right. But it was all wrong. I hated him for his kindness. I hated him until he hated me back. He said I'd tricked him into marriage. And somehow that seemed as it should be. He said I tricked him, that I did dreadful things and that's why the pregnancy. Maybe he doesn't really think it now. But sometimes things are said and they're not just words. They are everything that one person thinks of another in a sentence. Just one sentence. You tricked me, he said, and that's why the marriage. There are words and words and none mean anything. And then one sentence means everything.

Amy lay on her side as she gazed out towards the sea. Lying at her back, he felt jealous of her pillow. They lay silently together for a long time. With a finger he swept the hairs that fell across her face behind her ear. The shape of its shell always moved him. He felt a terrible vertigo, as if he were being swept into a gigantic maelstrom that had no ending. The green Bakelite clock was reduced to its phosphorescent arm and numbers, a ghostly floating circle that seemed now to hover above them as it ticked away. She rolled into him and he could feel her breath brushing his chest. He saw her eyes open, stare intently across his body as if gazing at something far beyond, and then close.

Much later, he awoke to the sound of her voice.

You hear that? she said.

Through the open window he could hear waves, some men leaving the bar four storeys down, talking about football. Footsteps, the occasional car in the unhurried and largely empty esplanade street, a woman talking to a child, people being together, being allowed to be together.

The waves, she said, the clock. The waves, the clock.

He listened again. After a time his ear attuned, the

street below fell quiet, and he could hear the slow rise and boom of the beach, the velvet ticking of the clock.

Sea-time, she said as another wave crashed. Man time, she said as the clock ticked. We run on sea-time, she said and laughed. That's what I think.

If he's so awful, why do you stay?

He's not awful, that's the thing. Maybe I even love him in my way. It's not us.

But love is love.

Is it? Sometimes I think it's a curse. Or a punishment. And when I am with him I am lonely. When I am sitting opposite him, I am lonely. When I wake in the middle of the night lying next to him, I am so lonely. And I don't want to be. He loves me and I can't say . . . It would be too cruel. He pities me, I think, but it's not enough. Maybe I pity him. Do you understand?

He didn't understand and he couldn't understand. Nor did he understand why if he wanted her, and the more he wanted her, the more he allowed himself to become tied up with Ella. He couldn't understand how what she had with Keith was *love* but it only seemed to make her miserable and lonely, yet its bonds were somehow stronger than their love that made her happy. And as she went on talking, it was as if everything that was happening to them could never be decided by them, that they lived in a world of many people and many ties, and that none of it allowed for them to be with each other.

We're not just two, he said.

Of course we're two, or we're nothing, Amy said. What do you mean, we're not two?

But he didn't know what he meant. At that moment he felt that he existed in the thoughts and feelings and words of other people. Who he was he had no idea. He didn't have words or ideas for what they were or what would become of them. It seemed to him that the world simply allowed for some things and punished others, that there was neither reason nor explanation, neither justice nor hope. There was simply now, and it was better just to accept this.

But still she talked on, trying to decipher an undecipherable world; still she asked of him his intentions, his ideas, his desires; still he felt she was trying to trap him into some expression of commitment that she could then reject outright as impossible. It was as if she wanted him to name whatever it was they had, but if he did that he would kill that very same thing.

In the dim light he heard her vow—

One day I'll go. One day I'll go and he'll never find me.

It was hard to believe her. He said nothing. She was silent. He felt he had to say something.

Why are you telling me?

Because I don't love Keith. Don't you see?

And these words struck them both as a new and unsettling revelation.

For a time they were both silent. Other than the green circle of time that waited opposite them they were in complete darkness in which their bodies dissolved. They found not each other in the dark, but pieces that became a different whole. He felt he might fly apart into a million fragments were it not for her arms and body holding him.

Listen, she said. We're sea-time.

But the sea had died off and the only sound was that

of the one-handed Bakelite clock. He knew it was untrue; that when he kissed the shell of her ear she was asleep, and that the only true thing in the universe at that moment was them together in that bed. But he was not at peace.

# 21

The morning air was already like an oven before the sun was properly up. She helped Dorrigo make the bed so their disgrace would not be visible to the maid. She watched him washing himself: his hands a wet bowl, his gleamy face falling from them a steaming pudding. It was his arms that she noticed above all, dark-skinned, the way he picked up and held things, the jug of cold water, the shaving brush, the safety razor. With a gentle power, not brute force. His tautness. The difference of him.

He was leaning down and burying his head in the water basin now, an arm splayed either side like a lamb's wonky legs. But he was nothing like a lamb—more like a wolf, she thought, holding himself there steady, poised, waiting, a black wolf, his gorgeous black hair in his armpits slicked with soap. His chest. His shoulders as he held up an arm as if stopping something—cars, trains, her heart—and then dropped it as if it were nothing.

She wanted to bury her face in those armpits there and then and taste them, bite them, shape into them. She wanted to say nothing and just run her face all over him. She wished she wasn't wearing that print dress—green, such a bad colour, such a cheap dress, so unflattering and her breasts she wanted up and out, not lost and covered up. She watched him, his muscles little hidden animals running across his back, she watched him moving, wanted to kiss that back, those arms, the shoulders, she watched him look up and see her.

The eyes, the black eyes. Unseeing and seeing.

She said something to hurry away from that look but she stayed. What he was thinking she never knew. She had once asked; he said he had no idea. Later, she thought he was scared. He was handsome. She didn't like that about him either. Too sure, she felt, too knowing—one more thing she later realised she had been wrong about. The knowing and the unknowing.

Him. To a tee.

When he saw her still staring at him, he looked away and down, his face flushed.

She longed to know everything about him, to tell him everything about her. But who was she? She had come down from Sydney to visit with a friend who had family in Adelaide and she had ended up staying, getting a job behind the King of Cornwall's bar. There she met Keith Mulvaney. He was a boring man but kind in his way, things had happened, and who was she? The daughter of a Balmain sign painter who had died when she was thirteen, one of seven children who made their way the best they could. She had never met a man like Dorrigo.

Is the floor more interesting than me? she said.

Why on earth did she say that? She was a wicked woman, she was a disgraceful woman; she knew it, and sometimes she didn't care if the world knew it, she would not regret it if she were on her deathbed now. She regretted nothing. She handed him his shirt.

No, he said.

He smiled. His smile, his bicep moving like a ball back and forth under his skin as he took the towel from her and buried his smile in it. Moving and unmoving.

But she thought he seemed unsure. All men were liars and he was no doubt no different—only one tongue and more tales than the dog pound. She had lived the lot, walked in each and every direction. She longed to have his lovely cock in her mouth now, in front of them all down in the dining room, that'd put some cream in their coffee.

Suddenly she wished he would just disappear. She wanted to push him away, and would have but she was terrified of what might happen if she touched him.

Dorry?

The asking and the wanting.

It could not be and it was, and she wondered if it would ever go, this feeling, this knowing, this *us*.

Dorry?

Yes.

Dorry, *would* it?

Would it, what?

Scare you, Amy said. If I said I love you?

Dorrigo made no answer and turned away, while Amy searched the blue bedspread for individual cotton strands, plucking at them.

Oh, she was a wicked woman and she had lied to herself and to Keith, but she regretted nothing if it had all led to this. She did not want love. She wanted *them*.

Though it was still morning, they lay back down together on their freshly made bed. His forearm ran over her breasts and his hand formed a nest under her chin. He ran his nose up and down her neck. She shuffled. His lips, open; her neck, rising.

No, he said.

When he was asleep she stood up, stumbled, gained her balance, stretched and went out into the shadow of the balcony. A distance up the beach there were some children squealing in the waves. The heat was like a maternal force, demanding she sit down. She sat there a long time, listening to the waves crack and boom. When she felt the shadow shortening on her extended legs she finally went down the three storeys to the rooms where she lived with her husband.

She smelt Dorrigo everywhere, even after she took a bath. He had scented her world. She lay down on her marital bed and slept there until well after dusk, and when she awoke all she could smell was him.

## 22

Half days, full days, free nights, whatever time off Dorrigo Evans could scrounge for leave he now spent with Amy. He had a new-found mobility in the form of a baby Austin baker's van. A fellow officer had won it in a card game and, having his own car already, happily lent it to Dorrigo whenever it was wanted. Keith enjoyed Dorrigo's visits and declared himself glad to have his nephew chaperoning Amy when he was away with his various commitments, which, as summer progressed, seemed to be ever more frequently.

Dorrigo's life at the King of Cornwall, which was

measured in hours and which could have added up to no more than a few weeks, seemed to be the only life he had ever lived. Amy used expressions such as *When we return to our real lives*, *When the dream ends*, but only that life, those moments with her, seemed real to him. Everything else was an illusion over which he passed as a shadow, unconnected, unconcerned, only angry when that other life, that other world wished to make claim on him, demanding that he act or think about something, anything other than Amy.

His army life, which once consumed him, now failed even to interest far less excite him. When he looked at patients they were just windows through which he saw her and only her. Every cut, every incision, every procedure and suture he made seemed clumsy, awkward, pointless. Even when he was away from her he could see her, smell her musky neck, gaze into her bright eyes, hear her husky laugh, run his finger down her slightly heavy thigh, gaze at the imperfect part in her hair; her arms ever so slightly filled with some mysterious feminine fullness, neither taut nor flabby but for him wondrous. Her imperfections multiplied every time he looked at her and thrilled him ever more; he felt as an explorer in a new land, where all things were upside down and the more marvellous for it.

She lacked the various conformities that made Ella so admired and drew comparisons with various Hollywood stars; Amy was far too much flesh and blood for that. When he was away from her he tried remembering more of her perfect imperfections, how they aroused him and delighted him, and the more he dwelled on them, the more there were. That beauty spot above her lip, her entrancing snaggle-toothed smile, the slight awkwardness in her gait—a pensive roll that was almost a swagger, as though she were trying to control the uncontrollable, to pretend to being demure without also exposing something at once feminine and animal. She was always inadvertently tugging at her blouse, pulling it up over her cleavage, as though if she didn't her breasts might at any moment escape.

He would remember how the more she tried to evade and cover her nature, the more it rioted in the gaze this brought. She was a moving paradox, at once embarrassed and yet excited by the very thing she oozed. When she laughed she cackled, when she moved she swung, and for him there was always about her the smell of musk and the erratic breath of sea wind puffing through the hotel's verandah and softly rattling the open French doors. In bed she sometimes ran her hand over parts of her body and stared at her hips or thighs in strange perplexity: her body was as unanswerable a mystery to her as it was to him. She described herself in terms of a faulty construction—the shape of her legs, the width of her waist, the shape of her eyes.

Her feeling for him he at first refused to believe. Later he dismissed it as lust, and finally, when he could no longer deny it, grew puzzled by its animality, its power and its scarcely believable ferocity. And if this life force sometimes felt too large and too inexplicable for a man with as low an estimate of himself as Dorrigo Evans it was also, he came to recognise, inexorable, inescapable, and overwhelming, and he surrendered himself to it.

Desire now rode them relentlessly. They became reckless, taking any opportunity to make love, seizing shadows and minutes that might abruptly end in discovery, daring the world to see them and know them *as* them, partly willing it, partly wanting it, partly evading it and partly hiding it, but always thrilling in it. The ocean rising and breaking through the King of Cornwall's thick bluestone walls; their exertions inside, slowly merging into one, bodies beading and bonding in a slither of sweat. They made love on beaches, in the ocean, and, less easily, in the Cabriolet, the street behind the King of Cornwall, over a barrel of Coopers Red in the cool retreat of the cellar, and once in the kitchen very late at night. He could not resist the undertow of her.

After lovemaking he was haunted by her face, expressionless, so close, so far away; looking up into him and through him, beyond him. At such times, she would seem lost in some trance. The eyebrows so definite, so strong; the burning blue of her eyes, silver in the night light, seemingly not focused on him but staring straight at him; her slightly opened lips, not smiling, only the gentlest of slowing pants that he would lean down and turn his cheek to, in order to feel their slightest breeze on his skin, so he might know that this was not a vision, but her, her in bed with him. And he knew not joy, or pride, but amazement. In the darkened hotel room he thought he had never seen anything so beautiful.

Once, when Keith had gone to town early for a meeting, she came to his room in the morning. They chatted, and when she went to leave they embraced, kissed and fell to the bed. With her legs spilling over the bed and him half-standing, half-crouching, he entered her. And when he looked down at her face she seemed not to be there or even conscious of him.

Her eyes grew brighter and brighter but were strangely

unfocused. Her lips were parted just enough for her shallow pants to escape, a short, repetitive cascade of sighs in part response to him and in part to some ecstasy that was hers alone. It frightened him how lost her face seemed to be. As though what she really sought from him was this obliteration, an oblivion, and their passion could only lead to her erasure from the world. As if he was only ever a vehicle for her to ride to another place, so distant, so unknown to him that a dull resentment momentarily rose in him. And as she began violently clutching and pulling him into her, he understood that his own body was somehow making the same journey. Did she think all this was him? he wondered. It was not him. It was a mystery to him also.

So it went on, that never-ending summer that ended like a joyriders' car smash on the Sunday night Keith told Amy he knew, and that he had always known.

# 23

Keith Mulvaney began at the beginning, and it was clear nothing had escaped him. He drove even more slowly than he normally did, for with the blackout laws there were no streetlamps, no visible houselights, and all car headlights were covered with slotted shades.

I know, he said. I've always known.

The car floor shuddered beneath Amy's feet. She tried to lose herself in its vibrations but the vibrations just seemed to be saying to her *DORRY—DORRY—DORRY*. She did not dare look at her husband, instead staring straight ahead into the night.

From the first, he said. When he came to the bar asking for me.

Miles seemed to pass between sentences. The car seemed to be lost in an endless, rattling blackness. She was trying very hard to push it out of her mind but all she could feel was the sadness emanating from Keith, a sadness that seemed to empty the world. Though the car shuddered and thrummed, all about her seemed only silence, solitude and the most terrible stillness. She had only ever known him like this when his beloved sister had died of tuberculosis the summer before.

Perhaps this, too, is a form of grief, she thought. There is no joy, no wonder, no laughter, no energy, no light, no future. Hope and dreams are cold ash from a dead fire. There is neither conversation nor argument. For, in truth, what is there to be said? It is death. The death of love, thought Amy. He sat there, leaning ahead, so many split sticks of despair protruding out of a sack of ill-fitting clothes: brown Oxford bags, green twill shirt, a muddy woollen tie.

I thought that was cheeky, Keith said.

Amy Mulvaney objected as best she could without telling the truth, that the truth was there was nothing going on then. She said that they were at that time strangers, save for one chance meeting—at the bookshop, which, as she reminded Keith, she had told him about, which, after a fashion, she had—where nothing had happened.

*Nothing*? Keith Mulvaney said. He was as ever smiling, a smile that horrified her and shamed her in equal measure. Your stomach didn't bunch up? he continued. You didn't feel somehow excited or nervous talking to him?

Not wishing to lie, she said nothing, knowing that silence was a damning admission but that words were somehow worse.

You see, I know you, Amy. And I know you were.

How could he know? she wondered. How could he have known when they hadn't? And yet he did.

If he had been a different man, she might have thought he was bluffing. But Keith Mulvaney was guileless. He had an unfortunate relationship with truth that she had made herself lose since meeting Dorrigo. She never said the first thing that came to her, but rather the third or fourth, and then only after it had been tested and checked for faults and flaws. But when Keith spoke, he said exactly what was on his mind. He had known, he had always known, and he had carried his terrible knowledge as he did so much else, silently, patiently, uncomplainingly until that night, returning from the Robertsons', something had opened up in the blackness in front of him and made it impossible for him to carry it any longer.

Their marriage had remained comfortable over the summer—perhaps, when Amy thought about it, it had grown even more so. It felt like the Edwardian horsehair furniture he had refused her requests to replace after their marriage: sagging, comfortable if one nestled in the soft spots and avoided the hard. He was unselfish and he was kind. But he was not Dorrigo. And she was finding it more and more difficult to delude herself that this was love. She felt their marriage withering. She returned to his presence, to their bed, with its thinning yellow corduroy cover she folded back each hot night, amicably, quietly, but hiding an inner life, a turmoil, that took her elsewhere.

Sometimes she had the strongest urge to fall to her knees and confess. Her guilt she could live with of a day. But of a night, early in the hours of the morning, it filled her stomach and pressed so hard on her chest that she had to slow her breathing to bear its crushing weight. She did not want his absolution, only the purity of reconciling her truth and her life, and, having done so, of standing up, turning away and leaving forever.

## 24

If Amy had enjoyed the attentions, the gifts and the flattery of the ageing, bearish publican in the first few months that she worked at the King of Cornwall—perhaps even unconsciously encouraged them—she had also begun to be disturbed by them. One night, after the bar had closed, she ended up with Keith alone. She did so because she thought it would offer the right moment when she could tell him kindly that his silly attentions must end, that nothing would or could come of them. But instead of that happening she found herself in a labyrinth of caresses and touches. She did not know when or how to escape him, and finally it just seemed easier and wiser to go along with it all, and wait for another moment to tell him.

And one thing, as they sometimes do, led not to another, but shattered a world.

After the abortion, when guilt took hold of Keith and his mind turned to marriage, Amy was too undone and too lost to make any decisions, and Keith worked assiduously at bringing her so fully into his world and that of the hotel that she had little time for anything else. Perversely, his proposal of marriage—in its certainty and its respectability—seemed the only way out of the mire. She told herself that their differences, which seemed so pronounced, were perhaps really no greater or less than those of any other couple.

And perhaps they weren't. She came to discover a gentle, generous, caring man. She had for the first time in her life security and moderate wealth. And in deference to the difference in their ages—some twenty-seven years—Keith accorded her a certain freedom to come and go as she wished, and she was not ungrateful. No, it was not hellish.

She knew there was much to like about Keith. He could be easy company. He made sure the hotel was in good repair, provided well for her, kept the fires loaded with wood in winter, the kitchen with ice in summer. He cared for her. She felt she existed as the hotel did for him, as a part of his life with needs that must be serviced, in all of which he had an interest but no fundamental passion. The emptiness of their life he kept at bay with industry, working hard at the hotel, and in what little spare time remained in his capacity as secretary of several sporting clubs and as an alderman.

But Amy wanted more than maintenance, comfort, split kindling and iced milk; more than a fading yellow corduroy bed cover falling neatly into creases worn into the fabric by years of identical folding back. She wanted disrepair, adventure, uncertainty. Not comfort, but the inferno.

Sometimes of a night he would lie at her back, caress her hips, her thighs. She would feel his hand on her breast and think of a fat huntsman spider. Then those same fingers would be between her legs, seeking to pleasure her. She never responded. She found that the best way to deal with his attentions was to do nothing. She neither resisted nor accepted. When he placed one leg here, when he entered her there, she just went with him, saying nothing. But always she refused his kisses. Her mouth was her own.

Sometimes this enraged him, and he would grab her by the chin, bring her face round to his and roll his lips on hers, his tongue snaking back and forth over her clenched mouth—she imagined it must be like licking a door lock—and then he would let her face fall out of his hands and sometimes moan, a strange, terrible, animal lowing.

Over time, he came to accept her compliance on her terms. At the end, she would throw off the bedclothes and, without a word to him, without a gesture, stride to the bathroom in sullen anger.

It hurt her to hurt him, but she felt it somehow truthful and necessary. And if he was left feeling like dirt, slime, a disgusting vile thing, there was reason for it, strange, contradictory reason. She at once wanted him to know and know everything, and equally she would do anything in her power to keep her affair with Dorrigo secret from him and not hurt him so. She wanted a crisis that would end it all, she wanted nothing to change; she needed to provoke him and desperately desired that he never be provoked.

When she returned she would never touch him or talk to him, but lie in bed with her back turned to him. He would lean across and try to kiss her forehead over and over, perhaps in a panic, perhaps wanting some sign, some affirmation that he was not mistaken, that she did love him, that she did feel for him as he did for her. But there was none.

Amy would feel his body behind her short of breath, and she would know that love is not goodness, and nor is it happiness. She wasn't necessarily or always unhappy with Keith, nor were her feelings about Dorrigo always or exactly those of happiness. For Amy, love was the universe touching, exploding within one human being, and that person exploding into the universe. It was annihilation, the destroyer of worlds.

And as she lay in bed feeling Keith silently sobbing behind her back, she understood that love does not end until all its power is exorcised in misery and cruelty and obliteration as much as in goodness and joy. And every night as she lay there, she could feel rolling in her stomach shards of broken glass—cutting, cutting, cutting.

## 25

There was no one to whom Amy could talk of such things. Love is public, one of her friends had said during the evening of playing five hundred that she and Keith were now returning from, or it's not love. Love is shared with others or it dies.

Keith and Amy played cards with the Robertsons on the first Sunday night of each month, and they had been discussing a recent scandal in which a well-known lawyer had left his wife for a doctor's daughter. This had led to several stories of lurid abandonments and contemptible adulteries. Invariably, the sympathy of the table was with the partner who was left. The spouse who found another was a figure of contempt, of mockery and exorcism. Mostly exorcism. A casting out.

Amy longed for that, for its dramatic finality. But instead things bled. They bled and bled and would not stop bleeding. There would be no dramatic end, she realised, only a slow withering, like Keith's sister's wretched end with tuberculosis. Bleeding and more bleeding.

There were so many things that she wanted to ask, to know. Do you really think *that*? she wished to ask. Is a hidden love not love at all? Is it really doomed never to exist? Does it never stop bleeding until it dies?

She wanted to upend the card table and scatter the cards to the winds, to stand up and demand that they said what they really thought. Answer me, she wanted to say. Can a love that is not named not be love too? Could it even be a greater love? I love another man, she wanted to say to them all. As the cards fluttered to earth, as everyone's hand was revealed as worthless, as every point won was shown to be a pointless charade, she would tell them how wonderful this other man was, and how if she didn't see him for another thirty years she would still love him, how she would still love him if he was dead until she was dead too.

But instead she watched as Harry Robertson played the right bower, and he and Keith, who always played as partners, won the hand.

Cheating is so easy, said Elsie Robertson, sweeping up the cards and shuffling the pack in readiness for the next round. It's pathetic. You just lie and abuse trust.

Amy thought they were talking about love. Cheating

wasn't easy, thought Amy. It was hard; so very, very hard. It wasn't some failure of character. It just was. It wasn't even cheating. Because if it was being true to yourself, then wasn't the real cheating the charade you played out with your spouse? And wasn't this, the real cheating, what the world and the Robertsons wanted and approved of?

She waited for some sign, some insight, some words from another woman that she was not alone. But there was none. Dorrigo had told her that very afternoon that his unit was shipping out on Wednesday. And perhaps he would die, or perhaps he would live but never return to her. She thought back to what he had said about the Greeks and the Trojans—were the Greeks to win again?

And she wondered: was hers a great love that was no love at all? And why, when she felt that she had come to exist only through another person, did she feel such a terrible solitude?

For this much Amy did know: she was alone.

When they left the card evening, Amy found Keith uncharacteristically quiet. Normally he babbled, but of late he said less and less, and through the hands of five hundred he had said next to nothing. The sadness emanating from Keith seemed to empty the world. She tried to lose her thoughts in the Cabriolet's rattling side windows, the road noise, the slight clatter of its motor. But all she was aware of was Keith's deep turn into himself, and the rattle and the thrum and the clattering points remained just that.

The magic's gone, he said.

The council will see the sense of what you're arguing, Amy said, picking up on a conversation earlier in the evening.

The council? Keith said, looking at her as if he were a grocer and she a customer who had walked into his shop and inexplicably ordered a bag of common sense. The council has got nothing to do with it, he said, his gaze returning to the road.

And though she knew she shouldn't, she said brightly, Who does then?

It was a lie of sorts. Everything was a greater or lesser lie now.

For a moment, Keith turned and looked at her. In the darkness she could make little out, but she could see he was staring at her not in rage, which would have been understandable, nor in accusation, which would have been helpful, but in a terrible judgement she could not escape for as long as he kept on looking at her—with pity, with horror, with a hurt that the blackness could not obscure and which she feared would stay with her forever after. She suddenly felt very frightened.

I didn't know, you know? he said. Not really.

She could not love him, she told herself. She could not, must not, could never, ever love him.

He went on, never raising his voice: I hoped I had it all wrong. That you'd prove what a horrible, jealous old man I was thinking such awful things. That you'd make me feel ashamed thinking such things. But now. Well, now I do. Everything is . . . *clear.*

For some moments he seemed lost in thoughts, calculations, some calculus of betrayal. And then he said in a vague and slow way—

And when you tell me something, it's, like . . . *like* . . .

He looked back to the road.

It's like hearing the hammer click back on the rifle.

She wanted to hold him. But she didn't and wouldn't do any such thing.

Perhaps I should have done something, said something, Keith continued. But I felt, well, what is there to say? He's her age, I told myself, more or less; I am an old, fat fool. I had—

He paused. Were his eyes moist? She knew he would not cry. He was braver than her, she thought. And better. But it was not virtue she wanted, but Dorrigo.

Had suspicions. Yes, Keith said, his tone as though he were speaking to Miss Beatrice on his lap. And I thought, well, Keith, old fellow, make yourself scarce when he comes around. They can be together, and it'll burn out, and she'll come back to you. It wasn't my first mistake, though.

An army truck passed them, and in the brief dim slit of light it threw into the Cabriolet she stole a glimpse across. But his face, shadowed, intent, staring far away down that long straight Adelaide street, told her nothing.

I should have let you keep the baby, he said.

He dropped gear and the car floor shook beneath Amy's feet. Its vibrations seemed to be shouting to her *DORRY!—DORRY!—DORRY!*

I had, I guess, Keith went on, ideas. That you, me . . . His tongue was stumbling. Each word was a universe, infinite and unknowable. *Us*, he continued.

She recognised within herself a deep feeling for him. But though she felt a great deal, what she felt was not love.

There's nothing going on, Keith.

No, no, he said. Of course. Of course, there's not.

What do you want me to do?

Do? Do? What can be done? he said. The magic's gone.

Nothing has happened, she lied a second time.

*We*, he said, and turned to her. We? he asked. But he seemed unsure, lost, as defeated as France. We *could*. That we could be something. Yes, said Keith.

Yes, she said.

That we could. But we couldn't. Could we, Amy? I killed the baby and that killed us.

## 26

On Monday morning Dorrigo Evans was about to lead a route march into the Adelaide Hills when he was called to regimental administration to take an urgent call from his family. The office was a large corrugated-iron Nissen hut in which staff officers worked in temperatures unknown outside of bakeries and pottery kilns. The infernal heat was trapped and further stifled by the hut's partition into unworkable offices delineated by single-sheet Masonite walls painted a grimy mustard. Out of frustration everyone seemed to smoke more, and the air had a haze about it that was only rivalled by its odour—compounded of tobacco smoke, sweat and the stale, ammoniacal scent of overcrowded animals—that left everyone coughing incessantly.

The phone where Dorrigo's call waited was mounted on a wall opposite the duty officer's front desk, past which flowed all those seeking to get outside on any pretext. Offsetting this insurmountable lack of privacy was a crazed cacophony of typewriter keys being pounded and typewriter carriages returning, phones ringing, men yelling and coughing, electric fans here and there droning as they hacked the unbearable heat into intolerable hot tufts.

Dorrigo picked up the Bakelite earpiece and, leaning down into the voice cone, coughed to make his arrival known. For a moment there was no sound, and then he heard her unmistakable voice utter two words.

He knows.

He felt himself falling through the cosmos, with nothing to stop him. Somewhere far below was his body, attached to an earpiece that was attached to a wire that ran through other wires all the way to where Amy Mulvaney stood in the King of Cornwall. He could see his body turn its back to the other men. He coughed again, this time inadvertently.

What? Dorrigo said. He cupped his hand around the end of the earpiece, both to better hear Amy and to ensure no one else could.

Us, said Amy.

Dorrigo ran a finger between his wet collar and his neck. The heat was impossible. He was breathing in long pants to try to get enough air.

How?

I don't know, she said. How, what, I don't know. But Keith knows.

Dorrigo understood that Amy would next say she would leave Keith, or perhaps that Keith had thrown her out. In any event, he and Amy would now start a life together. He understood all this, and he knew to this he would say yes—yes, he would end it with Ella Lansbury, and yes, he would immediately begin to arrange his affairs so he and Amy could become a real couple. And all this seemed to him inevitable and as it should be.

Amy, whispered Dorrigo.

Go back, she said.

What?

To her.

Dorrigo felt himself tumbling, returning into the oven-like office. He longed to talk to her anywhere but here—in a bookshop full of dust, at the beach, in the corner room he now thought of as theirs, with its peeling French doors and breezes and softly rusting wrought-iron balcony.

Go back to Ella, Amy said.

He replied as flatly and unemotionally as he could, breaking his words up so that the duty officer sitting behind him would not understand what he was saying.

What. Do you mean. Go back?

To her. That's what I mean. You must, Dorry.

She didn't want this, he thought. She couldn't want it. Why then was she saying it? He had no idea. His face was flushed. His body felt too hot and too large for his uniform. He was angry. He needed to say so many things and he could say none of them. He could feel the mustard Masonite walls closing in on him, the weight of khaki around him, of discipline and rules and authority. He felt he was choking.

Go to Ella, she ordered.

His body just wanted to flee the awful oven-like room of the Nissen hut, to escape, to—

Amy, he said.

Go, she said.

I—

I what? Amy said.

I thought, he replied. That—

That what? Amy said.

Everything now was inverted. The more he wanted her, the more she pushed him away. And then Amy said that she could hear Keith coming, that she was sorry, that she had to go. He would be happy, she said.

And though he wasn't happy, Dorrigo Evans felt the most unexpected and enormous relief. In a moment he would be outside the furnace of regimental administration, and he would no longer have the overwhelming confusion close to paralysis that Amy Mulvaney had brought into his life; henceforth, he would be able to live life on his own terms, in a straight and honest way with Ella Lansbury. He understood that he would be free, that he would no longer have to swim in a maelstrom of swirling lies and deceits, that he could with full heart devote himself to the task of finding love with Ella Lansbury. So, afterwards, he never understood why he then said what he did, only that he meant every word of it. That in one sentence he forsook that freedom and with it that reasonable hope of love being built.

I'll be back, Dorrigo Evans said. When it's over. For you, Amy. And we'll marry.

He was aware it was a path to misery and even damnation. What a moment before he had never even thought about now seemed inevitable, and it was as if it could never have been any other way—their meeting in the bookshop of wild dust motes, the bedroom of flaking paint and lazy curtains ruffling in ocean breezes, a tin hut as hot as a smokehouse. The Bakelite earpiece was so wet with sweat that it slid off his ear, and it was a moment or two before he understood that she had hung up and possibly not heard a word of what he had just said.

He had to see her—that was all he could think. He must see her. In one of the two nights he had left, he would have to somehow steal out of the barracks and arrange a meeting so that they might talk.

You're out of it, Evans, a voice behind him said. He turned to see a 2/7th staff officer with a clipboard.

Dorrigo's mind was awhirl with how he would get out of Warradale without permission, where he would find a vehicle, where they might secretly meet.

The 2/7th CCS are catching the train to Sydney tonight. On arrival, you'll be advised of what ship you're embarking on. Final destination to be advised somewhere in the middle of the bloody Pacific. You've been ordered to cancel all planned activities and be prepared to leave at 1700.

Dorrigo's mind was pitching and reeling. The import of what he was being told was beginning to sink in.

But—I thought it was to be Wednesday?

The staff officer shrugged his shoulders.

Bloody relief to get going, if you ask me, he said. You've got five hours. The staff officer raised his wrist and looked at his watch. Or less, he said.

And Dorrigo realised he might never see Amy again. And with this knowledge, he knew he would have to work, to operate, to go to bed and rise again and live, and now go wherever the war took him, without another soul knowing what he carried deepest in his heart.

# 27

Of a night, the heat seemed without end. But it was not like the summer of two years before. The war ground on, the families on the beach were mostly fatherless, uniforms rather than suits or singlets drank in the bar now, and their talk was full of new words, naming places hitherto unknown to either the front or back bar of the King of Cornwall—El Alamein, Stalingrad, Guadalcanal. It was the eleventh day of the heatwave, the King of Cornwall's bars were as busy as on a pre-war Cup day. A man who had killed his wife with a poker blamed the murder on the heat, and Amy had just returned home early after cutting her foot on a broken beer bottle while taking an evening walk along the beach. She washed her foot in the bath, bandaged it, and came into the room of the hotel that served as their parlour to find Keith Mulvaney standing over the wireless as he switched it off.

That was a good episode tonight, he said as the static softly died. You would have liked it.

And Amy had once liked it well enough, but now she could no longer abide her husband's domestic rituals, not least this, the silent listening to his favourite weekly radio serial—only broken by his match-striking and pipe-sucking, by the dog slobbering—and now she tried to escape it when she could. She hated the radio serial, his pipe, his old man's movements; she hated the very air she had to share with him, the stifling, unbreathable, stinking air that she was drowning in every day.

Keith sat down in an armchair, Miss Beatrice hopped into his lap, gasping and slobbering as he tamped his pipe. The windows were all open but still Amy found it stifling after the sea breath of the beach. She sat down. Her foot ached. The evening sea breeze found its way in, but seemed only to heighten the smell of brilliantine embedded in the antimacassar, to enhance the odour of stale pipe tobacco in the russet armchairs, to remind her of the scent of stale dog that always made her want to walk straight back out and leave forever.

After the council meeting tonight, Keith Mulvaney began, and Amy looked down at the dog hair on the rug, fearing another tale of municipal drudgery.

The council clerk, Ron, Keith Mulvaney said. You remember Ron?

No, Amy said.

Of course you do. Ron Jarvis. You remember Ron Jarvis.

No.

Ron Jarvis was saying he had heard on the by and by that it's very bad news about our boys in Java.

Amy looked up. Keith's rictus smile betrayed nothing—a dreamy, half-demented look, she felt. Yet at that moment she understood he had always seen further than she had known.

I have never heard of Ron Jarvis, Amy said, though she could now put a small, whippet-like face to the name. Was Keith seeking to gloss over the worst with some good? He lit his pipe, chugged on it till the tobacco was a ripe coal, and then, his smile never once faltering, leant forward in his armchair. Miss Beatrice, sandwiched in his lap, squawked as she adapted to the billow of Keith's belly.

I was asking, Keith Mulvaney said. Well, more than that. I said to Ron, I have a nephew, Dorrigo Evans—can you find out anything about him or his unit? Gave him details. Well, he came back yesterday. The thing is, Amy, the news is not so good.

Amy stood up, wincing, and hobbled over to the sash window.

No, he went on, not so good at all. Grim, really. Which is why it's hush-hush. Very hush-hush.

She stood next to the window, and although the night air outside was of a lower temperature than inside, the exterior heat still felt a brutish, menacing thing. She could hear the disturbing small sounds of things drying, crackling, breaking—grass, wood, God knew what else. She could make out the corrugated iron on the roof far above aching loudly as it contracted from its sunlit excesses. She leant hard on her cut foot to make the pain stab hard up into her.

Grim? Amy Mulvaney said. What's grim? They're prisoners, we know that. And the Japs are brutes. But they're safe.

The Australian prisoners in Germany you can correspond with. May as well be on holiday. But the POWs in Asia, well, it's not such a pretty picture. There's no news, no reliable testimony. There's been no real word of them since the surrender of Singapore. Nothing has been heard of his unit for nine months. They think thousands of the POWs have perished over there.

Maybe. But there's no proof Dorrigo's dead.

They've been told—

Who told? Who said it? Who, Keith?

I . . . Their intelligence, I guess. I mean—

Who, Keith?

I can't say. But Ron—well, he knows. *People.*

People?

Well-placed people. Defence Department people.

Keith Mulvaney halted; his mask-like smile seemed to be signalling something else—pity? uncertainty? rage?—and then continued with an implacable force.

And they expect very few of them to survive to tell the tale.

Amy realised he had abandoned his normal practice of asking a question only to immediately answer it. He wasn't trying to win an argument. He was trying to tell her something. It was as if he had already won.

He wrote to us, said Amy, but she could hear that her voice was shrill.

That card?

The card, yes. And his brother Tom wrote you that his family in Tasmania had one after us.

Her voice, she knew, was thin and unconvincing even to her.

The card he sent us, Amy, was dated May 1942, and we got it in November. That was three months ago. It's getting close to a year since we've had any word from him. Not a word—

Yes, Amy Mulvaney said. Yes, yes. Quickly, definitely, as though this somehow proved her point rather than demolished it.

Not a word since.

Yes, Amy Mulvaney said. Though she pressed down even harder on it, her foot didn't really hurt that much at all. Habit and circumstance, the reassurance and security of marriage, were no longer enough for her. She would leave him. But having thought this bitter thought, she immediately felt confused. How? Where? And what would she live on?

The card his family got in December was dated April.

Yes, Keith, Amy Mulvaney said. Yes, yes, yes.

Her body was being tossed and rolled, and she was reaching for words to help keep her balance. She did not say she had written over a hundred letters to Dorrigo since they had heard he had been taken prisoner. Surely, Amy Mulvaney thought, one would have got through.

Ron Jarvis also said there are reports coming from other sources. Not good. Saying the men are skin and bone and being starved to death.

There's been nothing in the papers.

There was. Atrocities. Massacres.

That's propaganda, Keith, Amy Mulvaney said. To make us hate them.

Though she put all her weight on her cut foot, it merely ached.

If it's propaganda, Keith Mulvaney said, it's very bad propaganda.

But nothing else, no follow-up.

It's a war, Amy. Bad news is no news. It vanishes. There's the best part of a fifth of the Australian army missing, and only a few reliably traced.

That doesn't mean he's dead, Keith. It's like you want him dead. He's not dead. I know. I know.

The sea breeze, she realised, had ceased. Even the world struggled to breathe. From outside, she thought she heard the sound of a dried leaf snap. Keith coughed. He was not finished.

Ron Jarvis made some more enquiries for me, he said, wiping his lips with a handkerchief. There was a POW who made it out. They're not telling the families yet. National morale, I suppose. And, I suppose, they wait for confirmation through other channels. Red Cross and so on.

Telling the families what, Keith?

I knew you'd want to know, Amy. I can't bring myself to tell his family, though—it's not my place, in any event. I'd be breaching a confidence. To say nothing of national security. This is strictly between us.

There's nothing to tell, Keith. What are you carrying on about?

The escapee confirmed that Dorrigo Evans died in one of the camps.

Amy's thoughts were distant and odd. It occurred to her that Keith loved her, something she had not thought for a very long time.

Amy, believe me, Dorrigo's dead. He died six months ago.

Keith Mulvaney's words, his boyish voice, spilled out onto the corridor floor tiles, black and white squares.

I knew you'd want to know, he said.

His words ran down the empty hallway and over its threadbare coconut mat runner, searching for Amy. But she was gone from the room.

Keith Mulvaney felt as a man who has killed something so that he might eat. He had wanted to say something else, something so true that it would justify the terrible lie he had just told. He wanted to say, I love you. Instead, he whistled Miss Beatrice onto his lap.

I think that'll do, Keith Mulvaney said to the dog as he tickled her under the ear. Yes, that'll do her.

He took solace in the knowledge he had not lied. It was true that the death was not yet confirmed, but Ron Jarvis had been unequivocal: among the list of names the

POW had provided the authorities was a Major D. Evans. He thought that they could be happy together. It was a matter of work and time.

Surely, he said to Miss Beatrice. Surely.

Later that evening he found Amy by herself, cleaning the dining room's kitchen. The room's perpetual odour seemed if anything stronger, but its wet cream tiles and steel gleamed in the electric light. She was without emotion, telling him she still had more to do, and renewed her scrubbing as he stood watching from the doorway.

Only after he'd gone did she drop the rag she had been using and crumple. She crouched on the floor, like a child. She banged her foot up and down on the tiled floor. But she felt nothing. She wanted to pray to whatever might exist. But she knew he was dead, that the world does not allow for miracles, that people die, and that she could not stop them dying; that they leave you and you love them more, and still she could not stop them dying.

Sitting in his russet armchair in their lounge room, tamping his pipe in readiness for a pre-bedtime smoke, his head laid back on the antimacassar, Keith Mulvaney felt a runnel of sweat down his left temple. He never heard the explosion that, with the subsequent fire, reduced the gracious four-storey stone hotel to smouldering rubble, charred beams and a two-sided façade.

A world of dew
and within every dewdrop
a world of struggle.

*Issa*

# 1

A drop dripped.

Tiny, whispered Darky Gardiner.

The noise of the monsoonal rain flogging the canvas roof of the long, A-framed shelter—bamboo-strutted and open-walled—meant Darky Gardiner could hardly hear himself. The clamour of the rain made such nights only more desolate, worse, in a way, than the days when he was just trying to survive but at least had company to do it with. The jungle shuddering in sheets of noise, the incessant drumming of mud churning as the rain slammed into it, the strange slaps and punches of invisible water runs, all of it he found dismal.

Another drop dripped.

Carn, cobber, hissed Darky Gardiner. Move over.

Darky Gardiner had no idea how long it was since he had got back to his tent after helping fetch an abandoned Japanese truck; he had looked for his place among the twenty POWs who slept up and down its length on two lice-infested bamboo platforms, only to find Tiny Middleton, the prisoner who lay to the right of him, had rolled over and taken up almost all of his sleeping spot on the platform. It left Darky jammed on his side next to Tiny, directly under a bamboo pole along which beads of water ran and fell onto his face. Tiny felt like a brick wall collapsing on him, yet, thought Darky, he would be lucky to weigh six stone. Now that Tiny was covered with ringworm, Darky hated touching him. And so he hissed again—

*Fucksake*, Tiny.

It was clear Tiny Middleton heard nothing. Darky Gardiner raised a wrist over his face to check the time. There was nothing to see; he had sold his illuminated watch for a tin of Portuguese sardines some months before. He dropped his arm. The good thing, Darky told himself, was that it was still dark. He was wet and weary, but he could rest a few more hours. Darky was always looking for the good thing, no matter how small, and consequently he often found it. Though he was awake now, the good thing was that he didn't have to get up and go to work on the railway but could sleep longer. That was good, and he would enjoy that sleep, if he could just get Tiny to move. Putting thoughts of ringworm aside, he pushed against the body lying next to him.

Move over, you fat prick.

After a while Darky gave up and lay on his side, with his back to Tiny, and his head tucked into his body in such a way that put it just out of range of the drip. He figured, he knew stupidly, that somehow his back was less likely to catch ringworm than his front. Curled up in his own darkness, safe in the knowledge no one would know, Darky reached above his head to his kitbag and pulled it down the platform to his chest. After some awkward fossicking in the dark, he removed from it what he knew to be two small miracles: a boiled duck egg and a can of condensed milk.

The milk or the egg? he wondered. Which one?

In the end he decided that the milk—which he had stolen from the Japanese truck—could be saved for an indefinite period without going off, and hence was better kept, if only for a few more days. Rabbit Hendricks had traded him the duck egg for a paintbrush Darky had stolen from the field satchel of a Japanese officer passing through the camp on his way to the battlefields of Burma. His method in thievery was based on speed and discretion: he never took so much as to demand investigation, just enough, instead, to help him *jog along*.

Rabbit Hendricks, in turn, had been given two duck eggs by the camp's Japanese commander in return for sketching some postcard pictures of him and some of his cronies—presumably to send back to lovers and families in Japan. While the Japanese occasionally made use of Rabbit's talents in this way, they would most likely kill him if they saw the sketches and watercolours he had made of the daily life of the camp—the hideous labour, the beatings, the torture—and for this reason Rabbit Hendricks kept them carefully hidden. But his work was at an end. The evening before, finishing their shift on the Line, Rabbit had been gripped by a horrific cramp and had to relieve himself immediately. Before he had even stood up, Chum Fahey, who was working near him, was staring. Rabbit Hendricks turned. Beneath him, he saw that his bowels had written his fate in a puddle of rice-water coloured shit. The POWs had come to fear this more than the Japanese since the cholera had broken out nine days earlier.

Chum Fahey and two others had helped Darky carry Rabbit back on a crudely improvised stretcher up and down the Dolly—a jungle track that connected the Line with their camp three and a half miles away—a painfully slow task that was not quickened by a search in the dark for Rabbit's dentures, lost in a violent bout of retching. With difficulty they made their way through the night jungle—their only guides home muddy ruts and the distant groans of the sick POWs who were ahead of them—finally arriving back at camp a little before midnight covered in mud and watery vomit. Rabbit Hendricks, along with his watercolour set, his sketchbook and his secret drawings, had then disappeared into the cholera compound where ever more were sent and from where only a handful returned. And all that remained of him was the blackened duck egg, the shell of which Darky Gardiner now adroitly peeled off in just three pieces.

The rain fell once more with a great heave, and the movement made a fresh, damp breeze that blew for a moment through the pitiful shelter that served as their barracks, washing away the stench of shit and decay that was all the men who slept up and down the hut on two long bamboo platforms. Darky felt the breeze as a form of hope, and he tried to tell himself that this was another good thing. But the rain began dripping on his face again, and when he tried to roll over, Tiny was still there, and, when he again shoved him, Tiny remained immovable, snoring, dead to the world.

Can you just bloody well shove over, Tiny?

Fuck the fuck up, Darky, yelled someone down the platform.

There was nothing Darky could do with Tiny. He stank too. The rain came back strong, and what with his feverish head and the noise it was sometimes hard to know what was inside his head and what was outside. He was thinking of when he first met Tiny, a bull of a man, who had stripped down and strutted around in his magnificent body flexing, rearing, crowing. Like a rooster rooting on a Sunday morning, Chum Fahey had said.

Even on the starvation rations they were given, Tiny's loss of weight seemed only to emphasise the magnificence of his body. It seemed to hone rather than waste his physique. Tiny's body had triumphed over everything: the malaria, the dysentery, the pellagra and the beri-beri. None of the diseases that laid low and began killing the other men seemed to affect him, as though his magnificence was in itself a form of immunity. Somehow the camps had not reduced him, nor the Japanese broken him.

Tiny's job was to make holes in the rock by slowly pounding a steel bar into the face with his sledgehammer until the hole was the required depth. When there were enough holes, a Japanese engineer filled them with explosive and blew that section. Darky was Tiny's offsider, holding the steel bar, giving it a quarter-turn after each blow to help it drill down. Tiny worked with energy uncharacteristic of any other prisoner and prided himself on finishing his work quota before anyone else. It was his triumph over his Japanese captors.

Show them little yellow bastards what a white man is, he would say.

He didn't seem to notice that the Japanese then demanded everyone else do the same.

That fucking Tarzan will do for us all, said Sheephead Morton.

If Tiny set a new record for the work—as he seemed regularly intent on—the Japanese engineers would make that the new daily quota, and others less strong would suffer while working to fulfil it.

For fucking fuck's sake, tell him, Sheephead Morton said to Darky.

Tell him what?

Ee-fucking-nough. *Nough*.

Nough nough or just nough?

Fuck off.

Cobber, Darky said later to Tiny, you might want to back off.

Tiny smiled.

Just a bit. Not every bloke can work at your rate, Darky said.

Tiny was a devout gospel-haller. With an eerie smile, he said, The Lord gave us this body to work with, to rejoice in.

Well, there's another bugger you don't hear from much these days. But we'll all be seeing Him soon enough if you don't back off. Because otherwise you'll be the death of everyone, Tiny.

The Lord will see us right. That's the way I look at it.

And Tiny, the muscular Christian, held himself like a runner at the end of the hundred-and-ten-yard sprint, hands on hips, slightly relaxed, body halfway between exertion and relaxation, taut, perfect, staring at Darky Gardiner with his thin, maddening smile.

Slowly, Darky grew to hate Tiny. Each new quota the Japanese engineers demanded in the alien metric measurement—first a metre a day, then two metres, then three metres—Tiny met in less time than the Japanese allowed, and then everyone else—the fevered, the starving, the dying—had to match that mad-man's work load. All the others tried to go slow, to do less, to save their diminished energies for the necessary task of survival. But not Tiny, his stomach rippling, his chest heaving, his brutish arms flexing. He treated it like the shearing sheds in which he had once worked, as if it were all still some stupid competition, and come evening he'd be the gun ringer yet again. But his vanity was only benefiting the Japanese and killing the rest of them.

The Speedo came. Now, there was only the Japanese pushing them with ever more beatings and ever less food to work ever harder and ever longer during the day. As the POWs fell further behind the Japanese schedules, the pace grew more frantic. One night, just as the POWs were falling exhausted on their bamboo platforms, to sleep, the order came to return to the cutting. So the night shifts began.

The cutting was a slit through rock, six metres wide and seven metres deep and half a kilometre long. Lit by fires of bamboo and crude torches made of rags stuffed in bamboo and fed with kerosene, the naked, filthy slaves now worked in a strange, hellish world of dancing flames and sliding shadows. For the hammer men it required greater concentration than ever, as the steel bar disappeared into the darkness of shadow as the hammer fell.

That first night, for the first time, Tiny struggled. He was malarial, his body was shuddering and his movement with the sledgehammer was not a beautiful rise and fall, but a painful effort of will. Several times Darky Gardiner had to jump out of the way when Tiny lost control of the hammer. After less than an hour—or maybe it was a few hours—after, Darky could not remember exactly how long—Tiny raised the hammer halfway and let it fall to the ground. Darky watched in astonishment as Tiny staggered round in a half-circle, a sort of jig back and forth, and dropped to the ground.

A guard with a short, muscular body and a mottled complexion came up: the Goanna. Some said the Goanna had vitiligo and that was why he was mad, and others just said he was mad and best avoided in any situation. A few said he was the devil himself—inexplicable, unavoidable, pitiless, and also, on odd occasion, as if in a final torment, bewilderingly kind. But as no one up there on the Line much believed in God anymore, it was hard to believe either in the devil. The Goanna just was, much as many wished he was not.

The Goanna looked at them working for a moment and very slowly turned away to look elsewhere, as if thinking, and equally slowly turned back. These strange, stilted movements were an inevitable precursor to an outburst of violence. He thrashed Tiny with a long piece of heavy bamboo for a minute or two, and afterwards gave him a few almost desultory kicks in the head and stomach. As bashings by the Goanna went, Darky didn't think it was so bad. What was different was Tiny Middleton.

Where once he had tensed and absorbed blows and kicks in a manner that bordered on insolent, as though his body was harder than any beating, now he rolled around on the blasted rock cutting like a thing made of rag or straw. He absorbed the blows and whacks like a sack. And at the beating's end, Tiny did something remarkable. He began to sob.

The Goanna was stunned. With Darky, he looked on in amazement. No one ever cried on the Line. It couldn't have been the pain or the humiliation, thought Darky, nor could it be the despair or the horror, because everyone lived with that.

Shaking his head, shadows of flames clutching at his sweat-greased, filthy body, Tiny now half-slapped, half-clawed at his chest as if he was trying to beat the shadows away and failing. It seemed to Darky that he was accusing his body, because this mighty body had always triumphed, had carried that small mind and tiny heart so far, only for it now—in that strange, hellish half-tunnel of flame and shadow and pain—to cruelly and unexpectedly betray him. And with his body wavering, Tiny was lost.

Me! he cried out as he beat and tore at himself. Me! Me!

But what he meant, none of them really knew.

Me! he continued to cry out. Me! Me!

Darky helped Tiny to his feet. With one eye on the Goanna, Darky took the sledgehammer and handed Tiny the steel bar. Tiny squatted, held the bar in the hole they had been working on, watery eyes firmly fixed on it, and Darky raised and dropped the sledgehammer. When he raised it a second time he had to ask Tiny to twist it a quarter-turn. The hammer fell and rose, Tiny was immobile, clutching the steel bar as though it were some necessary anchor, and again Darky asked Tiny to twist the steel bar a quarter-turn. He asked Tiny as gently as he would a toddler for its hand, and in the same voice he kept saying to Tiny the rest of the night, Turn'er—turn'er, mate—turn'er. And in this manner they continued with their work, as though everything was normal. Turn'er—turn'er, mate, Darky Gardiner would incant, turn'er.

But something had changed.

Darky knew it. He watched over the next few weeks

as Tiny's magnificent body began to fade away. The Japs knew it and seemed to bash Tiny regularly now, and with more vicious intent. And Tiny seemed not to care about this either. The lice knew it. Everyone had lice, but Darky noticed how they began to swarm over Tiny from that day. And Tiny seemed not to care that his body was overrun with them, no longer worried about washing or where he shat. Then came the ringworm. As if even fungi knew it, sensing the moment a man gave up on himself and was already as good as a corpse rotting back into the earth. And Tiny knew it. Tiny knew he had nothing left inside him to stop what was coming.

Darky stuck by Tiny, but something in him was revolted by that formerly big man, that once proud man, now a shitting skeleton. Something in Darky could not help but think Tiny had let go, that it was a failing of character. And such a thought, he knew, was simply to make himself feel better, to make him think he would live and not die because he still had the power to choose such things. But in his heart he knew he had no such power. For he could smell the truth on Tiny's rancid breath. Whatever that stench was, he worried that it was catching and he just wanted to escape it. But he had to help Tiny. No one asked why he did; everyone knew. He was a mate. Darky Gardiner loathed Tiny, thought him a fool and would do everything to keep him alive. Because courage, survival, love—all these things didn't live in one man. They lived in them all or they died and every man with them; they had come to believe that to abandon one man was to abandon themselves.

# 2

When the egg was ready—damp and waxy between his fingers—Darky Gardiner could smell its overpowering promise, slightly sickly in its richness. He had it almost to his lips when he stopped, considered and sighed. He shook Tiny's sleeping form not hard but insistently.

As Tiny finally roused, Darky held the egg near his nose and hushed him be quiet. Tiny grunted, and Darky halved the egg with his spoon. Tiny held out his hands in a cup, as if it were a sacrament he was receiving, to make sure no crumbling yolk was lost. And into Tiny's cupped hands Darky now added half a small fried rice ball that he had saved beneath his blanket from a previous meal.

In the wet dark where no one could see or hear them, in the black solitude where no one would ask how it was that they had extra food, they began surreptitiously to eat. Darky ate slowly, enjoying every morsel, his mouth salivating so wildly that he worried at the loud sloshing sound he made. But it was lost in all the other wet noises of the night.

He licked the sooty grease off his fingers. The egg and rice ball sat in his stomach a rancid lump, stayed in his throat a sour, fatty flame. He was not going to die. He no longer cared that Tiny had taken up most of his space. He could still feel the rice grains on his lips, still taste the gorgeous grease and rich yolk in his mouth, and his mind felt dizzied, then sleepy. He was unsure whether he was drowning or in some bed that was also a table full of crayfish and apples and apricot crumbles and roast legs of lamb, a dry bed of clean blankets and a fire at its foot, sleet slapping the small bedroom window beyond.

He had eaten, he wished to eat more, he was sinking deeper and deeper, he was at the table, and he was asleep.

When he next awoke, his stomach was a fist. It was still dark. His mouth tasted of soap, and a terrible gripping pain contorted his shrivelled belly. He sat up, half-groaning, half-gasping with the effort, grabbed a kerosene tin he kept full of water at the base of his sleeping spot, and began walking barefoot through the dark and mud and rain towards the benjo, as the Japanese insisted the camp latrine be known.

Some distance from the tents, the benjo was a trench twenty yards long and two and a half yards deep, over which the men precariously squatted on slimy bamboo planking to relieve themselves. The bobbing excrement below was covered with writhing maggots—like desiccated coconut on lamingtons, as Chum Fahey said. It was a vile horror. When the prisoners competed in devising ways of doing in their most hated guard, they joked of one day drowning the Goanna in the benjo. Even for them, a more terrible death was hard to conceive.

The tiger fires which the Japanese had ordered to be kept burning all night had long ago been swamped and killed by the incessant rain. The world was dark, with the monsoon clouds blocking much of the light of the stars and moon; the jungle soaked up most of what else was left. Darky Gardiner made his way in short awkward hops as he clasped his stomach with his free hand, trying not to wrench his guts with any large or abrupt movement into giving way too early. Half-doubled up, he made his way by vague black outlines through the shanty camp of rickety bamboo shelters. From within came the groans and snores and sudden gasps of other POWs, which may have been from pain or grief or memory or dying. Or all of these. And washing every sound of exhaustion and anguish and hope into the mud was the inexorable drone of the torrential rain.

By now fully awake from the pain that gripped his abdomen, and panting with the intense effort of walking without shitting himself, Darky was still some way from the benjo when he slid off the greasy shoulder of the path and into its muddy centre, up to his ankles in filthy mud. He momentarily panicked. His sudden, frantic effort to get back up on firmer ground excited his bowels. He felt an abrupt loss of extreme tension and, with a relieving rush, realised he was shitting himself in the middle of the camp's main path.

A terrible exhaustion overwhelmed him, his arse burnt like fire, his head swam wildly, and he just wanted to lie down in the mud and shit and sleep forever. But he fought this feeling because his stomach was again tightening like a garrotte, and once more he felt a stinking gravy exploding out. He was panting now with the effort; having emptied himself completely, his bowels felt immediately full again.

He gave himself over to his body, strained once more and hated himself that he had done this, that he could not even make it to the benjo, that he had spread his filth where other men would walk in the morning. He thought of the Big Fella's injunctions to observe strict hygiene, how they all now saw cleanliness—in so far as it was possible—as essential to their survival. And though there was nothing he could do about it, he still felt ashamed and defeated.

There was no way of separating his shitty stream from

the deep mud, that endless and ceaseless muddy, shitty world. It was already being ploughed by the rain and transformed into something else, an inescapable and deadly decay that was everything and everybody and returning them all to the jungle. Next time, he told himself, no matter what, he would make it to that fucking awful shitter. Finally there was an unsatisfactory motion that he knew would have produced nothing more than some mucous with an oily blood-streak striping it.

Finished, dizzy from the effort, Darky slowly drew himself back up to a fully erect posture, staggered a few short steps off the path, and with the water in his kero tin began washing himself as best he could. His buttocks felt little more than ropes. He spent some time cleaning his anus, which, in its strange prominence amidst his wasted flesh, left him with a deep sense of disgust. He was suddenly chilled, and his thighs and calves shivered wildly as he washed them down. He stifled a scream with a strange gulp as he splashed water over the tropical ulcer the size of a teacup on his leg, and consoled himself that keeping this wound clean was a good thing. It had to be kept clean. His mind felt not right—the malaria, he guessed—his senses at once too sharp and too blurred. But this much remained vivid and strong within him, this much he knew: it was easy to give up. Which was, to Darky's mind, however fevered, not just a bad thing, but the very worst thing. The path to survival was to never give up on the small things. Giving up was not getting to the benjo. Next time, he vowed, he would get there, no matter how hard it was.

His feet, lost in the mud, were condemned to exist in filth, and so, cleaned as much as was possible, he walked back through the shit and slush to his tent and his place on the bamboo platform. He crawled back under his filthy and foul-smelling blanket, dragging his shitty feet up with him. His last thought before a bedraggled exhaustion carried him off to sleep was how he was again hungry.

## 3

As the last notes of Jimmy Bigelow's bugle playing of 'Reveille' dribbled away into the dank dawn, Rooster MacNeice opened his eyes. A spreading grey light painted the wall-less tent he slept in and the fetid mud, the filth, the hopelessness of the POW's jungle camp beyond, into flat shades of iron and soot. Further away the teak rainforest was a black wall.

Before he was even properly awake, Rooster began that morning as he did every morning, with the first of several exercises in the self-discipline which he knew would ensure his survival, mentally, physically and morally. He commenced by reciting under his breath the page of *Mein Kampf* he had memorised the night before. He found that the parts with Jews in them—which was much of the book—were the easiest. They had a galloping rhythm that made them less difficult to memorise, the word *Jew* a helpful recurrent chorus. But now he was lost in the early history of the Nazi Party in Bavaria and he was struggling. Where were the Jews, wondered Rooster MacNeice, when you really needed them?

Bomb landed on Buckingham Palace, a voice nearby said. Took out the King and Gracie Fields.

As he pulled himself to the edge of the bamboo bench and scratched his thigh, and then more vigorously his crotch, Rooster MacNeice continued whispering to himself about the bravery of the early stormtroopers. He felt something hard and shell-like in his crotch and crushed it, then felt another and another, and only then did he begin to feel the itch and bite of the lice that lived in the bamboo slats.

One thing I'll say for the Japs, an old man said on noticing his itching, they bugger you so completely you can even sleep through lice eating your balls for breakfast.

Rooster realised it was Sheephead Morton talking. He looked a haggard seventy, but he couldn't have been more than twenty-three or twenty-four.

I thought someone said that Gracie Fields was with a dago, said Jimmy Bigelow, dented bugle in hand, as he walked back into the tent. Didn't they defect to Mussolini?

That was just a rumour, Chum Fahey said. This time I got the good oil from some Dutchies who came through the camp the other day. Dutch as I am. Half-caste wops, most of 'em. They said the Russkies lost at Stalingrad, the Yanks have invaded Sicily, Musso's been overthrown and the new dago government is calling for peace.

Rooster MacNeice had a scraggly ginger beard and the habit, when concentrating, of sucking it up from his lower lip and chewing on it. As he chewed on his whiskers he recalled that, the previous week, the rumour had been that the Russians won at Stalingrad. That was clearly bolshie propaganda, he thought. Most likely from Darky Gardiner. He'd say that sort of thing. Rooster MacNeice hated bolshies but on balance he hated Darky Gardiner more. He was a common and dirty man, and like most half-castes not to be trusted. He also couldn't abide Gardiner's habit—until the Speedo put an end to anything that wasn't work or sleep—of sometimes standing on a teak stump at the camp's edge singing 'Without a Song' as the POWs hobbled in of a night from the Line. Other men seemed to like it; Rooster MacNeice hated it.

And hate was a powerful force for Rooster MacNeice. It was like a food to him. He hated wogs, wops, gyppos and dagos. He hated chinks, nips and slopes, and, being a fair-minded man, he also hated poms and yanks. He found so little in his own race of Australians to admire that he sometimes found himself arguing that they deserved to be conquered. He returned to reciting *Mein Kampf* under his breath.

What you rabbiting on about now, Rooster? asked Jimmy Bigelow.

Rooster MacNeice turned to the bugler who had only recently been transferred into their tent and had no idea of his morning ritual. Rooster MacNeice thought Jimmy Bigelow was a Victorian, and so he freely told him that to stop his intellect stagnating amidst the convict-bred, card-playing, football-worshipping, horseracing-addicted Tasmanians—in whose tent they had both ended up and who were anything but what Australians should be—he had set himself the task of committing to memory an entire book, a page a day.

Rightio, Jimmy Bigelow said, not daring to tell Rooster MacNeice that he was from the Huon Valley and had enlisted with Gallipoli von Kessler. But as a way of passing a war, he went on, there are worse things than four-a-game crib.

The mind! said Rooster MacNeice. The mind, James!

Gallipoli von Kessler asked him if he had thought of playing five hundred, saying that though some people said that five hundred was perhaps a brainier game than crib, he didn't necessarily agree, but it might be more Rooster's fancy. It was really bridge without the bad company.

Of course, I am not sure if any book would help them, said Rooster MacNeice, looking around at his other tentmates to avoid looking at von Kessler. They have the *fatal stain.*

Rightio, Jimmy Bigelow said, having no idea what Rooster was on about, and Rooster just kept on, about how he hated *Mein Kampf*, how he hated Hitler, and how he hated having to memorise a page of this sausage-eater's nonsense every day. But in the Javanese POW camp at the time he began this exercise in mental discipline it was the only book he had been able to find; besides, he said, his beard glistening slightly with saliva, it was good to know the arguments of the enemy and, in any case, the content was meaningless for the purposes of his exercise. He didn't say he was surprised by how much of Hitler's manifesto made sense to him.

One of the Dutchie wops was on to it, I tell you, Chum Fahey said. I'd trust him. I sold him my greatcoat.

Rooster MacNeice asked what he got for his coat.

Three dollars and some palm sugar. And a book.

A coat's worth ten at least, said Rooster MacNeice, who also hated Dutchies of any origin. What's the book?

It's a good Western.

This infuriated Rooster MacNeice.

You may want nothing better than *Murder at Red Ranch*

or *Sunset on the Corral*, he burst out, but God help Australia if that's the Australian mentality.

Chum Fahey asked if Rooster MacNeice would be willing to swap his *Mein Kampf* for this? He held up a well-thumbed and very grubby copy of *Sun Sinking, Sioux Rising*.

No, Rooster MacNeice said. No, I would not.

The morning light, though still dim, was slowly bringing their tent into indigo relief. The rising conversation of waking prisoners abruptly halted, and all turned in one direction, looking over Rooster MacNeice's shoulder. A muted laughter rippled up the platforms, and one after another the prisoners wiped their eyes to make sure that what they were seeing was what they were seeing. Rooster MacNeice turned his head. It was the strangest, most unexpected thing ever. He sucked his whiskers back in.

Many men had begun to worry that their post-war performance would be permanently affected by the complete loss of desire that starvation and disease had brought to almost all. The doctors reassured them it was merely a matter of diet; and with that sorted, they would be fine. But still the prisoners had wondered if they would be functioning men at the end of their ordeals. None of them could remember the last erection they'd had. Some worried if they'd be able to keep their wives happy when they got home. Gallipoli von Kessler said he didn't know a bloke who'd had a hard-on for months, while Sheephead Morton claimed not to have *cracked a fat* for over a year.

It was, then, a most miraculous sight—as unmissable as it was remarkable—that they saw rising before them.

Old Tiny, said Gallipoli von Kessler. There he is, knocking on death's door, and he's like a bloody bamboo in the wet.

For rising up from the still-slumbering, skeletal form of Tiny Middleton—the once muscular Christian himself, asleep on his back, oblivious to all attention, happily dreaming of some sinful pursuit, his depravity unaffected by starvation and sickness—there stood, sticking up like the regimental flagpole, a large erection.

It was, they agreed, a heartening thing, no less so given how low Tiny Middleton had sunk in recent weeks. The sight was so remarkable that everyone kept their voices down as they wakened others and motioned at them to look. Amidst the low laughter, lewd jokes and general joy the sight brought, one man objected.

Is that the best we can do? Rooster MacNeice asked. Laugh at a man when he's down?

Chum Fahey observed that Tiny looked pretty up to him.

You men have no decency, Rooster MacNeice muttered. No respect. Not like the old Australians.

I'll cover him for you, Rooster, said Darky Gardiner. Picking up a large fragment of duck eggshell by his thigh, he leant across and carefully placed it atop the erect penis.

Tiny slumbered on. His hatted cock rose above them like a fresh forest mushroom trembling ever so slightly in the early-morning breeze.

It's wrong to mock, Rooster MacNeice said. We're no better than the lousy nips if we do that.

Darky Gardiner pointed at the eggshell, which looked like a mitre cap of sorts.

He's been promoted to pope, Rooster, Darky Gardiner said.

Damn you, Gardiner, Rooster MacNeice said. Leave the poor man alone and allow him some decency.

He pulled himself up to a full sitting position, stood up and walked to where Tiny Middleton slept. Leaning up between Tiny's splayed legs, Rooster MacNeice reached out to take away what was to him a degrading joke.

Just as his fingers closed around the eggshell, Tiny Middleton awoke. As their eyes met, Rooster MacNeice's hand froze on the eggshell, perhaps even crushed it slightly. Tiny Middleton drew himself up with a rage and an energy wholly out of proportion to his wasted body.

You fucking *pervert*, Rooster.

When—in humiliation and to the mockery of all, and the laughter of Darky Gardiner in particular—Rooster MacNeice returned to his place on the sleeping platform, he made a distressing discovery. On rummaging around in his kitbag for *Mein Kampf* to check his memorisation, he found that his duck egg—bought three days earlier and hidden in his kitbag—had vanished. He thought on that missing egg, and on the duck eggshell Darky Gardiner had placed on Tiny Middleton, and he knew that the Black Prince had stolen his egg.

There was of course nothing that could be done about it—Gardiner would deny the theft, the others would laugh even more, perhaps even enjoy the idea of the theft. But at that moment he hated Gardiner—a man who had stolen off him and then used that theft to humiliate him—with an intensity and savagery that far exceeded any ill feeling he had towards the Japanese. And hate was everything to Rooster MacNeice.

# 4

Darky Gardiner dressed, and because, like everyone else, he had no clothes other than the slouch hat he put on his head and the cock rag he wore night and day—a filthy G-string that covered the cock and little else—it took no time to dress. He made his bed and, because it was no bed, that also took Darky Gardiner no time. He folded his blanket in the regulation Imperial Japanese Army fashion, and then put it in the place defined by Imperial Japanese Army regulations—at the foot of his sleeping space on the bamboo bench. The rain stopped. The sound of dripping jungle gave way to jungle birds calling in droplets of sound.

He picked up one of his eight remaining possessions, his dixie mess kit—two battered tin bowls nesting inside each other, serving as plate and mug and food box—and was clipping the wire handle hairslide-like to his cock rag when a cry went up. Some guards were making their way to their hut for a surprise inspection. There was a flurry of desperate activity as blankets were folded, kitbags made plump and neat, and various contraband hidden as best could.

Two guards led by the Goanna made their way down the hut's central aisle as the prisoners stood to attention in front of the communal bunks on either side. The Goanna upended one kitbag into the mud outside, slapped another man for no apparent reason, and then halted in front of Darky Gardiner.

The Goanna took his rifle off his shoulder, and with a long, slow movement picked up Darky Gardiner's blanket with the tip of his rifle barrel and dropped it onto the muddy ground. For a moment he looked down at the filthy blanket, and then he looked back up. He screamed, and with all his strength slammed the rifle butt into the side of Darky Gardiner's head.

The prisoner dropped but was too slow in raising an arm to shield himself as another guard kicked him across the face. He managed to writhe sideways under the protection of the bamboo sleeping bench, but not before the Goanna got a good kick in on his head. And then, as abruptly as it started, it was over.

The Goanna continued with his strange, stilted walk down the hut aisle, slapping Chum Fahey for no discernible reason, then disappeared with his entourage out the other end. Darky Gardiner rose to his feet, somewhat unsteadily, his head still confused, his mouth salty with blood, his body covered in the foul mud that lay beneath the sleeping platform.

The fold, Jimmy Bigelow said.

It wasn't that bad, Darky said.

He meant the bashing. He spat out a gob of blood. It tasted too salty and too rich for a body as wasted as his. He felt dizzy. He put a finger in his mouth and felt the molar that had taken the kicks. It was wobbly, but with luck it would hold. His head was not right.

You forgot the fold, Sheephead Morton said.

I folded the fucking fucker, Darky Gardiner said.

With a smouldering cigarette butt he had just lit and now held between his thumb and forefinger, Jimmy Bigelow pointed at his own blanket.

See, he said.

The fold was facing outwards.

Your fold faced inwards, Sheephead Morton said. Against nip regulations. You know that.

The Goanna thought you was taking the piss, Jimmy Bigelow said, having a puff. Here—he held out the soggy cigarette butt for Darky.

Jimmy Bigelow's hand was covered with cracked scales, and was badly infected, all yellow and reds. Sickness terrified Darky Gardiner. It got hold of you and it would not let you go.

Here, Jimmy Bigelow said. Take it.

Darky Gardiner didn't move.

Only death is catching round here, Jimmy Bigelow said, and I ain't got that. Rightio?

Darky Gardiner took the smoke and—without letting it touch his lips—held it up to his open mouth.

Yet, Jimmy Bigelow said.

Darky took a pull on the cigarette. He watched four men carrying a bamboo stretcher stumble up towards the hospital.

Think that's Gyppo Nolan, Chum Fahey said.

The smoke rolled into Darky's mouth. It was sour and sharp and good.

That's our four-a-side crib competition down the gurgler, Sheephead Morton said. He turned to Rooster MacNeice. You interested in taking his place?

What? Rooster MacNeice said, still smarting from the humiliation of the eggshell.

Gyppo. He's . . . He's—well. Gone. And he loved the crib. He'd hate to think him just—

Dying?

Well. Sort of. I mean, the bloke could be an idiot. But he loved his cards. That was the gyppo I remember. And I know he'd want us to go on.

Playing crib?

Why not? Bridge wasn't ever Gyppo's lurk.

Darky Gardiner drew slow and long on the butt end a second time, dragging the smoke deep inside him and holding it there. For a moment the world was still and silent. With the rich, greasy smoke came peace, and he felt it was as if the world had stopped, and would stay stopped for as long as that smoke stayed within his mouth and chest. He closed his eyes, and whilst holding the butt end out for Jimmy Bigelow to take back, gave himself over to the nothingness that pervaded his body with the rich smoke. But his head was not right.

I hate cards, Rooster MacNeice said.

The rain returned. It was noise without comfort. It did not sweep faintly through the teak trees and the bamboo, it did not sigh, it did not create a tranquil hush. Rather, it crashed into the thorny bamboo, and the deluge sounded to Darky Gardiner like the noise of many things breaking. The rain was so loud it was impossible to talk.

He went out and stood in the tempest to wash the mud off. Filthy little creeks appeared around his feet as the rain formed rills and courses through the camp. He watched a dixie bob by their hut, and a moment later he saw a one-legged West Australian on bamboo crutches hopping in pursuit of it.

But his head was not right.

## 5

Every morning Dorrigo Evans shaves because he believes he must keep up appearances for their sake, because if it looks like he no longer cares, why should they? And when he looks in the small service mirror, he sees its cloudy reflection blurring the face of a man no longer him: older, skinnier, bonier, hard in a way he never was, more remote and relying ever more on a few sorry props: his officer's cap, raffishly angled; a red scarf, tied bandana-fashion around his neck, a gypsy touch perhaps more for himself than for them.

Three months before, walking to a downriver camp to get drugs, he had come upon a Tamil *romusha* in a ragged red sarong sitting next to a creek, waiting to die. The old man was uninterested in what help Dorrigo Evans could offer. He waited for death as a traveller for a bus. Walking back along the same path a month ago he came upon the old man for a second time, now a skeleton picked clean by beast and insect. He took the red sarong from the skeleton, washed it, tore it in half and tied the better piece around his neck. When death comes for him he hopes to meet it similarly to the Tamil *romusha*, though he doubts he will. He does not accept the authorities of life, and nor will he, he thinks, of death.

He notices how they, his men, are also far older than they will ever be if they survive to grow old. Somewhere deep within them, do they know they only have to suffer but not inflict suffering? He understands the cult of Christ makes of suffering virtue. He had argued with Padre Bob about this. He hopes Christ is right. But he does not agree. He does not. He is a doctor. Suffering is suffering. Suffering is not virtue, nor does it make virtue, nor does of it virtue necessarily flow. Padre Bob died screaming, in terror, in pain, in hopelessness; he was nursed by a man Dorrigo Evans knew was said to have been a brutal standover man for a Darlinghurst gang before the war. Virtue is virtue, and, like suffering, it is inexplicable, irreducible, unintelligible. The night Padre Bob died, Dorrigo Evans dreamt he was in a pit with God, that they were both bald, and that they were fighting over a wig.

Dorrigo Evans is not blind to the prisoners' human qualities. They lie and cheat and rob, and they lie and cheat and rob with gusto. The worst feign illness, the proudest health. Nobility often eludes them. The previous day he had come across a man so sick he was lying face-down, nose just out of the mud, at the bottom of the rock face that marks the end of the Dolly, unable to make it the final few hundred yards home. Two men were walking past him, too exhausted to help, striving to conserve what little energy they had left for their own survival. He had to order them to help the naked man to the hospital.

Yet every day he carries them, nurses them, holds them, cuts them open and sews them up, plays cards for their souls and dares death to save one more life. He lies and cheats and robs too, but for them, always for them. For he has come to love them, and every day he understands that he is failing in his love, for every day more and more of them die.

It has been a long time since he has thought of women. But he still thinks of her. His world beyond here has shrunk to her. Not Ella. Her. Her voice, her smile, her throaty laugh, the smell of her asleep. He has conversations with her in his head. Does he love them because he cannot have her? He cannot have her. He cannot answer himself. He cannot.

Dorrigo Evans is not typical of Australia and nor are they, volunteers from the fringes, slums and shadowlands of their vast country: drovers, trappers, wharfies, roo shooters, desk jockeys, dingo trappers and shearers. They are bank clerks and teachers, counter johnnies, piners and short-price runners, susso survivors, chancers, larrikins, yobs, tray men, crims, boofheads and tough bastards blasted out of a depression that had them growing up in shanties and shacks without electricity, with their old men dead or crippled or maddened by the Great War and their old women making do on aspro and hope, on soldier settlements, in sustenance camps, slums and shanty towns, in a nineteenth-century world that had staggered into the mid-twentieth century.

Though every dead man is a reduction of their number, the thousand POWs who first left Changi as Evans' J Force—an assortment of Tasmanians and West Australians surrendered in Java, South Australians surrendered at Singapore, survivors of the sinking of the destroyer, HMAS *Newcastle*, a few Vics and New South Welshmen from other military misadventures, and some RAAF airmen—remain Evans' J Force. That's what they were when they arrived and that's what they will be when they leave, Evans' J Force, one-thousand souls strong, no matter, if at the end, only one man remains to march out of this camp. They are survivors of grim, pinched decades who have been left with this irreducible minimum: a belief in each other, a belief that they cleave to only more strongly when death comes. For if the living let go of the dead, their own life ceases to matter. The fact of their own survival somehow demands that they are one, now and forever.

# 6

A sack of letters from Australia had arrived with the bogged truck. This was a rare and unexpected pleasure. The POWs were aware that the Japanese withheld almost all mail, and such was the excitement that before breakfast was over the sack had already been opened and its contents distributed. Dorrigo was delighted to receive his first letter in almost a year. Before he even looked at the handwriting, he knew from its stiff card envelope that it was from Ella. He resolved not to open it until the evening, holding off on the pleasure of feeling that, somewhere else, another, better world continued on, a world in which he had a place and to which he would one day return. But almost immediately his mind rebelled and he tore open the envelope, so excitedly unfolding the two sheets that he partly ripped them. He began reading in a greedy fury.

Two-thirds of the way down the first page, he halted. He found himself unable to go on. It was as if he had jumped into a car and accelerated straight into a wall. The letters of Ella's elegant copperplate hand kept scattering and rising off the page as dust motes, more and more dust motes bouncing off one another, and he was having trouble bringing her face to his mind. It seemed too real and entirely unreal at the same time.

He didn't know whether it was the malaria attack he was still recovering from or exhaustion or the shock of receiving the letter, his first for the best part of a year. He reread it but was lost in a memory at once precise and imprecise, the dust motes brighter and wilder, the late-day sun more blinding than ever, and yet he could not see her face clearly. Thinking: The world is. It just is.

He could remember sitting in the baby Austin baker's van as he drove towards the coast, could smell its acrid horsehair upholstery and stale flour, feel its burning sting in the Adelaide heat as he began visiting his uncle's hotel regularly, his stomach wild with nervousness, his mouth dry, his shirt too tight, his heartbeat a conscious thud. The hotel, which came to his mind as if he were there once again: the verandahs deep and dark; the rusty filigree iron flaking crusts; the wind-raked sea topaz-scattered; the distant, crackling sound of Leslie Hutchinson singing 'These Foolish Things', heard as if while bodysurfing a shallow wave. But of Amy's face he could remember nothing.

What, he wondered, was this desire to be with her and only her, to be with her night and day, to hang off even the dreariest of her anecdotes, the most obvious of her observations, to run his nose along her back, to feel her legs wrapping around his, hear her moan his name, this desire overwhelming everything else in his life? How to name this ache he felt in his stomach for her, this tightness in his chest, this overwhelming vertigo? And how to say—in any words other than the most obvious—that he now was possessed of only one thought which felt more an instinct: that he had to be near her, with her and only her.

She craved demonstrations of affection. The tritest of gifts always moved her, reassured her that his feeling for her had not evaporated. For her the gifts, the declarations, were necessary. What else did she have as proof of them? Denied the possibility of being a couple, this was the only evidence she could have, now and later, that she had once known such joy. Perhaps Amy, in her heart, so unlike Dorrigo, was a realist. Or so he thought. And so one day when they were together in the city he had withdrawn almost his entire savings to buy her a pearl necklace. It was a single pearl exquisitely mounted on a silver chain. It reminded him of looking out over her waist at the road made by moon over sea. She had rued his folly, twice told him to return it, but her delight was undeniable. For she had what she wished for, though she could never wear it publicly: proof of them. Even now he could see the necklace. But of her face nothing.

When you first saw me in the bookshop, he had said as he did up the triangular necklace clasp and kissed the back of her neck. Remember?

Of course, she said, a finger on the pearl.

Now I wonder if it was at that moment that you somehow joined us?

What do you mean?

But he hadn't known what he had meant and he had been frightened by where his thoughts were leading. If it were so, did he have so little control over his life? He remembered swimming at the beach one morning, waiting for her to return from town. An undertow had grabbed him and swept him some hundreds of yards along before he could escape it.

The undertow, he had said. Of us.

She had laughed. It's a beautiful necklace, she said.

Even now, he could see the necklace's miniature moon rippling the shop's electric light; he could see the triangular clasp resting on the nape of her neck, framing that faintest, most beguiling conifer ridge of down. But the dust motes were suddenly everywhere, the noise of the rain was rising and he could not see her face, he could not hear her voice, Bonox Baker was at his side saying it was tenko, and Amy was not there.

If we don't go now, Bonox Baker said, we'll be late and Christ knows what poor bastard they'll send out to work.

For a moment Dorrigo Evans was bewildered as to where he was. Still not entirely sure, he laid the letter down next to his bed and went out into the rain.

Thinking: The world is. It just is.

## 7

Rooster MacNeice was late in joining the weary mob making its way through the rain and mud of their village of the damned to the cookhouse. Save for their cock rags and AIF slouch hats, most were naked, and the less they had in the way of clothing, the more wasted and wretched their bodies, the more they seemed to wear their slouch hat with a larrikin lair, as if off out once more for a night of beer and brothels in Palestine. But they cut no dash as they once had.

The smell of wood smoke, the small sanctuary of dry, warm dust around the crude clay fireboxes, the ease of men about to be fed, the low hum of conversation, all these in most circumstances gave the cookhouse a homely, welcoming feel in an alien and unwelcoming world. But that morning the rain was pouring into the cookhouse. Several small streams fell from its attap roof, steaming as they hit the fireboxes, garnishing the rice in the wide cast-iron cooking pans with the soot they dragged down from the blackened rafters. The floor was a good two inches under water.

Rooster MacNeice, wading through, unclipped his dixie, and when his turn came held both bowls out. A small cup of a watery rice slurry that served as breakfast was slopped in one dixie and a dirty rice ball that served as lunch dropped in the other.

Moving on or what? said a voice behind him.

Rooster MacNeice straightened up. Sloshing through the water, he shuffled back out into the monsoon rain. Now his choice was either to attempt to make it back down the slippery slope with his rice water to the relative shelter of their tent, and there sit and eat his breakfast, or, as many prisoners did, stand in the rain and swallow it as quickly as possible. After all, it wasn't food; it was survival.

He watched Darky Gardiner walk past, heading back to their sleeping hut to eat. Darky Gardiner was one of those prisoners who would make a small ceremony out of eating, as though he were setting up not for a few spoons of rancid rice but for a Sunday roast. Rooster MacNeice, on the other hand, though he tried hard not to gallop down his swill, always failed. He could see the sense of taking pleasure in holding the food for a minute or two—in just knowing that now you could eat, of enjoying the anticipation almost as much as the eating, in eating it slowly, savouring the few mouthfuls, and even multiplying them, breaking them into many dabs on the spoon, rather than the three or four mouthfuls that the ration of swill amounted to. But he could never do it himself.

And Rooster MacNeice hated the moment when, after he threw his own rice down, he looked up to see such a man as Darky Gardiner still eating, slowly and serenely, eating with food still left. At such times, Rooster MacNeice would try not to look, to ignore the jealousy that so painfully bloated his empty guts, to dismiss the anger that tore at his frantic mind. He would vow that next time he too would eat wisely, carefully, slowly; that next time he, Rooster MacNeice, would be one of those whom all those miserable skull faces, all those bony snouts and large dreamy eyes, would turn to and watch enviously, desperate for some of his swill. That next time, he would be the one with this strange dignity that made of eating swill an act of courage, defiance even.

But he could never do it.

His hunger was like a wild animal. His hunger was desperate, mad, telling him whatever food he found just get it down as soon as you can and as fast as you will; just eat, his hunger screeched—eat! eat! eat! And all the time he knew it was his hunger eating him.

He heard a cry. Looking up, Rooster MacNeice saw Darky Gardiner slipping in the mud, his rice porridge spilling everywhere. He caught Darky Gardiner's distraught eyes for a moment longer than he wished, then, looking down, he saw where, in the brown mud, the heavy rain was already dissolving the rice swill into a glistening grey stain.

Rooster MacNeice turned away and, with his back to Darky, gobbled down the rest of his swill. It was gone in a few moments. It was nothing, he thought. A man needed ten times that amount of food for breakfast.

The filthy yellow swine are starving us all to death, he said to no one in particular.

Finished, he turned back to see Tiny Middleton—a grotesque figure so thin that his hips stood out like elephant ears—awkwardly helping Darky Gardiner to his feet. As Rooster MacNeice licked his own dixie clean, he watched as the skeleton picked up Darky Gardiner's tin bowl, spooned half his own rice swill into it and handed it back.

Rooster MacNeice snapped his dixie shut, rice ball lunch enclosed, and clipped it to his G-string. It made no sense to him that a humiliated man would help his tormentor by sacrificing half his food. Such men, he could see, knew neither shame nor self-respect. Feeling an odd sensation of relief bordering on triumph that he hadn't had to share his own breakfast, he walked over to the pair and put a hand on Darky Gardiner's muddy shoulder.

Need a hand, Gardiner?

I'm good, Rooster.

Noticing other men now heading to the morning parade, Rooster MacNeice hurried away to join a ragged procession making its way to the camp's western edge. There, in front of a two-room bamboo-walled and attap-roofed shed on stilts that served as the Japanese engineers' administration hut, was a quagmire that served as the parade ground. Here the morning tenko was held and here they were counted and divided into the day's work gangs.

On arriving, Rooster MacNeice watched the others coming in from all over the camp, some limping, some held upright by mates, some being piggybacked, some crawling. He found himself next to Jimmy Bigelow, who cursed the day and God.

It's beautiful, said Rooster MacNeice, who felt finer thoughts the only appropriate ones to voice. Finer thoughts, he had discovered, also sometimes had the effect of discouraging the company of men like those standing next to him. The prisoners tended to stick in their tent groups. At the best of times—and this was anything but that—such camaraderie didn't do much for Rooster MacNeice, and after his humiliation earlier in the day it now meant even less. When he couldn't evade it, he tried to break it.

It's nature's cathedral, Rooster MacNeice said, pointing at a grove of tall bamboos.

Jimmy Bigelow, raising his sunken eyes skywards, could see only the still-dark early morning sky and the black jags of jungle below it.

Rightio, Jimmy Bigelow said.

Look at the way they lean into each other to form those great gothic arches, Rooster MacNeice said. And behind them, the teak trees tracing those filigree lines, like glass leading.

Jimmy Bigelow stared into the gloomy treeline. He asked if Rooster meant like *King Kong*. His tone was unsure.

I believe there are vitamins in beauty, Rooster MacNeice said.

Jimmy Bigelow said he thought that vitamins were in vitamins.

Beauty, I said, said Rooster MacNeice.

He believed no such thing but had heard Rabbit Hendricks going on with some such nonsense. Such higher sentiments, being higher, even when stolen from others, he saw as evidence of a finer character that set him apart from the lower order and would ensure his survival.

A black raincloud came over the sky at a crazy speed. The light falling through the bamboo abruptly faded, the teak branches dissolved back into grey, a few fat beads of rain stuttered earthwards and within seconds had transformed into a roaring deluge. The jungle fell into a single oppressive thing. Heavy rushes of water tumbled out of treetops and bounced up from the ground at the side of the parade ground, as if even the earth was sick of the rain and wanted it gone. But it would not go. It was as if the rain wanted dominion over all things. It fell all the more; heavier, harder, so loud that the men gave up even yelling until the worst of it ended.

Prisoners kept arriving. There were more sick than ever. The ones who couldn't stand sat or lay alongside a great teak log at the side of the parade ground, a site known as the Wailing Wall. Through sheets of rain Rooster MacNeice watched a digger crawling through the mud towards the parade ground. Another prisoner walked beside him, keeping him company, as though they were both heading off to the races. The man crawling seemed not to want help, and the man walking beside him seemed not to be offering any. And yet, as the torrent blurred them into one, it seemed to Rooster MacNeice that something joined them.

As they finally drew closer, he realised it was Tiny Middleton who was crawling, and that it was Darky Gardiner walking with him, as though this were the most natural thing in the world. Twice he saw Gardiner offer to support his companion, but Middleton seemed intent on making it there on his own.

And the sight of men whom he despised from the bottom of his heart, this sight of that crippled man and his friend, who might mock him but would not desert him, this sight of what even the lowest seemed to have, and which Rooster MacNeice understood he did not possess, made no sense to him and momentarily filled him with the most terrible hate. Rooster MacNeice turned back to the bamboos and tried once more to imagine them as gothic arches, his prison as a cathedral, and to fill his heart with beauty.

## 8

While the prisoners assembled in the downpour, Dorrigo Evans at their head, the Japanese waited in the administration hut until the worst of it was over, and only then came out. To Dorrigo Evans' surprise, Nakamura was with them. Normally, Lieutenant Fukuhara oversaw the selection. Unlike Fukuhara, who always managed to look parade-ground perfect, Nakamura's officer's uniform was bedraggled and his shirt had dark mould blooms. He stopped to tie up a puttee tape trailing in the mud.

As he waited, Dorrigo Evans flexed his body as he once had on the football field, readying himself for the encounter. The prisoners counted off, a tedious process in which each man had to yell out his Japanese number. As the prisoners' commanding officer and senior medical officer, Dorrigo Evans reported to Major Nakamura that four men had died the day before, two overnight, and that this left eight hundred and thirty-eight POWs. Of this eight hundred and thirty-eight, sixty-seven had cholera and were in the cholera compound, and another one hundred and seventy-nine were in hospital with severe illness. A further one hundred and sixty-seven were too ill for any work other than light duties. He pointed at the prisoners propped up against the log and said that there were in addition sixty-two reporting in sick this morning over there.

That leaves three hundred and sixty-three men for work on the railway, Dorrigo Evans said.

Fukuhara translated.

*Go hyaku,* Nakamura said.

Major Nakamura say he must have five hundred prisoners, Fukuhara translated.

We don't have five hundred fit men, Dorrigo Evans said. The cholera is destroying us. It—

Australians should wash like Japanese soldier. Hot bath every day, Fukuhara said. Be clean. Then no cholera.

There were no baths. There was no time to heat the water even if they had them. Fukuhara's comment struck Evans as the most bitter mockery.

*Go hyaku!* Nakamura exploded.

Dorrigo Evans had not expected this. For the past week they had been asked for four hundred men and after the theatre usually settled on about three hundred and eighty. But every day there were more dead and more sick and fewer able to work. And now there was cholera. But he continued as he had begun and repeated that there were three hundred and sixty-three men fit for work.

Major say produce more body from hospital, said Fukuhara.

Those men are sick, Dorrigo Evans said. If they are put to work, they'll die.

*Go hyaku*, Nakamura said, without waiting for the translation.

Three hundred and sixty-three men, Dorrigo Evans said.

*Go hyaku!*

Three hundred and eighty, Dorrigo Evans said, hoping they could now settle.

*San hachi*, Fukuhara translated.

*Yon hyaku kyū jū go*, Nakamura said.

Four hundred and ninety-five, Fukuhara translated.

There was to be no easy settling.

They haggled on. After ten or more minutes further argument, Dorrigo Evans decided that if there had to be a selection of the sick to work, it should be based on his medical knowledge and not on Nakamura's insane demands. He offered four hundred men, citing once more the numbers of the sick, detailing their myriad afflictions. But in his heart Dorrigo Evans knew his medical knowledge was no argument and no shield. He felt the most terrible helplessness that was also his hunger eating him from inside, and he tried not to think of the steak he had so recklessly refused.

But beyond four hundred, he concluded, we are achieving nothing for the Emperor. Men will die who would be of much use once they're better. Four hundred is the best we can muster.

Before Fukuhara could translate, Nakamura yelled to a corporal. A white bentwood chair was hastily brought out of the administration hut. Mounting it, Nakamura addressed the prisoners in Japanese. It was a short speech, and when it was finished he stepped down and Fukuhara stepped up.

Major Nakamura have pleasure to lead you on railway construction, Fukuhara said. He regret to find seriousness in health matter. To his opinion this due to absence of Japanese belief: health follows will! In Japanese army those who fail to reach objective by lack of health considered most shameful. Devotion until death good.

Fukuhara got down and Major Nakamura stepped back up on the chair and spoke again. This time when he finished he didn't get down, but remained standing, looking up and down the ranks of the prisoners.

Understand Japanese spirit, Fukuhara yelled from beneath him, his gannet neck undulating as though disgorging. Nippon prepared to work, Major Nakamura say, Australian must work. Nippon eat less, Australian eat less. Nippon very sorry, Major Nakamura say. Many men must die.

Nakamura got down off the chair.

Happy bastard, Sheephead Morton whispered to Jimmy Bigelow.

Something fell. No one moved. No one spoke.

A prisoner had collapsed in the front row. Nakamura strode over, making his way along the row of prisoners until he reached the fallen man.

*Kurra!* Nakamura yelled.

When there was no response to this or a second shout, the Japanese major kicked the fallen man in the belly. The prisoner staggered to his feet, before falling again. Nakamura kicked hard a second time. Again the prisoner rose to his feet and again he fell. His huge, jaundiced eyes were protruding like dirty golf balls—strange, lost things from another world—and no amount of kicking or yelling by Nakamura would move him. His wasted face and withered cheeks made his jaw seem oversized. It looked like the snout of a wild pig.

Malnutrition, thought Dorrigo Evans, who had followed Nakamura and now knelt down between him and the prisoner. The man lay in the mud, inert. His body was a wasted rack covered in sores and ulcers and peeling skin. Pellagra, beri-beri, Christ knows what else, thought Dorrigo. The man's buttocks were little more than wretched cables, out of which his anus protruded like a turkshead of filthy rope. A stinking olive-coloured slime was oozing out and over his string shanks. Amoebic dysentery. Dorrigo Evans shovelled the shitty mess of a man into his arms, stood back up and turned to Nakamura, the sick man hanging in his arms like a muddy bundle of broken sticks.

Three hundred and ninety-nine men, said Evans.

Nakamura was tall for a Japanese soldier, perhaps five foot ten, and well built. Fukuhara began translating, but Nakamura put up a hand and stopped him. He turned back to Dorrigo Evans and backhanded him across the face.

This man is too sick to work for Nippon, Major.

Nakamura slapped him again. And as Nakamura went on slapping him, Evans concentrated on not dropping the sick man. At six foot three, Dorrigo Evans was tall for an Australian. This difference in height at first helped him ride the blows, but they slowly took their toll. He focused on keeping his feet equally weighted, on the next blow, on keeping his balance, on not admitting to any pain, as though it were some game. But it was not a game, it was anything but a game, and he knew that too. And in a way he felt it was right he was being punished.

Because he had lied.

Because three hundred and sixty-three wasn't the real number. Nor was three hundred and ninety-nine. Because, thought Dorrigo Evans, the real number was zero. No prisoner was up to what the Japanese expected. All were suffering varying degrees of starvation and illness. He played games for them like he always played games, and he played games because that was the best he could do. And Dorrigo Evans knew there was a number other than zero that was also the real number, and that number was the one he now had to calculate, the addition of the least likely to die to the now three hundred and sixty-two least sick. And every day this terrible arithmetic fell to him.

He was panting now. As Nakamura's blows continued falling he concentrated on running through the hospital admissions again, the ones recovering, the light duties men; as Nakamura hit him on this side of his face, then that, he counted again the number of sick in the hospital—perhaps forty—who, if properly handled, might just be capable of being transferred onto light duties—as long as they were very light—and the same number of the best of the light-duties men could then be put into the work parties. The combined number was four hundred and six. Yes, he thought, that's the maximum number he could find, four hundred and six men. And yet today, as Nakamura hit him again and again, he knew it would not be enough. He would have to give up to Nakamura even more men.

As suddenly as he had begun, Major Nakamura stopped beating him and stepped away. Nakamura scratched his shaved head and looked up at the Australian. He stared hard and deep into his eyes, and the Australian returned his stare, and in that exchange of glances they expressed everything that was not in Fukuhara's translation. Nakamura was saying he would prevail, come what may, and Dorrigo Evans was replying that he was an equal and that he would not submit. And only with that silent conversation finally done did the haggling resume in this strange bazaar of life and death.

Nakamura named the figure of four hundred and thirty men and would not budge. Evans blustered, held firm, blustered some more. But Nakamura had begun scratching his elbow furiously and now spoke forcefully.

The Emperor wills it, Fukuhara translated.

I know, Dorrigo Evans said.

Fukuhara said nothing.

Four hundred and twenty-nine, said Dorrigo Evans and bowed.

And so the day's deal was done and the business of the day began. Dorrigo Evans momentarily wondered whether he had won or lost. He had played the game as best he could, and every day he lost a little more, and the loss was counted in the lives of others.

He went over to the Wailing Wall and laid the sick man down by the log with the other sick, and was about to go to the hospital and begin the selection when he had the feeling he had lost or misplaced something.

He turned back around.

In the same way it covered logs, sleepers, fallen bamboo, railway iron and any number of other inanimate things, the rain now snaked over Tiny Middleton's corpse. It was always raining.

# 9

Yours, isn't it? Sheephead Morton asked, proffering Darky Gardiner a sledgehammer at the depot where the prisoners collected their tools. He had huge hands like vices and a head that he himself described as rougher than the road out of Rosebery. His name came not from his looks, but from his childhood growing up in Queenstown—a remote copper mining town on the Tasmanian west coast, a land made in equal parts of rainforest and myth—where for a time his family had been so poor that they had only been able to afford sheepheads for food. His gentleness when sober was only matched by his violence when drunk. He loved fighting, and once drunk he had challenged an entire busload of diggers returning from leave in Cairo to take him on. When told to shut up and sit down, he had turned to Jimmy Bigelow and, shaking his head in disgust, summed up a world of contempt with just eight words: You don't get rats out of mice, Jimmy.

Tiny's, Darky Gardiner said.

Tiny had marked the best hammer in the camp's collection by notching a T at the top of the handle so that he or Darky would recognise it each morning.

It's the best hammer, said Sheephead Morton, to whom such things mattered. The handle's a bit splintered but the head's a good pound heavier.

And while Tiny had his strength and they had been on a piecework system, it had been the best sledgehammer. Every blow had the extra power of its weight, slamming the drill harder and deeper and helping Tiny and Darky finish their quota early. You just had to be as fit and strong as Tiny had been to keep lifting it and dropping it accurately.

He thought it helped, said Sheephead Morton, waiting for Darky Gardiner to take the hammer.

For all of them now, though, it was not about getting the work done but surviving the day. Darky Gardiner was too weak to lift the heavy hammer, hour after hour, each time holding its drop accurately so that it hit the bar flatly and cleanly, blow after blow. Now he only looked for the light hammers, the useless hammers, and tippy-tapped away, trying not to hurt himself or whoever was holding the bar, trying to conserve enough strength for the next blow, trying to survive another day.

Helped him into the grave, said Darky Gardiner, picking up a light sledgehammer with a loose head.

They all just wanted whatever was lighter to carry now, lighter to lift, easier to survive another day with. He could jam the head with some bamboo, thought Darky Gardiner. Come the day's end he would be that little less exhausted. He balanced the hammer handle across his collarbone to have the most comfortable support for its weight. Feeling the lightness of the hammer there, he was almost happy, were it not that his head felt ever heavier.

A low murmur swept the prisoners like a breeze and then was gone. For really, what was there that could be said? They shuffled away and began the walk to the Line along the Dolly. With two Japanese guards up front and several coming up behind, they fanned out into single file. The least sick prisoners led the way, followed by the men with the seven stretchers carrying those too sick to walk but decreed by the Japanese fit enough to work, a position in the Line where they could be helped along but would not hold up everyone. Behind them followed men in various stages of decrepitude, with those on makeshift crutches bringing up the tail.

Fucking Christmas pageant, said someone behind Darky Gardiner.

He concentrated on the legs in front of him. They were filthy and skeletal, the muscles of their calves and thighs ragged sinews that disappeared where their buttocks should have been.

Even before this grotesque caravan reached the small cliff at the camp's far edge, where the prisoners had to climb a bamboo ladder tied together with wire—a rickety affair that had to be tested at each rung and never taken for granted—Darky Gardiner wanted to lie down and sleep forever. Above the ladder was a series of foot holds, slimy with rain and stinking, muddy shit, where the early-morning exertion had brought on an inevitable response in the near-naked prisoners as they climbed.

They worked together, passing up tools through a human chain, hauling up the weaker, somehow getting the stretchers up without mishap. The communal strength that this spoke of left Darky Gardiner feeling a little less weary and a little stronger when he reached the top of the cliff. And he needed all his strength, for he was that day the sergeant in charge of a gang of sixty men.

The morning light was still dim, and once they left the cliff and entered the jungle the world grew black and the track seemed darker and more confused than Darky Gardiner recalled it. Darky Gardiner did all he could to be a good gang leader, to get around the guards as much as it was possible, finding ways of cheating their quotas, of taking whatever opportunity presented itself to steal something of value, as long as the theft could not be traced, of keeping the bashings down, of helping the men of his gang survive another day. But today he was not himself. He had some bad fever—dengue, malaria, scrub typhus, cerebral malaria—it was hard to know what it was, and it didn't matter anyway, and he instead tried to focus on helping his men. He took a heavy coil of wet hemp rope off young Chum Fahey, whose shin was an ulcerated mess. Chum had borrowed his cousin's birth certificate to enlist, had been in the army for three years and was yet to turn eighteen. Darky had seen boys like Chum break like a stick once life turned against them. He threw the coiled hawser over his left shoulder to balance the sledgehammer on his right.

As they moved up the track, Darky Gardiner devoted his mind to reading the path in front of him and disciplining his exhausted body to place a foot or leg this way and not that, in order that he not injure himself. He had always been nimble. Even when he felt about to fall, he still had in his weakened state the ability to recover. He still retained enough strength in his thighs and calves to make the adept small leaps and twists to miss one obstacle, and use another—a rock, a log—to avoid some energy-sapping puddle or mess of fallen thorny bamboo.

And again he tried to tell himself how this was a good day and how lucky he was in his strength, which helped preserve itself; for Darky Gardiner understood that weakness only created more weakness, that every misstep led to a thousand more, that every time he balanced on his toes on one craggy piece of limestone it mattered to concentrate on getting the next step to the next craggy rock or slimy log right, so that he would not fall and hurt himself, so he might do the same again tomorrow and all the days after that. But he did not believe, as Tiny Middleton had, that his body would save him. He did not want to end up clawing his chest crying out *Me!* Darky Gardiner did not have many beliefs. He did not believe he was unique or that he had some sort of destiny. In his own heart he felt all such ideas were a complete nonsense, and that death could find him at any moment, as it was now finding so many others. Life wasn't about ideas. Life was a bit about luck. Mostly though, it was a stacked deck. Life was only about getting the next footstep right.

The prisoners heard a curse and their Indian file stopped. When they looked up and back they could see that Darky Gardiner had snagged his boot in a limestone cleft. Darky twisted back and forth and finally freed his foot. There was a laugh. The boot's upper was on Darky's foot, but the sole had completely separated, the makeshift stitching having torn apart, and was still stuck in the rock cleft.

Darky reached down and the sole tore in two when he pulled it out. He dropped the pieces, his shoulders sagged, maybe he swore, maybe he didn't. They were far too lost in their own battles to notice, and they all just had to start on their way again. He too kept stumbling forward, shuddering, the remnant of the boot flapping around his ankle. Then he yelled in pain as he jerked his leg back, fell and could no longer get up.

He's looking fucked, said Chum Fahey.

His shoe's fucked, said Sheephead Morton.

Same thing, said Chum Fahey.

Without boots or shoes most men struggled to last

long. Without boots or shoes it was only a matter of days or hours before a foot was cut or wounded by bamboo thorns, rocks, the endless blasted sharp rock fragments that were the floor of the cutting. Sometimes, within hours, an infection began that in days would turn septic and within a week become a tropical ulcer, the ulcers that were leading so many men to their deaths. Some men who had spent their lives in the bush didn't seem to be too affected and survived well enough, some even preferring to go bare footed. But Darky Gardiner wasn't a West Australian stockman like Bull Herbert, or a black-fella like Ronnie Owen. He was a Hobart wharfie and his feet were soft and vulnerable.

The column halted, waited, relieved for the break. Darky Gardiner was thinking of a pie he had once had, steak and kidney with a shortcrust pastry and a lush chutney, anything that took him away from that jungle. His mouth was salivating; the chutney was apricot, the gravy peppered. But he could not stop panting.

Mate? Sheephead Morton said.

Yeah, mate, Darky Gardiner said.

Getting better, mate?

Sure, mate.

Gotta get better, mate.

Yeah, mate, Darky Gardiner said.

As he panted and puffed for a good half-minute more, trying to get his breath, he watched a monkey. It sat hunched up in the lowlying branch of a tree a few yards down the track, shivering, hair wet through.

Look at that poor little bloody bugger, Darky Gardiner said finally.

He's free, you idiot, Sheephead Morton said, parting

his own wet hair with his saveloy fingers and putting his slouch hat back on. When I'm free I'm going to get back home to Queenstown, I'm going to get on the piss and I'm not going to get off it till I get to a hundred.

Yeah, mate.

Ever been to Queenie, mate?

The rain kept on. Neither man said anything for a while. Darky Gardiner wheezed.

Nuh, mate.

There's a big hill there, Sheephead Morton said. Mountain, really, and on one side there's Queenie and on the other side is Gormanston. Middle of nowhere. Two mining towns. Rainforest once. The mines killed the lot. Not a fern left to wipe your arse with. Nowhere else like it in the world. Looks like the fucking moon. On a Saturday night you can get pissed, go over the hill, have a fight in Gormy and then come back home to Queenie. Where else in the world can you do that?

## 10

As they waited, there was little further talking because there was really little to talk about. Every man was trying to rest, to give his body what respite he could before the onslaught of labour for which he had neither the reserves of strength nor energy that might have made it bearable. Sheephead Morton lit up a rollie made from some local tobacco and a page of a Japanese army manual, inhaled deeply and passed it on.

What we smoking?

The *Kama Sutra*.

That's Chinese.

So?

How's his foot? asked someone from up the back.

No good, Sheephead Morton said, lifting Darky's foot up and flicking some mud away. He moved the foot around his face as though it were a navigational instrument he was using to take a bearing.

The webbing's split between his big toe and the next. Pretty bad.

Someone suggested that they could make a new sole for his shoe upper come the evening back at camp.

That's the good thing, Darky Gardiner said. Still got the boot, eh?

No one spoke.

And I just need to rustle up a new sole and I'm back in business.

Reckon so, Darky, Chum Fahey said.

Everyone knew that there was no leather or rubber in the camp worthy of the name that could be pressed into service for a sole that would last even the walk to the Line, far less a day of labour.

There's always a good thing if you think about it, Darky Gardiner said.

You betcha, Darky, Sheephead Morton said, opening his dixie, splitting his lunch rice ball in half and putting one portion in his mouth.

And that was that. There was nothing that could be done, and soon they would have to start moving again. As he lay there, Darky Gardiner felt his tin dixie press hard into his side and was reminded how hungry he was, and how in that small tin box was a golf ball of rice that he could eat now. It was muddy from his fall, but it was food. And back in camp was his condensed milk, which he now resolved he would have that night. And that was a good thing too.

He forced himself to sit up. So many good things, really, thought Darky Gardiner. If only it wasn't for the pain in his feet, his aching head, and that the more he thought about the possibility of food, the hungrier he felt, it would be as good as it could get, all things considered.

Next to him, he could hear Sheephead Morton swallowing. A few others followed suit. Some took just a few grains of rice from their ball; some scoffed the whole thing in a gulp.

What's the time? Darky Gardiner asked Lizard Brancussi, who somehow had managed to keep a watch.

Seven-fifty a.m., Lizard Brancussi said.

If he ate his rice ball now, thought Darky Gardiner, he would have nothing more to eat for another twelve hours. If he kept it, he would have five hours until their short lunch break—five hours in which he could at least look forward to the prospect of food. But if he ate it now, he would have neither food nor hope.

It was as if there were two people inside him, one urging sense, caution, hope—for what is the rationing of nothing, but the act of a man who hopes to survive?—and the other declaring itself for desire and despair. For if he waited until lunch, wasn't there then a further seven hours without food? And what difference does it make if you don't have food for twelve hours or seven hours? What is the difference, after all, between starving and starving? And if he ate now, wouldn't that better his chances of surviving the day, of evading the blows of the guards, of having the energy not to misstep or make a mistaken blow that could lead to a potentially life-threatening injury?

And the demon of desire was strong in Darky Gardiner now, and his hand was reaching around to grab his dixie from his G-string when Sheephead Morton pulled him to his feet. The rest got back up, and Lizard Brancussi took the sledgehammer Darky had been shouldering, not out of any spirit of compassion but because they were in this, as in so many things, a strange animal, a single organism that somehow survived together. And Darky Gardiner was at once enraged that he was being so cruelly robbed of his food and relieved he would still have his rice ball for lunch. And in this strange mood of fury and relief he began trudging along again.

Then Darky Gardiner fell for a second time.

Give me a mo, boys, he said when they went to pull him back up.

They stopped. Some of them put down their tools, some squatted, some sat.

You know, Darky said, as he lay there in the wet darkness of the jungle floor, I always think of those poor bloody fish.

What you on about now, Darky? Sheephead Morton asked.

He was on about Nikitaris's fish shop. In Hobart. How he used to take his Edie there for a feed after they had been to the flicks on a Saturday.

Couta and chips, he told them. Flake's good, but couta's sweeter. There was a big tank there, full of fish swimming round. Not goldfish—real fish, mullets and cocky salmons and flatties—fish like what we were eating. And we'd watch them, Darky Gardiner said, and even then Edie thought it must be sad for them, pulled out of the sea and ending up in that bloody awful fish tank, waiting for the fryer.

He's always on about Nikitaris's fish shop, Lizard Brancussi said.

I never thought how that's their prison, Darky Gardiner said. Their camp. And I feel sick now thinking about those poor bloody fish in Nikitaris's tank.

Sheephead Morton told him he was a potato cake short of a packet.

Darky Gardiner told them to go on or the Goanna would be into them. He said he'd make his own way in his own time.

None of them moved.

Go on, cobbers, he said.

None of them moved.

He said he would just lie there a few minutes longer and think about Edie's breasts, that they were very beautiful and he needed to spend some time alone with them.

They said they weren't leaving him.

He said he was the NCO and to get going.

Go! he suddenly yelled. It's a fucking order. Go!

A fucking order? Sheephead Morton asked. Or just an order?

Yeah, funny, Darky Gardiner said. Funny as Rooster MacNeice reciting *Mein Kampf*. Go on. Fuck off.

They got to their feet if they were sitting or straightened up if they were standing and slowly got moving again. Darky was almost immediately lost to sight and to mind. The path grew muddy and treacherous, passing through slimy slots in jagged limestone, where feet could be and often were badly slashed. They began to quickly spread out, a prisoner's place in the line more or less determined by his illness. A small band, no more than a dozen men, still miraculously well and fit out front, at the other end those who kept falling and stumbling, sometimes crawling, and in between those who were now taking their turn carrying the stretchers of the sick. And then were the men, fit though they were, who stayed with their mates, helping, holding, never giving up.

And so their hapless column went on, making its way along the narrow corridor they had made through the great teak trees and thorny bamboo of the jungle, too thick to allow any other form of passage. They went on trudging and falling, they went on stumbling and slipping and swearing as they thought of food, or as they thought of nothing, they went on crawling and shitting and hoping, on and on in a day that had not yet even begun.

## 11

Dante's first circle, Dorrigo Evans said to himself, as he walked out of the ulcer hut and headed across the creek and down the hill to continue his morning rounds at the cholera camp, a forsaken collection of open-walled shelters, roofed with rotting canvas. Here all with cholera were isolated. And here most died. He had a classical name for many of their miseries: the track to the Line was the Via Dolorosa, a name the prisoners in turn had picked up on and turned into the Dolly Rose, and then, simply, the Dolly. As he made his way, he ploughed his bare feet through the mud as a child, head bowed as a child, interested as a child neither in where he was going nor in what might happen next but only in the furrow his foot opened that vanished a moment later.

But he was not a child. He jerked his head up and walked erect. He had to project purpose and certainty, even when he had none. Some were saved, yes, he thought to himself, perhaps trying to persuade himself he was something more than a bad actor. Some we save. Yes, yes, he thought. And by keeping them isolated, they save the others. Yes! Yes! Yes! Or some of the others. It was all relative. He could count himself king, he thought—but he would not count and he would not think, for he was north-north-west of no south, that was all he could think, nonsense words, even his thoughts were not his own, hawks being handsawn. In truth, he no longer knew what to think, he lived in a madhouse beyond allusion, far less reason or thought. He could only act.

At the cholera compound perimeter, beyond which only those with the terrifying affliction and their carers were permitted to pass, he was met by Bonox Baker, who had volunteered to be an orderly, with the news that two more orderlies had themselves gone down with cholera. To volunteer to be an orderly was a sort of death sentence in itself. Though Dorrigo accepted the risk he ran as part of his calling as a doctor, he never understood why those who could avoid it chose such a fate.

How long have you been here, Corporal?

Three weeks, Colonel.

Bonox Baker's stripling body rose up from two absurdly oversized and now battered brogues. He had acquired these while working in a Japanese work gang on the Singapore wharves, along with a carton of Bonox powder cans that had disappeared within a day and a new name that would remain with him for life. While everyone else was ageing by decades, sixteen-year-olds turning seventy, Bonox Baker was proceeding in the opposite direction. He was twenty-seven and looked nineteen.

Bonox Baker attributed his rejuvenation to the failure of Japan's war. Though not evident to anyone else in that POW camp deep in the Siamese jungle, to Bonox Baker this failure was obvious. He regarded the war as an immense personal campaign directed by Germany and Japan against him, with the sole aim of killing him, and so far, by staying alive, he was winning. The POW camp was just an irrelevant oddity. Bonox Baker always aroused a certain curiosity in Dorrigo Evans.

Since the cholera started, Bonox? he asked.

Yes, sir.

They walked to the first shelter, where the most recent cases were put. Few ever made it to the second tent, where the survivors recuperated as best they could. Many in the first shelter were dead in a few hours. It was for Evans always the most despairing of the tents, but it was also where his real work lay. He turned to Bonox Baker.

You can go back, Bonox.

Bonox Baker said nothing.

Back to the main camp. You've done your share. More than your share.

I think I'd rather stay.

Bonox Baker halted at the tent entrance, and Dorrigo Evans with him.

Sir.

Dorrigo Evans noticed he had lifted his head and was for the first time looking directly at him.

I'd rather that.

Why, Bonox?

Some bloke has to.

He raised a crumbling canvas flap and Dorrigo Evans followed him through the flared nostril of the tent into a stench, redolent of anchovy paste and shit, so astringent it burnt in their mouths. The slimy red flame of a kerosene lantern seemed to Dorrigo Evans to make the blackness leap and twist in a strange, vaporous dance, as if the cholera bacillus was a creature within whose bowels they lived and moved. At the far end of the shelter, a particularly wretched-looking skeleton sat up and smiled.

I'm heading back to the Mallee, fellas.

His smile was wide and gentle, and served to make even more grotesque his monkey-like face.

Time to see the old dears, the Mallee boy said, flower-stem arms waving, yellow-ulcered mouth blossoming. Bugger me! Won't there be some laughs and tears when they see their Lenny's come home!

That kid started out half a larrikin and ended up not quite the full quid, Bonox Baker said to Dorrigo Evans.

Won't there just? Eh?

No one answered the monkey-faced Mallee boy with the moony smile, or if they did, it was with low moans and soft cries.

Them Vics took any bugger, Bonox Baker said. How he conned 'em into taking him into the army I don't know.

The Mallee boy lay back down as happily as if he were being put to bed by his mother.

He turns sixteen next month, Bonox Baker said.

Amidst the slurry of mud and shit was a long bamboo platform on which lay forty-eight other men in various stages of agony. Or so it seemed. One by one, Dorrigo Evans examined the strangely aged and shrivelled husks, the barked skin, mud-toned and black-shadowed, clutching twisted bones. Bodies, Dorrigo Evans thought, like mangrove roots. And for a moment the whole cholera tent swam in the kerosene flame before him. All he could see was a stinking mangrove swamp full of writhing, moaning mangrove roots seeking mud forever after to live in. Dorrigo Evans blinked once, twice, worried it might be a hallucination brought on in the early stages of dengue fever. He wiped his running nose with the back of his hand, and got on with it.

The first man seemed to be recovering; the second was dead. They rolled him up in his filthy blanket and left him for the funeral detail to take away and burn. The third, Ray Hale, had made such a recovery that Dorrigo told him he could leave that night and go onto light duties the following day. The fourth and the fifth Dorrigo Evans also pronounced dead, and he and Bonox Baker similarly furled their corpses in their reeking blankets. Death was nothing here. There was, Dorrigo thought—though he battled the sentiment as a treacherous form of pity—a sort of relief in it. To live was to struggle in terror and pain, but, he told himself, one had to live.

To make sure there was no pulse here either, he reached down and picked up the wrinkled wrist of the next curled-up skeleton, a still pile of bones and stinking sores, when a jolt ran through the skeleton and its cadaverous head turned. Strange, half-blind eyes, bulging glassily and only dimly seeing, seemed to fix themselves on Dorrigo Evans. The voice was slightly shrill, the voice of a boy lost somewhere in the body of a dying old man.

Sorry, doc. Not this morning. Hate letting you down.

Dorrigo Evans gently placed the wrist back on the dirty skin of a chest that sagged over its protruding ribs as if pegged out to dry.

That's the way, Corporal, he said softly.

But Dorrigo's eyes had momentarily looked up and been caught by Bonox Baker's gaze. In his fearless superior's eyes the orderly thought he could see a strange helplessness that for a moment approached fear. Abruptly, Evans looked back down.

Don't say yes, he said to the dying man.

The skeleton slowly rolled his head back around and returned to his strange stillness. The few words had emptied him. With the tips of his fingers Dorrigo Evans traced the lank, wet hair on his wrinkled forehead, combing it away from his eyes.

Not to me or any bugger.

And so the skeletal pair continued on—the tall doctor, his short offsider, both nearly naked—the orderly with the absurd pair of oversized brogues and army slouch hat, its brim outrageously wide on his pinched face; the doctor with his greasy red bandana and his slanting officer's cap looking as though he were about to hit the town in search of women. Everything about their procession felt to the doctor an immense charade, with his the cruellest character: the man who proffered hope where there was none, in this hospital that was no hospital but a leaking shelter made up of rags hung over bamboo, the beds that were no beds but vermin-infested bamboo slats, the floor that was filth, and him the doctor with almost none of the necessities a doctor needed to cure his patients. He had a greasy red bandana, a cap on an angle and a dubious authority with which to heal.

And yet he also knew that to not continue, to not do his daily rounds, to not continue to find some desperate way to help was worse. For no reason, the image of the sickly Jack Rainbow playing Vivien Leigh meeting her lover on a bridge after a lifetime separation came to his mind. He thought how the shows the men had formerly put on—for which, with great ingenuity, they had made up sets and costumes out of bamboo and old rice bags to resemble movies and musicals—were not half so absurd a representation of reality as his hospitals and doctoring. And yet, like the theatre, it was somehow real. Like the theatre, it helped. And sometimes people did not die. He refused to stop trying to help them live. He was not a good surgeon, he was not a good doctor; he was not, he believed in his heart, a good man. But he refused to stop trying.

An orderly was battling to set up a new camp drip—a crude catheter cut out of green bamboo connected to some rubber tubing stolen by Darky Gardiner from the Japanese truck the night before—which ran up to an old bottle filled with a saline solution made from water sterilised in stills fashioned out of kerosene tins and bamboo. His name was Major John Menadue and technically he was third-in-command of the camp's POWs. He coupled the looks of a screen idol with the conversation of a Trappist monk, and when compelled to speak it was mostly to stammer. He was happiest as an orderly, being told what to do.

The Japanese, with their respect for hierarchy, while compelling all the lower ranks to work, made no such demands on the officers, who stayed in camp and, bizarrely, were paid by the IJA a minuscule salary. Evans had no respect for hierarchy except when its theatre was of help. In addition to levying the officers' pay, he compelled them to work around the camp, helping with the sick and sanitation, building new toilets, drainage and water-carrying systems, as well as looking after general camp maintenance.

John Menadue was trying to find a vein in the ankle to insert the bamboo catheter. For a scalpel he used a sharpened Joseph Rodgers pocket knife. The ankle was little more than bone, and the orderly was tracing a line back and forth on the drawn skin.

Don't be frightened of hurting him, Dorrigo Evans said. Here.

He took the knife and mimicked a precise and definite cut, then repeated the movement deftly, slicing down into the flesh just above the knob of the bone, opening the vein. He quickly inserted the home-made catheter. The cholera flinched, but the speed and sureness meant it was over almost as soon as it began.

He'll hang in now, Dorrigo Evans said.

The rehydration had, other than his firm insistence on hygiene, been his greatest success. It had saved several lives in the last two days alone, and a few men were now walking out of the cholera compound alive, rather than being carried off to the funeral pyres. That, he felt, was hope for all.

Here you're either dead or hanging in, whispered another digger.

I ain't fucking dead, croaked the man who had just had the drip inserted.

The choleras seemed to shrink away from them as they continued down the side of the bamboo sleeping platform, inspecting, checking saline levels, fixing drips, sometimes moving the lucky few into the much smaller shelter used for recovery. All seemed less than men when Dorrigo Evans came close to them, the terrible disease having wasted away much of their bodies in the few hours it took to strike and often kill. Some moaned in agony with the cramps that were dissolving their bodies and eating up their lives, others begged for water in a low monotonous drone, some stared like stones out of sunken and shadowed eye sockets. When they reached the man with the monkey face who was going home to his mum and dad, he was dead.

They do that sometimes, said Bonox Baker. Get happy. Want to catch the bus home or go and see Mum. And that's when you know it's the end.

I'll give you a hand, said Dorrigo Evans when an orderly nurse known to one and all only as Shugs—famed for having carried into the heart of the Siamese jungle a battered and now mouldy copy of Mrs Beeton's cookery book—arrived with a stretcher. It was a makeshift affair of two large bamboo poles, between which was stretched some old rice bags.

His work now done, Dorrigo Evans helped Shugs and Bonox Baker with Lenny's desiccated body. He seemed to weigh, Dorrigo thought, little more than a dead bird. Nothing. Still, it felt like it helped, it felt like he was doing something. There were not enough rice bags to run the length of the stretcher—Was there enough of anything here? wondered Dorrigo Evans—and Lenny's legs dragged.

As they made their way out of that home of the damned, Lenny's corpse kept slipping down. To stop it falling off the stretcher they had to roll the corpse over onto its stomach and spreadeagle the scrawny legs so that they hung over the bamboo poles. The shanks were so wasted that the anus protruded obscenely.

Hope Lenny don't feel a final squirt coming on, said Shugs, who was bringing up the back of the stretcher.

## 12

Since the cholera began, Jimmy Bigelow had been put on camp duties so that he would be able to perform his duty as bugler at the now daily funerals. He had been summoned and was waiting on the perimeter of the cholera compound when they came out with the stretchers. The last of these was being carried by Dorrigo Evans with his jaunty cap and red bandana, and Bonox Baker, in his ridiculous shoes that always reminded Jimmy Bigelow of Mickey Mouse, at the front, with Shugs at the rear, walking with his head held at an odd backwards slant.

Jimmy followed this pitiful funeral cortège through the dark, dripping jungle, his bugle strung over his shoulder with a knotted rag with which he had replaced its leather strap when that had rotted. He was thinking of how he loved his bugle, because of all things in the jungle—bamboo, clothes, leather, food and flesh—it was the only one that seemed impervious to decay and rot. A prosaic man, he nevertheless felt there was something immortal about his simple brass horn, which had already transcended so many deaths.

The POW pyre makers awaiting them in a dank clearing had learnt it took a lot to burn a man. Their pyre was a great rectangular mound of bamboo chest-high. One cholera corpse was already arranged on the top, along with his few meagre possessions and blanket. Jimmy Bigelow recognised it as Rabbit Hendricks. He was always surprised to feel how little he felt.

Anything a cholera had touched could not be touched by another—other than the pyre makers—and everything a cholera possessed had to be burnt to control the contagion. As the rest of his gang lifted the three new corpses and their possessions onto the pyre, one of the pyre makers walked up to Dorrigo Evans with Rabbit Hendricks' sketchbook.

Burn it, Dorrigo Evans said, waving it away.

The pyre maker coughed.

We weren't sure, sir.

Why?

It's a record, Bonox Baker said. His record. So people in the future would, well, know. Remember. That's what Rabbit wanted. That people will *remember* what happened here. To us.

Remember?

Yes, sir.

Everything's forgotten in the end, Bonox. Better we live now.

Bonox Baker seemed unpersuaded.

Lest we forget, we say, Bonox Baker said. Isn't that what we say, sir?

We do, Bonox. Or incant. Perhaps it's not quite the same thing.

So that's why it should be saved. So it's not forgotten.

Do you know the poem, Bonox? It's by Kipling. It's not about remembering. It's about forgetting—how everything gets forgotten.

*Far-called, our navies melt away;*
*On dune and headland sinks the fire:*
*Lo, all our pomp of yesterday*
*Is one with Nineveh and Tyre!*
*Judge of the Nations, spare us yet,*
*Lest we forget—lest we forget!*

Dorrigo Evans nodded to a pyre maker to set the bamboo alight.

Nineveh, Tyre, a God-forsaken railway in Siam, Dorrigo Evans said, flame shadows tiger-striping his face. If we can't remember that Kipling's poem was about how everything gets forgotten, how are we going to remember anything else?

A poem is not a law. It's not fate. Sir.

No, Dorrigo Evans said, though for him, he realised with a shock, it more or less was.

The pictures, Bonox Baker said, the pictures, sir.

What about them, Bonox?

Rabbit Hendricks was convinced that, no matter what happened to him, the pictures would survive, Bonox Baker said. And that the world would know.

Really?

Memory is the true justice, sir.

Or the creator of new horrors. Memory's only like

justice, Bonox, because it is another wrong idea that makes people feel right.

Bonox Baker had a pyre maker open the book to a page that showed an Indian ink drawing of a row of severed Chinese heads on spikes in Singapore after the Japanese occupation.

There's the atrocities in here, see?

Dorrigo Evans turned and looked at Bonox Baker. But all Dorrigo Evans could see was smoke, flames. He could not see her face. There were severed heads that looked alive through the smoke but they were dead and gone. The fire was rising at their back, its flames the only living thing, and he thought of her head and her face and her body, the red camellia in her hair, but as hard as he tried now, he could not remember her face.

Nothing endures. Don't you see, Bonox? That's what Kipling meant. Not empires, not memories. We remember nothing. Maybe for a year or two. Maybe most of a life, if we live. Maybe. But then we will die, and who will ever understand any of this? And maybe we remember nothing most of all when we put our hands on our hearts and carry on about not forgetting.

There's the tortures here too, see? Bonox Baker said.

He had turned the page to a pen-and-ink sketch of an Australian being beaten by two guards. To a watercolour of the ulcer ward. To a pencil drawing of skeletal men labouring, breaking rock on the cutting. Dorrigo Evans found himself growing irritated.

Better than a Box Brownie camera, old Rabbit was, Bonox Baker smiled. How the hell he got hold of the paints I'll never know.

Who'll know what these pictures will mean? Dorrigo

Evans said tersely. Who'll say what they're of? One man might interpret them as evidence of slavery, another as propaganda. What do the hieroglyphs tell us of what it was like to live under the lash, building the pyramids? Do we talk of that? Do we? No, we talk of the magnificence and majesty of the Egyptians. Of the Romans. Of Saint Petersburg, and nothing of the bones of the hundred thousand slaves that it is built on. Maybe that's how they'll remember the Japs. Maybe that's all his pictures would end up being used for—to justify the magnificence of these monsters.

Even if we die, Bonox Baker said, it shows what became of us.

You'll need to live, then, Dorrigo Evans said.

He was angry now, and angrier yet that he had allowed one of the men to see him lose his temper. For, as the flames began to build, he knew he was forgetting her already, that even at that moment he was having trouble trying to reconstruct her face, her hair, the beauty mark above her lip. He could remember pieces, bright embers, dancing sparks, but not her—her laughter, her earlobes, her smile sweeping up to a red camellia—

Come on, Dorrigo Evans said, let's get him on before the fire takes hold.

## 13

They lifted Rabbit Hendricks with his filthy, shit-smeared blanket and laid him alongside the other corpses, placing his kitbag—which contained nothing more than a dixie, a spoon, three paintbrushes, several pencils, a child's watercolour set, his dentures and some stale native tobacco—at his side, and put the sketchbook with it. The choleras were always eerily light. Since Padre Bob died, the funeral services had been conducted by Lindsay Tuffin, a former Anglican pastor who had been defrocked for some unspecified moral turpitude. But there was no sign of him and the fire was starting to scorch the corpses.

Colonel? said Shugs.

And so, because time pressed and duty called and rank obliged, Dorrigo Evans improvised a funeral service. He had no real memory of the official service because it had always bored him, and he performed what he hoped would prove an adequate piece of theatre. Before he began he had to ask the names of the other two corpses.

Mick Green. Gunner. West Australian, Shugs said. Jackie Mirorski. Stoker from the *Newcastle*.

Dorrigo Evans committed the names to an inviolable memory that recalled them only twice, the two occasions that mattered: the service he then conducted, and a reverie at the moment of his own death many years later. He concluded the funeral service by saying that these were four good men whom they commended to God. But he didn't really know what God had to do with it. No one spoke much about Him anymore, not even Lindsay Tuffin.

As Dorrigo Evans bowed his head and stepped away from the flames, Jimmy Bigelow stepped forward, shook his bugle to dislodge whatever scorpions or centipedes might have taken shelter there, and raised it to his lips. His mouth was a mess, the palate having shed its skin in rags. His lips had swollen up as well, and his tongue—so swollen and so sore that rice tasted like hot grapeshot—sat in his mouth like some terrible plank of wood that would not properly do its work. The Big Fella had told him it was pellagra brought on by the lack of vitamins in their food. All he knew was that his tongue now obstructed the air the bellows of his mouth had to pump into the bugle.

Yet when he brought the bugle to his lips to play that tune he now knew far too well, he was able to lose himself in the strangeness of the melody. At first, with only the slow notes, he could manage. Then, when the tune sped up, that moment where he had always believed the 'Last Post' gained its terrible power, he had to fight his whole body with an overwhelming effort to make the necessary short stops on the notes as the melody built and then died away. As he played, it felt to him that his tongue was gone and he was instead tapping the mouthpiece with a piece of four-by-two, desperately hoping that this would serve to halt notes and tongue the melody, to put the magic in.

As with everything else in that dark, dreary jungle world, Jimmy Bigelow had to improvise, tricking his tongue by sliding breaths around its whale-like form, deceiving his screaming nerve ends by concentrating on just hitting those notes, holding it together one more time for all of them who would stay in that jungle and never find their way back home. And at the end, embarrassed by tears that came not from any emotion—for he felt no more at that moment than at the five funerals he had played at yesterday or the day before that—but from the physical pain of playing, he quickly turned away, so that no one would know what an ordeal playing a simple tune had become or think he had grown oddly soft.

And though his whole body was aflame while playing this terrible bugle call, this music of death, still he played on, hearing it all anew, not understanding what it meant, hating that they had died, knowing that he had to keep playing this music he hated above all other music, but was determined never to stop playing. It did not mean those things he had been told it meant, that the soldier could now rest, that his job was done. What job? Why? How could anyone rest? That's what he was playing now, and he would not stop playing those questions for the rest of his life, at Anzac Days, at gatherings of POWs, at official functions, and occasionally at home late of an evening when overwhelmed by memory. He hoped what he was playing would be understood for what it was. But people made other things of it and there was nothing he could do. Music asked questions of questions, and of these questions there was no end, every breath of Jimmy's amplified in a brass cone spiralled out towards a shared dream of human transcendence that perished in the same sound, that was just out of reach, until the next note, the next phrase, the next time—

Immediately after the war it was quickly like the war had never been, only occasionally rising up like a bad bump in the mattress in the middle of the night and bringing him to an unpleasant consciousness. After all, as Shugs later said, it wasn't really that bloody long, it just seemed to never bloody end. And then it was ended, and for a time it was hard to recall that much at all about it. Everyone had stories far more incredible—fighting at El Alamein and Tobruk, Borneo, sailing in a North Sea convoy. And now, besides, there was a life to live. The war had been an interruption to the real world and a real life. Jobs, women, houses, new friends, old family, new lives, children, promotions, sackings, sicknesses, deaths, retirements—it became hard for Jimmy Bigelow to recall whether Hobart came before or after the camps and the Line, before or after, that is, the war. It became hard to believe that all the things that had happened to him had ever really happened, that he had seen all the things he had seen. Sometimes, it was hard to believe he had ever really been to war at all.

There came good years, grandchildren, then the slow decline, and the war came to him more and more and the other ninety years of his life slowly dissolved. In the end he thought and spoke of little else—because, he came to think, little else had ever happened. For a time he could play the 'Last Post' as he had played it during the war, with a feeling that had nothing to do with him, as a duty, as his work as a soldier. Then for years, then decades, he never played it at all until at the age of ninety-two, as he lay dying in hospital after his third stroke, he put the bugle to his lips with his good arm and once more saw the smoke and smelt the flesh burning, and suddenly he knew it was the only thing that had ever happened to him.

I've got no argument with God, Dorrigo Evans said to Bonox Baker as they pushed and poked the pyre to keep the flames wrapping around the corpses. Can't be bothered arguing with others about His existence or otherwise. It's not Him I'm shitty with, it's me. Finishing that way.

What way?

The God way. Talking about God this and God that.

Fuck God, he had actually wanted to say. Fuck God for having made this world, fucked be His name, now and for fucking ever, fuck God for our lives, fuck God for not saving us, fuck God for not fucking being here and for not fucking saving the men burning on the fucking bamboo.

But because he was a man, and because as a man he

was the most conventional of unconventional men, he had instead gabbled God God God during his funeral service whenever he had nothing else to say, and about untimely, pointless death he had found that there was very little that he had to say. The men seemed satisfied but Dorrigo Evans could not swallow the toad of disgust that rolled around in his mouth after. He did not want God, he did not want these fires, he wanted Amy, and yet all he could see was flames.

You still believe in God, Bonox?

Dunno, Colonel. It's human beings I'm starting to wonder about.

As the bodies burnt they crackled and popped. One raised an arm as the nerves tautened in the heat.

One of the pyre makers waved back.

Have a good one, Jackie. You're out of here now, mate.

Guess that's how it is, Bonox Baker said.

I'm not sure it's how it should be, Dorrigo Evans said.

Meant something to the men. I suppose. Even if it didn't for you.

Did it? Dorrigo Evans said.

He remembered a joke he had heard in a Cairo café. A prophet in the middle of a desert tells a traveller who is dying of thirst that all he needs is water. There is no water, replies the traveller. Yes, the prophet agrees, but if there was you would not be thirsty and you would not die. So I will die, says the traveller. Not if you drink water, replies the prophet.

As the flames leapt higher and the air filled with smoke and gyrating cinders, Dorrigo Evans took a step back. The smell was sweet and sickening. To his disgust, he realised he was salivating.

Rabbit Hendricks sat up and raised both arms, as though embracing the flames that were now charring his face, then something inside him popped with such force that they all had to jump backwards to miss being hit by pieces of burning bamboo and embers. The bamboo pyre transformed into an ever more ferocious fire, and Rabbit Hendricks finally fell sideways and was lost in the flames. There was a loud bang as another of the corpses exploded, and everyone ducked.

The Big Fella stood up and, grabbing a bamboo pole, helped the pyre makers push the corpses back into the centre of the fire, where they would be incinerated most fully and quickly. Together they all laboured, poking and levering and flicking the bamboo back to feed the ever-rising flames, sweating, puffing, not stopping, not wanting to stop, just losing themselves in the soaring flames for a few moments more.

When they were done and went to leave, Dorrigo Evans noticed something lying in the mud. It was Rabbit Hendricks' sketchbook, slightly charred but otherwise unscathed. He guessed it had been blown off the fire by the force of the small explosion. The card cover was gone, along with the early pages. Its front page was now a sketch of Darky Gardiner sitting in an opulent armchair covered in little fish, drinking coffee in a ruined street of a Syrian village, with some others standing around behind him, including Yabby Burrows with his hot boxes. Rabbit Hendricks must have sketched Yabby in *after* he was blown up, Dorrigo realised. The picture was all that was left of him.

Dorrigo Evans picked the sketchbook up and went to toss it back into the fire, but at the last moment changed his mind.

# 14

Men and more men began to overtake Darky Gardiner, shapeless empty sticks, their mouths grim set or gaping and their eyes like dry mud, moving no longer fluidly but fitfully jerking and jolting, and he fell further and further back in the column. All was gone from him. And what remained, he knew, what was strong and burning in his head and flesh, was sickness. His ulcerated legs only had to brush against leaves for a rush of agony to part his body in strange oscillations of pure pain.

Still, Darky Gardiner counted himself lucky: he had his boots, he told himself, and if one was temporarily soleless, tonight he would somehow fix it. No doubt about it, Darky Gardiner thought, even when they were buggered it was a good thing to have boots. And bolstered by this thought of good fortune at such a bleak moment, he dragged the coil of thick hemp rope back across his collarbone to stop it falling off, shrugged to better position it against his neck, and kept going.

And though he kept falling ever further behind, he still managed to make his way deeper into the jungle. His day he understood as a series of insurmountable battles that he would nevertheless surmount. To get to the Line, and at the Line to work till lunch, then after lunch—and so on. And each battle now reduced to the next impossible step that he would make happen.

He fell into a thicket of thorny bamboo, gashing his hand as he put it out to stop the fall. When he got back to his feet, he no longer had the agility and strength to poise on one rock and leap to the next, to take the long step up and over. Everything began to go wrong. He stumbled repeatedly. He swayed and lost what reserves of energy he had left trying to keep his balance. He fell again and again. And each time it was harder to get back to his feet.

When he next looked up as he lurched forward into the green bleakness he realised he was alone. The men out front had disappeared over a rise, and whoever was behind him was a very long way behind. The hemp hawser soaked up more rain and grew heavier on his shoulder. It kept losing its furl, spooling out into uneven bands of rope that snagged in roots, causing him to stumble. Each time he halted, refurled the rope and rebalanced the coil on his shoulder, the heavier and more awkward it became.

He stumbled on. He felt terribly weak and his head felt sloppy and unbalanced. The rope snagged again, he tripped, fell face-first into the mud, slowly turned onto his side and lay there. He told himself he needed to rest for a minute or two, then he would be fine. Almost immediately he passed out.

When he awoke he was in a dark jungle with a mess of rope beside him. He staggered to his feet, put a finger to a nostril, snorted snot and mud out of his nose, and shook his groggy head. Taking a stuttery step forward, he fell against a rock outcrop and dislodged some crumbling limestone from an overhang, which hit him on the shoulder.

I've got to get going, he thought—or thought he thought, his mind now so frayed that it felt a separate thing, a weight, a boulder; and all he knew for sure was that he was panicked and that he had momentarily passed out.

He gathered his balance, and, angry at the rock, the world, his life, he leant down, picked up a piece of the limestone and, with what strength his small fury could drag out of his fevered body, he hurled it at the jungle.

There was a soft thud and a simultaneous curse. His body tensed.

Fuck you, Gardiner, a familiar voice hissed.

Darky Gardiner looked about. Rooster MacNeice stepped out from a bamboo grove, hand on his head.

You coming with us or giving us away?

And behind Rooster MacNeice there appeared six other prisoners he didn't recognise, and behind them Gallipoli von Kessler, who gave Darky his familiar, somewhat casual Nazi salute.

We thought you were onto us, Kes said.

Onto what? Darky Gardiner asked.

We thought you knew and were just going careful, pretending to have a quick kip, Rooster MacNeice said.

Knew what? Darky Gardiner said.

Our rest day. Japs won't give us one so we're taking our own.

Darky Gardiner looked back up the track.

We've been counted this morning, and the Japs don't count again till evening parade back at camp, Rooster MacNeice went on. Out on the Line they never count and never notice. We hide away and rest up and just fall back in with everyone else as they head back to camp. Fall in, get counted, Tojo's your uncle.

You can't expect others to cover for you, Darky Gardiner said. It won't work.

We did it last week, not a squeak out of the squint-eyed bastards. And we're doing it again today.

But you blokes are in my gang today, Darky Gardiner said.

So? Rooster MacNeice said.

So how's it fair on the other blokes?

Kes said they'd found an overhanging cliff half a mile away, out of the rain. No one could hear or see them, and they had a good pack of cards, only missing the jack of diamonds. How was his five hundred?

They'll flog the hide off you, Darky Gardiner said.

How will they know? Rooster MacNeice said.

They'll work it out and they'll flog you.

You'll cover for us, Rooster MacNeice said. You're sergeant in charge of the gang today. Micky did it last time. Said nothing. Sliced and diced it a bit different so there were still men on each job. Just one less on each of the gangs.

Kes said that not having the jack of diamonds made five hundred a lot more interesting. And—

That's not the point, Rooster MacNeice interrupted. At all. It's about refusing to collaborate with the nips' war effort. We have to make a stand somewhere, sometime, and this is it.

Darky Gardiner thought about it, but not a lot.

I can't stand five hundred, Darky Gardiner said.

Kes said that, to be honest, there wasn't that much else to do. Five hundred or sleep. Maybe patience, but who ever saw the point of that?

Fuck it, said Darky Gardiner, to whom sleep sounded good and whose head was once more throbbing. I'm too buggered to argue. But it's an order. I don't mind you skiving, but I do mind if others suffer for it.

No one's going to suffer, said Rooster MacNeice.

You will, said Darky, if you disobey me. Let's go.

But when he picked up the rope, furled and shouldered

it once more, and resumed his hapless march to the railway cutting, only Gallipoli von Kessler went on with him.

Gardiner's too weak a sergeant to ever say anything, said Rooster MacNeice to the other men as they turned and headed away from the path and into the jungle. Not a leader like the old leaders.

## 15

Colonel Kota was less than surprised that his fears had been realised. The Thais were not to be trusted in the mass and were spectacular thieves in the individual. In the four hours of night between him and his driver leaving their truck in the middle of the jungle and a rescue crew of POWs arriving to push it into camp, some Thai bandits had stolen several hoses, rendering the truck undriveable. He was forced to stay at the camp until a guard—expected by dusk—returned from the closest camp with some new hoses.

Having been delayed for the day, Colonel Kota decided on an inspection of the work on the railway line. With the Goanna as his guide, he was making his way to the Line when they came upon two prisoners, one sitting, the other lying in the mud. The sitting prisoner leapt to his feet, but the one lying across the track did nothing. He seemed unaware of anything. They thought he was dead, but after the Goanna rolled him over with his foot they realised their error and yelled at him. When that did no good, the Goanna gave him a good kick, but the man only moaned. They could see that he was beyond threats and blows.

Colonel Kota found it despairing. How can we build

a railway, he thought, when they can't even walk to the job? And then he noticed Darky Gardiner's neck.

Colonel Kota ordered the Goanna to manhandle Darky Gardiner into a kneeling position, with his head bowed. He examined the Australian prisoner's neck more closely. It was skinny, filth in its folds.

Yes, Colonel Kota thought. The flesh was muddy, grey, like dirt you piss on. Yes, yes, Colonel Kota thought. Something in its strangely reptilian wrinkling and dark patterning rumpled a memory in him that craved repetition. Yes! Yes! Colonel Kota knew he was in the power of something demented, inhuman, that had left a trail of endings through Asia. And the more he killed, so casually, so joyfully, the more he realised his own ending would be the one death beyond his own control. To control the deaths of others—when, where, the craft of ensuring it was a cleanly sliced ending—that was possible. And in some strange way, such killing felt like controlling whatever remained of his own life.

In any case, Colonel Kota now reasoned, it would just waste the other prisoner's precious energy carrying the sick man back to the camp, and at the camp precious food would be wasted on him when he was likely to die soon anyway.

Unsheathing his sword, he gestured to the Goanna to give him his water bottle. Colonel Kota could see his own hands were trembling, which was strange. He felt no fear or conscience.

*Only the moon*
*and I, on our meeting-bridge,*
*alone, growing cold.*

Colonel Kota recited Kikusha-ni's haiku twice. But he had to stop his hands trembling. He took the cap off the water canteen and, as it shuddered in the air before him, poured water onto his sword. He watched the water beads rolling together on its bright surface, wet whip snakes slithering away. The beauty of it steadied him.

Raising his head, he concentrated on slowing his breath before carefully lowering the sword blade until it rested on Darky's neck. He held it there, making his intention clear, readying his own body.

Eye shut! the Goanna yelled at Darky Gardiner. Eye shut!

And as he lit a cigarette, the Goanna blinked twice to illustrate his meaning.

Colonel Kota spread his legs, got his balance, with a scream raised the sword high into the air, and went to recite Kikusha-ni's haiku one last time. But he could not remember the correct sequence of the middle syllables. In his mind, he kept muddling the poem.

All waited—Colonel Kota with the sword poised above the kneeling POW, the Goanna holding a cigarette next to his lips, Gallipoli von Kessler watching transfixed. Alone unable to see, Darky Gardiner knew only the wet heat like a blanket and the sweat on his closed eyes. All he could feel with his wretched rag of a body, twisted with terror, was the sword poised between him and the sun.

He didn't dare gulp.

He could smell Colonel Kota, an overwhelming odour of rotting fish. He could feel the sword blade hunger in the air above. He could hear blood. His. Theirs. Growing louder.

And Colonel Kota, a man who believed in symmetry

and order in all things, grew confused as his mind railed against its own weakness. He was bewildered. He had lost control of the sequence of things—and in losing that, he had lost control of this ending and, in some strange way that was to him also perfectly logical, of his own life. And that he could not allow.

Darky Gardiner's neck seemed to him to be screaming. He longed for the blow of the sword so that it might be over. He wondered if the sword was already falling, if his head were already—

He's gone, he heard Kes say.

There were sounds of someone walking away, a short silence, and the same footsteps coming back.

He's fucked off, Kes said. I've checked. You can look, Darky.

And Darky Gardiner opened his eyes.

Kota and his sword had disappeared. The Goanna was gone. Only Kes remained, apple-pip eyes staring down at him. Darky looked around at the black line of the bamboos at the top of a nearby cliff and, beyond, the silhouette of teak.

Jeepers creepers, Kes said, look at those peepers.

He heard the screech of monkeys.

He smelt the reeking mud of the jungle.

And in all this life around him, Darky Gardiner for the first time sensed his own death. He understood that all this would go on, and of him nothing would remain, that even his memory, though held by a few family and friends for a few years, perhaps decades, would ultimately be forgotten and mean no more than a fallen bamboo, than the inescapable mud. As Darky Gardiner looked up and down the track, as he thought of the naked slaves only a mile distant toiling away, he felt the most terrible rage seize him. All this would go on and on, and only he would be gone. Everywhere he looked, he could see the most vibrant world of life that had no need of him, that would not think for a moment of his vanishing, and it would have no memory of him. The world would go on without him.

You all right, mate? Kes asked.

Darky Gardiner's eyes were darting everywhere, and everywhere all he could see was a world to which he was meaningless, nothing, that had no need of him. They would toss him on a fire of bamboo, say something or say nothing, Jimmy Bigelow would play the 'Last Post', and in ten years or twenty years perhaps those who survived would all be slaves in some new Japanese empire. And after fifty or a hundred years everyone would accept it as perfectly normal, and none of it would be better or worse than anything now, and the only difference would be that he would not be there. Suddenly he needed sleep. He just had to sleep. He rolled onto his back and lay there. His body felt as if it were dissolving back into the mud.

We gotta move on, Kes said. They'll kill you if you stay.

As he leant down to drag Darky Gardiner to his feet, Kes heard a guttural cry and to his horror saw the Goanna striding quickly back down the path. The guard shoved Kes aside, kicked Gardiner again and, yelling, Byoki house, byoki house, pointed down the track in the direction of the camp. Even in his delirious state, the prisoner seemed to find it hard to believe such a thing.

Byoki house? Darky Gardiner gasped, disbelieving, repeating the camp pidgin for hospital.

*Byoki house!* the Goanna yelled again and gave him another kick to emphasise the point.

With what energy he could summon, Darky Gardiner pulled himself to his knees and hands, and like a weary dog turned around and started to crawl back to camp before the guard changed his mind. Kes began quickly marching in the opposite direction, heading to the railway cutting. The Goanna sprinted past him to catch up with the visiting colonel. When he disappeared out of sight, Kes halted.

He watched in wonderment as his left leg went into a violent spasm for no reason, jumping about as if wired into a power line. And then his body shuddered uncontrollably for some minutes, a violent and wild shaking. Finally it ceased, and he was able to resume walking to the Line.

## 16

It was just after midday, Shugs had eaten his filthy grey rice ball for lunch and was on his way to the cookhouse in order to scrounge another kerosene tin boiler to fit into the broken still. He was also hoping that a cook might give him some peelings or rice scrapings.

Shugs was a lot older than most, maybe close to thirty even, and his eyes, which reminded everyone of overflowing ash trays, coupled to his odd, taciturn nature, made some suspect he was touched. He had been a trapper before the war, a nomad of the Tasmanian high country, and he carried nothing, not even a kitbag. The first time he had worn underwear was when he enlisted and received two pairs as part of his uniform issue. He had never got over the luxury of army life, the exoticism of which was summed up by the recipe book he had won in a game of pontoon in Java. Shugs said he'd been dreaming of a recipe of Mrs Beeton's for pork roulade when he came upon Darky Gardiner, collapsed in mud in the middle of the parade ground.

Christ knows how he made it back down the Dolly, Shugs told some of the other POWs later. But he did.

They wondered too how Darky Gardiner did it on his hands and knees, up and over the rocks and roots, through the mud and the puddles, down the cliff, and they feigned astonishment, which was really fear, because next day, next week it might be one of them, and they would just have to find within themselves whatever Darky Gardiner had.

His guts had gone on him completely and he was covered in shit, poor bugger, Shugs told them. I guess he just crawled up and down that miserable fucken track squirting away shit everywhere.

Shugs had their attention.

Poor fucken bugger, bugger me, you wouldn't know how bloody long he had bloody well been there. He was all away with fever like a wormy leaf on a windy day. I thought he was dead. He looked that fucken awful. Then I could see he was breathing. I thought, I just want to get him out of sight of any Jap, because even if you're dead you're still skiving to a Jap if you're not on the bloody sick lists. I got him up, this shitty skeleton, and he's leaning on me and me him, half-staggering, half-dragging Darky like a dirty old busted broom over to the bamboo showers. Got some water, got some rag, washed him down, cleaned him up, I washed his face, I cleaned his filthy arse.

They could see Shugs standing Darky up under the

bamboo shower. They knew how awkward it would have been, the two naked men like two trees collapsed on each other. They could see that stream of water falling from the bamboo piping they had run back from the creek, Shugs saying, It's good to be clean, cobs. They could see Darky flopping around in Shugs' arms everywhere. They could see the water running like roots over the holes of Darky's shoulders and his chicken-ribbed chest, Shugs saying, Get that fucken stink off you and out of you. And they wondered if any of them had half the decency of the foul-mouthed, half-mad Shugs.

Shugs told them how Darky came-to a bit when the Big Fella's 2IC, Squizzy Taylor, with his gangster dash and not a touch of the hard man about him, arrived, and Darky told him about how the Jap officer went to behead him but didn't, and how the Goanna then sent him back.

You can never accuse the Japs of consistency, Squizzy Taylor says, shaking his big gangster head, and he holds out his gangster hands and begins to examine him. By this time Darky's making no sense, Shugs went on, and he's rabbiting on about how before the war he used to take his missus to Nikitaris's fish shop in North Hobart for a feed of fish and chips. Goes on about how he can't stop thinking about the fish that used to swim around in the big tank in the shop window. Flathead and mullet and blackback salmon. Nothing special, says Darky, as Squizzy prods him a bit, lifts his eyelid a tadge, taps his chest, all the doctor bizzo.

Just fish? Squizzy asks.

Yeah, Darky says, just fish. Poor bloody things, locked up in that glass box looking out.

Poke your tongue out, Darky, Squizzy says.

After the matinee at the Avalon, Darky goes on

rambling. Always, Nikitaris's fish shop. Two couta—chips—battered scallops—buttered bread.

First they demand everyone on death's door work, Squizzy says, then they send this poor bastard back. Get your tongue out, Darky.

And Darky kept going on about how Edie loved that. A flick then a feed of fish.

And then? I wanted to ask, Shugs said. But he's going on about how he can't stop thinking about all those fish swimming about in Nikitaris's tank. How it's not natural. How they're POWs too. How when he gets back he's going to Nikitaris's fish shop. How he's gonna scoop all them fish up and take 'em down to the docks and set them free. I don't care what old Nikitaris thinks, says Darky. I'll buy 'em, I'll rob the fucking joint, I'll do whatever and get those fish out and put them back in the sea where they belong.

Squizzy tells him not to get so excited, how he's got every disease going and he's going into the hospital for as long as it takes, and after he gets out neither the fish nor his missus will be safe.

Darky was swaying like a grass stalk, Shugs said. It was hard to know what he was thinking or even if he knew where he was. Maybe he was imagining him and Edie there for a feed after an evening at the Avalon, Shugs said, maybe he was laughing at the fish in the tank. Maybe he doesn't really notice them at all, maybe he is just looking at Edie's breasts, maybe Edie is telling him to stop looking at the fish and pay more attention to her. Or maybe not. Maybe she is saying, What are you looking at? and Darky goes all shy and looks at the fish, thinking maybe he is one of the fish swimming in the tank, maybe he is a naked prisoner of war in the jungle with his arm around me, as Squizzy Taylor tells me to take him up to the hospital.

Have them dose him up on whatever quinine they can scrounge, he says, and some emetine for the dysentery. He turns to me with his big gangster eyes looking at me and he says under his breath, There is no quinine, there is no emetine, there is next to no food. But at least he can rest.

And then, Shugs said, you won't believe me, but Darky starts laughing and it was like he wasn't with us here in the middle of the bloody jungle but had headed back to Nikitaris's fish shop before the war. No quinine, he says, no emetine. Two couta, a dozen battered scallops and some buttered bread. Squizzy says, What'd he say? And I say, Two couta, a dozen battered scallops and some buttered fucken bread. Sir.

And Squizzy starts laughing, Shugs said. And me too. And Darky laughs. Couldn't stop laughing. Two couta, Darky says, a dozen battered scallops and some buttered bread. Just holding on to each other, in the middle of that fucking mud, laughing our heads off. I don't have a clue what pork roulade tastes like. But hot, salty, greasy battered fish? No bugger forgets that.

## 17

As he came close to the ulcer hut, Dorrigo was enveloped by the stench of rotting flesh. The stink of foul meat was so bad that Jimmy Bigelow—who accompanied Evans on his rounds outside of the cholera compound to help as an orderly nurse—would on occasion have to leave, go outside and vomit.

Once they were inside the ulcer hut, the stench grew stronger. Dorrigo Evans brought a hand to his nose, then quickly took it away, considering it one further affront to men who had already suffered too much. He headed down an aisle that ran between two bamboo platforms, which were full of his ulcer patients. The stench was now different, once more growing stronger and also sharper, so foully pungent that Dorrigo's eyes were watering. Rows of naked men lay like stick insects dying after some strange swarming, so many cicada husks rising and falling on the woven bamboo, lying not parallel but at strange angles to one another, dulled bug eyes wide and vacant, chicken carcass chests rising and falling the only outward sign of life. Occasionally he felt he did see something in their eyes but they were terrible things—envy or a terrifying fatalism, or a dizzying terror into which they were falling ever deeper. It was hard to look, harder not to. Many were oblivious and most paid no attention; some were silent; some were delirious, their heads rolled side to side; some mumbled and muttered; some groaned incessantly as pain coursed through them as rain through bamboo.

Dorrigo Evans made his way between the platforms, as chatty as if it were a country pub on a Saturday afternoon and he was meeting old mates, but his good spirits fled and he felt his stomach cramp when he saw two orderlies carry Jack Rainbow in. One orderly was holding some filthy rags, trying to staunch the blood that was seeping out of the little stump that was all that was left of Jack Rainbow's right leg. Dorrigo Evans had operated on him twice before, the first time amputating the leg below the knee when the ulcer there had eaten through to his shin and anklebone. The second time gangrene had set in around the stump and he had had to amputate high up the thigh. And that had been three weeks ago, and here he was again. The orderlies placed him on a bamboo table used for patients when their ulcers were cleaned out with sharpened spoons. Dorrigo Evans came across to inspect the leg.

But before he looked, he smelt.

It was all he could do not to vomit.

The same thing had happened again, and where there should have been healing there was just black rot and infection, and blood pulsing out of the little stick-like stump. Dorrigo Evans realised the stitches he had used on the femoral artery must have sloughed off.

Gangrene, he said to no one in particular, because everyone with a nose already knew. Tourniquet.

Nobody responded.

Tourniquet? Oh, Christ, no, said Dorrigo Evans, realising he was in the ulcer tent and there were no tourniquets or any such equipment. He hastily unbuckled his belt, drew it out of his shorts and wrapped it around what remained of Jack Rainbow's thigh, a thin thing not much thicker than a drainpipe. It looked like a paper cup made of foul bitumen. He gently cinched the belt tight. Jack Rainbow gave a low moan. The bleeding slowed.

Get him up.

The orderlies pulled Jack Rainbow up to a sitting position in their arms. One of them offered him water in a tin can but he could not catch the rim of it with his shaking mouth and the water spilt.

We're taking you to the operating theatre, Corporal Rainbow, said Dorrigo Evans. And when one of the orderlies halted momentarily to scratch his nose, Dorrigo Evans said quietly, Quickly.

The orderlies knew the more quietly he spoke, the more pressing and urgent the order. They hurried away with the stretcher, as Evans turned to another orderly.

Find Major Taylor. Say I need him now in the operating theatre. And can you get me some string or rope or something for my shorts?

Together the colonel and his orderly ran to the operating theatre, Jimmy Bigelow doing his best to keep up with the colonel, whose speed seemed unaffected by having to use one hand to hold up his shorts as his long legs loped through the mud.

The operating theatre was a small hut. Its chief virtue was its situation: halfway between the hospital hut and ulcer ward, and thus separate from the sick and the near insuperable problems of hygiene that went with them. It had an attap rather than a canvas roof, which meant it was more or less dry. Such equipment it possessed resembled a child's idea of an operating theatre. Contrived out of bamboo, empty food and kerosene tins, and bric-a-brac stolen from the Japanese—bottles, knives and tubes out of trucks—it was a triumph of magical thinking. There were candles set in reflectors made out of shaped tin cans, a steriliser made out of kerosene tins, a bamboo operating table, surgical instruments made out of honed steel stolen from engines and kept in a suitcase that sat on a table so the rats and mice and whatever else couldn't crawl over them.

What could he do? wondered Dorrigo, as he began

readying his instruments for sterilising. He had no idea. What on earth comes into your head? Squizzy Taylor had asked him after Dorrigo once played cards for a prisoner whom Nakamura wanted to punish. My only idea ever, Dorrigo had confessed, is to advance forward and charge the windmill. Taylor had laughed, but Dorrigo had meant it. It's only our faith in illusions that makes life possible, Squizzy, he had explained, in as close to an explanation of himself as he ever offered. It's believing in reality that does us in every time.

He made life up every day, and the more he trusted in his fancy, the more it seemed to work. But how now to advance forward? At the far end of the hut, away from the operating table, he began scrubbing his hands, washing the greasy blood off under the steady stream of water that ran out of a bamboo pipe, another makeshift piece of plumbing the men had rigged up to bring water from a nearby stream, which he now suspected might carry cholera. Everything seemed poisoned, and sometimes every effort seemed to do nothing other than worsen the situation, to lead to ever more deaths. Dorrigo Evans called Jimmy Bigelow over to the table with a kerosene tin of precious distilled water and had him slowly pour it over his hands.

As he rinsed, Dorrigo Evans tried to steady himself, to compose his mind and body.

He was panicking. He knew it, and he steadied himself, trying to settle into his pre-op routine of cleaning. Make sure each finger is thoroughly clean. He could do this, he told himself. Nails—make sure nothing is under the nails. He had no belief he could do it, but others believed he could do it. And if he believed in them believing in him, maybe he could hold on to himself. Wrists—don't forget wrists. It was all ridiculous, and yet to live, he told himself, demanded above all else a ridiculous belief that you could live.

The orderlies arrived with Jack Rainbow, who was now quiet. As they laid him on the operating table, Squizzy Taylor came in. The orderly who had found him had procured some pieces of coloured rag that were knotted together into a crude rope. He proffered them to the colonel.

That's my belt?

Saris. Apparently. Some time ago.

The colonel smiled.

It's good that they help keep my pants on for a change. Here, he said, indicating his shorts with his elbows as he kept washing his hands.

The orderly ran the makeshift rope around his shorts and knotted it on one side, giving the tall surgeon's narrow hips a buccaneering dash.

Named after the noted Melbourne gangster, because of both his surname and a dark charm—emphasised by damp marsupial eyes, at once alert and vulnerable, and underlined by a pencil moustache—the once sleek Squizzy Taylor was now very thin, a form that lent him a villainous look he had never before had, further adding to the aptness of his nickname. His background as a suburban doctor in Adelaide was as plain as his looks were exotic. Other than what he had learnt assisting Evans, he knew surgery only from his medical training and anecdote.

Colonel?

Amputate, Dorrigo Evans said without looking up from his hands. Again.

Dorrigo, Squizzy Taylor said. You've looked at the stump?

I know.

There's nothing left to cut off.

Dorrigo felt his hands crushing each other. They had to be clean.

I know. You can—Dorrigo Evans began, and then hesitated.

He wrung his hands harder. Could he?

For Christ's sake, Jimmy, he snapped, this fucking water's more precious than single malt. It's not for irrigation. Go slowly with it, I said.

He'll die from the shock, Dorrigo.

He'll die if we don't. It's gangrene. There's . . . There is a chance if we amputate at the hip.

Is there? Squizzy Taylor said. Even in the most modern hospitals hip disarticulation only kills people. You're just cutting through too much of the body. Out here, it's pointless.

How much anaesthetic have we got?

Enough.

I assisted on a hip disarticulation once, Dorrigo said. In Sydney, back in thirty-six. Old Angus MacNamee did the job. The best.

Did he live?

She. An Aboriginal woman. For a day. Maybe two. I can't recall exactly.

Why don't you just go for a very high thigh amputation? There's a chance then.

The gangrene is too high.

I am not a surgeon. But it's not that high. Take the leg off where the tourniquet is.

Either way, high up on the thigh or at the hip, there's nowhere left to put any tourniquet and he bleeds to death. There's no fucking leg left, Squizzy. That's the problem.

If I can push down hard with something round and flat about here, said Taylor, prodding around his own groin with his fingers, feeling the arteries, the flesh, the span of the dilemma. Here, he said, pushing two fingers into his groin. *Here*—on the femoral artery, that might stop the blood enough.

It might not.

It might not.

Maybe something like a spoon with the handle bent around? That might.

Might.

Might.

That'd do the job. And hopefully staunch the flow enough that you can work. He'll still bleed. But you get the stump off, clamp the arteries and then sew up. He'll still be bleeding but not so badly he'll die.

I'll have to go quickly.

You were never a man to dawdle.

Jack Rainbow's wasted body was trembling slightly. A low hiss pulsed in and out of his mouth.

Okay, said Dorrigo Evans, shaking his hands dry. He sent Jimmy Bigelow for a tablespoon and went back to the bamboo table.

We're just going to whittle that leg back a bit more, Jack, cut that stinking gangrene away and—

I'm cold, said Jack Rainbow.

# 18

Dorrigo Evans looked at the gaunt face, grey as beef dripping, with white stubble stiff as fuse wire, the large possum eyes, the snub nose and dirty freckles.

Get a blanket, Dorrigo Evans said.

You got a Pall Mall, doc?

I'm afraid not, Jack. But after, I'll make sure you get a good smoke.

Nothing like a Pall Mall to warm you up, doc.

And Jack laughed and coughed and shook once more.

Van Der Woude arrived with his homemade anaesthetic. Jimmy Bigelow returned with a tablespoon from the kitchen and a soup ladle as backup. The candles and two kerosene lamps were lit, but the mass of them only seemed to accentuate the darkness of the hut. An orderly switched on a torch.

Not yet, Dorrigo Evans said. We've got no spare batteries. Wait till I ask.

He motioned Jimmy Bigelow and Squizzy Taylor to stand with him alongside the table and slide their hands under Jack Rainbow.

On the count of three, gentlemen.

They rolled Jack Rainbow over. When Squizzy Taylor slid the needle into Jack's spine, Jack made a plunging noise like a drain being suddenly emptied. They began drip-feeding him the anaesthetic. Wat Cooney, a cook of impossibly small proportions with ears that looked as if stolen from a bag of brussel sprouts, arrived with the meat saw from the kitchen.

Van Der Woude's concoction was good but variable in strength. Jack Rainbow lost feeling quickly and they prepared for the amputation, boiling the kitchen saw and the few surgical instruments they had. When all was finally ready, Dorrigo Evans gave the signal they were about to begin. The drip was removed and Jack Rainbow was rolled back around.

We will be as quick as we can, Dorrigo Evans said. Normal procedure. The key here is to keep bleeding to an absolute minimum. Hold him, he said, turning to Jimmy Bigelow and Wat Cooney. Spoon ready? he asked Squizzy Taylor. Taylor raised the now bent spoon in a mock salute.

Charge the windmill, Dorrigo Evans said.

He took a deep breath. Taylor pushed the spoon head gently but with growing firmness into the base of Jack Rainbow's wasted belly.

Torch, Dorrigo Evans said. Jimmy Bigelow came forward and shone the torch on the stump.

There was noise from the general hospital huts but it was almost immediately drowned out by Jack's screaming as Dorrigo Evans began cutting away his leg stump. The stench of the dead flesh was so powerful it was all he could do not to vomit. But Jack Rainbow's screams confirmed to Dorrigo Evans that he was doing what he had to do: cut into living flesh.

An orderly came running into the operating hut.

What do you want? Dorrigo Evans asked, not looking up.

The Goanna's taken Darky Gardiner out of the hospital.

What?

We couldn't stop him. They dragged him out by his arms. Something about men missing up on the Line. There's a tenko happening now. They're going to punish him.

Later, Dorrigo Evans said, his face down almost at the

level of Jack Rainbow's stinking remnant of leg, concentrating on the job at hand.

Major Menadue said only you can stop them.

Later.

When he severed the femoral artery it bled badly, but not wildly.

Clamps, Dorrigo Evans said. Nothing I can do about it at the moment. Fucking yellow bastards. Clamps? Bastards. Clamps!

He clamped the femoral artery but the tissue just broke away and the fleshy tube spat blood out over the table and then continued pumping blood.

Push harder, he said to Taylor. He was thinking how he should have been there to stop such an outrage. He thought also of the broken still, the need to buy more anaesthetic from the Thai traders, and how in future he must always make the first amputation as low as possible to allow for such future horrors as this.

He clamped the femoral artery a second time, and for a second time it fell away, and he had to push up into the stinking dead flesh and clamp again. He stopped, waited. This time it held.

Okay, he said, okay.

He cut away more flesh. Within a minute he had cut off the rest of the rotting meat. There was bleeding, but Taylor was right, it was not too much, there had been enough leg left, just enough to amputate. For the first time in an hour he relaxed a little.

Spoon away? Taylor asked.

Not yet, Dorrigo Evans said. Pointing to the rotting meat on the table, he said to Jimmy Bigelow, Get rid of it, for Christ's sake.

Next Evans flensed enough skin to form a flap to cover the final wound. Then he neatly filleted the living leg muscles back from the bone, so that he could remove the bone higher up and the flesh could in time heal below and around it to form a tolerable stump.

Saw, he said.

An orderly handed him the kitchen meat saw. It was hard to get the traction he needed, so he worked with gentle small strokes, scoring the upper thighbone, seeking to avoid splinters and any further damage to the flesh. And soon enough a piece of bone the length of a finger dropped away.

The three men were now intensely focused on the operation. Dorrigo Evans set to work sewing up the femoral artery with a gut twine Van Der Woude had improvised out of a pig's intestine casings. These had been cleaned, boiled and pared into threads, then cleaned and boiled again, then boiled a third time before the operation. Compared to surgical ligatures, they were coarse, but they held. But this time he was sewing into nothing, wetness, a blur of tissue and blood. The torchlight was dimming, and he concentrated with all his being on getting each suture in exactly the right place.

And then the bleeding stopped.

He had done it. He had managed to suture the artery, and Jack Rainbow would live. He realised he was breathing heavily. He smiled. He began to prepare the rest of the muscles and skin flap for binding over the bone stump. He looked up at Squizzy.

Spoon away, Major. Gently.

Squizzy Taylor lifted the spoon. Dorrigo Evans kept working, more slowly now, more carefully. Jack would live. He would save this man's life. There was the recuperation to get through, the chance of infection. But his chances were now good. Not great, perhaps, but still good. He concentrated on doing the best job he could now, imagining a middle-aged Jack Rainbow with children, his stump on a cushion. Alive. Loved. And he knew that what he did was not pointless, without reason; that he had not failed.

Torch off, he said.

He was finished.

He stood up straight, rubbed his back, winked at Jimmy Bigelow and looked back down at the stump. It was a surprisingly neat job. He felt proud of his handiwork. He noticed a small seep of blood where he had just stitched the flaps of flesh together, but the orderly was cleaning the stump and wiped it away.

Dorrigo lit a cigarette, breathed in the welcome smoke deeply, and laughed.

A spoon, he said.

A bloody bent spoon, said Squizzy.

That's one for *The Lancet*.

When he glanced back at Jack, a few fresh beads of blood had appeared on the stump.

Why aren't you dressing and bandaging the stump? Dorrigo asked Wat Cooney, as he wiped away the blood a second time.

As if in answer, the blood almost as quickly reappeared. The stitched flaps were swelling, the small seepage was transforming into a persistent oozing, and then blood began to drip from every part of the wound. Wat Cooney looked up at Dorrigo in horror.

The stitches holding the femoral artery together must

have given way, Squizzy Taylor said, giving words to a thought Dorrigo did not wish to have. For a moment he was frozen.

Spoon! he suddenly yelled.

What? asked Jimmy Bigelow, who was on the other side of the hut.

The ligatures are gone on the femoral artery. We've got to open it back up.

Squizzy Taylor ran back with the spoon.

Torch! Jimmy, torch! We've got half a minute.

For after half a minute, he knew, Jack Rainbow's heart would have emptied his body of blood. Before he could get the spoon back in position Jack Rainbow's body jolted.

Spoon!

Jack Rainbow's body had gone into convulsions.

*Spoon!* Dorrigo Evans yelled.

Squizzy Taylor went to push the spoon down but couldn't keep it pressed against the bucking body. Jimmy Bigelow switched the torch on and got back in position, but the torch dimmed further and then died altogether.

Torch! Dorrigo Evans was yelling. Where's the fucking light?

The body was jumping wildly.

Hold him! Hold him down! Hard. Spoon! Hard! Hold the fucker!

I'm pushing as hard as I fucking can but the fucker won't stop, yelled Squizzy Taylor.

Blood was everywhere, blood over the bamboo, blood over them, blood dripping oily lines in the dark mud below. It took a few more moments for Jimmy Bigelow and Wat Cooney to get a good grip of Jack Rainbow and hold him, but still that emaciated tiny body jolted up and down as if electricity were coursing through it, and their grips slipped in the blood that now seemed to grease everything.

The leg, said Dorrigo Evans. Get the leg!

But there was really no leg left to get, only a weirdly moving and bloody thing that seemed just to want to be left alone. The tiny piece of thigh that remained was now so slippery with blood that it was very difficult to work on, and in the dim light and the confusion of blood Dorrigo Evans was having trouble seeing anything clearly. The tremors eased then stopped, and he managed to find the sutures holding the flesh together so that he could get back to the femoral artery, but when he snipped them Jack Rainbow jolted again. Squizzy's spoon slipped in the bloody slime, and blood spurted in a wild arc that reached as far as the foot of Jack Rainbow's good leg.

He was frantically searching the muck of Jack's stump with his fingers, trying to find something to stitch, pinching vaulting slime, groping pitching slop, there was nothing, nothing to stitch into, *nothing* that might hold the thread. The artery walls were wet blotting paper. There was, realised Dorrigo Evans, with a rising horror as the blood continued to pump out, as Jack Rainbow's body went into a terrible series of violent fits, nothing he could do. But there must be, he told himself. Think! Think! Look!

With each galvanic jolt blood was spewing out in a small fountain. It was as if Jack Rainbow's body were willingly pumping itself dry. Dorrigo Evans was trying to stitch as far up the artery as he could go, the blood was still galloping out, Squizzy Taylor was unable to staunch the flow, blood was everywhere, he was desperately trying to think of something that might buy some time but there was nothing. He was stitching, the blood was pumping, there was no light, the stitches kept ripping, nothing held.

Push harder, he was yelling to Squizzy Taylor. Stop the fucking flow.

But no matter how hard Squizzy Taylor pushed, still the blood kept surging, spilling over Dorrigo Evans' hand and arm, running down into the Asian mud and the Asian morass that they could not escape, that Asian hell that was dragging them all ever closer to itself.

The convulsions gave way to shivering. Dorrigo Evans was pushing deeper into the stump, the flesh was tearing and falling away as he worked; his needle at one point hit the bone. He was trying to think, he was trying to find some way, he was trying not to give up hope when he heard Jack speak a few low words that were not much more than gasps and cracks of breath.

Big Fella?

Jack?

Will I die?

I think so.

Cold, he said. So fucken cold.

Dorrigo Evans kept steadily working on Jack's stump, his bare feet ankle-deep in the bloody mud below the makeshift bamboo operating table, his outer calm a strange thing he knew he preserved at the moments of greatest inner turmoil. He kept looking for that piece of artery, trying to find something in his work to hold on to, unconsciously clawing at the mud with his toes.

And then finally he had it, and he worked with the utmost care and delicacy to make sure his work would hold and Jack live, and when it was done and he lifted his head he knew Jack had been dead for some minutes and no one had known how to tell him.

## 19

Colonel Kota found the Korean sergeant ever more irritating. Everything about the guard seemed untrustworthy and unreliable. Even his affected way of walking and his exceedingly slow way of turning seemed somehow false. As he looked up and down the tangle of sleepers, rock, dirt, irons and naked slaves working like cockroaches, Colonel Kota understood why Koreans could never be used as frontline troops.

While he inspected the railway works—the embankments and sidings, the great cuttings through rocky hills, grey limestone cliffs holding up black clouds, and the magnificent teak trestle bridges over jungle gorges, bowing like rainbows in the monsoon deluge—all he could think of was how he had not killed the prisoner back along the track, and how the Korean sergeant had witnessed his strange behaviour. And yet, even now, he could not remember the exact order of the haiku's syllables. The Korean sergeant annoyed him immensely, seeking to please him with his affected smile, his ridiculous agreement with every comment Kota made, his boasting of the efficiency of their operation. Colonel Kota was convinced that behind every compliment was contempt, behind every agreement mockery, beneath every boast insolent superiority. On a hunch that he thought at best might embarrass the Korean and at worst annoy him, he ordered a head count of the prisoners for no reason other than that he could.

To the guards' astonishment, the count came up nine short—nine prisoners missing. Alerted to this discovery, eight men mysteriously appeared at the second head count, held half an hour later. The hatchet-faced Japanese colonel demanded the eight men who had been hiding come forward to be punished, and that they reveal the identity and whereabouts of the ninth missing man.

When no one came forward, he ordered that the POW sergeant responsible for the gang be found and severely punished as an example. After some confusion, it was established that the ninth man *was* the sergeant, and that he was not on the Line but back in camp.

On returning to the camp late that afternoon, Colonel Kota gave Nakamura a dressing down, his rage driven by his own shame at having forgotten a haiku and thus having been unable to behead a prisoner—and this in front of a Korean guard. In turn deeply ashamed, the Japanese major found the Korean sergeant whose name he could never remember, slapped him hard a few times, got the name of the prisoner who was apparently—of all things—hiding out in the hospital, and ordered a parade to be called and the prisoner to be punished in front of the assembled POWs.

For his part, the Goanna was unconcerned by his slapping, but he was less than thrilled with the order: he did good business with the prisoner Gardiner, and the charge was to his mind even more pointless than most. While Gardiner annoyed him with the way he sometimes sang and whistled, the prisoner occasionally proved useful. Only a few days before, the Goanna had scored fresh beef from

Gardiner for all the NCOs. But so it went. It was a shame, but he supposed that, after the beating, Gardiner would still need him and he Gardiner. So it went on and it never stopped. You could go to war with the world, but the world would always win. What could he do?

And so Gardiner was found where the Goanna had sent him, in the hospital. As he was unable to walk, the Goanna ordered the two guards who were with him to drag the prisoner to the parade ground to be punished.

# 20

The day was passing, it was cooling down, and the men were thinking how, here at least, they did not have to work. For a few minutes or however long it took, they could rest, and rest was always welcome, the most welcome thing in their world other than food. But they did not want to be here.

They stood in the middle of the parade ground, a hundred or so prisoners who had been on light duties and who had, that early evening, been assembled in the monsoon rain to witness Darky Gardiner, a man who pitied wet monkeys, being beaten by the Goanna for a crime he had not committed. Their number slowly swelled as prisoners returning from the Line were made by guards to join this desolate gathering.

When the Goanna tired, two other guards stepped forward to continue his work. A fruity, wet fragrance momentarily swept in from the jungle, and it reminded some of sherry and made them think of Christmas with the family and the trifle their mothers used to make. While one of the guards slapped Darky's face back and forth and a second punched him in the torso, some of the prisoners tried to be happy in their memories of roast pumpkin and roast lamb and plum pudding with beer washing it all down. And though they would carry the memory of Darky's beating to their own deaths six days or seventy years later, at the time the event seemed no more within their control, and therefore no more within their consciousness, than a rock falling or a storm breaking. It simply was, and it was best dealt with by finding other things to think of.

Sheephead Morton—slowly, carefully, so as not to draw attention to his forbidden movement—speared mud beneath his toes and was once more concreting, as he had sometimes as a labourer before the war, laying a house foundation. Jimmy Bigelow rolled the tip of his thumb along the side of his index finger, and this gentlest of touches took him to a bed where a woman's fingers whispered a line along his hip. He remembered the marvel of her faint down moustache as she drew him in to kiss.

After a further ten minutes the Goanna, finished resting and perhaps sensing the absence of their attention, ordered that the prisoners all take six steps forward. Now the very sound of the hits and slaps and punches, dull and muted as they were, could be felt by the assembled men. Now there was no way not to look at the near-naked man being beaten by the uniformed guards. His wet, swelling face wore a strange look of astonishment each time the guards hit him with their fists or bamboo poles.

Help! Darky Gardiner moaned. Help me!

Or perhaps his punctured cries just sounded that way.

Every strange, laboured breath of Darky's—part wheeze, part bloody gargle, occasional grunt, as his body worked at this, too, the very surviving of the beating—every sound could not now be entirely blocked out. And yet they did block them out.

Lizard Brancussi was trying to see his Maisie's face. Daily, he looked lovingly at Rabbit Hendricks' pencil sketch, but when he tried to look beyond it—when he tried to recall her—everything grew hazy. The fantasy of Mae West was growing ever stronger, and Maisie, as she was, growing ever weaker. Still, as the beating went on, he kept trying, for he understood the measure of his life now to be his capacity to believe in something—anything—other than what was happening in front of him.

So they saw, but they did not see; so they heard, but they did not hear; and they knew, they knew it all, but still they tried not to know. At times, though, the prisoners were tricked back into seeing the beating by some novelty, such as a small teak log the Goanna found and threw at Darky Gardiner's head, or when he thrashed Darky Gardiner's body with a bamboo pole as thick as his arm, as if the prisoner were a particularly filthy carpet. Blow after blow—on the monster's face, a monster's mask.

The prisoners were starving, and increasingly their thoughts were of their evening meal, which, however meagre it was, was still real and still waiting for them; the beating was denying them the pleasure of eating it. They had been at work all day with nothing more to sustain them than a small ball of sticky rice. They had laboured in the heat and the rain. They had broken rock, carried dirt, cut and hauled giant teak and bamboo. They had walked seven miles to and from work. And they could not eat until the beating was done or Darky was dead, and their one secret hope was that, either way, the affair would be over with sooner rather than later.

More men staggered in from the Line, the number of prisoners grew to two hundred and then over three hundred. And they had to keep watching other men breaking in the mud a man like other men, and none of them could say or do anything to change this unchangeable course of events.

They wanted to rush the guards, seize the Goanna and the two others, beat them senseless, smash their skulls in until watery grey matter dribbled out, tie them to a tree and run their bayonets in and out of their guts, drape their heads with necklaces of their blue and red intestines while they were still alive so the guards might know a small measure of their hate. The prisoners thought that and then they thought they could not think that. Their emaciated and empty faces grew only more emaciated and empty the longer the beating went on. Then these men who were not men, humans unable to be human, heard a familiar voice cry out—

Byoki!

And their spirits momentarily rose as they turned to see Dorrigo Evans running towards them. When his ulcerated ankle brushed a slashed bamboo clump, Dorrigo Evans yelled harder—

Byoki! Byoki!

But the Goanna ignored the Australians' commanding officer completely. Another guard shoved him into the front row of the prisoners as across the parade ground Major Nakamura came striding towards them with Lieutenant Fukuhara in tow, come to inspect the punishment.

Stepping out of the line, Dorrigo Evans pleaded with the Japanese officers to stop the punishment. Some men noticed how Nakamura bowed slightly, respectfully acknowledging the colonel's superior rank, and how their colonel, rather irritatingly for the Japanese, did not return the bow.

They heard him say: This man is severely ill. He needs rest and medicine, not a beating.

And, behind him, the beating went on.

## 21

Nakamura was rocking on his heels as he listened. He was itching, his mouth was dry, and he felt angry and agitated. He needed shabu, just one pill. Watching the prisoner being beaten gave him no pleasure. But what could you do with such people as these? What? Good and gentle parents had raised him as a good and gentle man. And the pain brought on in him by such suffering as he had ordered proved to him how deeply he was a good and gentle man. For, otherwise, why would he feel so pained? But precisely because he was a good man—who understood his goodness as obedience, as reverence, as painful duty—he was able to order this punishment.

For the beating served a greater good. Overnight, the task of completing their section of the railway line had increased immeasurably. And because the prisoners had today been particularly difficult, and because the guards sensed that and were in turn uneasy, the punishment of a prisoner offered a way for the guards to reassert their authority and for all the prisoners to be reminded of their sacred duty.

There was the other matter of Colonel Kota having been the one who discovered the missing POWs—thereby shaming him, Nakamura, and all the engineers and guards under his command. The punishment wasn't about guilt, but honour. There was no choice in any of this: one existed for the Emperor and for the railway—which was, after all, the embodiment of the Emperor's will—or one had no reason to live or even die.

Fukuhara told him the Australian colonel was going on yet again about medicine. What medicine? thought Nakamura. The central command sent them nothing—not machinery, not food, certainly not medicine, just a few old broken hand tools and impossible orders to build a miracle out of nothing in this green desert. And Koreans. Useless Koreans. No wonder they didn't use them as front-line troops. You couldn't even trust them to guard Australian prisoners. He needed medicine too. He needed shabu. Because if he failed to complete his section of the railway on time, he would have no choice but to kill himself out of shame. He did not want to kill himself, but he could not return to the Home Islands having failed the Emperor. He was a better man than that. And to get done what had to be done over the next few hours, he just needed a little shabu.

As the beating went on, Nakamura noticed that the Korean sergeant seemed to be putting less force into his blows, a lack of purpose that annoyed Nakamura immensely. The Koreans were, well, Koreans, and he was simply not doing the job properly. Perhaps he was weary, but it was no excuse. Nakamura had ordered the punishment, the order was necessary and justified, yet the guard seemed not to be taking the order seriously.

As Fukuhara continued translating the Australian colonel's claims that the prisoner was guilty of nothing and had been sent back to the hospital by one of the guards because he was so sick, Nakamura continued standing there, itching badly, wasting his time, watching the Korean featherdusting the prisoner. The prisoner appeared groggy but was still managing to ride the guard's weak blows with his body. When the prisoner staggered, it seemed to Nakamura that he was using the stagger to sway and roll with the blows of the bamboo pole and the guard was doing nothing to end this farce. The prisoner was making a joke of the punishment. It maddened Nakamura, it made his skin even itchier—he just needed to get that shabu pill, but how much longer did he have to wait, watching such ineptitude, such stupidity?

The Australian colonel had changed tack and seemed to be fashioning an argument of offended authority to stop the beating. Fukuhara told Nakamura that the Australian colonel claimed that the Korean sergeant had completely ignored him—a colonel and commanding officer—when he had spoken to him, demeaning his rank and honour.

Nakamura swung around to Fukuhara. He would end the punishment now and they could all be done with it—poor show as it had been, it had served its purpose. But as Nakamura turned, his left foot trod on his perennially trailing puttee tape, his right boot corkscrewed around, and somehow, as he tried to pick up his left foot, he tripped over his right boot and fell sprawling in the mud.

No one said anything. The beating momentarily stopped, then hastily resumed as the Japanese major got back to his feet. One side of a trouser leg was smeared with mud and his shirt was filthy.

As he scanned the faces of enemy and ally alike, Nakamura was acutely aware that everyone had seen his humiliating fall. Prisoners. Koreans. Fellow Japanese officers. He had had enough. He was tired. He had been up since three a.m. He had much yet to do, the day was already dying, and the railway was further behind schedule than ever. Nakamura—humiliated, enraged, muddy—saw a pile of tools that the prisoners had dumped. His mind was abruptly clear. He understood the intolerable Australian colonel's issue—as an officer he felt he had been insulted. And he saw how he could resolve both the Australian colonel's problem and his own.

He went over to the tools, chose a pick handle, weighed it in his hands and, brandishing it like a baseball bat, walked straight past the Australian colonel to where the Korean sergeant was thrashing the prisoner. He called the guard to order. Nakamura planted his feet, drew the pick handle back and, wielding it like a samurai's sword, hit him hard across his left kidney.

The Korean groaned, swayed and almost toppled, and only with some difficulty drew himself back to attention. Nakamura raised the pick handle above his head and with a powerful swing drove it into the Korean's neck. He finished with a backhanded sweep of the pick handle into the side of his head, and the Goanna dropped to one knee. Nakamura yelled at him in Japanese, threw the pick handle at his head, walked back to Dorrigo Evans and bowed. Without meaning to, Dorrigo Evans bowed in return.

Nakamura spoke quietly. Fukuhara translated for the Australian colonel, saying that the guard had been punished for his insolence to the Australian colonel, and now the punishment of the prisoner could continue.

In front of them, the Goanna got back on his feet, grabbed the pick handle, staggered the few steps to Darky Gardiner, steadied himself, then raised the pick handle high before bringing it down on the prisoner's back with a new-found zeal. Darky Gardiner fell to his knees and was gathering himself to stand back up when the Goanna kicked him full in the face.

As the Australian colonel began remonstrating again, Nakamura waved his translator away.

It's not a question of guilt, he said wearily.

Darky Gardiner's movements were no longer graceful as his wasted, naked body tried to recover, coordinate and move again in time to defend itself from the next blow. His timing was growing jagged. As he got back up, a blow of a guard's bamboo pole caught him in the side of the face. His head snapped sideways, he gasped and reeled backwards, trying not to fall, but his body had grown clumsy. He tripped and fell to the ground.

As the guards took turns kicking Gardiner, Nakamura murmured a haiku by Basho. Fukuhara looked at him queryingly.

Yes, Nakamura said. Tell him.

Fukuhara continued staring.

He likes poetry, Nakamura said.

It is very beautiful in Japanese, Fukuhara replied.

Tell him.

In English I think not.

Tell him.

Smoothing the side of his pants with his hand, Fukuhara turned to the Australian. He drew himself up straight, so that his neck seemed even longer, and recited his own translation:

*A world of pain—*
*if the cherry blossoms,*
*it blossoms.*

## 22

Dorrigo Evans looked at Nakamura, who was scratching violently at his thigh. And Dorrigo Evans understood that for the railway to be built, that railway that was the only reason for the immense suffering of hundreds of thousands of human beings at that very moment—for that senseless line of embankments and cuttings and corpses, of gouged earth and massed dirt and blasted rock and more corpses, of bamboo trestling and teetering bridges and teak sleepers and ever more corpses, of innumerable dog spikes and inexorable iron lines, of corpse after corpse after corpse after corpse—for *that* railway to exist, he understood that Darky Gardiner must be punished. At that moment he admired the terrible will of Nakamura—admired it more even than he despaired of the beating of Darky Gardiner—the grim strength, the righteous obedience to codes of honour that allowed no doubt. For Dorrigo Evans could find in himself no equivalent life force that might challenge it.

With his fixed face and ascetic's ragged tunic, in his

thrashing of the Goanna, in the bark of orders he had just given, Nakamura no longer seemed to Dorrigo Evans the strange but human officer he had played cards with the night before, not the harsh but pragmatic commander he had bartered lives with that morning, but the terrifying force that takes hold of individuals, groups, nations, and bends and warps them against their natures, against their judgements, and destroys all before it with a careless fatalism.

The Goanna had stooped down and scooped Darky Gardiner up in a fireman's lift. He threw him onto his shoulder and then back up to a standing position. There was an odd pause, as though the beating was over, but once Darky had his balance the three guards started once more with the bamboo poles and pick handle until he fell again. And so began a pattern of beating, falling, kicking and dragging back up to beat again.

And watching this—as the Goanna yet again stood Darky Gardiner up in order to beat him down again, as he quickly backhanded him twice—Dorrigo Evans felt as if some terrible vibration was shaking the earth, and that all their beings could not help but drum with it. And that ominous drumming was the truth of this life.

This must stop, Dorrigo Evans was saying. It's wrong. He's sick. He's a very sick man.

It wasn't even an argument, though, and Nakamura just raised a hand and talked over him in a new, kindly voice.

Major Nakamura say he have some extra quinine, Fukuhara said. To help sick men work. The Emperor's will decrees it, the railway needs it.

And the drumming went on, louder and louder.

Dorrigo Evans understood that Nakamura was trying to help, but that he could do nothing about the beating he had ordered. Quinine would help others. Nakamura could help whom he could help, and quinine would help him help them. But he could not stop the drumming. He could not help Darky Gardiner. The railway demanded it. Nakamura understood that. Dorrigo Evans had to accept it. He too had a part in the railway. Nakamura had a part. Darky Gardiner had a part, and his part was to be brutally beaten, and all of them—each one in his own way—had to answer to the terrible drumming.

The jerking movements of Darky Gardiner's body and arms and legs as he tried to protect himself—all these were for the guards now just natural obstacles, like rain or bamboo or rock, to be ignored or cut or broken. Only when he ceased to struggle did they stop standing him up, and his cries gave way to a long, slow wheezing, like a torn fire bellows, and their grim work slowed to a more moderate tempo, taking on the nature of manual labour.

Something was happening inside Dorrigo Evans as he watched. Here were three hundred men watching three men destroying a man whom they knew, and yet they did nothing. And they would continue to watch and they would continue to do nothing. Somehow, they had assented to what was happening, they were keeping time with the drumming, and Dorrigo was first among them, the one who had arrived too late and done too little and now somehow agreed with what was happening. He did not understand how this had come to be, only that it had.

For an instant he thought he grasped the truth of a terrifying world in which one could not escape horror, in which violence was eternal, the great and only verity, greater than the civilisations it created, greater than any god man worshipped, for it was the only true god. It was as if man existed only to transmit violence to ensure its domain is eternal. For the world did not change, this violence had always existed and would never be eradicated, men would die under the boot and fists and horror of other men until the end of time, and all human history was a history of violence.

But these feelings were too strange and overwhelming to hold on to, they floundered for a moment in Dorrigo Evans' mind, and then vanished. Behind him, Nakamura was walking away. The Japanese officer's thoughts were also confused and too disturbing to make sense of, far less hold on to. Other, more reassuring, comforting ideas of duty and the Emperor and the Japanese nation and the immediate practical worries of tomorrow's railway building took their place, and, again, as a mouse in a wheel, Nakamura's mind returned to obediently fulfil that role which had been assigned to him.

Within ten minutes he had completely forgotten the beating, and it was only an hour later, when he walked back past the parade ground and saw the prisoners still at attention, that he realised it had not ended. Two extra guards held hurricane lamps to light the scene now it was night, the prisoner had somehow lost what rags he had and was naked, and the uniforms of the three guards administering the punishment were dark with rain, mud and blood. The prisoner no longer sought to resist or evade his beating but absorbed it as passively as a bag of chaff. When the guards weren't hitting him with their sticks, they kicked him around like an old ball. But then he no longer looked like a man, but something wrong and unnatural.

Nakamura would have preferred that the beating had stopped some time ago, but it seemed best not to interfere.

Fortified by three tablets of shabu, he was on his way to find Corporal Tomokawa and have him head over to the river camp to buy a bottle of Mekhong whisky from a Thai river trader. Some shabu and whisky, thought Nakamura, that was what was needed.

And the drumming went on and when the other guards had tired and stopped, still the Goanna went on, diligently, obediently, rhythmically beating Darky Gardiner with the pick handle.

And to his drumming there could be only one end.

## 23

Darky Gardiner opened his eyes and blinked. Raindrops fell on his face. He pushed his hands into the mud but they kept sinking. He was swimming in shit. He tried to get back to his feet. It was impossible. He was swimming in ever more shit. He tried to curl up to protect himself. It did no good and he only sank back into the foul hole. If he closed his eyes he was back there being beaten. If he opened his eyes he was drowning in shit, trying to stay afloat, trying to climb out. But it was so slippery and so dark and he could not find a hold, and when he did he had no strength to climb out. His body could not help him. It answered only to the kicks and blows that twisted him wherever they wished. He had no idea how long he had been there. Sometimes he thought it seemed forever. At other times it seemed no time at all. At one point he heard his mother. He was having difficulty breathing. He felt more soft raindrops, saw bright-red oil against the brown mud, heard his mother calling again, but it was unclear what she was saying, was she calling him home or was it the sea? There was a world and there was him and the thread joining the two was stretching and stretching, he was trying to pull himself up that thread, he was desperately trying to haul himself back home to where his mother was calling. He tried calling to her but his mind was running out of his mouth in a long, long river towards the sea. He blinked again. A monkey shrieked, its teeth white. Above the ridge, the smiling moon. Nothing held and he was sinking. He heard the sea. No, he said, or thought he said. No, not the sea. No! No!

## 24

They found him late that night. He was floating head-down in the benjo, the long, deep trench of rain-churned shit that served as the communal toilet. Somehow he had dragged himself there from the hospital, where they had carried his broken body when the beating had finally ended. It was presumed that, on squatting, he had lost his balance and toppled in. With no strength to pull himself out, he had drowned.

Always shit in the shitter, said Jimmy Bigelow, who volunteered to be lowered on a rope into the hole of shitty water to manhandle the corpse out. Rightio, he yelled to those holding the rope at the top when he was up to his thighs in the filth. Rightio!

And as he tied a second rope around the corpse, he spoke to it.

Oh, you fucking stupid bastard, Darky. Couldn't you just have shat yourself on the bunk like every other dopey bugger? Couldn't you just have folded their fucking blanket the right way out?

As they raised Darky Gardiner's body, Jimmy Bigelow glimpsed it by the light of the kerosene lantern. Coated in maggots, it was something so oddly bruised, crushed, filthy, so dirty and broken, that for a moment he thought it could not be him.

They carried the body to the hospital. With a kerosene tin of water and his miner's hands, so violent, so gentle, Sheephead Morton cleaned the filth off the blackened body and prepared it to be buried the next day.

It had been a day to die, not because it was a special day but because it wasn't, and every day was a day to die now, and the only question that pressed on them, as to who might be next, had been answered. And the feeling of gratitude that it had been someone else gnawed in their guts, along with the hunger and the fear and the loneliness, until the question returned, refreshed, renewed, undeniable. And the only answer they could make to it was this: they had each other. For them, forever after, there could be no I or me, only we and us.

## 25

The following morning Rooster MacNeice rummaged deep in his kitbag for his copy of *Mein Kampf* to begin the day with his ten minutes of memorisation. He had woken in the middle of the night, harrowed by just one thought—that if he had stepped forward to say it had been his idea to hide from work, Gardiner would not have died. But, he reasoned, if he had done that, perhaps he would have died instead. Or not. Or maybe both of them would have died. He told himself it was impossible to know with the Japanese. He reassured himself that Gardiner was doomed in any case, as sergeant in charge of their gang, as a sick man.

When Rooster MacNeice had stood there in the cutting the day before, as the Japanese had demanded the guilty prisoners step forward, what had been loudest in his mind was not the Japanese roaring but Gardiner's laughter after he had been caught with his hand around the eggshell. At the moment when Rooster could have stepped forward, all he could think of was the blackened duck egg Gardiner had stolen from him, the eggshell of which he had then used to mock him. The humiliation of the previous morning at Gardiner's hands remained with him as a more painful emotion than the later memory of Gardiner being beaten. No, Rooster MacNeice had thought, he would not help such a man. But he had not meant to kill him.

No. I did not mean it, he muttered to himself. No, I did not.

As he sucked on his ginger beard, he could feel at the bottom of his kitbag his dixie, then the damp, cupped clapboards of his copy of *Mein Kampf*. Just as he was about to pull it out, his hand brushed against a dress uniform shirt he had somehow kept through all his travails. He always had it neatly folded and flat, but it was now bulging. He let go of his book, felt around and pulled out of his kitbag a duck egg. His lower lip dropped out of his mouth. His feeling of relief at finding the egg was almost immediately overtaken by a horror beyond words. He quickly placed the duck egg back in the kitbag as if it were some gigantic shame that needed to be hidden, and got out *Mein Kampf*.

Much as he tried, he could memorise none of it.

# 26

Decades later, Jimmy Bigelow would insist that his kids always fold their clothes so, fold ever outwards. He would open the drawers of the chest of drawers in their suburban weatherboard home in Hobart to make sure they were safe and the fold was out. He would never hit or smack them for not folding their clothes with the fold out. He would beg and plead, he would order and demand and, in the end, exasperated, he would refold and restack their clothes himself as they stood by nervously waiting. He would feel some nameless terror that was beyond him to explain—a confusion they too would carry with them for the rest of their lives that was both love and fear, that was beyond the drawers opening and closing, beyond their father's frustration and mumbling. He knew they didn't understand. But could they not *see*? How could they not *know*? It should have been so obvious what had to be understood. You could never know when everything might change—a mood, a decision, a blanket.

A life.

They knew none of it. They only knew that, whatever they did, he would never hurt them. At the very worst, he would throw them over his knee, bring his hand up and then hold it there, hovering, over their bottom. Sometimes they would feel him shaking through his knees and thighs. They would steal a look upwards and see his hand trembling, his eyes watery. How could they know that their father was desperately trying to protect them from the unexpected smash of a rifle butt into their soft child's cheeks, to warn them of what horrors this hard world had ready for the unwary, the unwise and the unprepared—to prepare them for all those things for which no one could ever be readied? They knew only this one thing: that he would never hurt them.

As his body trembled back and forth through time, they knew what he meant when he said, Rightio, and suddenly threw them off his lap and back onto their feet. Averting his eyes, he would wave them away with an extended hand.

That's it. Rightio? Just. Just put the fold out next time. Out. Always out. Rightio?

And they would run outside into the sun.

Perhaps, he wondered, he didn't make the time or space he should for love. He fitted it in, and it flitted away. Perhaps he somehow chose—why, he couldn't say—the predictable lines of work over love's wild circling, the folding of a blanket over the unfolding of locked arms.

But sometimes it was just there: staring out an open window to see little Jodie look up and wave to him with the biggest smile, he was shocked to see love playing in a backyard of brown grass under a sprinkler's diamond spill—shocked to know he had been lucky enough to live and know it, to love and be loved. And he would watch his children playing outside in the sun. Ashamed. Amazed. It was always sunny.

## 27

And what of the Line? With the dream of a global Japanese Empire lost to radioactive dust, the railway no longer had either purpose or support. The Japanese engineers and guards whose responsibility it was were imprisoned or repatriated, the slaves that had remained to maintain the Line were freed. Within weeks of the end of the war the Line began welcoming its own end. It was abandoned by the Thais, it was dismantled by the English, it was pulled up and sold off by tribespeople.

After a further time, the Line began to bend and warp. Its banks broke, its embankments and bridges washed away, and its cuttings filled in. Abandonment ceded to metamorphosis. Where once death stalked, life returned.

The Line welcomed rain and sun. Seeds germinated in mass graves, between skulls and femurs and broken pick handles, tendrils rose up alongside dog spikes and clavicles, thrust around teak sleepers and tibias, scapulas, vertebrae, fibulas and femurs.

The Line welcomed weeds into the embankments the slaves had carried as dirt and rock in their tankas, it welcomed termites into the fallen bridge timbers the slaves had cut and carried and raised, it welcomed rust over the railway irons the slaves had shouldered in long rows, it welcomed rot and ruin.

In the end all that was left was the heat and the clouds

of rain, and insects and birds and animals and vegetation that neither knew nor cared. Humans are only one of many things, and all these things long to live, and the highest form of living is freedom: a man to be a man, a cloud to be a cloud, bamboo to be bamboo.

Decades would pass. A few short sections would be cleared by those who thought memory mattered, transformed in time into strangely resurrected, trunkless legs—tourist sites, sacred sites, national sites.

For the Line was broken, as all lines finally are; it was all for nothing, and of it nothing remained. People kept on longing for meaning and hope, but the annals of the past are a muddy story of chaos only.

And of that colossal ruin, boundless and buried, the lone and level jungle stretched far away. Of imperial dreams and dead men, all that remained was long grass.

This world of dew
is only a world of dew—
and yet.

*Issa*

# 1

Scattered like sesame seeds along the Shinjuku Rashomon's ragged crest, the crows—startled by a rock thrown at them—rose up over a Tokyo yet to concrete over the ash of its past. Beneath their beating wings the city scarcely existed. Not so very long ago the same crows had thrived on the black corpses that had been so common in the fire-stormed city. Now they flew over a vast and charred, churned-up plain, in the weird warrens and labyrinths of which wandered widows and orphans, broken and crippled ex-soldiers, the mad and the dying and the despairing, their paths occasionally crossed by a jeep of American GIs. In that bitter winter of 1946 reconstruction amounted to little more than tents, lean-tos and tin shelters, in which the more fortunate huddled, while the rest made do with the subways, railway stations or burrows and caves in the rubble.

The man who had thrown the rock, Tenji Nakamura, formerly a major in the Imperial Japanese Army's 2nd Railway Regiment, was sheltering from the bitter rain in an erratic archway made of the fallen beams and debris of fire-bombed buildings that had, by chance destruction and some judicious burrowing, formed over a back street. As though this pile of rubble was a grand gate to their great city, those locals who had to pass through this chaotic tunnel to and from the devastated pleasure district of Shinjuku called it the Shinjuku Rashomon. Foxes, rats, whores and thieves were the Shinjuku Rashomon's most common inhabitants, living in its burrows, nests and the half-collapsed rooms. Mount Fuji, which Nakamura could glimpse even from this ramshackle gateway, again stood above their world, as it had a century and a half before for the great Hokusai to paint, once more fully visible, ever-changing and immutable, still and immortal.

Yet the world Mount Fuji now presided over was ferociously mortal, and in it people died every day but had to continue living. The streets were full of people senseless on *kasutori*, the cheap, lethal drink of choice for the starving and despairing, or shabu stolen from army warehouses, or both. Nakamura's poverty had broken Nakamura of his own shabu habit and he was determined not to return to it. Hungry dogs roamed the sunken lanes that had once been roads in large and threatening packs, and hungrier children would appear to work the streets as pickpockets and beggars and pimps.

Wolves, all of them, thought Nakamura.

With their slow eyes and sudden movements, there was about them something Nakamura found eerie, at once vulnerable and threatening. They looked an emaciated six or seven years of age but were often already teenagers. Women sold themselves everywhere, a few finding a curious honour and reduced income in refusing to service the American devils. Most, however, revelled in the affluence being a pan pan girl brought. One night, after he had been with such a woman, he grew angry at her trade, in which he now saw his own life reflected, and he asked her how she could go with the Americans. A freshly lit Lucky Strike on her smiling red lips, she asked him—

Aren't we all pan pan girls now?

Since being demobilised two and a half months earlier,

Nakamura had lived amidst such ruins of people and place, and among their number he was nothing and glad of it. He was armed only with a crowbar that served both as the means by which he procured a precarious living and as a weapon of self-defence on the spine of which every few minutes he crushed some more lice ripped from his itching body. With it, he extricated broken pieces of timber framing from destroyed buildings, from the silt and mud and ash of what had once been Tokyo, pulled them apart as best he could and then sold the pieces to a charcoal burner. As he turned over the charred remnants of the once great capital of the Empire, Nakamura's thoughts tended to turn to where he might be able to get some miso soup or a bowl of rice. Occasionally, such scrounging yielded unexpected rewards: the day before, he had unearthed some stale acorns that even the rats had missed, buried deep in the rubble. Since eating them, though, he had had nothing.

To divert his thoughts from hunger, he picked up a newspaper that lay trampled on the ground. It was several days old, and he managed to read a few stories without taking in a word, until one suddenly brought his mind to white-hot attention. He read carefully, desperately. It was about warrants being issued by the Americans for the arrest of more ex-POW camp staff in relation to possible war crimes. The article ended with a list of the wanted suspects' names, and halfway down the list he found what he had for so long dreaded—his name mentioned as a possible Class B war criminal.

Nakamura began again to itch. He was no war criminal, yet the Americans who were the real war criminals would kill him if they could and make a lie out of his life. Rage began to rise within him. But underlying his anger, punctuating his day-to-day thoughts of survival, was the dull but ever-present fear of an animal that knows destiny is searching for it. For Nakamura had heard how the Americans, whose hulking, loud bodies seemed to him to be everywhere, were hunting down those they believed to be war criminals with a grim efficiency, and high on their list were those who had had anything to do with POWs. He was determined to survive, to not be caught and not be executed, because his honour demanded it. His itching grew violent, and he reached inside his pants and tore at his crotch. He pulled out a scabby mix of skin, hair and lice and threw it on the ground.

As he waited for the weather to improve, Nakamura ran his finger up and down the weary green paint of the crowbar, crushing the few lice that still remained on his hand between his fingernail and the iron. He thought on his situation: scrounging timber was no way to survive; his crowbar had lost half a tooth from its nail pull, and the side of his face throbbed from a gouge made by a jagged beam that had fallen unexpectedly across his body two days before; the terrible, inescapable cold only made him hungrier and now the Americans were after him. As he again looked at his name on the newspaper list Nakamura realised with horror that for several days at least now the Americans had been hunting him—methodically pursuing leads, eliminating false trails, homing in on others—and every hour drawing closer to him, and he to his death at the end of a gallows-rope. To survive, Nakamura realised, he had to do something, and that meant he would now have to contemplate doing anything. But then this feeling of defiance gave way to one of utter hopelessness and defeat. What could he do?

What? The honourable thing, Nakamura thought, would be to do as others had done and kill himself.

And at the moment he resolved to take his destiny into his own hands and die honourably, Nakamura heard some muffled shouts from above. He found his whole being filled with an insatiable curiosity as to what those shouts were, as though doing something, anything, was better than contemplating his wretched fate.

He crawled out of the hollow, stood up in the rain and slowly turned his head, listening intently. Then he heard a woman hissing. The sound came from somewhere above, in a pile of rubble that formed the left-hand side of the Rashomon.

As quietly as was possible on rubble, Nakamura crept up the large mound of loose masonry and broken buildings that formed the left wing of the archway, hand gripping his crowbar tightly. He came upon a small hole in the rubble, the size of a fist. Looking through it he saw into the remains of a bombed-out room, lit from an opening where the top half of the far wall ought to have been. Nakamura could see that the room had perhaps once been a neat and pleasant place, but now the chrysanthemum wallpaper was only just visible through a thick smear of dust and soot, and it seemed to Nakamura that it had been turned into a sort of animal den. The remnants of a rotting tatami mat and some cushions formed a bed, and by it was a three-legged table, propped up with broken bricks, on top of which sat a dirty mirror.

The woman's hissing began again, very close now, and by twisting his body in the direction of the woman's voice, Nakamura was able to see into a far corner of the room. There stood a pan pan girl and a young boy, perhaps sixteen or seventeen years old, holding a long kitchen knife. Below them lay the uniformed body of an American serviceman whose throat had been so recently cut that it was still weakly spurting blood. The pan pan girl was remonstrating with the boy, asking why he had killed the American, but she was not sad, only angry.

Hidden from their view, Nakamura quickly took all this in, but what caught his eye was not this drama—about which he couldn't have cared less—but what sat on the makeshift dressing table: two gyoza dumplings and a bar of American chocolate.

## 2

Nakamura carefully and quietly crawled down from his peephole and crept over the top of the Rashomon and around to the opening in the wall. As he slowly raised his head over a loose sheet of roofing iron, the pan pan girl was rifling through the dead man's pockets. When she rolled the American's body over onto its side, it gave a low murmur. She jumped back up, but, realising it was just air being forced out of his lungs, she went back to searching his clothes. From a back pocket she pulled a roll of American dollars.

But it was the gyoza dumplings that Nakamura was focused on. He was remembering how they ate them all the time when he had served in Manchukuo and thought nothing of it. He felt his mouth filling with saliva at the memory of them then, and the possibility of them now.

Unable to think of anything other than how much he

wanted those gyoza dumplings, Nakamura braced himself and threw himself through the hole. He rolled into the room and jumped to his feet, brandishing the crowbar. For a moment all stared at each other over the body of the dead American—the pan pan girl in an expensive floral print shirt, wide slacks and glossy black geta sandals holding the wad of American dollars, the boy with the knife, and Nakamura with his crowbar.

With a roar the boy leapt at Nakamura with his knife, and Nakamura, feeling some heightened sense of himself that was at once terror and calm experience, dropped to a slight squat to balance better, and swung the crowbar as if it were a sword. It passed through the air in a wide upward arc that ended with the soft, sloppy sound of it hitting the boy's head. That sound—of a hammer burying itself in a watermelon—seemed to Nakamura to stay in the air for a long, long time. And in that same odd eternity that was also only an instant, all the boy's violent forward momentum ended. There seemed to Nakamura to be a strange break in time before the boy dropped noiselessly to the floor.

Both Nakamura and the pan pan girl said nothing. Though the boy's body spasmed violently, they knew he was dead. As blood began to appear, the spasms slowed, then stopped, and Nakamura noticed lice swarming in seeming sudden panic around the boy's filthy long hair. He became acutely conscious of the chill odour of damp dust that filled the room.

The pan pan girl began to whimper. Nakamura took two steps over to the three-legged table and stuffed both gyoza dumplings into his wet mouth. As he gobbled them down, he kept his eyes firmly fixed on her. A new idea came to him.

Using the crowbar to talk, he pointed at the wad of dollars in her hand. With a shaking hand she passed it to him. He pocketed the cash, and then with the tip of his outstretched crowbar lifted the edge of her floral print shirt. Slowly, she raised her eyes from the crowbar to his eyes, and then she bowed and took a step backwards. She began to strip.

Naked, she was bowlegged. Her unpleasantly thin thighs were covered with little sores, buttercup-yellow. The silky hair of her crotch contrasted with the scaly white skin underneath. Her breasts were still more swellings than breasts, and her skin was sickly in colour. Nakamura could smell her now, unwashed and sweaty, like a stabled cow at the end of winter.

She went over to the three-legged dressing table and lay down on the filthy tatami mat, feet pointing towards him. He could hear her breathing, short pants. She disgusted him, selling herself to the American devils and now offering her filthy, sullied body to him. He picked up the pan pan's clothes, pocketed the chocolate bar and went to climb out of the cave. For a moment he halted and looked at the two corpses.

The American was already nothing. The Japanese boy had a badly pimpled face. Too much was made of killing, thought Nakamura. Maybe one should feel remorse, guilt, and at first in Manchukuo he had. But the dead soon ceased to be faces. He struggled to remember any of them. The dead are dead, he thought, and that's it. Still, two corpses and one of them American . . . it would mean trouble for him if he wasn't careful, and he was a wanted man already.

Avoiding stepping in the large puddle of dark blood, Nakamura knelt down over the American. He smelt of the DDT they had deloused Nakamura with when he had been demobilised. He felt the American belonged to some other species, so oversized and strange did he look. The Australians had not looked anything like this in the jungle, like this large and too-dead American.

Making sure he never touched the corpse, he artfully wormed one end of the crowbar into the American's half-closed fist and laid it across his chest. Then, thinking on it, he rubbed the bar around in the man's hand, pushing it hard on his fingers, then dropped it in the puddle of blood. As long as the pan pan disappeared and kept her mouth shut, the Americans and the police would draw the obvious conclusion: a pimp tried to roll the American, a fight ensued and both lost their lives.

And with that he turned and went to pull himself up into the chest-high hole that served as this den's entrance, when behind him he heard the pan pan get to her feet. Nakamura paid her no heed till he felt her trying to clutch at his ankles. To free himself, he had to give her two good kicks that sent her sprawling back onto the American's corpse.

As he slid down the rubble outside, he could hear a yelling behind him. He turned to see the pan pan girl, arm over her little blood-slicked breasts, leaning out of the hole, saying something about how the American raped her and her brother arrived and was just trying to protect her. Nakamura didn't really follow her story and wasn't interested in trying. He scrambled back up to the hole, grabbed her by the shoulder and held a brick near her whimpering head.

Forget it, said Nakamura. Forget him, forget your brother and forget me.

The pan pan girl wailed more loudly. He shoved the brick against her mouth.

You survive if you forget, he said angrily.

He pushed her back into her hole, scrambled down the Shinjuku Rashomon and headed into the city.

With the fifty American dollars he stole from the pan pan girl he was able to buy false identity papers. With the money he made from selling her clothes to another pan pan, he bought a train ticket to Kobe. In a third-class carriage with all its windows blown out, he now travelled through a brutal winter's night, away from his past as ex-railway regiment major Tenji Nakamura and into his future as ex-IJA private Yoshio Kimura.

Things were no better in Kobe than they had been in Tokyo. That city, too, was just craters and mud, hills of bricks and steel twisted like wire, with Japanese crawling around like cockroaches in the mess. But Nakamura felt he had put the distance he needed between him and the dead American and the dead boy. For several months he made a hand-to-mouth living from such petty thieving and black marketeering as was possible. But he never felt safe. On one occasion he thought he had recognised at a distance a tall Australian officer from one of the POW camps. Such was Nakamura's fear that, for a week after, he only ventured out on the streets of a night.

He began following the war crimes trials closely. He read how one Japanese soldier who had beaten a POW who had escaped several times was found guilty as a war criminal and hanged. Nakamura found this impossible to fathom.

One beating?

He had been beaten all the time in the Japanese Army,

and it had been his duty to beat other soldiers. Why, when he was training he had been knocked out twice, and once suffered a ruptured eardrum. He had been beaten with a baseball bat on his buttocks for showing 'insufficient enthusiasm' when washing his superior's underwear. He had been beaten senseless by three officers when, as a recruit, he had misheard an order. He had been made to stand-to all day on the parade ground, and when he had collapsed they had fallen on him for disobeying the order and beaten him unconscious.

So how did one beating make one a war criminal? And what was a prisoner of war? Did not the Field Service Code specifically state that a captured officer was to kill himself? What was a prisoner of war? Nothing, that's what. A man without shame, a man with no honour. A no man.

One beating?

He had been a good officer, and some of the other officers had chided him for dealing with most infringements of discipline just with face slapping.

You're too warm-hearted, he recalled Colonel Kota telling him after Nakamura had slapped Corporal Tomokawa for some misdemeanour. Just slapping a man for that? I would have thrashed him so hard he never forgot.

And after that, Nakamura wanted to scream to the clear Kobe sky, what was a prisoner of war? What?

## 3

Choi Sang-min was sitting in the dark on a bamboo stool, a luxury he had been allowed as a condemned man. He had heard that some ex-POWs had simply tossed Kim Lee from the top floor of a brothel in Bangkok when they had found him there. That seemed to him reasonable and sensible. He hoped Kim Lee had spat on them as they threw him to his death. Kim Lee had been a guard like him, he had killed POWs, and when the war was ended they had killed him. It seemed perfectly understandable, unlike his own situation, which did not. He despised the Australians' hypocrisy, dressing up their vengeance with rituals of justice. In his heart he knew they had always wanted to kill him too, so why all this pretence?

He had neither watch nor clock. Other than his intuition, he had no way of knowing how much longer the night might go on. But his intuition no longer seemed to work. The night was never-ending and yet it was already racing away from him. The Changi prison had been locked down for the evening, perhaps two hours earlier. If he had thought about it, he may have reasoned it was somewhere near midnight. But he did not think about it or anything, really. Choi Sang-min was lost in a place beyond thought. His mind beat time between two emotions. One was a panic that would come on him like a mad, nagging cough and have him once more frantically pacing his Changi prison cell trying to discover a way of escaping, only to discover there was no escape possible, either from the cell or from his imminent death.

And then his mind would pitch to anger, not at his fate or the impossibility of escaping, but at a fact he found tormenting. As he was imprisoned as a member of the Japanese military, he must surely still be owed his fifty yen monthly pay, none of which he had seen since before the war's end, two years earlier. His anger arose not out of arithmetic or greed, but an idea of motivation that was also a sense of injustice. Fifty yen was the only reason he was there. Why, then, was he not receiving it?

And because in his heart he knew he would never receive any money ever again, that the fifty yen was an absurdity and yet he had somehow been robbed of it, his mind would abruptly swing back to panic, and he would once more begin pacing his cell, running his fingers over the walls, his hands over the cell window bars, the door, pushing, touching, searching for a way out, until he once again realised no escape was possible and his mind swung back to the anger he felt at being denied his fifty yen.

His trial had been held in an Australian military court and had lasted two days. Other than when he was being directly questioned, the proceedings were all in English and he understood almost none of it. At its end, the judge—a man with the face of a windswept candle and the voice of a gravedigger—for the first time looked directly at Choi Sang-min and spoke. An interpreter, his gaze fixed resolutely on the judge's lips, whispered in Choi Sang-min's ear broken branches of Japanese sentences.

Because of—of the contradictory nature, said the interpreter, evidence presented—form of written testimonies—the charge of having participated in the murder—Australian Imperial Force Sergeant Frank Gardiner—is dismissed. The translator switched to a more informal tone to add, This is very good news, very good.

And then he returned to his fragmented translation.

The charges—of having ordered the murder of Private Wat Cooney—these are upheld—as are several other lesser charges of—ill-treatment, including the withholding of food and medical supplies leading to avoidable suffering and death. Having—having been found guilty of being a Class B war criminal—you will—be—be executed by hanging.

The translator this time added no gloss of his own.

There were more words but Choi Sang-min was no longer hearing anything. When he had been questioned in court, Choi Sang-min had tried to explain how, as a Korean sergeant, he could never have ordered the death of a prisoner, but the Australian lawyers quoted from the interrogation of a Japanese officer called Colonel Kota saying he had. Kota's evidence had already helped convict several Korean and Formosan guards and, Choi Sang-min had also heard, he had later been released without charge. Choi Sang-min had pointed out that Cooney was no longer in the camp when the order to execute him was supposedly given. But the camp records, confused and incomplete, offered no proof that this was so.

After his sentencing, his Australian defence counsel, a flabby man with wet, glistening eyes that reminded the condemned Korean of scalpel blades, pleaded with him to lodge a petition for clemency. Choi Sang-min was resolved to dying in a foreign land and could not see the point in drawing out the agony. It had not escaped the notice of Choi Sang-min, along with the other Koreans and Formosans held at Changi as Class B and Class C war criminals, that the Allied victors often seemed to free officers who had links to the Japanese nobility and let others more lowly, like themselves, be the scapegoats whom they hanged. Choi Sang-min thought of Major Nakamura, who had never been arrested and no doubt never would be; of Colonel Kota, who was once more free. Both were probably working for the Americans somewhere.

All the same, said Choi Sang-min.

What? asked his counsel, wet eyes cutting back and forth.

All the same, said Choi Sang-min, a comment he made to demonstrate his fatalistic acceptance of life, but which his counsel understood as an assent to his attempt to prevent his execution and have the sentence commuted. The lawyer submitted the petition, and Choi Sang-min's life and torment were extended by another four months.

Choi Sang-min noticed how every man at Changi conceived of his destiny differently and invented his past accordingly. Some men had point-blank denied the charges, but they were hanged or were imprisoned for lengthy periods anyway. Some had accepted responsibility but refused to recognise the authority of the Australian trials. They too were hanged or were jailed for greater or lesser periods. Others denied responsibility, pointing out the impossibility of a lowly guard or soldier refusing to recognise the authority of the Japanese military system, far less refusing to do the Emperor's will. In private they asked a simple question. If they and all their actions were simply expressions of the Emperor's will, why then was the Emperor still free? Why did the Americans support the Emperor but hang them, who had only ever been the Emperor's tools?

But in their hearts they all knew that the Emperor would never hang and that they would. Just as surely as they had beaten and tortured and killed for the Emperor, the men who didn't accept responsibility were now to hang for the Emperor. They hanged as well and as badly as the men who accepted responsibility or the men who said they never did any of it, for as they jiggled about beneath the trapdoor one after another, their legs jerked all the same and their arses shat all the same and their suddenly swollen penises spurted piss and semen all the same.

During his trial, Choi Sang-min became aware of many things—the Geneva convention, chains of command, Japanese military structure and so on—about which he had hitherto only the vaguest idea. He discovered that the Australians he had feared and hated had, in a strange way, respected him as one who was different: a monster they called the Goanna. And Choi Sang-min wasn't displeased to learn that he loomed so large in their hate.

For he sensed in the Australians the same contempt for him that he had known in the Japanese. He understood that he was once more nothing, as he had been in Korea as a child, standing at the back of his class after being caught whispering in Korean instead of speaking in Japanese; as he had been when working for the Japanese family, where his position was worse than that of the family pet; as he was in the Japanese army, a guard, lower than the lowliest Japanese soldier. Better Kim Lee's fate than his now. And yet some men who he knew had done far worse things than him or Kim Lee had their lives spared. How? Why? None of it made any sense.

Beating the Australian prisoners, on the other hand, had made a lot of sense. However briefly, he felt he was somebody while he was beating the Australian soldiers who were so much larger than him, knowing he could slap them as much as he wanted, that he could hit them with his fists, with canes and pick handles and steel bars. That had made him something and someone, if only for as long as the Australians crumpled and moaned. He was vaguely aware that some had died because of his beatings. They probably would have died anyway. It was that sort of place and that sort of time, and no amount of thinking made any more or less sense of what had happened. Now his only regret was that he had not killed many more. And he wished he had taken more pleasure in the killing, and in the living that was so much part of the killing.

As the Australians talked to each other during the trial, it dawned on Choi Sang-min that this was something beyond hate. It was a certainty about life that he had never had but that the Japanese above him had always had. And when he had been given power over the life and death of the Australians, he had at first beaten them only because it was the Japanese way that he had been brought up with, and he saw nothing remarkable about thrashing a man who you felt was too slow or shirking work.

At Pusan he had undergone the same strict military training as that for Imperial Japanese Army privates. Only they were not Japanese, they were all Koreans and were never to be soldiers: their job was to be guarding enemy soldiers who had surrendered because they were too cowardly to kill themselves. As well as marching and shooting and bayoneting, he had been taught *binta*, the face slapping that the Japanese insisted on for even the most minor error. Even if only one person made a mistake, everyone had to be slapped. Every day they had all the trainee Korean guards line up in two rows facing each other, and each trainee had to slap the trainee opposite him, right hand on left cheek, left hand on right cheek, taking it in turns and only stopping when the face of the one being hit was badly swollen. All orders had to be obeyed. *Binta* and obeying orders, that was now Choi Sang-min's life—right hand on left cheek, left hand on right cheek. He longed to run away and go home, but he knew there would be trouble for his family with the Japanese authorities if he did. And besides, he would shortly be earning fifty yen a month.

He remembered how he had whispered to the trainee opposite him that he would go easy on him if he returned the favour. Their ruse was quickly spotted by their Japanese officer. He was a fine-looking man whom the recruits admired. Choi Sang-min even imitated his way of walking and his slow, precise way of turning when spoken to. Now the officer was shouting in Choi Sang-min's ear.

Want to pretend? he yelled. Pretend this doesn't hurt.

And with a short steel rod he hit Choi Sang-min in the kidneys on both sides so hard that he pissed blood for several days afterwards. The next morning, when the recruits were once more lined up in rows to slap each other, Choi Sang-min beat his counterpart with a desperate rage that never quite left him, right hand on left cheek, left hand on right cheek.

And, at first, when he—a small, skinny Korean kid of sixteen—had been sent to the jungle in a distant land, he had been frightened of the larger, taller and older Australian men, orang-utangs with their wide-set backs, thick arms and hairy thighs. They were always whistling and singing. In his experience, Koreans and Japanese didn't do much of either in public, and he hated this strange cheerfulness. And so he went further than he strictly needed to with his punishments—to impress upon them that he was more man than they were, to make clear that their cheerfulness should end. And after a time the men began to shrink and shrivel, their arms withering and legs wasting; they whistled less and only sang sometimes.

And in truth the prisoners deserved what they got.

They tried to avoid work, and when they couldn't avoid it they did it badly and lazily. Though they did it much less, they would still sometimes whistle or sing when he was about. They stole anything and everything—food, tools and money. If they could do a job badly they saw it as a triumph. They were skin and bones, and they'd just give up while they were working and die there on the railway. They'd die walking to work and they'd die walking back from work. They'd die sleeping, they'd die waiting for food. Sometimes they died when you beat them.

It made Choi Sang-min angry with the world and with them when they died. It made him angry because it wasn't his fault that there was no food or medicine. It wasn't his fault that there was malaria and cholera. It wasn't his fault that they were slaves. There was fate, and it was their fate and his fate to be there, it was their fate to die there and his fate to die here. He just had to provide whatever number of men the Japanese engineers needed each day, make sure they got to work and kept at the work the Japanese engineers wanted done. And he did his job. There was no food and no medicine and the line had to be built and the job had to be done and things ended up as they were always going to end up for them and for him. But he did these things, he did his job and their section of line got built. And Choi Sang-min was proud of that achievement, the only achievement he had ever known in his short life. He did these things, and these things felt good.

The moments when he completely lost his temper were the most euphoric to him. In his world of darkness and ignorance, he felt free—and more, he felt alive for the first time in his life. All his hate and his fear, his anger and his pride, his triumph and his glory, came together when he hurt others, or so it seemed to him now, and his life had for that short time meant something. And at such moments he escaped his hate.

Though the pressure was on from the engineers to get the railroad built, there was a pleasure and interest too in watching how the more he bashed them the less of men they became, how little they now whistled or sang, and how much more of a man he knew he was. For as long as he kept kicking and punching and beating, he was liberated. He had heard the stories of the IJA eating Australians and Americans in New Guinea, and he understood it was about something more than just starvation. And he knew none of this was a defence, and none of it would mean anything to the Australians, to their scalpel-eyed lawyers or candle-dripping judges. For when he was a guard, he lived like an animal, he behaved as an animal, he understood as an animal, he thought as an animal. And he understood that such an animal was the only human thing he had ever been allowed to be.

He was not ashamed at his discovery of his humanity in being an animal, only perplexed as to where it had led him. When his sentence of death by hanging was translated for him, he bore it like an animal, without understanding but with a dull awareness that he had had his freedom and now his end had come.

The judge's candle-wick eyes had looked down at him with flickering flames, and he had looked up with eyes he knew were dead already; and he had shaken his head back and forth and he had felt something large and terrible come down on him. He had wanted to ask about his fifty yen, but said nothing, and now he once more found himself pacing his cell, looking for a way he might escape. But there was none, and there never had been.

## 4

They died off quickly, strangely, in car smashes and suicides and creeping diseases. Too many of their children seemed born with problems and troubles, handicapped or backward or plain odd. Too many of their marriages faltered and staggered, and if they lasted it was sometimes more due to the codes and customs of the day than to their own capacity to make right all that was wrong; and what was wrong was too large for some of them. They went bush by themselves; they stayed in town with others and drank too much; they went a bit crazy like Bull Herbert, who lost his licence drunk and took to riding a horse into town when he wanted a drink, and he wanted a drink a lot after he made a suicide pact with his wife, shared poison with her and woke up to her dead and himself alive. They went silent or they talked too much, like Rooster MacNeice, run to fat and showing off his appendix scar and carrying on about the Japs bayoneting him. Like fuck they did, Rooster, said Gallipoli von Kessler, walking in on the performance one day in the Broadmeadows RSL.

Don't worry, Rooster MacNeice said. That's just Kes. He always was a commie but he's okay. It was a guard they called the Mountain Lion; I testified about the bastard after the war.

They drank though. They drank and they drank, and they couldn't get drunk no matter how much they drank. When they were demobbed the army quacks told them and their families not to talk about it, that talk was no good. It was hardly a hero's tale in the first place. It wasn't Kokoda or a Lancaster over the Ruhr Valley. It wasn't the *Tirpitz* or Colditz or Tobruk. What was it, then? It was being the slave of the yellow man. That's what Chum Fahey said when they met up at the Hope and Anchor.

Isn't exactly something to boast about, Sheephead Morton said.

Blokes were funny. Some disappeared. Ronnie Owen married an Italian woman, and she told Sheephead Morton's missus, Sally, that it was two years before she even knew he'd been a soldier. It was like that.

Bonox Baker said nothing for years, then one night took a shotgun to his oven, Jimmy Bigelow said. Shot the shit out of it. Looked like the back of a bloody cheese grater. Then he went quiet again. It was like that too.

Poor old Lizard Brancussi, Sheephead Morton said. And that story was too sad for anyone to repeat. He had carried the pencil sketch of his wife through the camps, on the hellship to Japan, held on to it when the Mitsubishi shipworks in Nagasaki, where he was slave labouring, vanished in the A-bomb and he somehow survived. He made it to safety in the hills, walking past the dead who filled the river like floating firewood, and the living fleeing with skin falling away in long ribbons like seaweed; he'd stumbled on past carbon sculptures of human beings walking, cycling, or running; past all those Japanese in agony in that roiling hell of blue fire and black rain, who, like the POWs he remembered, called for their mother as they were dying. And all the time he tried to see Maisie as Rabbit Hendricks had sketched her that morning in a Syrian village that smelt of human beings in trouble.

He tried to imagine her as the one thing in the world that was not this, and as long as she was there, he would not die or go mad, that as long as she was there, the world was good. On his way to Manila on a US aircraft carrier he had shown the postcard to the American sailors, who agreed he was a very lucky man. He finally got to Fremantle on a ship that was going through to Melbourne, and there he had telephoned home.

Dave and Maisie's phone, a man's voice answered. Dave speaking.

Lizard Brancussi had hung up. When his ship steamed out of Fremantle he was spotted slipping over the side on the first night and was never found.

Suddenly the beer was like fuel for a fire. They drank to make themselves feel as they should feel when they didn't drink, that way they had felt when they hadn't drunk before the war. For that night they felt ferocious and whole and not yet undone, and they would laugh at all that had happened. And when they laughed the war was nothing, and everybody dead was alive in them, and everything that had happened to them was just this vibrating jumping thing beating inside them so hard they needed another drink quickly to slow the feeling.

And that night Lizard Brancussi was alive in them, and little Wat Cooney was alive in them, and Yabby Burrows and Jack Rainbow and Tiny Middleton were alive in them, all the many dead, and Sheephead Morton said he even sometimes remembered fondly that dirty miserable bastard Rooster MacNeice who should have been dead. And Gallipoli von Kessler—who had turned up in an old pair of worsted trousers so frayed around the cuffs they looked as if he had bought them from a scarecrow—mentioned Darky Gardiner, and then Jimmy Bigelow started singing—

Every day in every way it's getting a little bit better.

They were standing around the pub fire at the Hope and Anchor that night, until the backs of their trousers got so hot they pushed them forward into another beer. It was forty-eight or maybe forty-seven. Whenever it was, it wasn't much of a night, and it felt good to be inside, warm. They hadn't all got together since being demobbed. Jimmy Bigelow wasn't saying much. The marriage he had come back to wasn't the marriage he had left. Or he had come back different.

I'm doing the best I can, he said at one point.

There were kids. He had four of them in the end and was called a family man. He wasn't. He was a man who had four kids. No one said anything much more about Darky Gardiner, except for Gallipoli von Kessler who said, Nikitaris's.

Yeah, said Sheephead Morton. Bloody Nikitaris's fish shop. Never shut up about it, did he?

## 5

Jimmy Bigelow said nothing. He was trying, that was the point, surely? But he didn't speak. His hopes of becoming a musician, somebody, something, hadn't worked out. He worked at the zinc works as a storeman. The big-band music he loved was no longer in fashion. The new music, the bebop and modern jazz, wasn't music to him. It was choppy noise pretending to make music out of traffic jams. You couldn't dance or fall in love with it, thought Jimmy. It wasn't Al Bowlly. It wasn't Benny Goodman or the Duke. It was the end of music. And the end of hope for someone like Jimmy Bigelow. The big bands were all folding, if not gone.

The things he believed in were heading out to sea, vanishing, lost forever. The things he thought he was coming home to. The things that he had hoped to become and make his life. It turned out that they weren't worth a brass razoo. He didn't fit with his own life anymore, his own life was breaking down, and all that did fit—his job, his family—seemed to be coming apart. He wanted to set things right with Dulcie, with his life, with bebop and swing, but it was over. He'd like to set things right, he thought, but it wasn't possible.

But that wasn't why they left the pub and headed up Elizabeth Street towards Nikitaris's fish shop. To make all the wrong right. They left because it was near midnight, way past closing, and they were drunk and thrown out and they had nothing better to do.

It was one of those Hobart spring nights, cold as charity, snow coming down hard on the mountain, the harbour a lather, sleet slapping and scratching at windows and tin roofs like a wild drunk who's been locked out.

They tramped up Elizabeth Street to Nikitaris's fish shop, following the frayed trousers of Gallipoli von Kessler as he strode out the front. You could have fired a mortar down the street and hit no one. The fish shop wasn't how they had imagined it in the camps, with people everywhere and steam and the smell of frying food and Darky's girlfriend sitting up there waiting for them to walk in and do what they had to do. No, it was nothing like that.

As closed as a nun's proverbial, Sheephead Morton said when they arrived.

Nikitaris's was shut—the doors were locked, the shop interior lifeless, the lights all off save for those that illuminated the long fish tank at the front of the shop. The fish swam round and round in the window. A couple of flatheads, a trumpeter, two silver trevally and a leatherjacket. Other than them staring in at an aquarium, the night-slicked street was empty.

Well, Sheephead Morton said. You can't say they look *exactly* unhappy.

Maybe in the camps we didn't either at any given moment, Jimmy Bigelow said.

They stood around, hands in pockets, shrugging shoulders for warmth, hopping leg to leg, as if waiting for a midnight train to arrive. Or leave.

Nothing as clueless as a mob of drunks, Gallipoli von Kessler said. Even chooks do something.

Jimmy Bigelow felt himself all appearance with nothing inside. He had trouble feeling. He wished to feel, but it was not something one could have by wishing for it. He picked up a rock and rolled it around in his palm. He looked up at the shop window. It was a big plate glass number, all beautifully painted with NIKITARIS'S FISH SHOP on it, very flash and fancy. He brought his hand back past his shoulder and, without warning, threw the rock as hard as he could at the window.

They heard the glass crack. Not all at once. But, like

time, a long fracture slowly opened with a sigh. Jimmy Bigelow was smiling as if someone had sliced his mouth at the corners.

Then they were all throwing rocks, the window broke apart and fell away, and they were in. Gallipoli von Kessler, with an orchardist's gift for improvisation, grabbed a chip fryer and used it to scoop the fish out. After a few mishaps they had all the fish in two mop buckets, and they walked back down to the docks, trying not to slop the water away.

There were some cray and couta boats rocking in the long swell that penetrated even this far into the harbour, and a cruel wind beyond the cove. Standing at the edge of Constitution Dock, Sheephead Morton put his head into a bucket and yelled:

You're fucking free!

And tipped the bucket.

The fish fell into the sound of water.

## 6

At the Hope and Anchor the next night, the story was told with gusto, albeit beset by a growing shame. Finally, Jimmy Bigelow said they had to go and see Nikitaris and fix him up for the window. It was still early and the shop lights were on. The window had already been replaced, though it was not yet painted.

Inside there were some old women working the fryers and a boy in the fishmonger's part of the shop, scrubbing the display stand. Sheephead Morton asked if Mr

Nikitaris might be about. The strap disappeared and returned from out the back with a small, old man, whose wizened body preserved intact the quiet resolution of the stonemason he had been as a young man. His hair was silver and his skin had the colour of a stain someone had tried to bleach out and failed. There was about his dark eyes a damp emptiness. He smelt of tobacco and aniseed.

Mr Nikitaris, said Jimmy Bigelow.

What you boys up to? the old man said. His accent was heavy. He sounded weary and annoyed. I've had a shocking day. What do you want?

Mr Nikitaris, said Jimmy Bigelow, we—

Just place your order with the lady over there.

We—

Mrs Pafitis there, he said, pointing with a knobbly finger. She'll fix you up.

We've come to say sorry, said Jimmy Bigelow.

We had a mate, began Sheephead Morton. And this time the old Greek said nothing. He was so stooped it was hard to see his eyes, which roamed the black and white tiled floor as Sheephead Morton told him their tale.

When it was done, Jimmy Bigelow said that they wished to pay old man Nikitaris for the broken window, for the fish and any other damage.

The old Greek was a time in replying. His eyes looked up and around, and as his head roamed, taking in each man in turn, it nodded slightly.

He was your cobber?

Like all immigrants, he seemed to have an unerring instinct for the oldest, truest words in his new language.

The way he said the word, it felt free of the treacherous weight of *mate.*

He was, said Sheephead Morton. *Our* cobber.

Sheephead Morton took out his wallet. How much do we owe you, Mr Nikitaris?

My name is Markos, he said. But call me Marco.

Mr Nikitaris. It was your window and we broke it.

He put out a shuddery old hand and shook it.

No, he said, put it away.

He asked if they were hungry and without waiting for an answer said they must eat as his guests.

Sit down and eat, said the old Greek. It's good to eat, boys.

The men looked at each other, uncertain about what to do.

You are my guests, he said, pulling out a seat and putting a hand on Jimmy Bigelow's shoulder. Please, he said. Sit down. You must eat.

And so the men sat down.

You like wine? I have some red wine you might like. I am not supposed to serve it so don't make a show of it, but have as much as you want, boys.

He went over to the fryers, filled a mesh strainer with chips, and then turned back.

Do you like flake or do you like couta? Some people prefer the shark, but trust me; the couta is bony, sure, but sweet. Very sweet. You must eat, he said. It's good to eat.

He brought the fish and chips to their table, then filled some small glass tumblers behind the counter with red wine and brought them out too. Then he sat with them. As they ate, he let them talk. When they flagged he talked of how such a winter meant it would be a good summer for apricots, yes. Then he started up about his own life, of the island of Lipsos he came from, the beautiful but harsh life there, of his dead wife, of how they, as young men, had a life before them. A rich life. A good life. Yes. How people told him coming to his fish shop made them happy. He hoped that was true.

I really do, he said. That's a life.

Do you have children? Jimmy Bigelow asked.

Three daughters, he replied. Good girls. Good families. And the boy. Good boy. Good—

And the old Greek stammered for a moment, something unintelligible, and his face seemed to wobble off its awkward axis. He brought a hand of knobbly fingers up to his face, like old pruned apricot branches shaking in an autumn gale. As if trying to prop his face back into a picture of certainty.

He was killed in New Guinea in 1943, he said. Bougainville.

The shop slowly emptied, the staff cleaned up, locked up and left, and outside the street died away to the very occasional car slashing a puddle. Inside, they just kept talking to the old Greek about many things until it was so late that not a pub was left open. But they didn't care. They sat on. They talked about fishing, food, winds and stonework; about growing tomatoes, keeping poultry and roasting lamb, catching crayfish and scallops; telling tales, jokes; the meaning of their stories nothing, the drift of them everything; the brittle and beautiful dream itself.

It was hard to explain how good that fried fish and chips and cheap red wine felt inside them. It tasted right. The old Greek made his own coffee for them—little cups, thick, black and sweet—and he gave them walnut pastries his daughter had made. Everything was strange and welcoming at the same time. The simple chairs felt easy, and the place, too, felt right, and the people felt good, and, for as long as that night lasted, thought Jimmy Bigelow, there was nowhere else in the world he wished to be.

# 7

Stepping down from the Douglas DC-3 at Sydney in the autumn of 1948, Dorrigo Evans was both horrified and impressed to see her waiting for him. The Japanese and the Germans may have surrendered in 1945, but Dorrigo Evans hadn't and wouldn't for some time. He valiantly tried to keep his war going, lapping up any opportunities for adversity and intrigue and brinkmanship and adventure that presented themselves. Inevitably, they presented less and less. Many years later he found it hard to admit that during the war, though a POW for three and a half years, he had in some fundamental way been free.

And so Dorrigo Evans had put off returning for as long as he could, but after nineteen months working around various army instrumentalities throughout south-east Asia—dealing with everything from repatriation to war graves to post-war reconstruction—he had run out of cover and faced either a conventional career in the army or the possibilities of civilian life. He had no sense of what these possibilities might be, but they suddenly seemed attractive, and the army no longer the wild jaunt it had been with its defeats and victories and the living—the living!—constantly tearing anything established into ribbons, melting everything solid into air. Wealth, fame, success, adulation—all that came later seemed only to compound the sense of meaninglessness he was to find in civilian life. He could never admit to himself that it was death that had given his life meaning.

Adversity brings out the best in us, the podgy War Graves Commission officer sitting next to him had said when the DC-3 had bounced around rather disturbingly as they circled down through a squall into Sydney. It's everyday living that does us in.

As he walked across the tarmac towards a small crowd of people he didn't know, he resolved to meet his new civilian life as he had met and overcome so many other obstacles over the seven years since they had last met—with charm and daring, and with the knowledge that time would soon wash over the follies of long ago, as it seemed to do, or so it seemed to him, with almost all things.

Forward, he whispered to himself, gathering his face into a smile that he understood was thought charming. Charge the windmill.

A conventionally pretty woman was waving a gloved hand in a conventional gesture that he knew was meant to convey a conventional glory chest of emotion: joy, ecstasy, relief—*love*, he supposed; fidelity vindicated, he feared. None of them meant much to him, for he was outside of it all. Though after the first few words he recognised her voice, the summer air seemed mild and empty and somehow disappointing after the steamy must of Asia, and even after they kissed he still couldn't remember her name. Her lips seemed dry and disappointing—like kissing dust—and finally, thankfully, it came to him.

Ella, he said.

Yes, he thought, that was it. It felt more than rusty.

Oh—Ella.

Oh, Ella, he said more softly, hoping some other words that made sense of that name and him and them might stumble onto his tongue if he just said her name enough. They didn't. Ella Lansbury just smiled.

Don't say anything, darling, she said. Just don't say anything bogus. I can't stand bogus men.

But I am, he said, completely bogus. That's all I am.

She was already smiling, that dull, all-knowing, knowing-nothing smile he was to find ever more unpleasant, those unexpectedly dry lips telling him that everything was arranged, that he was to worry about none of it. He recalled now that he had proposed to her in 1941 as a way of kissing her breasts. In as much as he could remember, it had been the final night of what would transpire to be his last leave with Ella before embarkation, and he could not stop thinking of Amy. To gain some relief from Ella's constant questioning him as to why he had not proposed, to escape from his incessant thoughts about Amy and the guilt he felt in consequence, he sought to find his way through the complex maze that led into Ella's cleavage and that demanded he put to her the ultimate riddle: Ella, will you marry me?

Hadn't she known what he was really thinking? Hadn't she?

There had been no oblivion in her breasts. Everything about Ella only reminded him ever more painfully of Amy. He had felt ashamed then, and worse now.

That's why I love you, Alwyn, she said.

Alwyn? For a moment he had no idea who she meant.

And then he remembered it was him. That too felt more than rusty.

Because you're anything but bogus.

And in the way she had then embraced him, in a smother that was inescapable, all the people he met in the next few days similarly and unquestioningly embraced the idea that they were to marry—that there could be no question that an engagement made hastily in the looming shadows of war seven years earlier and his imminent departure overseas was now to be rushed to a conclusion that did not bear any reflection or second thoughts. In the intervening years he had lived several lives, while her only life—or so it appeared to Dorrigo Evans—had been devoted to an idea of him that he scarcely recognised. Occasionally he felt something within him angry and defiant, but he was weary in a way he had never known, and it seemed far easier to allow his life to be arranged by a much broader general will than by his own individual, irrational and no doubt misplaced terrors. His mind, in any case, he felt was a prison camp of horrors. He did not wish to give it any more weight than was necessary. He recognised the many people around him who were excited by his impending marriage as far more sober and sane than he, and he gave himself up to their sobriety and their sanity—so at odds with his ever-stranger thoughts—in the hope that they might draw him to a new and better place. In that childish way that was also part of his nature, he was inevitably attracted to the excitement of anything new and unknown, particularly when it was frightening. And because nothing frightened him more than the prospect of marrying Ella Lansbury, that is what he did three weeks later, in an alcoholic haze and a new suit that she chose and he forever after felt looked as affected as their wedding at Saint Paul's Cathedral.

Even before they kissed, he once more forgot his name—he felt lost in her smell of powder—and then finally it came to him. Alwyn, yes, that was it—I, Alwyn, he said. He turned and looked at her, all made up and framed in lace and orange blossom, but he could see only the narrow face and that strange nose he had always found slightly repugnant and the high-arched, thin eyebrows, and he could find nothing attractive in her. Take you, Ella, he said more softly, and Ella Lansbury, soon to be Ella Evans, just smiled, lips slightly parting but saying nothing.

I am not Alwyn, he wished to say at the reception, and I am entirely bogus. But he instead lied and spoke of a love that had survived seven years of a separation, a mythical amount of time worthy of Ulysses and his men. And though the only classical hero he really resembled was the ram—much laughter—Ella truly was his Penelope, and he was glad to have finally arrived at his Ithaca—much applause.

For the rest of his life he would yield to circumstance and expectation, coming to call these strange weights duty. The guiltier he felt about his marriage, about his failure first as a husband and later as a father, the more desperately he tried to do only what was good in his public life. And what was good, what was duty, what was ever that most convenient escape that was conveniently inescapable, was what other people expected. What was bad and wicked was himself, he thought the first time he slept with someone other than his wife, her best friend,

Joan Newstead, a woman with mesmerising damp lips and a sly smile, a month after his honeymoon. It was at a shack in Sorrento in the mid-afternoon when everyone else had conveniently gone everywhere else.

*Yet all experience is an arch wherethro'*
*Gleams that untravell'd world . . .*

he whispered to her after, running a finger up and down the mosquito net before turning back to her, dropping his head and catching her dark nipple with the edge of his lower lip as he continued reciting Tennyson with soft breaths on her breast:

*. . . whose margin fades*
*For ever and for ever when I move.*

That evening there was a barbeque because the meat, left to hang in a Coolgardie safe, was beginning to spoil in the heat, and although meat rationing had only just ended, they still felt bad that good meat might be wasted. Perhaps he drank too much, perhaps he didn't drink enough, he thought after, but his head spun, his stomach was full of nails. He felt bloated and taut with something large and wrong and hidden that came between him and Ella, Ella from whom he henceforth wanted to have nothing hidden, while Joan Newstead was now jealous of the attention Dorrigo was paying to her best friend, his wife. What was he doing? he wondered. Did he hope to be found out?

The porterhouse steak was grilled over a ferociously

hot bed of redgum coals, but when he cut into it the meat was still not right and for a moment he was back there, heading across the camp towards the second part of his daily rounds on that day in the middle of the monsoon and the Speedo. As he came close to the ulcer hut, Dorrigo was enveloped by the stench of rotting flesh. And he remembered how the stink of foul meat was so bad that Jimmy Bigelow would on occasion have to go outside to vomit.

## 8

After being convicted, Choi Sang-min was transferred to Changi's P Hall in which all the condemned men lived together as equals, Japanese and Koreans and Formosans. He was given a dirt-brown uniform marked with the English letters 'CD'. The letters, he was told, signified that he was convicted to die. Choi Sang-min noticed that every CD there desperately tried to fill in his days with some sort of activity, and every man seemed to be neither depressed nor overly concerned by what the future might hold. And he himself felt something lift from him, as surely as something else was slowly enshrouding him, as though some lifelong feeling of fear and inferiority had evaporated. None of those things any longer meant anything. And that was because it was now his turn to be killed.

Each morning they were turned out of their cells, made to wash, and began another day of occupied nothingness. They sat shirtless in the baking gallery at the centre of the cells, playing *go* or *shogi* or rereading one of the few books or magazines available, or just sitting alone. Every few weeks an Indian captain, with silver spectacles behind which his glistening tadpole eyes swam slowly back and forth, would arrive with a notice of execution. The prisoners would wait silently, frozen with dread, wondering who was to die, every man intensely relieved when it was not himself but the man next to him.

On the third such visit, Choi Sang-min realised he was going to die, but not because his own feelings told him so, for at that moment his feelings seemed not to exist. Nor did he know it from the piece of paper he was handed. He held that piece of paper, but he could not connect himself and his life with what he was told that piece of paper said.

He looked up and around P Hall. It was paper—nothing—and he was a man. A man, Choi Sang-min reasoned, was something. A man, Choi Sang-min wished to say, was full of so many things, so many changes. A man, good or bad, was magnificent. It was not possible that this thing that was nothing and would never change could mean the end of everything that moved and changed within him—the good, the bad, the magnificent.

Yet it did.

And it was from the terrible relief the other men showed, relief that he felt like a burning flame, that he finally understood he was to be executed the following morning.

For the four men who were to die, a Japanese meal and cigarettes were provided. A Buddhist monk attended. Choi Sang-min, who had never thought much about religion, remembered that his father, about whom he had also never thought much, had once said he was Chongdoist, and so the presence of the Buddhist monk made him angry.

Choi Sang-min looked down at his rice, miso soup and tempura. He longed for his mother's spicy kimchi and hated the bland Japanese food. But hate and anger were no good to him now. He could not eat his last meal. If he ate his last meal, it would be his last meal. If he did not eat his last meal, he could not die until he had. Perhaps there would be other meals until he agreed which one would be his last. But he did not agree with this last meal. A last meal was an agreement with the inevitability of his death. And he did not agree with his death.

He smoked his cigarettes and said nothing as the other condemned men talked of loved ones. He did not agree with their talk, with a piece of paper against which his life seemed a cosmic force.

He said nothing after the meal as the guards carried the scales in, placed them down and gestured for him to mount them. They weighed Choi Sang-min. They measured his height. He knew why because the others had told him. How they knew was a mystery. They told him as if their knowledge of the gallows had come to them with their mother's milk.

The hangman, they said, would set his hemp rope at the right length for a man of his height and weight in order to get the correct drop and maximum force to snap his neck as he fell. Then he would fill a sandbag to the same weight as Choi Sang-min and tie it to his hemp rope and leave it dangling overnight in order to stretch it, so that when tomorrow Choi Sang-min fell through the trapdoor there would be no bounce in the rope. With no bounce, his neck ought to snap immediately.

He remembered a Japanese officer who had shown remarkable poise the night before he was executed. When the guards came to weigh him, he told them in broken English that he was dying for Japan, that he was not ashamed of having made the POWs work hard for the Emperor, and that as a military man, he understood he was to die simply because his country had been defeated.

Choi Sang-min longed for such clarity and certainty. The Japanese had it—at least, he had always felt that the Japanese had it. And now he could see what he had sensed as he had tried to smash it out of the POWs with his fists and boots—that the Australians had it too. Everyone had it; everyone in the world had it. Except perhaps him.

The gallows were behind the gallery in which Choi Sang-min and the three other men now sat waiting for their last ever lock-up. On the days of executions the CDs yet to have their date of execution confirmed waited inside this hall in silence, able to hear the condemned's steps up the scaffold and his final words. The Japanese officer had shouted, Long live the Emperor! The trapdoor had slapped open and a dull thud followed almost immediately.

But what good was such an attitude for him, a Korean? thought Choi Sang-min. He had not done anything for his country and his country had done nothing for him. He had no particular beliefs. He thought of his parents, imagined their anguish on hearing of his death, and he realised he could offer them not one good reason as to why he died, other than fifty yen a month.

As they waited in this anteroom of death, a condemned guard called Kenji Mogami sang songs. They had briefly worked together in the same POW camp. They called him the Mountain Lion, but he, who had never hurt anyone, was also to die. Choi Sang-min remembered an Australian singing and how he had stopped him singing, but about Kenji Mogami's singing he could do nothing. A Japanese officer waltzed alone. Then they were taken to their cells.

He was unable to sleep. He felt almost painfully alive and awake and now wanted to taste and know every second of his life. To stop his mind wildly pitching between panic at not being able to escape and anger at not getting his fifty yen he tried to remember how some of the others had met their executions.

Hurrah for the Great Korean country! cried out one Korean as he walked the fateful thirteen steps.

What great Korean country? wondered Choi Sang-min. What about my fifty yen? I am not Korean, he thought to himself. I am not Japanese. I am a man of a colony. Where's my fifty yen? he wanted to know. Where?

His father, a peasant, had wanted him to have an education, but times had been hard and after three years at elementary school learning some Japanese myths and history, he left to work for a Korean family as a servant. They gave him his board, two yen a month and regular beatings. He was eight years old. At twelve he went to work for a Japanese family, who gave him board, six yen a month and an occasional thrashing. At the age of fifteen he heard the Japanese were hiring guards to work in prisoner-of-war camps elsewhere in the empire. The pay was fifty yen a month. His thirteen-year-old sister had signed up with the Japanese to go to Manchukuo to work as a comfort woman for similar pay. She told him she would be helping soldiers in hospitals and, like him, was very excited. As she could neither read nor write, he had never heard from her again, and now that he knew what comfort women did, he tried not to think about her, and when he did, he hoped for her sake that she was dead.

Though he had many names—his Korean name, Choi Sang-min; the Japanese name he had been given and made to answer to in Pusan, Akira Sanya; his Australian name that the guards now called him, the Goanna—he realised he had no idea who he was. Some of the other condemned had strong ideas about Korea and Japan, the war, history, religion, justice. Choi Sang-min realised he had no ideas about anything. But the ideas the others had seemed no better to him than having no idea. Because they were not their ideas, but the ideas of slogans, wireless broadcasts, speeches, army manuals, the same ideas they had absorbed with the same endless beatings they too had endured in their Japanese military training. In Pusan they had slapped him because his voice was too low or his posture wrong, they had slapped him for being too Korean, they had slapped him to show how to slap others—as hard as he could. Choi Sang-min hated it. He wanted to run away, back to his home. But he knew that if he did he would be punished, and, worse, his family would be punished. They slapped him, they said, so he would be a strong Japanese soldier, but he knew that he would never be a Japanese soldier. He would be a prison guard, guarding men who were less than men—those who had chosen surrender before death.

Sitting on death row, Choi Sang-min desperately wanted to have an idea of his own. He hoped that long night that an idea would finally come to him, open him up, an idea that would allow him to understand and at the same time to know peace. He hoped to be like the Japanese officer who believed in the Emperor, or the Korean guard who believed in Korea. Perhaps he should have asked for more than fifty yen. But no idea came, and far too quickly morning did.

As the cell began lightening, he wanted calm, he needed that feeling he had first known as a child working for the Japanese family. The Japanese father was an engineer who had trained in Scotland. He wore tweeds and, like the British, had a pet dog that used to eat far better than Choi Sang-min, being fed all the choice bits from the Japanese family's table. The family loved the dog, and one of Choi Sang-min's daily tasks was to walk it. The dog had large eyes and a head that jerked when it looked at Choi Sang-min, waiting for him to throw another stick. One day the dog went with Choi Sang-min on an errand to the market. Choi Sang-min took a short cut through some back streets and stubbed his toe on an old brick that lay in his way. He picked it up in a fury, and the dog gave him its look of complete trust and affection, jerked its head side to side, and waited for Choi Sang-min to throw the brick as if it were a ball or stick. And Choi Sang-min brought the brick down hard on the dog's head, again and again, until his hands were dark and sticky with its blood and gristle.

He had sold the dog's body to a butcher for ten yen and then walked back to his Japanese family. The air smelt sweet, a soft wind felt cool and good on his face, every person he passed seemed to be smiling and friendly, and he felt an enormous sense of tranquillity and fulfilment.

How he longed for that feeling again, to again know that exhilarating moment of strange power and freedom that had come with the killing of another living thing. But there was nothing in his cell that he could kill to recover that feeling, and it was others who would soon take pleasure in his death, as he once had in his killing of the Japanese engineer's dog. As his cell lit up ever more brightly—as he could see clearly first his hands and next his thighs and then his feet—he felt a sudden terror gather inside his stomach. For Choi Sang-min knew he would never again see himself in the morning light.

He fought the guards when they came to take him to the gallows. He had seen a cockroach and wanted to kill it. There wasn't time. After they had strapped his wrists together behind his back, a doctor was called for, and through a translator Choi Sang-min was asked if he wished for drugs to calm him. Choi Sang-min screamed. He could still see the cockroach. He was given four phenobarbital tablets to steady his nerves, but his body was too excited and he vomited the pills straight back. Before the doctor gave him an injection of morphine, he managed to crush the cockroach beneath his boot heel. Feeling nauseous and slightly dizzy, he walked the short distance out of P Hall and across to the gallows with a soldier supporting him on either side. Everything was happening very quickly now. He saw two sandbags leaning up against a wall as they entered the courtyard. There were perhaps a dozen men, perhaps more, six on the scaffold, most below. They walked him up a ramp covered in straw matting to the top of the scaffold. He was struck by how the rope was far thicker than he had expected. It reminded him of a ship's hawser. He sensed a joyous brutality about the large, powerful knot. I understand, he wished to say to the rope. You long for me. His thinking was calm, even vaguely pleasant, but his face was twitching. So many people and no one was talking and his face would not stop twitching. To his side, perhaps five metres away, a second trapdoor lay open, spent, and rising out of it a taut rope. He realised at its end, out of sight, dangled Kenji Mogami.

He was asked if he wished to say anything. He looked up. A bell somewhere tolled some hour. He wanted to say he had an idea. Someone laughed quietly. He looked down at the soldiers and pressmen. He had no idea. He had been paid fifty yen, and fifty yen was not even a good deal, far less an idea. Fifty yen was nothing. On the trapdoor in front of him he saw chalk lines marking what he knew were the correct places for his feet. Fifty yen! he wanted to say. The soldiers continued to hold his arms. He could see the chalk dust as if they were white boulders. He bowed his head and a hood was dropped over it. He closed his eyes, then opened them. After months that had passed by interminably slowly, everything was now happening too fast. He could feel the canvas, and its blackness seemed somehow more frightening than the night of his own eyes, so he closed them again. The morning was already hot. It was stuffy in the hood. He felt the noose dropping over his head, and at the same time he realised his ankles were being bound together. He went to ask them to slow down, to wait, but with a hard, decisive shove he felt the noose tighten hard around his neck and the only sound he made was an involuntary gasp. He was finding it hard to breathe. His face was jumping wildly. He could not even spit on them, as he hoped Kim Lee had done when they killed him. The soldiers holding either arm frogmarched him two steps forward, and he knew he was now standing on the chalk lines on the trapdoor. His last thought was that he needed to scratch his nose as he felt the floor beneath him suddenly vanish and heard the crashing noise of the trapdoor slamming down. Stop! he went to yell. What about my fifty—

## 9

The years passed. He met a nurse called Ikuko Kawabata, a young woman whose parents had been killed in the firebombing of Kobe in the final months of the war. After the peace her brother had died of starvation. That city, too, was a wasteland of rubble and ruins, and Ikuko's story was so commonplace that she, like so many others, found it better not to talk about it.

Ikuko had lustrous skin and a large birthmark on her right cheek, both of which inexplicably moved Nakamura more than he wished to admit. She also had a lazy smile, which he found both erotic and irritating. She would seek to end any disagreement between them with it, something that was at once agreeable to him but also suggested, he sometimes felt, stupidity and weakness of character.

Through Ikuko, Nakamura found work in a hospital, first as an orderly and then as a storeroom clerk. He was glad to leave behind his black-market work, as it was neither overly lucrative nor particularly safe, and he worried at all times about being exposed and handed over to the Americans. Even in his new work he avoided others—but then there were many doing the same, and it seemed to Nakamura that everyone seemed to understand why so many wanted no one to either know or understand them. He moved in with Ikuko, as much to preserve his solitude as for any wish for human company. She was healthy and a good housekeeper, and he was grateful to have found a woman with such virtues.

In spite of his solitary ways, he grew into the habit of playing *go* with a doctor at the hospital by the name of Kameya Sato, and over several years the habit grew into a trust, and the trust in turn grew into a quiet friendship. Sato, who came from Oita, was devoted to his patients and was a quiet and humble man, and unlike other doctors had the eccentric habit of never wearing a white jacket. Sato was a far better *go* player than Nakamura, and one evening the ex-soldier asked the surgeon what the secret of playing *go* well was.

It's like this, Mr Kimura, said Sato. There is a pattern and structure to all things. Only we can't see it. Our job is to discover that pattern and structure and work within it, as part of it.

It was evident to Sato that his answer didn't make much sense to the old soldier. And so, pushing two fingers gently into one side of Nakamura's belly, he continued.

If I am to remove an appendix, I will proceed in here, separate the muscles according to the pattern and structure that I was taught at Kyushu, and there be able to remove the inflamed appendix with the least danger and stress for the patient.

This led them to talking about Kyushu, one of Japan's great universities for training doctors. Nakamura remembered reading a story in a newspaper about some doctors who were tried and jailed for what the Americans claimed was the vivisection of live American airmen, without the use of anaesthetics. The reports and convictions had angered Nakamura at the time, and he now brought the subject up with some fury, concluding vehemently—

American lies!

Sato looked up from the *go* table, then back, placing a black stone down.

I was there, Mr Kimura, said Sato.

Nakamura stared at Sato, till the humble surgeon raised his eyes and stared back with strange intensity.

I was an intern there near the war's end, under Professor Fukujori Ishiyama. One day I was asked to fetch a US airman from a ward where he was under guard. He was so tall, with a very narrow nose and red curly hair. He had a wound from where he had been shot by a soldier who had helped capture him, but he trusted me. I showed him the gurney and he got himself on it. I had been told to take him not to the operating theatre but to a dissection room in the anatomy department.

Nakamura was intrigued.

And there?

And there he trusted me again. I pointed to the dissection table. The room was crowded with several doctors, nurses and other interns, as well as some army officers. Professor Ishiyama hadn't yet arrived. The American actually stood up and then laid himself down on the dissection table. And winked at me. You know how the Americans wink. Winked and smiled. As if I was in on a joke with him.

And then, said Nakamura, he was anaesthetised, and Professor Ishiyama operated on his wound.

Sato held another *go* stone in the palm of his hand, rubbing his thumb back and forth over its polished, lens-shaped sphere, as if massaging a blind black eye.

No, said Sato. Two orderlies bound his limbs, torso and head to the table with leather belts. Professor Ishiyama arrived while this was going on and began addressing the others. He spoke of how the dissection of subjects before death helped obtain important scientific data that would help our soldiers in the great battles to come. Such work was not easy, but all great scientific achievement required sacrifice and commitment. In this way, as doctors and scientists, they were able to prove themselves worthy servants of the Emperor.

Nakamura looked at the *go* board but his thoughts were no longer with the game.

I remember feeling proud to be there, said Sato.

All that Sato was saying made perfect sense to Nakamura—after all, the same argument, formulated differently for different circumstances, had determined his entire adult life, and though he did not think this, the familiar patterns and rhythms of Sato's story reassured Nakamura that Professor Ishiyama, even if he didn't use anaesthetic, was acting correctly and ethically.

And still the American didn't struggle, continued Sato. He couldn't dream of what was about to happen to him. Before Professor Ishiyama began we all bowed towards the patient, as though it were a normal operation. Maybe that reassured him. Professor Ishiyama first cut into his abdomen and cut away part of his liver, then sewed the wound up. Next he removed the gall bladder and a section of his stomach. The American, who looked an intelligent and vital young man at the beginning, now looked old and weak. His mouth was gagged but he was quickly beyond any screaming. Finally, Professor Ishiyama removed his heart. It was still beating. When he put it on the scales the weights trembled.

Sato's story ran over Nakamura like a rising river over a boulder outcrop. It trickled around him, then it flushed over him, and finally it covered him. But nothing in him moved. And while it meant that all that the Americans said was true, and that he, Nakamura, had been wrong, the reasons for which it had been done made such complete sense to Nakamura that he felt there was nothing remarkable about this story of a man being cut up while alive and fully conscious.

It felt strange, but at first I didn't think so much about it, continued Sato. It was war, after all. And then over the next few days there were other operations on other airmen—opening up the mediastinum of one, severing the facial nerve roots on another. At the last I attended they made four holes in the serviceman's skull, then inserted a knife into the brain to see what would happen.

They were playing *go* in a small garden that had been made for the staff. It was spring, and when Sato halted, Nakamura could hear early evening birdsong. There was a maple tree that turned the last long rays of sunlight into shimmering threads of dark and light.

After the war Professor Ishiyama hanged himself in prison, Sato said. They got some others, sentenced them to death, then commuted their sentences and finally let them all go free. I thought for a time I might be tried too, but now that time is long past. The Americans want it forgotten, and so do we.

Sato pushed the paper he had been reading across to Nakamura.

Look at this, he said.

He pointed to a small article accompanying a photo. It was about the charitable work of Mr Ryoichi Naito, the founder of the Japan Blood Bank, a successful company that bought and sold blood.

I have colleagues who worked with Mr Naito in Manchukuo. Mr Naito was one of the leaders of our very best scientists in similar work there. Vivisection. And many other things. Testing biological weapons on prisoners. Anthrax. Bubonic plague, too, I am told. Testing flamethrowers and grenades on prisoners. It was a large operation with support at the highest levels. Today Mr Naito is a well-respected figure. And why? Because neither our government nor the Americans want to dig up the past. The Americans are interested in our biological warfare work; it helps them prepare for war against the Soviets. We tested these weapons on the Chinese; they want to use them on the Koreans. I mean, you got hanged if you were unlucky or unimportant. Or Korean. But the Americans want to do business now.

We, too, are victims of the war, said Nakamura.

Sato said nothing. Nakamura felt in the deepest part of his being that he, like the Japanese people, was an honourable, good man falsely accused. A victim, yes—him, Ikuko, his executed comrades, Japan itself. This sentiment explained to him all that had befallen him, even lent a certain grandeur to his miserable life of secrets and evasions, of false identities and growing distance from other people. But he felt excited by Sato's story. A distant prospect of some divine liberation seemed to exist within it.

You know that strange sound near an earthquake's end? Sato asked. In the dying light his weary face was growing dim. After the shaking and wild swaying is done, Sato went on, and all things—hung paintings, mirrors, windows in their frames, keys on hooks—all things shudder and make this strange sound? And outside, everything you know may have vanished forever?

Of course, Nakamura said.

As if the world is making this shimmering sound?

Yes, Nakamura said.

When the stainless-steel pan of the dissection room scales was being rattled by the American's heart, that's what it was like. As if the world was trembling.

Sato pulled his face into a strange smile.

You know why he trusted me?

Professor Ishiyama?

No, the American airman.

No.

Because he thought my white coat meant I would help him.

## 10

Nakamura and Sato never spoke of Sato's past again. But something in his story began to trouble Nakamura. Over the following months their games of *go* grew less frequent. Nakamura now found the surgeon—who had formerly seemed to him such an interesting and genial companion—somehow dull and tedious, and the games became a burden to be endured rather than a pleasure to be enjoyed. And he sensed the feeling was, in some strange, inexplicable way, becoming mutual. Sato stopped turning up in the storeroom office to have a smoke with Nakamura, and Nakamura found himself avoiding those parts of the hospital where Sato might be found. Finally, they stopped playing *go* altogether.

As he grew distant with Sato, Nakamura drew closer to other people, found the strength within himself to somehow be more truthful as a human being. He came to understand that there were many men like him—proud, good men who had done their duty and were determined not to be ashamed—who also saw themselves as victims of the war. And he realised that the period of no one being who they said they were and no one being what they seemed and everyone remembering only the things that could be spoken about had now ended. As the last of the remaining imprisoned war criminals were released, Nakamura gave up any pretence of subterfuge, and, resolving that it was best to live a life of honour by acknowledging the truth, he reverted to his real name. The following year he married Ikuko.

They had two daughters, healthy children who, as they grew up, came to deeply love their gentle father. At the age of six, their younger daughter, Fuyuko, nearly died after being hit by a school bus. Fuyuko's overriding memory of that time was of her father by her bedside day and night, head bowed. He almost seemed to his daughters to be of another world, misbuttoning shirts, forgetting to wear a belt, and concerned not to hurt spiders, which he would catch and take outside, or mosquitoes, which he would refuse to swat.

He alone sensed the strangeness at the heart of his transformation into his idea of a good man. Was it hypocrisy? Was it atonement? Guilt? Shame? Was it deliberate or unconscious? Was it a lie or was it the truth? He had, after all, overseen many deaths—perhaps, he sometimes felt, with an almost savage pride that he found undeniable and not in the least contradictory, he had even been party to some deaths. But he felt no responsibility, and time eroded his memory of his crimes and allowed his memory instead to nurture stories of goodness and extenuating circumstance. As the years passed, he found he was haunted only by the way he was haunted by so little of it.

More out of curiosity than optimism, Nakamura applied for a position with the Japan Blood Bank in the spring of 1959. To his surprise, he got an interview. He took the train to Osaka early on a winter morning. At the Japan Blood Bank's headquarters he was made to wait till almost lunchtime, when he was finally ushered not into a meeting room as he had expected, but a large executive's office. He was seated and again told to wait. There was no one there. After a quarter of an hour, the door behind him opened and a voice told him not to turn around and look but to stay seated. He felt fingers trace a crescent across the back of his neck. And then, behind him, a man's voice began reciting:

*Across the sea, corpses in the water,*
*Across the mountains, corpses upon the grass . . .*

Of course, Nakamura knew *Umi Yukaba*, the ancient poem that had become so popular during the war that every radio announcement of a battle—in which it was invariably announced that Japanese soldiers had met with honourable deaths rather than the dishonour of surrender—began with it. Nakamura recited the last two lines as if they were a password:

*We die by the side of our Emperor,*
*We never look back.*

He felt the hand on his neck once more.

Such a good neck, a great neck, said the man behind him.

Nakamura turned and looked up. The hair had grown white and spiky, the body burlier, but the face, albeit sagging a little more and now smiling, remained a shark fin.

I had to see your neck. I just had to be sure you were the man I thought you were. You see, I never forget.

When he caught Nakamura's querying look, Kota explained.

Some old Manchukuo comrades felt I might do some good work here.

The rest of Nakamura's interview was perfunctory, as though everything was long ago settled. As he went to leave, Kota congratulated him on his new position. On returning home that evening, Nakamura almost sobbed when he told Ikuko what had happened.

What, he asked Ikuko, can prepare you for such kindness?

★ ★ ★

Many decades later, a young Japanese nationalist journalist, Taro Ootomo, who wished to rectify the many misunderstandings that had grown about Japan's role in the Greater East Asia War, went to interview the distinguished soldier, Shiro Kota, who was now one hundred and five. He had read some articles Kota had published in some Zen magazines in the late 1950s that spoke of the deep spiritual basis of Japanese *bushido*. Kota had argued that it was the way the Japanese—inspired by Zen—had been able to recognise that there was ultimately no distinction between life and death that had rendered them such a formidable military power, in spite of their material shortcomings. But when Taro Ootomo went with ward officials and a local TV crew to congratulate Kota on his one hundred and fifth birthday, there was no one home.

Taro Ootomo was young and keen, and he persisted, going to the length of visiting Kota's elderly daughter, Ryoko, to reassure her of his good intentions, hoping through her some entree to the old veteran. But Ryoko discouraged Taro Ootomo, saying her father was not up to talking to strangers, particularly about the war and his service, which was so easily misrepresented. He was attempting in his great old age to become a living Buddha, she told Taro Ootomo.

It was clear to Ootomo that Ryoko had little interest in her father. Deciding it was best to ignore her, he began to organise a celebration of Kota's one hundred and fifth birthday with some nationalist friends. It would be respectful and dignified, and would seek to honour war veterans as well as to publicise the misunderstood spiritual basis of Japan's twentieth-century wars. But each time Ootomo went to visit Kota, no one seemed to be at home.

Something in Ryoko's manner and Kota's strange refusal to answer his door began to disturb Taro Ootomo, and he said as much while drinking with his old schoolfriend and now police lieutenant Takeshi Hashimoto one night.

Hashimoto smelled a rat. With some difficulty, he managed to check welfare records and noticed that Ryoko had power of attorney over her father's affairs. Two months earlier, two million yen had been withdrawn from Kota's account. Hashimoto obtained permission for a search of Kota's apartment. It was in a formerly favoured part of the city, but the block of units, once fashionable, had in recent years fallen into disrepair. There were roughly assembled wire cages bolted on the exterior walls above the first floor to catch falling render. As the lift doors refused to open, Hashimoto and his three men had to climb the stairs to the seventh floor.

In an apartment lined with bookshelves of poetry, Hashimoto found the mummified body of an ancient man lying in bed. There was no smell. He had been dead for years, perhaps, thought Hashimoto, decades. Reaching down with his left hand, Takeshi Hashimoto very slowly lifted the flowery bedspread. The fluids of the slowly decomposing body had left a thick, dark stain on the sheets. At the centre of this halo, skin stretched like parchment over his bones, lay Shiro Kota.

On the bedside table by the living Buddha, now dead, was an old copy of Basho's great travel journal *The Narrow Road to the Deep North*. Hashimoto opened it to a page marked with a dry blade of grass.

Days and months are travellers of eternity, he read. So too the years that pass by.

# 11

As his commanding officer, it ought to have been John Menadue's job, but John Menadue had no heart for it; he had never had a heart for anything, not up on the Line, not back in Australia. Dorrigo Evans had received a letter from Bonox Baker telling him that he had heard no one had been to see Jack Rainbow's widow, that John Menadue had his medals to give her but just never seemed to get round to it. And so, some months after he had returned from his honeymoon and as it became clear to him that his marriage was what it was, and that what it was wasn't anything worth wanting, Dorrigo Evans took an ANA flight to Hobart. He found John Menadue in a pub two doors down from Nikitaris's fish shop.

Up in the jungle John Menadue had found he was no leader at all. Some people, like the Big Fella, it came to, thought John Menadue. But not him, which was strange—because John Menadue had been told by his father that he was a leader, and that leadership had nothing to do with anything other than character. At the Hutchins School he was told that he was a leader because only leaders were admitted into the Hutchins School. Leadership, he was told, was his natural destiny because it was the natural destiny of all people born leaders, who were all the boys at Hutchins. And so the world went on telling him, and so John Menadue—because of his schooling and his connections, because of his undeniable character and his irrevocable destiny—went straight into officer school. John Menadue had believed it all to be true and self-evident and himself a leader until he had arrived on the Line. Then he came to see that his primary interest was not in helping others but in saving his own life, and that his father had been right about character but wrong about his son.

John Menadue understood authority. And that day as he sat in the pub two doors down from Nikitaris's fish shop with a pound of couta fillets and his good looks intact, his life intact, John Menadue knew he had none. He wondered what it was that allowed it to exist in such a man as Dorrigo Evans—a despicable womaniser close to ugly, a loner who hid in crowds, a man oblivious to any sort of authority except that which he commanded by some insulting grace of God—who made the favour he was doing John Menadue look like a trivial act of no great consequence.

I'm sorry, John Menadue said to Dorrigo Evans. I went to see Mrs Les Whittle. I couldn't do it again after that. Do you remember Les?

I do. He was a rather marvellous Robert Taylor in *Waterloo Bridge*. It was opposite Jack Rainbow, of all people, wasn't it?

I don't remember. You heard about his death?

No.

He ended up in a camp in Japan. Slave labourer in a coal mine under the Inland Sea for the Japs. They were starving. When the war ended the Yanks parachuted supplies into the POW camps there. US Liberators dropping forty-four-gallon steel drums chockers with food. They're fluttering down—gentle as dandelions in summer, one bloke said. Blokes everywhere, excited. Then the forty-fours start landing, crashing through roofs, smashing up whatever they fell on. And a forty-four full of Hershey bars landed on Les. Crushed him to death.

He passed over a shoebox to Dorrigo Evans in which a few ribbons and medals rolled around. On the lid was sticky-taped the name and address of Mrs Jack Rainbow.

What sort of death is that? John Menadue said, his gaze fixed on the shoebox. A starving man killed by food? By our side? By Hershey bars. For God's sake, Dorrigo, bloody Hershey bars. What do you say?

What did you say?

The right things. Lies. She was a very dignified woman. Small, chunky thing. But dignified. And she listened to me lie. And for a long time she didn't say anything. Then she said, I never really knew him, you know. That's the sadness of it. I would have liked to have known him.

Mrs Jack Rainbow lived near Neika, a few miles beyond the small village that sat in forest halfway up the mountain above Hobart. Overhearing Dorrigo Evans asking for directions, the barman introduced him to a small man who drove the Cascade brewery truck and was heading that way with a delivery. He could drop Dorrigo off and pick him up on his return home, two hours later.

A little out of Hobart, it began to snow. The truck had one shuddering windscreen wiper that cleared a small cone into a winter world where eucalypts and great man ferns heavy with fresh fallen snow leant over the road. The rest disappeared into white, and Dorrigo Evans found his thoughts following. He held a hand out and pushed his fingers into the air, trying to see if there was some other way he had not known of stopping that femoral artery emptying. His fingers pushed and shoved emptiness, coldness, whiteness, nothing.

Nippy, eh? said the brewery driver, noticing him moving his fingers. That's why I have these, he said, lifting a wool-gloved hand from the steering wheel. Bloody well die of frigging frostbite otherwise. Scott of the bloody Antarctic, that's me, mate.

They made their way up the mountain, through Fern Tree and past Neika. As they came down on the range's far side, the brewery driver dropped Dorrigo Evans off at a farm entrance composed of two green lichen-bearded posts and a broken gate, which lay on the side of a snow-covered path. The farm looked dilapidated, and the whiteness and the intense hush that went with the snow made the place feel abandoned. Fences and hop frames were leaning, and in places fallen down. The sheds seemed weary; a little vertical-board oast house sagged.

He found her in a small concrete dairy shed, churning butter. She wore a cotton skirt decorated with swirling red hibiscuses and an old home-knitted woollen jumper that was unravelling at one elbow. Her bare legs were unshaved and bruised. Her face seemed to him only to hold broken hope, the line of her mouth a wobble that fell away at each end into thin lines.

He gave his name and his regiment number, and before he could say anything more she took him through her kitchen, which was warm from a fuel range crackling at its centre, into her parlour, which was cold and dark. She called him *sir*. When he said that wasn't at all necessary, she called him Mr Evans. He sat in an overstuffed armchair that felt damp.

Across the hall and through an open doorway he could see beaded wainscoting painted bright cream enamel rising to the ceiling, and in front an iron bed. He hoped she had known some happiness in it with Jack. He imagined them together on such a winter night as would come in a few short hours, and them together warm, perhaps watching a bedroom fire dying into embers, Jack puffing on his Pall Malls.

## 12

We have five children, she said. Two boys, three girls. Little Gwennie, she's the dead spit of her father. The youngest, Terry, was born after Jack left and has never seen his dad.

There was a long silence. Dorrigo Evans had learnt in his surgery to wait for people to say what they really wished to say.

I couldn't bear to be alone, she said finally. I have a terrible fear of being lonely. When he was away at the war I slept with all the kids. She smiled at the memory. Bloody six of us in the bed. Ridiculous, eh?

A kettle whistled and she disappeared to the kitchen. He regretted letting her take his army greatcoat. She returned with tea in a chipped green enamel pot and the remnants of a large cream cake.

It's very quiet, she said, on account of the snow falling. Like a great big blanket. That's why I like the kids round. But the little ones are at Jack's sister's today and the big kids are at school. She paused. Jack loves the snow but, Lord, I feel it sometimes.

She offered him some cake and he declined. She put the cake plate down on a side table, swept the crumbs at its edge inwards with her index finger for a few moments, then, without looking up, said—

Do you believe in love, Mr Evans?

It was an unexpected question. He understood he did not need to answer.

Because I think you make it. You don't get it given to you. You make it.

She halted, waiting perhaps for a comment or judgement, but when Dorrigo Evans made neither she seemed emboldened and went on.

That's what I think, Mr Evans.

Dorrigo. Please.

Dorrigo. That really is what I think, Dorrigo. And I thought Jack and me, we were going to make it.

She sat down and asked if he minded if she lit up. She never did when Jack was about and puffing like a steam train, she said, but now, well, it was sort of him and it sort of helped—him not being here and that.

Pall Malls, eh? she said, taking a cigarette out of the bright-red pack. Not Woodbines for Jack. Something a little posh to make up for all that cursing. He always was quarterflash, Jack. Quarterflash and half-cut with a fulsome woman, he used to say, what fool isn't happy?

She took a puff, put the cigarette in the ashtray and stared at it. Without looking up, she said, But do you believe in love, Mr Evans?

She rolled the cigarette end around in the ashtray.

Do you?

Outside, he thought, beyond this mountain and its snow, there was a world of countless millions of people. He could see them in their cities, in the heat and the light. And he could see this house, so remote and isolated, so far away, and he had a feeling that it once must have seemed to her and Jack, if only for a short time, like the universe with the two of them at its centre. And for a moment he was at the King of Cornwall with Amy in the room they thought of as theirs—with the sea and the sun and the shadows, with the white paint flaking off the French doors and with their rusty lock, with the breezes late of an afternoon and of a night the sound of the waves breaking—and he remembered how that too had once seemed the centre of the universe.

I don't, she said. No, I don't. It's too small a word, don't you think, Mr Evans? I have a friend in Fern Tree who teaches piano. Very musical, she is. I'm tone-deaf myself. But one day she was telling me how every room has a note. You just have to find it. She started warbling away, up and down. And suddenly one note came back to us, just bounced back off the walls and rose from the floor and filled the place with this perfect hum. This beautiful sound. Like you've thrown a plum and an orchard comes back at you. You wouldn't believe it, Mr Evans. These two completely different things, a note and a room, finding each other. It sounded . . . *right*. Am I being ridiculous? Do you think that's what we mean by love, Mr Evans? The note that comes back to you? That finds you even when you don't want to be found? That one day you find someone, and everything they are comes back to you in a strange way that hums? That fits. That's beautiful. I'm not explaining myself at all well, am I? she said. I'm not very good with words. But that's what we were. Jack and me. We didn't really know each other. I'm not sure if I liked everything about him. I suppose some things about me annoyed him. But I was that room and he was that note and now he's gone. And everything is silent.

I was with Jack, he began. At the end. He was keen for a Pall Mall.

## 13

The mattress was lumpy and had a small crater at its centre unsatisfactorily padded out with an old North Hobart football jumper. He turned onto his side, manoeuvred his body around its contours, its wadis and plains, its inclines and depressions and ravines. Having formed himself into the shape of the mattress, he leant into her, pushing his knees up under her knees, his thighs under her thighs, and, resting an elbow on her hip, brought his hand around her, and in this way he held her. There seemed to be a deep relief to speak of so many things that troubled both of them without confusing any of them with words. She couldn't bear to be alone. Perhaps they lay together for warmth. Perhaps they held each other against the silence. Hoping for that sound to come back. Both knowing the person lying next to them understood it never would. He could hear sleet beginning to brush the tin roof. It was enough to be warm with her. Perhaps that's all there was. He felt an immense age. He would be thirty-four come July. They held each other without words until he heard the horn of the brewery truck at the top of the drive.

After he left she tipped the medals into the range fire. A few days later she raked out the ash, and for a moment was unsure what the melted slag in her hearth pan was as she threw it into the chook yard. Nineteen years later the great fire of '67 swept through, taking all before it. The hop farm, now run by her son, her timber home and his newer brick home, the photos of her and Jack, all went in the flames. And over half-buried slag that had once been medals in what had once been a chicken pen a new layer of ash deposited itself. After more years passed, there grew out of it water ferns and dogwood and myrtles, until what had been the dream of Jack's life was a forest and the forest dropped leaves and bark and branches, and over more time the ash disappeared under more layers of rot and peat and new life.

She married a younger man who was good to her and she to him, but it was not the same thing as Jack Rainbow and she had been. He died in a tractor accident and so she outlived him too.

Near the end of her life, she realised she could no longer remember what Jack looked like. Nor what he sounded like, or smelt like, or how he had held her and caressed her, slowly puffing on his Pall Malls while the snow fell outside. Sometimes she thought she smelt the smoke of his Pall Malls as she fell into sleep. Sometimes she remembered a room humming. But she could not hold the smell or the thought or the sound, and sleep was taking her somewhere deeper, ever further away. She was trying but she could remember nothing except that for a time, a short time, she had not been lonely and cold.

As the truck made its way back down the mountain, Dorrigo Evans talked with the brewery driver as strangers sometimes do, explaining a little why he was there.

They had something, he said. He's dead and I am alive, but he had something I've never known.

What's that?

He was a couple, said Dorrigo Evans.

A couple, said the brewery driver. My mum and dad, they were a couple. Me, the missus, well, we're D-day. Every day.

He double-declutched, almost standing up on the brakes to drop the truck back to a crawl to take one of the many hairpin bends that formed the writhing road through the forest. When the road straightened out, he got the truck back into second and continued talking.

But a couple? I mean, no. She's a good woman. But love?

Love, said Dorrigo Evans. Yes, I guess love.

The brewery truck driver pondered on it for a mile or two. And then he said:

Maybe a lot of people never know love.

The idea had never occurred to Dorrigo Evans.

Maybe not.

Maybe we just get given our faces, our lives, our fates, our happiness and unhappiness. Some get a lot, some bugger all. And love the same. Like different glass sizes for beer. You get a lot, you get bugger all, you drink it and it's gone. You know it and then you don't know it. Maybe we don't control any of it. No one makes love like they make a wall or a house. They catch it like a cold. It makes them miserable and then it passes, and pretending otherwise is the road to hell.

That's it?

So she goes, said the truck driver. Where did you say you're from?

The mainland.

Thought so, said the truck driver, for whom this revelation seemed both to explain and end an overly personal conversation.

As the afternoon flight to Melbourne banked around and levelled out, Dorrigo Evans could see the snowy mountain backdropped by a perfect blue sky through the plane porthole. The world is, he thought. It just is. Then it disappeared into white and he found his thoughts following. He held a hand out and he pushed his fingers into air, as though he might yet find that femoral artery in time.

You can feel the chill coming through from here, said a pleasant voice in the cocoon of intimacy that existed within the deafening throb of the great propellor engines. Dorrigo Evans turned and for the first time realised that there was an attractive woman sitting next to him. Her corn-blue jacquard blouse revealed the beginnings of a cleavage defined by the swelling cusp of very white breasts.

You can, he said.

And where are you heading? she asked.

He smiled.

Your hands look freezing, she said.

So she goes, he said, suddenly conscious of his fingers held outwards, pushing and shoving emptiness, coldness, whiteness, nothing.

In this world
we walk on the roof of hell
gazing at flowers.

*Issa*

# 1

TENJI NAKAMURA'S THROAT had been oddly hoarse for some weeks when, after a long interview for the position of deputy accounts manager he had sat in on, he rubbed his stiff neck and felt a strange swelling. He paid no heed—indeed, he could afford to pay no heed because his job in the personnel department was busier than ever, and he was in line for a senior manager's position and couldn't afford to give in to ideas of sickness.

But his throat grew sorer. When he began to find swallowing food painful, he reduced his eating to a minimum and lived on a diet consisting in the main of miso soup. Only after he began coughing up blood did he relent and go to the doctor. The diagnosis was unequivocal: Nakamura had throat cancer.

The tumour was removed, and though his speaking voice was somewhat affected by the surgery, Nakamura took this blow with grace. He had come to view himself as a survivor, and wore his new, thin, reedy voice as a badge of honour. He felt blessed beyond belief. But three months later, when he ran his finger along his neck, he felt a small bump, taut and strange. He put it out of his mind. But the bump grew and there was more surgery, along with radiotherapy that left him feeble and aged far beyond his years. His saliva glands were burnt out, and he now could swallow only wet food, and even that with difficulty. And through this ordeal he came to recognise what an extraordinary woman Ikuko was. For she devoted herself to his care, was unfailingly light and pleasant, and seemed not to mind his dry and reeking body. When he was recovering from the ravages of his treatment he grew very conscious of how fresh and pleasant she always smelt, of how lustrous her skin remained, as though her very body was the sum of goodness. Sometimes he felt overwhelmed by the health she radiated, which seemed best caught in her seemingly ceaseless lazy smile.

Every morning before she left for work, she would rise an extra two hours early in order to attend to all his needs. He admired her practical nature, but what he loved was simply her presence and touch. After a time he would do anything to have her sit next to him and gently run the backs of her fingers down the side of his face. And though she thought that doing nothing—as she put it—was a complete waste of her time, that same nothing was the most important thing in Nakamura's life. Then he felt no fear, his pain was again for a short time bearable, and he wondered how he could have been oblivious to his wife's goodness for so long.

And more, moreover: for his wife's goodness brought out so much that was good in him. He bore his illness with stoicism and humour. He made time to see others who were even sicker than he; and even did some work with a charity that took meals to the old. He was kinder and more thoughtful about one and all: his family, his friends, his neighbours, even strangers. Tenji Nakamura was stunned by this discovery of such goodness in himself. I am, he decided, a good man. And this thought gave him immense comfort and a tranquillity in the face of his cancer that amazed all who knew him.

## 2

It was at this time, when Tenji Nakamura was frail but regaining his strength, when he had come to realise how blessed he was in his life, that a letter found him from Aki Tomokawa, who had been part of his platoon on the railway. His old corporal had been searching for his commander for some years and wrote that he hoped that this letter might finally have found him.

Tomokawa had always irritated Nakamura with his narrowness and obsequiousness, but he now saw his old corporal in an entirely different light—as a noble and good man with whom he had shared much. And Nakamura was touched by Tomokawa's loyalty, which seemed to him of a piece with the goodness of his wife, with the kindness of his daughters, who every evening sat and talked with him, and which demanded of him some reciprocal act of goodness. Ever since that day at the Shinjuku Rashomon when he had read his name among the list of suspected war criminals, Nakamura had made it a rule to avoid any contact with his old comrades, and—other than the accident of his having ended up working for Kota—he had stuck by it.

But now this attitude struck him as both selfish and absurd. The time for retribution on the part of the Allies was long past. Tomokawa, who had ended up on the northern island of Hokkaido, seemed to have tracked down many of their old comrades and to know of their various and varied fates. Not only that, but a group of railway engineers from their old regiment had even been back to Thailand—as Siam was now known—and had found the rusting hulk of the first locomotive to have made its way along the full length of the Siam–Burma railway in 1944. They were in the process of restoring it, with the ultimate aim of bringing it back to Japan, where it might be displayed at the Yasukuni Shrine in honour of their great achievement.

Hearing of this marvellous work, Tenji Nakamura realised that, among the other blessings he was accumulating with age, he no longer had to fear. And with fear gone, he now wished to be proud, and to share in the pride of others. Tomokawa's letter marked in his mind the moment when he finally escaped the yoke of fear that he had lived under since that day at the Shinjuku Rashomon. Nakamura decided that, in spite of his illness, he would travel to the frigid town of Sapporo in the far north to once more meet with his old comrade.

It was midwinter when he arrived, and preparations for the city's annual snow festival were in full swing. Nakamura had seen on television how the snow festival's theme for 1966 was to be the monsters that had become so popular in Japanese movies and on Japanese television. As he travelled in a taxi from the Sapporo airport to the Tomokawas' apartment, he saw soldiers from the Japanese Self-Defence Force helping make gigantic ice sculptures.

The driver insisted on naming them as they drove by: Gamera, the fire-breathing turtle, Godzilla, Giant Robo, Red Cobra with his huge forehead and protruding upper teeth, Mothra, the giant caterpillar, and Guillotine the Emperor with his huge head and tentacles. None of the names meant anything to Nakamura, but he admired the exquisite Japanese workmanship, the indomitable Japanese spirit such an endeavour represented.

Tomokawa lived in a high-rise government housing

unit and Nakamura got lost in the complex. By the time he found the right unit, he was exhausted from the search and the cold. Still—Tomokawa! How good it was to see him again! He was fatter, balder and, thought Nakamura, even shorter, but the same old daikon-headed Tomokawa—even if the daikon was a little blemished from the liver spots that mottled his face, putting Nakamura in mind of something vaguely reptilian. And if he was still somewhat annoying, Tomokawa was so delighted to see his old commander, so frank and unaffected, that what Nakamura had once found irritating he was now determined to find endearing and even charming.

Tomokawa's wife was even shorter than her husband, with an unfortunate underbite that meant she sometimes gave the impression of eating her words rather than speaking them. In spite of this, or because of it, she was a confident woman—a little too much so for Nakamura's liking, but he chose to find her over-familiarity with him as evidence of warmth and kindness, and as such being qualities that marked Mrs Tomokawa out as a special woman.

Such a man of talents, Commander, said Mrs Tomokawa, showing him into their living room, done up in the western style, complete with two very large soft armchairs. A soldier, a businessman and our very own Hokusai!

Tenji Nakamura hid his confusion with a smile, unsure whether she had confused him with the immortal painter or just eaten half a word. But there was no confusion.

Do you still paint, Commander?

She was holding a military postcard and passed it to Nakamura. It bore a small painting of Tomokawa as he had been on the railway in 1943. It was clear Mrs Tomokawa thought Nakamura had painted it, for on the back of the card Nakamura had written a greeting and a short note saying Tomokawa was in the best of health.

Outside the day was black with snow clouds.

Forgive me, said Nakamura, but I must rest for a moment.

He asked to sit down. The western armchair he found spiritually coarse and physically unpleasant; sitting in it felt like being embraced and smothered by something monstrous. The trip had wearied him far more than he could have believed possible and the morphine medication, which he had tried to minimise for the trip so he wouldn't appear stupefied, seemed nevertheless to be affecting him more than usual.

He felt a strange sense of drift and separation that was not entirely unpleasant and at the same time he became intensely aware of every sound in the room, every odour and even the movement of the air. The furnishings were living things, even the wretched armchairs were alive to him, and he felt he understood all things, but every time he tried to put this understanding into words it ran away from him. Suddenly he wanted to go home, and he knew that would not be possible until the formalities of his visit to the Tomokawas were ended. He kept his eyes closed, conscious that all around him the world lived as he had never known it had lived, and, just as he finally opened himself up to this joy, he also realised that he was dying.

## 3

As Dorrigo Evans filled out in middle age, his looks grew to be outsized and quixotic, as though he was overdone and overwrought in every sense, as if, Ella was fond of saying, the volume was turned up to eleven: formidable in presence but with an odd remove and strange, inquiring eyes. For his admirers it added up to charm, elegance even. For his detractors it was one more element of his infuriating difference. His masculine resolve remained. Aided by his height and a middle-aged stoop, he understood that it was often misunderstood as gravitas, and he was not ungrateful for the mask such confusion afforded.

Through the decades following the war he felt his spirit sleeping, and though he tried hard to rouse it with the shocks and dangers of consecutive and sometimes concurrent adulteries, outbursts, and acts of pointless compassion and reckless surgery it did no good. It slumbered on. He admired reality, as a doctor, he preached it and tried to practise it. In truth, he doubted its existence. To have been part of a Pharaonic slave system that had at its apex a divine sun king led him to understand unreality as the greatest force in life. And his life was now, he felt, one monumental unreality, in which everything that did not matter—professional ambitions, the private pursuit of status, the colour of wallpaper, the size of an office or the matter of a dedicated car parking space—was vested with the greatest significance, and everything that did matter—pleasure, joy, friendship, love—was deemed somehow peripheral. It made for dullness mostly and weirdness generally.

He found himself no longer afraid of enclosed places, crowds, trams, trains—all the things that pressed him inwards and cut out the light—but he saw many other things now as an evasion of that light. He had seen too much to be frightened any longer of the rest of the filler that packs out evenings, days, years, sometimes the best part of a life, but he did find it dull. Still, he could do boring, and boring he did at countless memorial dinners, fundraising breakfasts, charity events, sherry parties and the vertiginous horror of dinner parties, and later at the meetings of hospital and college boards, of the numerous charities, clubs, and societies that prevailed on him to be a patron.

It all bored him. Ella bored him. Ella's friends bored him. Home brought on a weary headache. He bored himself. He was more and more bored by routine surgery, which was what he knew responsible surgery should strive to be; it was the non-routine where complications occurred, where things went wrong, where lives were ruined or abruptly ended but sometimes saved. He was bored by the sex of his adulteries, which was why, he presumed, he pursued them ever more ardently, imagining that there must be somewhere someone who could break the spell of torpor, his soul's strange sleep. Occasionally a woman misunderstood him and imagined a future life with him. He would quickly disabuse her of the malady of romance. Thereafter, they thought him only interested in the pleasures of the flesh; in truth nothing interested him less.

The more he advanced forward, the further the windmill receded. He thought of the Greeks' idea of punishment, which was to constantly fail at what you most desire. So Sisyphus succeeds in rolling his boulder to the top of the cliff, only for it to fall back down, and he must return to the bottom and repeat the identical task the next day. So the forever starving, thirsty Tantalus, who brought the food of the gods to mortals, is condemned to stand in a lake and watch the water recede every time he stoops to drink, and the fruit-laden branch above his head rise out of his grasp every time he reaches to pick something to eat. Perhaps that was what hell was, Dorrigo concluded, an eternal repetition of the same failure. Perhaps he was there already. Like Socrates discovering the undying soul as he dies drinking hemlock, Dorrigo discovered the true object of his love where it was always absent: with other women who were not Amy.

When ardour began to fail him, he reverted to a theatre of sensuality that he found even drearier than sex unadorned. It was ridiculous, comic, beyond belief and certainly beyond conversation at the Melbourne society events that were now his milieu. He would have liked to have laughed at himself in the company of others, but it was not possible.

There was, he knew, within him, hidden deep and far away, a great slumbering turbulence he could neither understand nor reach, a turbulence that was also a void, the business of unfinished things. He drank—why would he not drink? A few wines at lunch, sometimes a whisky in his morning tea, a negroni or two before dinner (a habit he had picked up from an American major while with the occupying forces in Kobe) and wine with it, brandy and whisky after and some more whisky after that and after that again. His moods came upon him now in a more unpredictable and uncontrollable fashion and were sometimes vile. A lion in winter, he hurt Ella frequently with his words, his indifference, his rage at her affections and industry. He shouted at her after her father's funeral for no good reason or even a bad reason. He wanted to love her, he wished he could love her; he feared he did love her but not in the way a man should his wife—he wanted to hurt her into the same realisation, a recognition that he was not for her, to elicit a response that might break him out of his sleep. He waited for a denouement that never arrived. And her hurt, her pain, her tears, her sadness, rather than ending his soul's hibernation, only deepened it.

## 4

Ella could not fathom living without loving. She had been loved by her parents and loved them deeply in return. Her love was simply what she was, looking for objects to pour itself out upon. She listened to Dorrigo's problems at the hospital, she grieved with him when he lost a patient. She sympathised with his struggles with the idiotic bureaucrats who, he said, were going to be the death not just of him but of medical care in Australia, with the surgeons who disapproved of his methods.

She had matured into a striking older woman, her raven hair more remarkable now dyed, dark-skinned, admired by other women for her elegant calm and style, her compassion for others and her easygoing nature. Whether it was her full figure or her radiant complexion, she had an appearance of vigour that belied her age. Men liked the way she looked, the way she moved, the sight of her dark legs in summer, and the way she smiled with such attention when the men talked about themselves. The only blemish on her beauty was a slight upturn at the tip of her nose, which at certain angles made her face somehow look almost a caricature. Most people never really noticed it. Over the years though Dorrigo saw it more and more, until sometimes—first thing of a morning or when he arrived home from work—he could see little else of her.

She so thoroughly believed in Dorrigo and Dorrigo's life that she repeated his opinions as if they were her own, and she did it in a way that always frustrated him. Damned bloody bureaucrats, she would say, they'll be the death of more than just patients. Or she would start going on in some detail about the medical ignorance of some stupid surgeons.

And as he listened, all he could see was the slight upturn of her nose, the way it made her face which once had seemed very beautiful rather comical, and he thought how she wasn't really that beautiful at all, but rather odd-looking. And every time he heard her repeat something he had said a month or a week ago, he'd be astonished at both the banality of the opinion and her loyalty in repeating something that he could now see was trite and stupid. And yet had she dared suggest that what *he* was saying was banal and ridiculous, he would have been furious. He wanted her agreement and, having got it so unconditionally, he despised it.

With their children she would agree also, much to Dorrigo's irritation.

It is the parent's job to parent, he would say to her, and their job to live.

And having said that, he would try to hide his frustration, and would have to look away from her face so he would not focus on the tip of her nose.

But I agree with you, she would say. I couldn't agree more. If a parent doesn't parent, what are we here for?

Dorrigo, the children, her friends, and her wider family—they all existed for her as a way of divining the world. It was a far larger and more wondrous place with them than it was without them. If she hoped for the same love from Dorrigo, and if she was disappointed in her hope, she did not feel its absence as a reason not to love him. The problem was that she did. Her love was without reason and would never yield to reason. Though it longed for requital, her love in the end did not demand it.

But when he was away at night, she would lie awake, unable to sleep. And she would think of him and her and feel the most overwhelming sadness. She may have been a trusting woman but she was very far from a stupid one. She repeated his words and echoed his opinions not because she was without thoughts of her own, but because her nature was one that wished to live through others. Without love, what was the world? Just objects, things, light, darkness.

Damn bloody bureaucrats. Stupid surgeon. Oh, that poor, poor man, she would say. Over and over. And then, inexplicably, she would cry until she could cry no more.

## 5

For some minutes Tenji Nakamura said nothing. He was trying to remember the Japan he had believed in before he went to war; a beautiful, noble Japan that he recalled as strong and good in spirit, which he had served in the fullness and purity of his soul. But something in his memory of the POW painting portraits of him and his men that day in Siam troubled him, but why it did so, he had no idea, and the effort of memory or the effect of morphine meant he next forgot about whatever it was he had just been thinking. All he could think of was how, beyond his vision, frozen monsters loomed over the city, frozen monsters past which he had travelled to come to the Tomokawas', frozen monsters beneath which he would travel going back to the airport. He realised Tomokawa was talking to him and he tried to concentrate, but the monsters seemed to be in the room now.

You know, Tomokawa was saying, but Tomokawa looked like the monster Gamera, at the beginning I was terrified they'd pick me up as a war criminal. And I used to think: What a joke! Because they only cared about what we did to the Allied prisoners.

Nakamura could hear Tomokawa's voice but he was seeing a huge turtle spurting flames.

And when I think about all that we did with the chinks in Manchukuo, the turtle was saying with his breath of brimstone. And the fun we had with their women!

Nakamura was fully awake now and looked around uneasily, but Mrs Tomokawa, he realised, was out of hearing range in the kitchen.

Well, you'd remember it all, I'm sure, the giant turtle—who, Nakamura had to remind himself, was really Tomokawa—went on. And so I think those POWs had it easy, and they should be proud of what they achieved with that railway and us. But to hang us for that and not for what we did to the chinks! Really—it defies any reasoning. That's what I think, anyway.

Mrs Tomokawa came back in to the room with food, and Tomokawa, who suddenly looked human again, changed the conversation. But all the time Nakamura was thinking about what Tomokawa had said and the common-sense wisdom of it all. For they had built a railway in fifteen months that the English had said could not be built in five times that period. He rubbed his neck, where the new bump had grown even that day, or so it seemed to Nakamura, for he believed he could feel the lump growing within him every hour of every day and every minute of every hour, eating him up. He tried, of course, not to feel it. He could with an effort not think about it and focus his mind instead on what concerned him more and more: the war, for that too was growing within him.

They had battled disease, starvation and Allied air raids. It was not easy making sick men work, but how would the railway have been built if they had relied solely on the almost non-existent ranks of the healthy? He understood that he once could have stood accused of the deaths of perhaps hundreds of romusha and POWs. How many? He had no idea how many.

But in a jungle without end, where transport was difficult, sickness and death everyday companions, he knew that he had selflessly performed his duty with devotion and honour. The railway had been a triumph of Japanese spirit. They had shown that spirit could triumph where the Europeans, with all their superior technology, had not even dared try. Without the capacity to make railway irons they had taken apart strategically unimportant lines throughout the Empire—in Java, Singapore and Malaya—and then transported them to

Siam. Lacking heavy construction machinery, they had fallen back on the miracles the spirit can achieve with the body. It was beyond his power to stop the deaths, because the railway had to be built for the Emperor, and the railway could not have been built any other way. He remembered with a sadness that felt ennobling the deaths of his and Tomokawa's comrades, both those who had died of disease in the jungle, and those later hanged by the Americans.

His mind raced away from them and hurtled towards his childhood, and here he tried to dwell with a child who had lived life in accordance with some unspoken natural order. But he knew he was no longer that child—that he had somehow, somewhere broken with that child's understanding of the world. Again, he heard Ikuko's voice, saw that irritatingly stupid smile, and he was possessed of a shame that was also a terror. The things he thought right and true had all been wrong and false, and he with them. But how was such a thing possible? How could a life come to this? He began to fear his imminent death, not because he would die but because he sensed that he had never really lived as he wished. And Tenji Nakamura did not understand why this was so.

He understood that somewhere in that goodness his wife and daughters loved in him, that goodness which had saved a mosquito's life, was the same unswerving goodness that had allowed him to devote his life, no matter the anguish and the doubts, to the Empire and the Emperor. And this goodness was unlike Ikuko's patient nursing, getting up two hours before work and the touch of her fingers on his cheek. It was a different goodness, and the Emperor was its embodiment both now and in the future. For it and for him Nakamura had shed the blood of others and would willingly have shed his own. He told himself that, through his service of this cosmic goodness, he had discovered he was not one man but many, that he could do the most terrible things he might otherwise have thought were evil if he had not known that they were in the service of the ultimate goodness. For he loved poetry above all, and the Emperor was a poem of one word—perhaps, he thought, the greatest poem—a poem that encompassed the universe and transcended all morality and all suffering. And like all great art, it was beyond good and evil.

Yet somehow—in a way he tried not to dwell upon—this poem had become horror, monsters and corpses. And he knew he had discovered in himself an almost inexhaustible capacity to stifle pity, to be playful with cruelty in a way he found frankly pleasurable, for no single human life could be worth anything next to this cosmic goodness. For a moment, as he was being eaten by Tomokawa's oppressive armchair, he wondered: what if this had all been a mask for the most terrible evil?

The idea was too horrific to hold on to. In an increasingly rare moment of lucidity, Nakamura recognised that what was imminent was a battle *not* between life and death in his body, but between his dream of himself as a good man and this nightmare of ice monsters and crawling corpses. And with the same iron will that had served him so well in the Siamese jungle, in the ruins of the Shinjuku Rashomon and at the Blood Bank of Japan, he resolved that he must henceforth conceive of his life's work as that of a good man.

His mind felt suddenly serene. He had always used his

powers for the sake of the Empire and the Emperor. He wished to tell his children that he was going peacefully, with good grace, to the land of the dead, where his parents and comrades awaited him. His idea of his own goodness, though, was becoming harder and harder to hold on to. It came close to collapsing altogether when Ikuko touched him, when he saw her skin still beautiful at her age, her slightly stupid smile, and he instinctively understood that her goodness was something that, at heart, was not within him. He tried to recall good things in his life—separate of the Emperor's will, of orders and authority—with which to build some other idea of goodness, that might offer evidence of a good life. He remembered offering quinine to an Australian doctor. And despairing of the violence of a beating. But these thoughts gave way to a general hopelessness that was mixed up with images of skeletal beings crawling through rain and mud, and among the monsters in Tomokawa's apartment he began seeing those crawling corpses everywhere, amidst ceaseless rain and the fires of hell. And Tenji Nakamura understood that these deaths would have been no more welcomed by those who inhabited those awful bodies than his own would soon be welcomed by his.

You remember that prisoner painter? asked Tomokawa. I've told her it wasn't you, but she never hears. It was an Australian. He used to get about with that sergeant. The one who used to sing of a night. All those horror stories they tell about us! And prisoners singing—it can't have been so bad.

How we lived, Nakamura thought.

It was the happiest time of my life, Tomokawa said.

Beyond Nakamura's thoughts, snow swept through the

world heavily, endlessly, erasing all that existed. Soon he would die, and all good and all evil would be as nothing. The monsters would melt and run into the black ocean. For a moment he thought he smelt DDT and saw many things: Sato looking up from the *go* board about to say something, lice fleeing a dead boy's body, a man less than a man crumpling in the mud of a jungle clearing. He had a fulfilling sense of having cheated destiny in his life. His body suddenly jolted and he was awake. He had no idea how long he had been asleep.

Some carp sushi, Commander? Mrs Tomokawa asked in her strange way, half-conversation, half-mastication.

Nakamura felt without emotion, yet his body was trembling as he imagined the hospital scales had once trembled when the American's heart was placed on them.

I get it from the market. It's a little salty, but we like our carp sushi a little salty.

Nakamura shook his head.

The following spring, the Tomokawas received a card from Mrs Nakamura saying her husband had died. She did not mention to them his final ravings, his petty bad temper, or his vicious attacks on her and her daughters, who were nursing him, for even the simplest things such as stroking his cheeks or just smiling. Instead, she wrote of how the night before he passed away, knowing his time was rapidly approaching its end, and being something of an amateur poet and in accordance with tradition, he set out to write his death poem.

A humble man to the end, continued Mrs Nakamura, he struggled for some hours, but, weakened by his illness, he concluded it was beyond his powers to better the death poem of Hyakka, which, he said, expressed everything he felt, but far more beautifully than he could ever manage. Mrs Nakamura added that she felt that Mr Nakamura had in this final act been inspired by his visit to wintry Sapporo the year before, and for that reason she was forwarding them a copy. His family had been with Mr Nakamura when he died, concluded Mrs Nakamura. They knew he was a kind man who could not bear to see even animals suffer. He knew he was a blessed and lucky man who had led a good life.

Mrs Tomokawa picked up the separate page on which the death poem was copied, and read it out to her husband:

*Winter ice*
*melts into clean water—*
*clear is my heart.*

## 6

Sometimes I think he is the loneliest man in the world, Ella Evans announced one night at a dinner for the College of Surgeons' executive committee. And everyone laughed. Dear old Dorry? she imagined them thinking. Every man's best friend? Every woman's secret desire?

But he knew she knew. He was alone in his marriage, he was alone with his children, he was alone in the operating theatre, he was alone on the numerous medical, sporting, charity and veterans' bodies on which he sat, he was alone when addressing a meeting of a thousand POWs. There was around him an exhausted emptiness, an impenetrable void cloaked this most famously collegial man, as if he already lived in another place—forever unravelling and refurling a limitless dream or an unceasing nightmare, it was hard to know—from which he would never escape. He was a lighthouse whose light could not be relit. In his dreams he would hear his mother calling to him from the kitchen: Boy, come here, boy. But when he would go inside it was dark and cold, the kitchen was charred beams and ash and smelt of gas, and no one was home.

Dorrigo Evans did not view his marriage as a wasteland though. Far from it. For one thing, he felt strongly that it wouldn't do to regard his marriage as a failure, or to think he hadn't loved Ella. For another, in the practical manner of arranged marriages—admittedly, arranged by themselves—they worked at love. When he first met Ella, because marriage was so much on everyone's mind, he saw Ella only through the prism of a prospective wife. In his youthful mind love was more or less marriage brocaded with lines of poetry. And, as a wife for a man who was clearly going to amount to something, Ella seemed to him perfect: loving, doting, more determined even than him to see him rise. Ella accorded with convention and mortised with literature. He presumed all this was love, and although after their marriage it quickly did not seem enough, he accepted it had to do.

And then, when Ella's body had changed into lustrous circles while bearing their children, her full breasts and dark nipples a wonder, her thinking unexpected, her aura strange and anything but boring, he had loved her very much. Before the sum of his adulteries meant she could no longer bear to have him in bed with her, he would lean into her back, smell her and know a peace that otherwise evaded him. He did not bother explaining to her that to him sex was not infidelity, that sleeping with someone was. And that he never did.

Their three children—Jessica, Mary and Stewart—he loved more deeply the further away he voyaged from them. His attitude was one of benign neglect; he had not expected that they would act out his relationship with Ella among themselves. Their enmities and coldness to each other were to him unbearable; it broke his heart, he hoped it was not permanent, he begged them not to be cruel or callous when he saw them echoing the cruelty and callousness he showed Ella. He recognised himself as unfit for fatherhood but stayed the course, because staying the course was what he did in all things. He wondered if it was surrender to his own private terror.

He and Ella were at their best in company, and found the other at such times admirable—even, as he heard Ella say at one dinner, adorable. Adorable! And he admired her and pitied her for being with him. He heard her telling her friends in all sincerity that the war and the camps would not let him go. She seemed to want to make of him a tragedy, and he, who had seen tragedies, was angry that she would be so naïve, so self-dramatising as to make her husband one more. He wished she would just damn him for what he had become—a bastard. But that would have been too straightforward for Ella, and, besides, she loved him in her way, which is to say she refused to give up on him long after he had given up on himself. She took to having her hair cut like Françoise

Hardy and smoking purple Sobranies in an attempt at chic distance that perhaps she hoped might also prove seductive to him. Her fragility—which to him was always her most interesting feature—remained, though it was increasingly enshrouded in a perfumed smoke he found abhorrent.

What do you want? Ella would ask, taking the Sobranie from her lips, and that was the question to which there really was no answer. And when he lied and said Nothing, or he lied and said, Serenity, or he lied and said, You, or he lied and said, Us, she would say, But what do you really want, Alwyn? Tell me, what? What?

What indeed? he wondered.

Is it just their bodies, sex, is that it? she said, and her calm hurt him far more than any anger. Just getting your end wet? she said. Is that it?

Her calm, her vile candour, her inestimable sadness—was that what he had led her to?

Is that all you are about? Ella would say, exhaling more Sobranie smoke. Is it?

Was it? How he hated that smoke. He feared he had made her coarse, she who had been anything but. He thought of how the world organises its affairs so that civilisation every day commits crimes for which any individual would be imprisoned for life. And how people accept this either by ignoring it and calling it current affairs or politics or wars, or by making a space that has nothing to do with civilisation and calling that space their private life. And the more in that private life they break with civilisation, the more that private life becomes a secret life, the freer they feel. But it is not so. You are never free of the world; to share life is to share guilt.

Nothing could wash away what he felt. He looked up at Ella.

Is *that* it? Ella said.

It is not so, he said.

The wording of his answer sounded stilted and unbelievable to them both; worse, it sounded weak, and she just shook her head. Despite what she said, she always preferred strong lies to weak truths.

Along with her new candour, Ella had taken to wearing heavy perfume in her middle age, and the fumes of that entwining with the fug of the Sobranie smoke gave her an aroma that he found occasionally exciting, even erotic, but mostly—and more and more—stale and claustrophobic, like a wardrobe of old clothes destined for charity. How he wished she wouldn't wear that perfume, that she wouldn't smoke Sobranies, that she wouldn't do her hair like Françoise Hardy. Because he felt in all these things a disguise made up of her bravery, her pride, her huge sadness so painful it throbbed through their home. How he wished he hadn't made her hard.

## 7

In his early years with Ella he thought of Amy frequently. He wondered what it was that he had known with Amy. He had no idea. It seemed a power beyond love. He recalled their first meeting as unremarkable. He had noticed her beauty spot above her lip obscured by the dust motes, not because she was pretty but because the sight of her through the shafts of dusty light was striking. He thought of their strange conversation, not because it was bewitching, but because it had vaguely amused him. He remembered how, the following day, when he went back to the shop to buy the Catullus, it was the book and not her of which he had the strongest memory. The chance meeting with the girl with the red camellia had been a curious encounter of a type he understood he would soon enough forget.

And if he hadn't forgotten her in those early post-war years, as surely as Amy had for a time become his entire reason for existence, so too she now began to recede from his thoughts. In trying to escape the fatality of memory, he discovered with an immense sadness that pursuing the past inevitably only leads to greater loss. To hold a gesture, a smell, a smile was to cast it as one fixed thing, a plaster death mask, which as soon as it was touched crumbled in his fingers back into dust. And as over the years his memory of Amy atomised, Ella became his most formidable ally and his most trusted adviser. She soothed him when he was enraged, encouraged him when he found obstacles, and little by little, event by event, in the tumble and mudslide of life, his memory of Amy was slowly buried, until he had trouble remembering very much about her at all. Whole weeks would pass and he would realise he had not thought about her, then that period became months, and then several months could run together and of her specifically he had thought nothing. He began smelling on himself the same strange, blanketing complicity of small things shared—food, towels, cutlery and cups, the combined purpose of lives pursued together—that he had once been repulsed to smell on Keith Mulvaney.

There grew between him and Ella a conspiracy of

experience, as if the raising of children, the industry of supporting each other in ways practical and tender, and the sum of years and then decades of private conversations and small intimacies—the odour of each other on waking; the trembling sound of each other's breathing when a child was unwell; the illnesses, the griefs and cares, the tendernesses, unexpected and unbidden—as if all this were somehow more binding, more important and more undeniable than love, whatever love was. For he was bound to Ella. And yet it all created in Dorrigo Evans the most complete and unassailable loneliness, so loud a solitude that he sought to crack its ringing silence again and again with yet another woman. Even as his vitality leached away, he laboured on in his quixotic philanderings. If there was no real heart to any of it, if it was dangerous in so many ways, that added to it for him. But far from ending the scream of his solitude, it amplified it.

As a meteorite strike long ago explains the large lake now, so Amy's absence shaped everything, even when—and sometimes most particularly when—he wasn't thinking of her. He flatly refused ever to visit Adelaide, even when major professional or veterans' events were held there. The only interest he ever showed in gardening—which he otherwise left to Ella and the gardener—was to have a large and very beautiful red camellia ripped out, much to Ella's fury, when they moved into a new house in Toorak. His perennial infidelity was, in a strange way, a fidelity to Amy's memory—as if by ceaselessly betraying Ella he was honouring Amy. He did not conceive of it in this way and would have been horrified if anyone had said it, yet no woman he met in those years meant anything in particular to him.

So the women came and went, angry, mystified, shocked; his marriage continued; his work went on and his standing grew. He headed departments, reviews, national enquiries into health, discovered that people's goodwill was frequently in inverse relationship to their position, and felt completely baffled when at a dinner he heard a speaker describe with such profligacy his own life as *a glittering career.* The feeling passed, and shaded into a bewildered disappointment. He was compelled to travel frequently; long periods of tedium and waiting, interspersed by unnecessary meetings with people similarly suffering the vertigo of achievement. During sleepless nights in hermetically enclosed rooms that had the persistent, unpleasant underscent of chemicals, he wondered why fewer and fewer people interested him. Inexplicably to him, his reputation continued to grow. Newspaper profiles, television interviews, panels, boards, the incommunicable tedium of social events to which *he had to go*, so flat and endless that he feared he might see the curvature of the earth if he looked too hard. The world is, he would think. It just is.

One evening he was called back to the hospital late for an emergency appendectomy. The young patient's name was Amy Gascoigne.

Amie, amante, amour, he murmured as he scrubbed up.

The head nurse at the next sink, used to the surgeon's recitations, laughed and asked what poem that came from. As they walked into the operating theatre, Dorrigo Evans realised it was the first time he had consciously thought of Amy in several years.

I've forgotten, he said.

He had stolen light from the sun and fallen to earth. For a moment he had to turn away from the table and compose himself, so that the rest of the team would not see his scalpel shaking.

## 8

It was during these years that Dorrigo Evans renewed his relationship with his brother, Tom. He found in this some salve for the loneliness he otherwise felt, even with—and sometimes most particularly with—Ella and their children. He found in the time he was able to spend with Tom—by phone once a month and what became after a time an annual visit to Sydney in midwinter, and then, as his reputation grew and he travelled to Sydney more frequently—that special closeness that siblings sometimes have. It was an ease of company that allows for most things to be unsaid, for awkwardness and error to be entirely unimportant, and for that strange sense of a mysterious shared soul to be expressed through the most trivial of small talk. If beyond their blood relation they had almost nothing in common, Dorrigo Evans still increasingly felt with Tom that he was but one aspect of a larger thing, of which his brother was another, different but complementary part, and their meetings were not so much an assertion of self as a welcome dissolution of it in each other.

Their father had survived their mother by only a few years, dying of a heart attack in 1936; as the youngest of seven, Dorrigo had little to do with his older siblings, who had scattered around Australia in the years before the Depression looking for work. Four sisters went to the woollen mills in the western districts of Victoria; he never really knew them, and he attended their funerals through the 1950s as they passed away, broken by life. He looked at their children and husbands as strangers, but he still helped them all when they came to him. The last of them, Marcy, who was also the oldest and whom he supported entirely for more than a decade, died in Melbourne in 1962 of an undiagnosed cancer. His eldest brother, Albert, who had found work as a cane-cutter in far north Queensland, had died there in an explosion in a sugar refinery in 1956. Tom had ended up in Sydney in a childless marriage, a labourer in the vast works of the Redfern railway yards, and after retiring had spent his days tending his vegetables in his Balmain backyard and playing darts at his local pub.

In February 1967 Ella planned a week's holiday in Tasmania with the children at the home of her sister, who had recently moved there with her husband. These planned holidays, conceived and booked without Dorrigo's involvement, under the pretence of being a high point of their shared lives, were rather the last vestige of them as a family. Accordingly, Ella created them and he agreed to them and they all loathed them as a form of corrective punishment known as *family time*.

On the Saturday they were to fly to Hobart, he thus took a phone call about his brother Tom's heart attack with mixed feelings. On the one hand he was upset; on the other it gave him good reason to evade at least the first day or two of Tasmania. He managed to get a flight to Sydney that evening, but Tom was too heavily sedated on the Sunday to make much sense. It wasn't until the Monday that Dorrigo was able to talk at some length with him.

Tom told him how he had the heart attack that felled him in the Kent Hotel, just as he was about to throw a bull's eye.

A bull's eye?

Had it in the bag, Tom said. Bloody embarrassing way to go, though. In a puddle of piss on the floor with a dart in your mitt. Would have preferred somewhere private, like the tomato patch.

His brother seemed unusually talkative, and Dorrigo soon found himself deep in reminiscences about their childhood in Tasmania. Tom was an endless song cycle of Cleveland stories, some of which Dorrigo knew, many of which he had never heard. Doughy Yates' name came up, and Tom recalled how Doughy would frequently boast that he could outrun the train. Challenged to prove it, he stripped to his long white underpants and raced the Launceston to Hobart express through the peppermint gums and silver wattles of the Cleveland bush. As the train disappeared with a whistle round the bend heading toward Conara Junction, Doughy fell to the ground scratched and exhausted and had to admit defeat.

He was into everything, Doughy, Dorrigo said.

Still dancing solo at eighty-five, Tom said. Collected Leyland P76s at the end. A car you couldn't give away. Had them bury him lying on his stomach so that everyone would have to kiss his arse forever after. But I always think of him running through the bush in those long white underpants. It's like life, isn't it? You think you'll outrun it, that you're better than it, but it makes a fool of you every time. It runs you into the ground and steams off whistling away, happy as buggery with itself.

They laughed.

You know Doughy was Jackie Maguire's cousin? Tom said.

Dorrigo didn't. He spoke fondly about his memories of reading poetry and Aunty Rose's advice columns for Tom and Jackie Maguire.

Old Jackie, said Tom. Good fella. Best of blokes. Knew the bush. His wife was a blackfella, you know?

For a moment or two Dorrigo couldn't place Jackie Maguire's wife at all. Then a long dormant memory—a memory that had in some way troubled and shaped him far more than he knew—pushed its way to the front of his mind. Though he had heard vague tales of aristocratic Spanish blood, one of the traditional Tasmanian alibis, Dorrigo hadn't known she was an Aborigine, and it led him to questions he had always wanted to ask.

Back then, all those years ago. Just before she vanished. I saw you with her.

Mrs Jackie Maguire?

You were kissing her.

Kissing? Where?

The old chook shed behind St Andrews Inn.

I weren't kissing.

I saw you both. She was holding you.

I was coming back from shooting rabbits. She was hanging washing. I had nothing doing so I gave her a hand. Looking back, I can see she must have been in a bad way. But it didn't feel quite that way. We were just talking. Stories of family. People. And I started saying what I hadn't really said to anyone. Things I had seen.

War things. And then it was too much. I remember that. I just started panting and not able to speak properly. Lost. And she held me like a child. That was it, more or less.

You had your face buried in her neck.

I was crying, Dorry. Crying, for Christ's sake.

What happened to her, Tom? Why did she vanish? I've always wondered what became of her.

Old Jackie, he used to knock her about a bit. He loved her, but she was twenty years younger, she wasn't happy and he knew it. Well, what could you do? Aunty Rose wasn't going to help you. A good fella, Jackie, but then he'd touch the bottle along and give her what for. That much I knew. But where she went I never knew. Not for many years. Then a letter from her found me here in Sydney. She had gone to Melbourne, then later New Zealand. She married a brickie over in Otago. Said nothing more about him. The letter really said nothing more about anything. There was a note with it from her daughter over there saying her mother had asked her to post this to me after her death. And that was that. I guess because others were going to read it there was no mention of old Jackie, or of her family here in Tassie.

The conversation swung to footy matches they had in Cleveland, to Jo Pike's dray, to the day Colonel Cameron's man came into their kitchen with his rifle after Tom's dog because, he said, it had been killing Colonel Cameron's sheep, and Tom had come out of his bedroom with his rifle, saying, Shoot my dog and I shoot you.

Tom was wearying now. Dorrigo said goodbye, made his brother comfortable, told him he was in the best of hands, and left. He was in the corridor when he heard an old voice rasping from behind.

Ruth!

Dorrigo Evans halted and turned around. In the arsenic-green glow of the ward, his brother, trying to push himself back up the steep slope of pillows, suddenly looked not like Tom at all—a man who, in his younger brother's mind, had until that moment remained fixed as the very image of youthful vitality and strength—but a very old and sick man.

Her name was Ruth.

Dorrigo Evans stood there, staring at the stranger who was his brother, unsure what Tom meant or what he wanted. He went back into the ward and sat down next to Tom's bed. Tom sucked his mouth in and out, readying it to speak again. Dorrigo waited. Tom drew his body up from its slump into something firm, and when he next spoke, he did not look at his brother but at the distant wall.

Mrs Jackie Maguire. Her name was Ruth, Dorry. Ruth. And Ruth had a baby.

Here he halted. Dorrigo said nothing. Tom hauled himself up on the pillows again, grunted and coughed.

Yeah, a baby. July 1920. It was her third. How she kept it hidden I don't know. But she did. Jackie was away, trying to get work on the mainland—I think he was getting some work up the Diamantina, he had a mate up there. Jackie never knew about the baby. No one in Cleveland knew. She dressed all baggy like—well, you remember how it was there, it wasn't Paris, it was the bloody middle ages, you could get away with whatever. So she did a good job, I reckon. She had the baby in Launceston. A boy. And they sent it to Hobart. That day I, sort of, well, broke down about the war, she held me like I said. And she told me about the baby. She had just found out what had happened to it.

But why, Tom?

Tom's watery eyes grew sharp, his frail body tensed, and Dorrigo felt that something of the man he had so admired as a child was again present.

I was the bloody father, that's bloody well why.

And Tom finally turned to look at his brother. His eyes bore into Dorrigo's; the pupils were strangely small and empty; they looked like holes burnt in old newspaper with a matchstick.

A family called Gardiner was bringing the kid up. Well-to-do people. It upset her. Upset me. But what could you do? Not that it was being looked after, but that we weren't doing the looking after. No one was going to chase after him and claim him back and bugger up everyone's life—his, theirs, hers, mine, Jackie's. No. No bugger was going to do that. It was just one of those things you had to live with. After the last war I ran into a Hobart bloke who knew the family. They called the boy Frank, apparently. He died during the war. My only son, and I never even met him. One of those bloody awful POW camps that you were in up in Thailand.

## 9

Sydney was full of American GIs from Vietnam on R&R. It was late afternoon, the city was sweltering, and to escape the heat and the GIs, to somehow come to terms with what Tom had just told him, Dorrigo Evans, who advised his patients that walking was the best medicine, decided to take his own advice.

He walked from the hospital to Circular Quay, and then he found himself setting out to walk away from the overly pressing crowds there, across the Sydney Harbour Bridge, with the aim of visiting a surgeon friend in Kirribilli. The sauntering sightseers were pleasant to lose himself among, the bridge walkway wide, and the views of Sydney from it he found expansive and reassuring.

He stopped in the middle of the bridge. A light easterly was blowing a cooling sea breeze in, and he gazed at the water far below coughing white and blue waves. On a near point, ochre-red tower cranes stood like sentinels around the giant unclad sails of the new opera house, its intricate skeleton reminding Dorrigo of the fine lace veins of dry gum leaves. Beyond, the late sun was folding the city into hard and bright bands of light and shadow. It was when he drew himself up from the side rail and resumed walking that he first glimpsed her in the distance, momentarily stepping out from one such bar of slanting darkness into the light.

A few moments later he saw her again, coming towards him, framed by the arch of the great sandstone pylon that supported the northern end of the bridge, her head bobbing like flotsam on the rolling swell of the walkers all around her. He was on the outer side of the wide walkway, in the shadow thrown by the bridge's vast iron-work. His whole being was concentrated on this stranger who was approaching him on the inner side, a ghost walking in the sunlight, when she again disappeared from his sight.

The third time he picked her out in the crowd she

was closer. She was wearing fashionable sunglasses and a sleeveless dark-blue dress with a white band around the hips. She had two children with her, small girls, each holding one of her hands. The traffic noise reverberating in the riveted iron ribcage of the bridge meant he could see the children, laughing, chattering, and her replying. If he could not hear, he still knew: she was no ghost.

He had thought her dead, but here she was, walking towards him, noticeably older, though to him time had made her more, not less, beautiful. As though, rather than taking, age had simply revealed who she really was.

Amy.

The abyss of years—with their historic wars, their celebrated inventions, their innumerable horrors and miraculous wonders—had, he realised, all been about nothing. The bomb, the Cold War, Cuba and transistor radios had no power over her swagger, her imperfect ways, her breasts longing for liberation and her eyes rightfully hidden. Her lighter, bleached hair seemed to him more becoming than her natural colour; her body, if anything perhaps a little thinner, making her more mysterious; her face, slightly gaunt with its defining lines, seemed to him full of some hard-won self-possession.

Over a quarter of a century after he had first seen her through dusty shafts of light in an Adelaide bookshop, he was shocked by how little her changes meant to him. So many feelings that he thought he had lost forever now returned with as great a power as when he had first known them.

Would he stop or would he walk on by? Would he cry out or would he say nothing? He had to decide. So few moments to weigh lives known and unknown, his life now, their life then, her unimaginable life now. He could see the children well enough to recognise in them what he felt to be her unmistakable features. And something in them that was not her and which pained him far more than he thought possible. Perhaps she was happy in her marriage. He was finding it hard to breathe. A thousand mad, maddening notions ran through his mind as he kept on walking towards her. He told himself that he could not barge into her life, causing chaos; he told himself he must, that all was not lost, that they could start again.

She was drawing nearer. He tried to slow his step as his mind sped ever faster. His stomach churned and his balance was uneven. He was close enough now to see the small mole that defined her upper lip. Now he did not think she was as beautiful as ever, or that she was beautiful at all. Only that he wanted her. She was wearing a necklace that sparked an uncontrollable insurrection of memory. Had she seen him? He would call out to her. He would! And then, with the full light of the sun behind her, he saw her pinch her dress between her thumb and forefinger and tug it back up her cleavage. For a moment, perhaps, he expected that in that transcendent light she would now welcome him into her arms and her life.

But there is only light at the beginning of things.

As he went to say something, he realised they had walked past each other without a word. He kept on walking in the shadow, continuing to look straight ahead. He had got it wrong. Her, him, them, love—especially love—so completely wrong. He had got time wrong. He could not believe it, yet he had to. Her death, his life, them, everything, *everything* wrong. And the gravity of his error was so great, so overwhelming, that he could not fight it and turn around, call out, run back. Only when he reached the other end of the bridge did he find the strength finally to turn.

Amy was nowhere to be seen.

He stood in the middle of the walkway, with people spilling all around him—as though he were just one more urban obstruction, a bollard, a bin, a body—and he thought of Lot's wife and what a lie that story was. You become a pillar of salt when you don't turn and look back. He realised he should have stopped her and he realised he now never could. He should never have walked on and yet he had.

Had he chosen? Had she? Was there ever a choice? Or did life just sweep people up, together and away?

Around him, behind him, beyond him were people, moving every which way. Wild flying particles in the light, lost long-ago, as he knew everything now was lost, in the steel and the stone, in the sea and the sun and the heat rising and falling in the cloudless blue sky, lost in the ochre cranes and the thundering expressway.

For a moment longer he remained there, an insignificant figure amidst the soaring iron half-circles and the roaring traffic, the blue day and the sparkling water. Thinking: How empty is the world when you lose the one you love.

And he turned back around and kept on walking, pathless on all paths. He had thought her dead. But now he finally understood: it was she who had lived and he who had died.

# 10

After they had walked across the bridge, Amy bought her two nieces ice-creams at Circular Quay and caught the ferry back to her sister's home in Manly. For many years she had thought him dead. She had become aware that he had not died during the war only in recent times, as his fame had begun to grow. Why, why, she thought once more as she sat on the ferry's rear deck, watching the coruscating waters recede, why if he had been alive, had he not come back to find her? Why? she thought on arriving back at her sister's home. Why? she thought as she lay down on her bed, so very tired. For she could not forgive him for having broken his promise.

It never occurred to her that he might have thought she had died in the explosion, rather than discovering it the next morning, as she had, when she drove the Cabriolet back from the coastal beach where they had first gone, and where—after Keith told her he was dead—she, undone with grief, had driven to think of Dorrigo and ended up sleeping the night.

In recent years she sometimes had the fancy of seeking Dorrigo out. She had been on the edge of it several times—even finding his number and writing it down—but she had not really been on the edge of anything. Every time she thought about contacting him she felt overwhelmed. What did she want of him? What would he want of her, if anything? Sometimes she wondered if he would even have a strong memory of her. And, in any case, what would she say? That she had thought him dead?

How to tell him of the inheritance, comfortable, in

the wake of Keith's death; of the second marriage, long after the war, pleasant, fun, to a bookmaker better at losing money than keeping it, who blew the lot then disappeared, it was said, to America. And that was about it. One or two others, brief encounters, more or less. Mostly less. How to tell him it had not been love, not even with the bookmaker? Something lighter—a hat or a dress or a cloud. But who remembers a cloud?

And whenever she came close to writing a letter, making a phone call, she saw before her the huge obstacle of his rejection of her in never having sought her out, in not having come back for her after the war, as he had promised. Now their positions were changed utterly: he was the famous Dorrigo Evans, forever rising, and she nobody, sinking. And then had come the diagnosis. How to tell him that?

Her sister called a second time.

Yes, she said, one minute more.

She was so weary. She had forgotten so much about him. But it had been him. He was not dead and nor yet was she. It was enough. She took her necklace off and rolled the pearl in her fingers. She felt many things. Then she put it down. He had become someone, or more than someone—she could see that he was passing into something not a person.

She, on the other hand, would soon be nothing. There were treatments—extreme and, her oncologist had told her, essentially futile. She'd had two cleaning jobs, and between them battled to get by, but had now thrown them in, after her sister agreed to nurse her. Her dreams were long ago spent.

Now she sought pleasure in sunsets, in her friends, few

but loved by her, in the charms of her city—the warmth of early morning, the smell of bitumen and buildings after wild rain, the daily summer carnival of its beaches, the view of it from the bridge of a sunny afternoon, the strangers she sometimes met, spoiling her nieces, the pleasant solitude of memory that the evening of a summer's day allowed. Sometimes she felt happy.

Occasionally, she remembered a room by the sea and the moon and him, the green hand of a clock floating in the darkness and the sound of waves crashing, and a feeling unlike anything she had known before or ever knew again.

She would not contact him. He had his life, she had hers: the merge was impossible to dream. And what we cannot dream we can never do.

In eighteen months—six more than she had been given—she would be buried in a suburban cemetery, an unremarkable lot amidst acres of similarly unremarkable graves. No one would ever see her again, and after a time even her nieces' memories would fade and then, like them also, finally be no more. All that would remain, luminous in the long night of the earth, would be a pearl necklace with which she had asked to be buried.

## 11

That night Dorrigo Evans flew to Melbourne, from there the next day he got the morning flight to Hobart; in the overwhelming drone of the 707's engines and the strange oblivion they invited he found a restful limbo. His flight's descent into Hobart was marred by violent winds and heavy smoke coming from bushfires in the island's south; the plane dropped, pitched and tumbled like a pea in a violently boiling pot. They disembarked into the odour of ash and the slap of wind-gusted heat.

He was welcomed by old Freddy Seymour, a surgeon of disputed years who ran the Tasmanian chapter of the College of Surgeons, and who, somewhat eccentrically, drove an old green 1948 Ford Mercury, kept, like Freddy, in a state of immaculate grace in denial of its age. The College of Surgeons was hosting a luncheon in Dorrigo's honour in a Hobart hotel that day. After that, Dorrigo was heading to Fern Tree—the village just out of Hobart, located in picturesque mountain forest, where Ella's sister lived—and his family. He rang Ella from the airport's public phone; her sister was gone till mid-afternoon with her car. In any case, it was too hot to do anything other than stay put with the kids. She said it was pleasantly cool in the shade of the vast eucalypts and she couldn't think of a better place to be.

The lunch was a more pleasant affair than Dorrigo had expected; at least, it was a diversion for his mind from everything else that was crowding into it. But just as they had got to the sherry and cigars there came word that the fire situation had considerably worsened, and that towns to the immediate south, among them Fern Tree, were now threatened by a firestorm.

Dorrigo Evans found a hotel phone and tried calling Ella's sister's number, but the connection was down, and so too, said the operator, were almost all the lines to homes on the mountain. Dorrigo Evans turned to Freddy Seymour—who had just lit up and whose sunken coral-pink cheeks wobbled as he chuffed the smoke in with tiny, quick breaths—and asked if he might borrow his car keys.

I love you, Evans, said the old surgeon, exhaling his own smoke plume. Like a son. And, like a son, you shall return my car not as it was, and like a father I shall forgive.

Fern Tree was twenty minutes' drive from the city. The winds by now were ferocious, the heat a gritty oppression. When he got into the Ford Mercury, he was startled to see his face in the rear-view mirror covered in smuts of the ash that was swirling outside in thick eddies, like black snow.

The Ford Mercury drove like a bucket with only a vague relationship to the road, but its V8 had a reassuring power. The mountain, normally a majestic presence, was invisible, lost in a pall of smoke so thick that within minutes Dorrigo's visibility was down to a few yards and he had his headlights on. Occasionally another car would appear out of the gloom, seeking to escape into the city with people inside looking as he had seen Syrian villagers once look as they sought to escape the war. Some of the cars were scorched; one, improbably, had no windscreen; another's paintwork was raised in big, blackened blisters. He passed from the outer suburbs of Hobart into a thick, tall forest through which the road now cut a deep and sinuous trench.

Coming round a corner, he came upon a police roadblock stopping any car from going further. A solitary policeman put his head into the 1948 Ford Mercury and told Dorrigo he had to turn back.

It's a death zone up there, mate, he said, jerking a thumb behind him in the direction of Fern Tree.

Dorrigo described Ella and his children and asked if

they had passed through the roadblock. The young policeman, who said he had been there for two hours, hadn't seen anyone like that. Perhaps they had fled earlier.

Dorrigo Evans calculated that there was perhaps an hour and a half from the time of his phone call when Ella and the children might have fled. But it was unlikely she would have left when the town was unthreatened, and, besides, she had no car. Dorrigo Evans hoped they had escaped, but reasoned that he had to act in the expectation that they hadn't.

The fire's coming up from the Huon, the policeman went on, and across from the east. I'm hearing crazy stories of it spot-lighting from embers in front of the main fire, up to twenty miles away. As he spoke, glowing embers fell onto the bonnet, as if in proof of the policeman's argument.

You'd be crazy to go up there, he said finally.

My family is up there, Dorrigo Evans said, dropping the column shift down into first. I'd be crazy if I didn't.

And with that he politely asked the policeman to step away. When the policeman refused, he dropped the clutch, smashed through the roadblock and mumbled the first of several apologies to Freddy Seymour.

Within half a mile flames surrounded him, but it did not seem ferocious enough to be the main fire front, though what a main fire front looked like Dorrigo Evans had no idea. He also had no idea where Ella's sister lived, having never visited her before, and while he had an address, no street signs were visible. Nor, hardly, was the road which had become a confusion of burning branches, the occasional burning abandoned car, raining embers and thick smoke. He drove at little more than walking pace along the same road he had travelled near twenty years before in a Cascade brewery truck. Where he had once tried to divine love in a snowstorm, he was now desperately searching for his family in dense smoke, scanning driveways, road verges, shelters, beeping his horn constantly. But there was no one. He presumed everyone was gone or dead. There was no longer sky, only an occasional glimpse of wildly billowing blue-black clouds backlit by a hellish red light. He kept driving, concentrating on his search, keeping his ear close to the window and the window just enough down that he might hear someone, somebody, anything.

And then he thought he heard somebody, but with all the other noise he dismissed it as the whistling the vaporising sap was making as the trees exploded. Then the noise came again, fainter, but different. He stopped the car and got out.

## 12

After the house five along from Ella Evans' sister's home exploded into flame, Ella found their three children—Jess, Mary and little Stewie—playing under what little water was now oozing out of the backyard sprinkler. She told them that they were going to walk to Hobart.

Hobart? How far away is that? Jessie asked.

Ella had no idea. Seven miles? Ten? She felt frightened.

We have to leave straightaway, she said.

The children were wearing only their bathers and plastic sandals, except for Stewie, who was in his aircel undies. The fire was jumping everywhere, and Ella couldn't be bothered arguing with Jess when she insisted on bringing with her a forty-five record player she had got for Christmas. Uniquely, it doubled as a hair dryer with a hose and plastic shower cap that she decided to wear to stop the sparks singeing her hair. In addition, she brought the only forty-five she had so far acquired, an old Gene Pitney single her aunt had given her.

They walked quickly down the road, brushing the burnt leaves and charred man fern fronds that fell out of the sky off their faces and out of their hair. They stared without wonder or surprise at the bitumen dripping away at the edges, at the red embers floating through the air like so many butterflies, their glow rising and falling with the wind gusts. They passed old Mrs McHugh, the piano teacher, whose paling fence was burning, and yelled at her to come with them, but she had an axe and was too busy chopping down the fence to stop the fire spreading to her house to be bothered with their cries.

At first, there was a magical excitement about it all, and something in their mother's terror that made the three children feel better, even superior. They had passed into another world—an adult world, where everything was weighted differently, where people said what they meant, where what you did mattered and where your own life, hitherto meaningless, now mattered to them and to you. It was their first taste of death and they would never forget it.

They must have walked a good mile or so down the mountain when their excitement began to ebb and their fear grew. The main fire, which had seemed a good distance away when they had left the house, was now close to them. Stewie had begun to cry because the embers were burning his skin. He complained, not without reason as flames filled the sky and ate the air, of the fire's *neverendingness*. They came to a brick house that had an aura of solidity and safety, unlike the weatherboard houses they had passed that, long before the fire reached them, were already smoking with small flames licking around their eaves.

Ella went to the front door and pushed the doorbell button. There was a sound of ludicrous chimes. The door opened only wide enough to allow conversation. Through its thin opening Ella made out an older lady dressed in a black-edged white-wool suit, as if about to go to a charity luncheon. By now Ella, who was wearing only a green cotton print dress and thongs, was covered in a dirty grease of sooty sweat. It was clear to her that the older lady felt Ella not to be of the same class and saw her near-naked filthy children as urchins. Ella had intended to ask for refuge, but when she opened her mouth she heard herself ask merely for drinks of water for the children. She had to ask twice. Without saying anything, the woman opened the door and showed them into a neat kitchen at the back of the house. She got out one old plastic cup.

Here, she said, holding it out, its rim pinched between her thumb and arched finger. The tap's there.

The children just wanted to go: they knew the old woman wanted them gone, and their hate of her and her house was even greater than their fear of the fire. But something about the woman's snobbery now made Ella determined to stay. Stewie was crying from his burns and Ella asked the older lady if she had some old children's clothes she might borrow to protect her son from sparks and embers.

The woman opened a cupboard, and inside Ella saw

shelf after shelf of neatly ironed and stored children's clothes. Good clothes. Most of it boys' stuff. She could smell the camphor, something she always associated with timelessness, a reassuring smell of place and things that never changed. The old woman turned around and passed to Ella a folded piece of clothing. Ella unfolded it with a flick of her wrists.

It was a girl's old, worn red dress.

Thank you, said Ella.

Somehow she could not reconcile the idea of a safe refuge with such implacable humiliation. With her son in the tatty red dress, she took her family back out into the fire, believing it not only to be right but also wise.

When they got back out onto the road, the fire no longer made any sort of sense. There was wind behind them and wind coming at them, fire everywhere and wind whipping up willy-willies of swirling red embers, glowing magic cones that turned everything they touched into flame. They had been fleeing from the flames but now the flames were all around them.

We're surrounded, Stewie said, and cried again.

That's enough, Ella said, grabbing him. We've just got to get to Hobart. Get behind me, hold each other's hands, and whatever you do, don't let go.

So linked, this thin line of hope and terror continued into the wind and smoke and flame. Mary started to cry because her feet were blistering.

We'll fix your feet when we get to Hobart, Ella said.

There were trees and houses burning around them and now in front of them and Ella kept urging them to hurry. She was carrying Stewie now, with Mary behind her holding the hem of her dress with one hand and Jess with the other, and all of them terrified of what would become of them if they did not keep holding on to each other. Through the noise of the flames and the wind there was a crash, and up ahead a tree fell onto the road in a ball of flame. Ella found a path skirting around the flames and they kept on, past it, past a burning car wreck and past a fallen, burning telegraph pole with electric cables running like knitting wool around them. But the fire grew worse in front of them than it was behind, Mary's feet were blistering badly, the heat was incredible, and suddenly Ella halted and turned to face her children.

We've got to go back, kids. Quickly, she said. No buggering around now.

She never swore. They knew something had changed.

Quickly, she kept saying. Quickly!

But what about Hobart? asked Jess, who had said nothing. If we get to Hobart we'll be safe. Her voice was panting. We've got to!

And Jess shoved around and starting heading past them into the flames. Ella grabbed her and slapped her hard across the face.

We'll be the Sunday roast if we go any further that way. We've just got to find somewhere to shelter from the fire.

Jess started screaming and Ella slapped her hard a second time. Jess burst into tears and dropped her record player, which smashed to pieces on the road. Their throats burnt with the tar of smoke, it was hard to breathe, their eyes were streaming and snot was running from their noses. It was impossible to see much more than a few steps in front, and they only knew where they were by occasionally sighting the beginning of a drive, a bend in the road, a sign.

They came to a house that had no garden and just one old apple tree and a fibro garden shed that sat in the middle of a dead lawn. There was nothing to burn and the fire was roaring up behind them; little fires were appearing on the dead lawn where there was nothing to burn but they were burning anyway.

Here, said Ella, opening the door of the fibro shed, thinking, *Here?—It's here we all die?*

They huddled inside, holding each other in spite of the ferocious heat, hardly able to breathe. It was as if the fire was eating all the air in the world. They heard a sound like a jet airliner bursting over the top of them. An obscene tongue of flame, a good yard long, licked in under the door like a hungry animal, and Jess leapt back screaming and bumped a shelf full of bottles.

Jess! Ella yelled.

She was holding the shelf. It was full of bottles of brushes in mineral turps and methylated spirits. She hung on to that shelf and told them not to move.

Whatever you do, she said, don't bump this shelf or me. Look at Gene, Ella said.

And Jess, still wearing her record player cum hair dryer plastic cap, speckled with black holes from sparks and cinders, held up in the gloom the forty-five Gene Pitney record she had carried all that way. In the heat it had drooped into the shape of a pudding bowl.

Look at Gene, kids, Ella said. Just look at Gene.

After a few minutes it was hotter than ever but the noise had died down and the flames had stopped licking under the door. They heard a strange noise. Very slowly, Ella opened the door. No one moved. They looked out.

Nothing made sense. The house was gone. Next to

where its remains were smoking, the apple tree was still there, a little singed but otherwise okay, while the forest on the other side of the road was burning ferociously.

They heard the strange noise again and realised it was a car horn growing weaker as the car continued on, away from them. Ella hauled Stewie into her arms, and her daughters ran out with her, all of them yelling through the flames, but the car had already gone past and was disappearing into the smoke up the road. They yelled harder.

And then the car stopped. It was a green 1948 Ford Mercury with white-walled tyres. None of the children would ever forget it. The driver's door opened and a man got out. And when he turned around, they saw that it was their father, come to find them.

They started running to him and he to them, through the smoke and heat and flames. When they met, Dorrigo grabbed Stewie, swinging him with one arm onto his hip. His free hand he opened out wide, cupped Ella's head and clutched her face hard against his. He held her against him and the girls against them both, as if they were entwined roots holding up a decayed tree. It was only a moment before he let her go and they all fled to the car. But it was more affection than his three children had seen their father show their mother in a lifetime.

## 13

Reasoning that their best chance of survival now lay in heading deeper into the forest that had already partly burnt, rather than heading into the fire that was now sweeping into Hobart, Dorrigo drove on in the direction from which his family had fled. Some houses and forest remained, but where the old woman who had not wanted them had saved her good boys' clothes for someone else, there was now nothing except smoking tin and ash and a naked chimney. Where Mrs McHugh had been chopping down her fence to save her house, it was hard to know in the smoke where either had been.

They found themselves driving into a strange night. Coming round a corner the black sky gave way to a huge, red wall of fire, perhaps half a mile away, flames rising far above them. This was a new fire, roaring up from a different direction, and it seemed to be joining several smaller fires into a single inferno. The noise of it was overwhelming. For a moment longer they continued staring as they kept driving. Ella broke the spell.

It's the fire front, she said.

Dorrigo braked, threw the Ford Mercury into a wild reverse swerve, crashed it into first and took off back down the road from where they had just come. Past the fallen wires and flaming car wrecks he drove like a man possessed. Within minutes though the fire front had caught up with them, and now he drove between walls of flame on either side, around burning tree limbs falling everywhere, past houses exploding, alternately speeding as fast as he could go when there was a clear stretch of road, and slewing and slowing when he had to. A fireball, the size of a trolley bus and as blue as gas flame, appeared as if by magic on the road and rolled towards them. As the Ford Mercury swerved around it and straightened back up, Dorrigo found he had no choice but to ignore the burning debris that appeared out of the smoke and hurtled at them—sticks, branches, palings—sometimes hitting and bouncing off the car. He grunted as he worked the column shift up and down, spinning the big steering wheel hard left and right, white-walled tyres squealing on bubbling black bitumen, the noise only occasionally audible in the cacophony of flame roar and wind shriek, the weird machine gun-like crackling of branches above exploding.

They came over a rise to see a huge burning tree falling across the road a hundred yards or so in front of them. Flames flared up high along the tree trunk as it bounced on landing, its burning crown settling in a neat front yard to create an instant bonfire that merged into a burning house. Wedging his knee into the door, Dorrigo pushed with all his strength on the brake pedal. The Ford Mercury went into a four-wheel slide, spinning sideways and skidding straight towards the tree, slewing to a halt only yards from the flaring tree trunk.

No one spoke.

Hands wet with sweat on the wheel, panting heavily, Dorrigo Evans weighed their options. They were all bad. The road out in either direction was now completely cut off—by the burning tree in front of them and the fire front behind them. He wiped his hands in turn on his shirt and trousers. They were trapped. He turned to his children in the back seat. He felt sick. They were holding each other, eyes white and large in their sooty faces.

Hold on, he said.

He slammed the car into reverse, backed up towards the fire front a short distance, then took off. He had enough speed up to smash down the picket fence in the garden where the burning tree crown had landed. They were heading straight into the bonfire. Yelling to the others to get down, he double-declutched the engine into first, let the clutch out and flattened the accelerator.

*Charge the windmill.*

The V8 rose in a roar, tappets clattering, and they crashed into the burning bush at the point closest to the house, where the flames were largest but, Dorrigo had gambled, the branches would be smallest. For a moment all was fire and noise. The engine screamed with wild intent, a heat of such ferocious intensity seemed to penetrate the glass and steel that to breathe hurt, everything was a dull red; there was the crack of flame, of branches snapping, metal scratching and groaning as panels distorted and bent, of wheels losing and gaining traction. The driver's side rear window smashed. Sparks, embers and a few burning sticks flew into the car, Ella and the children began screaming as the children cowed on the far side of the rear bench seat. For a terrifying second or two the car slowed almost to a halt when something caught underneath its chassis. And then, as quickly, the bonfire was somehow behind them, and they were accelerating towards another decrepit paling fence that Dorrigo also smashed through in a momentary blizzard of breaking timber. The windscreen transformed into a white cloud of fragments, he yelled at Ella to kick it out, and when it fell away they found themselves back on the road, past the fallen tree, heading towards Hobart. He was steering with one hand, while leaning over grabbing burning sticks from the back seat with his other—his surgeon's hands he had always tried so hard to protect—and tossing them out the smashed window.

As the 1948 Ford Mercury, green paint blackened and blistering, screeched and slithered its way back down that burning mountain, Ella looked across at Dorrigo, the fingers of his left hand already swelling into blisters the size of small balloons, so badly burnt he would later need skin grafts. Such a mystery of a man, she thought, such a mystery. She realised she knew nothing about him; that their marriage had been over before it began; and that it was not in the power of either of them to alter any of this. On what were now three tyres and one disintegrating wheel rim, the Ford Mercury careered round a long corner and, through the smoke, they finally glimpsed before them the sanctuary of the police roadblock.

I think this may be the last time Freddy Seymour invites you for lunch, said Ella Evans.

And in the back seat the three now silent, soot-smeared children absorbed it all—the choking creosote stench, the roar of wind and flame, the wild rocking of a car being driven that hard, the heat, the emotion so raw and exposed it was like butchered flesh; the tormented, hopeless feeling of two people who lived together in a love not yet love, nor yet not; an unshared life shared; a conspiracy of affections, illnesses, tragedies, jokes and labour; a marriage—the strange, terrible *neverendingness* of human beings.

A family.

## 14

The old are filled with remorse, Jodie Bigelow's father once told her. Her father. Jimmy Bigelow was never quite Jodie's dad. He seemed absent through not only her life, but much of his own. He worked as a mail sorter and never seemed interested in rising beyond it. One day in high school she had to do a project on Anzac Day, and she had asked her father to tell her what the war had been like for him. He said there wasn't really that much to tell. This and that. When she grew insistent, he went into his bedroom and returned with an old bugle. He wiped the mouthpiece and made a few farting noises with it to make her laugh. Then he found some real notes. He dropped the bugle, coughed, swelled up, raised his head in a martial manner entirely unfamiliar to his daughter and played the 'Last Post'.

That's it?

That's all I know, he said. That's about all anyone needs to know.

That's not a school project, Dad.

No.

It's sort of lonely, Jodie said.

Jimmy Bigelow thought on this, and then said he guessed it was, but it had never felt that way. It felt the opposite.

Jodie had browsed some books about the POWs.

It must have been hard, she said.

Hard? he replied. Not really. We only had to suffer. We were lucky.

What does that music mean? she asked.

It's a mystery, he said after a while. The bigger the mystery, the more it means.

Jodie's mother died of leukaemia when Jodie was nineteen. Jimmy Bigelow survived her for another twenty-eight years. He did not take himself seriously and came to believe the world was essentially comic. He enjoyed the company of others and found in his life—or in this way of looking at life—much at which he and others marvelled. There was a growing industry of memory all around him, yet he recalled less and less. Some jokes, some stories, the taste of a duck egg Darky Gardiner gave him, the hope. The goodness. He remembered when they went to bury little Wat Cooney. He remembered how Wat loved everyone; how he was always waiting at the cookhouse until the last man made it in, no matter how late, keeping some food for him, making sure, no matter how little there was, every man was fed something. Looking over his grave, no one had wanted to be the first to throw a sod. He did not remember that Wat Cooney had died during the march north to Three Pagoda Pass, nor any of the march's attendant cruelties. For him, such things were not the truth of it.

His sons corrected his memories more and more. What the hell did they know? Apparently a lot more than him. Historians, journalists, documentary makers, even his own bloody family pointing out errors, inconsistencies, lapses, and straight-out contradictions in his varying accounts. Who was he meant to be? The Encyclopaedia bloody Britannica? He was there. That was all. When he played 'Without a Song' on his cassette player that too was a mystery, because for a moment he saw a man standing on a tree stump singing, and he felt all those things he otherwise didn't feel; he understood all those things he otherwise didn't understand. His words and memories were nothing. Everything was in him. Could they not see that? Could they not just let him be?

His mind slowly distilled his memory of the POW camps into something beautiful. It was as if he were squeezing out the humiliation of being a slave, drop by drop. First he forgot the horror of it all, later the violence done to them by the Japanese. In his old age he could honestly say he could recall no acts of violence. The things that might bring it back—books, documentaries, historians—he avoided. Then his memory of the sickness and the wretched deaths, the cholera and the beri-beri and the pellagra, that too went; even the mud went, and later so too the memory of the hunger. And finally one afternoon he realised he could remember none of his time as a POW at all. His mind was still good; he knew he had once been a POW as he knew he had once been a foetus. But of that experience nothing remained. What did was an irrevocable idea of human goodness, as undeniable as it was beautiful. At the age of ninety-four he was finally a free man.

Thereafter he took great pleasure in wind, in the sound of rain. He marvelled at the feeling of dawn on a hot day. He exalted in the smiles of strangers. He worked at habits and friendship, seeing in them the only alternative to what he felt the alternative was. He cultivated a flock of vivid green, blue and red rosella parrots that came to his yard for the food and water he laid out for them. Then came the wrens and the bullying honeyeaters, the gossiping firetails and the occasional scarlet robin, the bright blue wrens with their dun-coloured harems, the shimmering cranky fantail, the cuckoo shrikes and silvereyes and chirruping pardalotes. He would sometimes sit on a bench seat on his verandah for hours watching the birds feed, bathe, rest, preen and play. And in the mystery of their flight and beauty, in their inexplicable arrivals and departures, he felt he saw his life.

After he died at the old-age home, falling off the top of a flight of stairs from where he was feeding birds, Jodie found her father's bugle in his wardrobe. It was old and filthy and badly dented. Instead of a proper cord there was a knotted piece of red rag. She sold it in a garage sale.

Sometimes his laugh would come back to her at an unexpected moment—in a supermarket aisle as she looked for dishwashing powder, as she browsed a celebrity magazine in a dentist's waiting room. At such times she would remember him unable to smack her, hand trembling above her, and hear him saying—

That's all I know. That's about all anyone needs to know.

And her once more asking, What does that music mean?

And the world around her, the supermarket aisle and its shelves, the dentist's waiting room and its tub chairs, the garage sale and her father's bric-a-brac on two trestle tables in front of her and a voice saying, You take five for it? And, as she passed it over, the battered bugle trembling with no answer.

Rightio, she thought she heard it say, as a stranger took hold of it. Or was it her? Rightio.

# 15

Dorrigo Evans was driving through an intersection in Parramatta at three in the morning—a place and a time subsequently never publicly explained, along with the small matter of an alcohol reading—when he first found himself flying, being suddenly thrown into the air, never to return to earth. A carload of drunken kids fleeing the police in a stolen Subaru Impreza had crashed a red light and run straight into Dorrigo Evans' ageing Bentley, totalling both vehicles, killing two of them and critically injuring one of Australia's greatest war heroes, who had hurtled through his car's windscreen.

He was three days in dying, and in that time possessed of the most extraordinary dreams of his life. Light was flooding a church hall in which he sat with Amy. Blinding, beautiful light, and him toddling back and forth, in and out of its transcendent oblivion and into the arms of women. He was flying and he was smelling Amy's naked back and he was soaring ever higher. Whilst around him the nation prepared itself to mourn while simultaneously debating the decline of youth, contrasting the noble heroics of one generation with the vile and murderous criminality of another, he was stunned to realise that his life was only just beginning, and in a faraway teak jungle that had long since been cleared, in a country called Siam that no longer existed, a man who no longer lived had finally fallen asleep.

## 16

Dorrigo Evans awoke from a terrible dream of death. He realised he was so exhausted that he had momentarily nodded off while the parade was assembling. It was almost midnight. He turned back to the seven hundred men assembled in front of him, and explained that it was his task to pick one hundred men to march to another camp one hundred miles deeper into the jungle of Siam. They would be leaving immediately after the morning parade.

The men were counted and then counted again, and somehow the numbers didn't tally. More men staggered in from the Line, confusing matters further. Sergeants sought to explain who was there and who wasn't and why they weren't. There was some heated discussion between Fukuhara—immaculately uniformed, even at this late hour—and the guards, one of the Australian sergeants was slapped around, and after some confusion the counting began again.

Major Nakamura had come to him an hour earlier with Fukuhara and given him the order that one hundred men were to be selected to march to a camp near Three Pagoda Pass.

None of these men should be asked to do any more, argued Dorrigo Evans. There is not one prisoner in this camp capable of such a march.

Major Nakamura insisted that a hundred were to be found.

Unless you change your treatment of prisoners they will all die, said Dorrigo Evans.

Major Nakamura indicated that he would choose if the Australian colonel would not.

They'll all die, said Dorrigo Evans.

Again Lieutenant Fukuhara translated; Major Nakamura listened and then spoke. The lieutenant turned to Dorrigo Evans.

Major Nakamura say that very good thing, Lieutenant Fukuhara said. It save Japanese army much rice.

Evans understood that if Nakamura chose, it would be indiscriminately and their number would include the sickest—and perhaps most likely the sickest, because they were of least use to Nakamura—and that all of them would die. If, on the other hand, he, Dorrigo, chose, he could pick the fittest, the ones he thought had the best chance of living. And most would die anyway. That was his choice: to refuse to help the agent of death, or to be his servant.

As the parade went on, as additional men on light duties or cooking or in the hospital were rounded up and brought in, as they stood there sick and starving, as the occasional man collapsed from exhaustion and was just left lying in the mud, the prisoners watched a long column of Japanese soldiers appear, marching along the rough track that ran along the far side of the parade ground, which, when not impassable from the monsoon, served as the supply road for the railway.

The Japanese soldiers were on their way to the Burmese front, hundreds of miles of weary jungle away. They were filthy and exhausted but still they pressed on into the night, with no more than grunts and groans, pushing and pulling artillery axle-deep through the mud. Some seemed ill, many so young that they might still have been in school, and all looked miserable.

Dorrigo Evans had not seen any Japanese troops up close for several months. In Java he had come to respect them not as the short-sighted buffoons the Australians had been told by their intelligence officers to expect, but as formidable soldiers. But these Japanese soldiers, who had clearly been marching all day and long into the night on their way to the horror of another front, looked as much the wretched of war as the POWs themselves, broken, bedraggled, exhausted. Dorrigo caught the eyes of one soldier who carried a hurricane lamp. They loomed large on his child-like face, and looked soft and vulnerable. He could not have been more than seventeen years old. What he saw in the Australian officer, Dorrigo Evans had no idea, but it was not hate or the devil. He stumbled, then halted, still staring at the Australian. Perhaps he saw something; perhaps he was too tired to see anything. Dorrigo Evans felt an overwhelming urge to put his arm around him.

Suddenly, a Japanese sergeant—seeing the soldier gawking—strode over and thrashed him brutally around the face with a bamboo cane. The soldier immediately drew himself erect, barked some word of apology and focused his gaze back on the jungle ahead. It was clear to Dorrigo Evans that this soldier no more understood his beating or purpose than the POWs did their miserable fate. How far away was his home? wondered Dorrigo. Was it a farm? Was it a city? Some place, some valley, some street, a lane, an alley, that he perhaps dreamt of, a place of sun and winds that caressed and rains that refreshed, of people who cared for him and laughed with him, a place far away from this stink of decay, the smothering green, the pain and brutal people who simply hated and taught hate, who made the world hate. As the boy soldier trudged away, Dorrigo could see he was bleeding about the face where he'd been whipped, that his simple uniform was filthy, torn and mildewed, and that he had no heart for any of this. And yet, when called upon, he—this soft-eyed boy with the lamp—he too would kill brutally and in turn be killed.

The Japanese sergeant who had so savagely beaten him now took a break. Watching the column file past into the blackness of the jungle, he lit a cigarette and took a puff. When another NCO approached, he handed the smoke to him with a smile and a joke. And as the column of children was swallowed by the darkness, Dorrigo Evans felt as if the whole war was passing before his eyes.

After the column had vanished into the jungle, the rain came in a deluge. The sky was black, and other than the few kerosene lanterns and guards' torches, there was no light. The only sound was that of the rain rolling down from the nearby teak trees in gushes, the rain sweeping back and forth, and the rain felt to Dorrigo Evans a solid, moving, living thing, and the rain and the great teak jungle in which their camp sat in that small clearing seemed to form a prison that was endless, unknowable, and slowly killing them all.

Finally, it was established that all the prisoners were there. Dorrigo Evans lifted his lantern and his gaze, worried that he might be giving the impression that he was downcast, his spirit broken by all that they had suffered. He could not do that to them. He had to do far worse. He looked at the seven hundred men, whom he had held, nursed, cajoled, begged, hoodwinked and organised into surviving, whose needs he always put before his own. Most wore only a Jap happy or wretched rags that masqueraded as shorts, and in the greasy, sliding lantern light their skeletal bodies for a moment horrified him. Many shook with malaria, some shat themselves as they stood there, and it was his task to find among them one hundred men to march one hundred miles further into the jungle, towards the unknown, into the passage of death.

Dorrigo Evans looked downwards, and though he could see nothing, it reminded him that few had that one key to survival, boots. Holding a lantern at ankle height, he walked slowly along the first row, looking at the bare feet, some badly infected, some swollen with beri-beri, some with stinking ulcers so large and vile that they were like angry craters eating almost to the bone.

He stopped at one: a severe, untreated ulcer that had left a thin strip of intact skin down the outer side of the calf, the rest of the leg being a huge ulcer from which poured offensive, greyish pus. Sloughing tendons and fasciae were exposed, the muscles were tunnelled and separated by gaping sinuses, between which he could glimpse a raw tibial bone that looked as if a dog had gnawed it. The bone, too, was starting to rot and break off into flakes. He lifted his gaze to see a pale, wasted child. No, Chum Fahey could not go.

Report to hospital when parade has ended, said Dorrigo Evans.

The next man was Harry Dowling. Dorrigo had successfully removed his appendix three months ago, a triumph in such circumstances of which he was proud. And now Dowling seemed in not the worst shape. He had shoes and his ulcers were only mild. Dorrigo looked up at him, put his hand on his shoulder.

Harry, he said, as gently as he could, as though waking a child.

I am become a carrion monster.

The next in line was Ray Hale, whom they had managed to bring through cholera. He too Dorrigo touched on the shoulder.

Ray, he said.

Thou art come unto a feast of death.

Ray, he said.

Dread Charon, frightful and foul.

And so Dorrigo continued on, up and down the lines of those he had tried to save and now had to pick, touching, naming, condemning those men he thought might best cope, the men who had the best chance of not dying, who would most likely die nevertheless.

At its end, Dorrigo Evans stepped back and dropped his head in shame. He thought of Jack Rainbow, whom he had made to suffer so, Darky Gardiner, whose prolonged death he could only watch. And now these hundred men.

And when he looked up, there stood around him a circle of the men he had condemned. He expected the men to curse him, to turn away and revile him, for everyone understood it was to be a death march. Jimmy Bigelow stepped forward.

Look after yourself, Colonel, he said, and put out his hand to shake Dorrigo's. Thanks for everything.

You too, Jimmy, Dorrigo Evans said.

And, one by one, the rest of the hundred men shook his hand and thanked him.

When it was done, he walked off into the jungle at the side of the parade ground and wept.

## 17

We're not sure what he knows, a nurse said. She had seen his dog-black eyes glistening with a life of their own under the neon tubes of the ward. I think he hears me, though, she said. I do.

Broken as he was, he could recognise that it was a fine room he had been given, looking out on giant fig trees with their flying roots and lush greenery. But he did not feel at home. It did not feel his place. It was not the island of his birth. The birds cried differently at dawn, harsh, happy calls of green parrots and gang-gang parrots. Not the soft, smaller, more complex trilling of birdsong, of the wrens and honeyeaters and silvereyes of his island home, the fetching return call of the jo-witty, all the birds he now wished to fly and sing with. It was not a road rolling from the cup of a woman's waist over a pewter sea to a rising moon.

*For my purpose holds*, he whispered—

*To sail beyond the sunset, and the baths*
*Of all the western stars until I die.*

What's he saying? asked one nurse.

He's raving, said a second. Better get a doctor. It's the morphine or the end, one or the other, or both. Some say nothing, some give up on breathing, some rave.

As politicians, journalists and shock jocks competed in their ever wilder panegyrics of a man they had never understood, he was dreaming of just one day: of Darky Gardiner and Jack Rainbow, of Tiny Middleton. Mick Green. Jackie Mirorski and Gyppo Nolan. Little Lenny going home to Mum in the Mallee. Of one hundred men shaking his hand. One thousand others, names recalled, names forgotten, a sea of faces. Amie, amante, amour.

Life piled on life, he mumbled, every word now a revelation, as if it had been written for him, a poem his life and his life a poem.

*Little remains: but every hour is saved*
*From that eternal silence, something more,*

—something more . . . something more . . . he had lost some lines somewhere and he no longer knew what the poem was or who had written it, so totally now was the poem him. This grey spirit, he thought despondently, or was he remembering?—yes, that was it—

*And this grey spirit yearning in desire*
*To follow knowledge, like a sinking star,*
*Beyond the utmost bound of human thought.*

And he felt shame and he felt loss and he felt his life had only ever been shame and loss, it was as though the light was now going, his mother was calling out, Boy! Boy! But he could not find her, he was returning to hell and it was a hell he would never escape.

And he remembered Lynette Maison's face as she slept, and the Glenfiddich whisky miniatures he had drunk before he left, and Rabbit Hendricks' illustration of Darky Gardiner sitting in an opulent armchair through which little silver fish swam, in a Syrian village in which Yabby Burrows and his spiked hair was about to dissolve into Syrian dust. And somehow it made no sense to him that the picture survived and would be reproduced endlessly, but Yabby Burrows was gone and to his life no future and no meaning could ever be attached. There was someone in a blue uniform standing above him. Dorrigo wanted to tell him he was sorry, but when he opened his mouth only drool rolled out.

He was in any case hurtling backwards into an ever faster swirling maelstrom of people, things, places, backwards and round and deeper and deeper and deeper into the growing, grieving, dancing storm of things forgotten or half-remembered, stories, lines of poetry, faces, gestures misunderstood, love spurned, a red camellia, a man weeping, a wooden church hall, women, a light he had stolen from the sun—

He remembered another poem, he could see the poem in its entirety, but he did not want to see it or know it; he could see Charon's burning eyes staring into his but he did not want to see Charon, he could taste the obol being forced into his mouth, he felt the void he was becoming—

—and finally he understood its meaning.

His last words, as witnessed by a Sudanese orderly:

*Advance forward, gentleman. Charge the windowsill.*

He felt a snare tightening around his throat; he gasped and threw a leg out of the bed, where it jerked for a second or two, thumping the steel frame, and died.

## 18

The long night waxed, the slow quarter-moon continued rising through black rungs, the night moaned with many groans and snores. Bonox Baker turned up at the officers' tent with the news of Darky Gardiner's drowning. By the light of a kerosene lantern, Dorrigo Evans entered it in his diary as murder. The word seemed inadequate. What didn't? In his small shaving mirror, which lay next to the diary, he glimpsed his frightful reflection, hair hoary and unkempt, fierce eyes lit with fire and a filthy rag hanging around his neck. Had he become the ferryman? He turned the mirror upside down. It was almost midnight, and he knew he should try to get a few hours' sleep so he might have the strength to make it through another day. He wanted to be first at the dawn parade to meet the hundred men as they arrived and wish them well before they left.

A bag of mail had arrived that morning with the truck, the first any of them had seen for nine months. As ever, the correspondence was random. Some men received several letters, many men none. There was one letter for Dorrigo Evans from Ella. He had intended to wait until now, the end of his day, for the immense pleasure of reading it, so that he might fall asleep with it filling his dreams, but he felt so home sick on seeing the letter when it was handed to him in the morning before the parade he had torn it open and read it there and then. He could not believe her news. All day it had haunted him. Rereading it now at the end of the day he still found it impossible to digest.

The letter was six months old. It ran to several pages. Ella wrote that although nothing had been heard from Dorrigo or, for that matter, from his unit for over a year, she knew he was alive. The letter talked of her life, of Melbourne in all its mundane detail. All this he could believe. But unlike other men, who pored over every sentence of their letters and cards from home, only one detail registered with Dorrigo Evans. Enclosed with the letter was a newspaper cutting headed ADELAIDE HOTEL

TRAGEDY. It told of how, after a gas explosion in its kitchen, the King of Cornwall hotel had burnt down with the loss of four lives, including that of the much-respected publican, Mr Keith Mulvaney. Another three people were unaccounted for and believed to have also perished, including two guests and Mrs Mulvaney, the publican's wife.

Dorrigo Evans read the newspaper cutting for a third and then a fourth time. Outside it was raining again. He felt cold. He pulled his army blanket round him tighter, and by the light of the kerosene lantern he once more read Ella's letter.

One of Daddy's friends high up made some enquiries for me with the coroner's office in Adelaide, Ella wrote. He said it had now been made official, but because of the tragedy and people's feelings and morale and all that they've kept it out of the paper. They had to use teeth. Can you imagine? Poor Mrs Keith Mulvaney is now among the confirmed dead. I am so sorry, Dorry. I know how fond you were of your uncle and aunt. Tragedies like this make me realise how lucky I am.

Mrs Keith Mulvaney?

For some time the name made no more sense than the news.

Mrs Keith Mulvaney.

She had only ever been Amy to him. He had no idea it was a lie, the only lie Ella ever told him.

He put out the kerosene lantern to conserve fuel and lit the stub of a candle. For a long time he watched the flame refusing to die. The smoke tapered into tiny smuts that played up and down in the pulsing areolae of candle-light. He looked at the light, at the smuts. As though there were two worlds. This world and a hidden world that was a real world of wild, flying particles spinning, shimmering, randomly bouncing off each other, and new worlds coming into being in consequence. One man's feeling is not always equal to all that life is. Sometimes it's not equal to anything much at all. He stared into the flame.

Amy, amante, amour, he whispered, as if the words themselves were smuts of ash rising and falling, as though the candle were the story of his life and she the flame.

He lay down in his haphazard cot.

After a time he found and opened a book he had been reading that he had expected to end well, a romance which he wanted to end well, with the hero and heroine finding love, with peace and joy and redemption and understanding.

Love is two bodies with one soul, he read, and turned the page.

But there was nothing—the final pages had been ripped away and used as toilet paper or smoked, and there was no hope or joy or understanding. There was no last page. The book of his life just broke off. There was only the mud below him and the filthy sky above. There was to be no peace and no hope. And Dorrigo Evans understood that the love story would go on forever and ever, world without end.

He would live in hell, because love is that also.

He put the book down. Unable to sleep, he stood up and went to the edge of the shelter beyond which the rain teemed. The moon was lost. He relit the kerosene lantern and made his way to the bamboo urinal on the far side of the camp, relieved himself, and on his return noticed growing at the side of the muddy trail, in the midst of the overwhelming darkness, a crimson flower.

He leant down and shone his lantern on the small miracle. He stood, bowed in the cascading rain, for a long time. Then he straightened back up and continued on his way.

## VINTAGE CLASSICS

Vintage Classics is home to some of the greatest writers and thinkers from around the world and across the ages. Bringing you not just the books you already know and love, but new additions to your library, these are works to capture imaginations, inspire new perspectives and excite curiosity.

Renowned for our iconic red spines and bold, collectable design, Vintage Classics is an adventurous, ever-evolving list. We breathe new life into classic books for modern readers, publishing to reflect the world today, because we believe that our times can best be understood in conversation with the past.